Athanasia: The Great Insurrection

Thomas W. Coutouzis

ISBN: 9781521180426

DEDICATION

I would like to thank my Lord and Savior Jesus Christ to whom I have been redeemed. He is the inspiration for this book and is the One who has equipped me with the desire and talent to write for His glory.

CONTENTS

ACKNOWLEDGMENTS

I would like to thank Brian Lloyd for taking my cover design ideas and breathing life into them. You did a fantastic job. A book is never complete without a cover, likewise, an author is never complete without a good designer. Many thanks to Issac Lewis for his many hours of edits/direction, and S.E.M. Ishida for her guidance. Lastly, I would like to thank my wife Kathy for the encouragement and sacrifices she made on many occasions which enabled me to write. I love you, Chloe, and Micah. You make your mommy and daddy very proud.

1 - SALEM, PORTUS

In the quarters of Mardok, leader of the Adelphos, a surreptitious meeting was starting to take place. A man with dark shoulder length hair entered the balcony but did not make eye contact with Mardok who was leaning and looking off into the distance on the railing of his balcony. The man walked to the railing of the balcony and looked down at the crowds of people. Mardok looked down from the balcony at all the people walking the streets as if he were a perched eagle ready to pounce on his unknowing prey. He smirked because the people were not aware of the secrets he was hiding. He looked over to the man with him on the balcony and said, "Arsinian, where do things stand?"

Arsinian smiled as he continued looking off into the distance and said, "Everything is ready. They will never know what has overtaken them."

Arsinian and Mardok had some similar features as both were of olive complexion and had dark eyes. Mardok was bald and clean shaven, while Arsinian's face looked like it had not seen a blade in many days. Mardok looked around at some of the nearby balconies and seeing no one close by he said, "Excellent work, my brother. Too long have we served an inferior race and bowed to men that are lesser than we! The time for my reign is at hand!"

Both turned and walked back into Mardok's royal quarters which were decorated with marble floors, fine linens and burgundy draperies as well as many solid gold ornaments and statues that he brought back as spoils from war. His quarters were very large potentially housing 10 families underneath its roof. On the walls hung portraits of the kings that he had protected since his creation in order from the most recent to the first. As they passed by the portraits the oldest ones looked somewhat faded because of time but others were without blemish. As they came closer to the portrait of King Argos one could notice what looked like dagger strikes in the more recent king's faces. Mardok scowled at the paintings as he passed them as if they reminded him of some former enemy.

The two then sat down at a large oak table where Mardok had intricate plans strewn all over its top. Mardok asked, "All but six Adelphos are committed to this and have pledged their loyalty to me?"

Arsinian replied, "Yes, my lord. Seventy eight of the eighty four have pledged their allegiance to you."

At that moment a bookcase in the room by the table creaked open and a hooded man wearing a black cloak entered the room. Mardok said, "Perfect timing, Romus. We were just reviewing the final plans. Is everything in place with the royal guard?"

Romus remained cloaked as he sat down and replied, "Everything is ready. The captain of the guard and my lieutenants are prepared and know what to say and how to react when the accusations take place."

Romus then turned to Mardok and said, "What will you do with Victus and Spiros?"

Mardok grinned before responding, "You will label Spiros as a fellow conspirator. Arsinian will eliminate Victus."

Romus asked, "I thought the Adelphos could not be killed? I know that those in your order do not age, and I have seen them gravely wounded in battle but continue to live, so how will this sword complete the task at hand?"

Arsinian's nostrils flared as he turned to Romus and said, "You fool!" He then drew his sword and put it on the table in front of Romus. "This is a sword of Helios! These are no ordinary swords as they were individually crafted by Sophos with drops from the sun. Each of the Adelphos carry one of these swords as do the 21 kings. They are the most lethal swords in existence as they can cut through metal and stone as if it were a loaf of bread."

Arsinian picked up his sword from the table and demonstrated its power as he ran it through a three foot stone wall on the other side of the table. He then withdrew his sword from the wall and put it on the table in front of Romus and said, "These are the only things in creation that can kill an Adelphos."

Beads of sweat began to form on Romus' face and his hands began to tremble. "My lords, it has never been tested before on one of your kind so how can you be absolutely sure?

Mardok gnashed his teeth and pounded the table with his fist. "It will do as Arsinian has told you!"

Mardok then looked up at Arsinian, "Keep a careful eye on Romus as my confidence in his abilities has faded because of his frail human disposition. Make sure that Victus dies and that Spiros is implicated as I no longer trust this vapor to carry out the task."

Romus replied, "Please forgive me, Mardok, I desire for you to be king more than any other. If this plan doesn't work than I and the other mortal men involved will be hung from the gallows for treason."

Mardok responded, "This plan will work, Romus, and you will be rewarded for your faithfulness to me." Mardok unsheathed his sword and pointed it at Romus and said, "Now, bow down to me as you would bow before King Argos. Show me your allegiance!"

Beads of sweat began pouring down the face of Romus as he fell to his knees and lay prostrate before Mardok. Mardok smiled, "Rise, faithful servant."

Romus wiped the sweat from his brow with the sleeve on his left arm and took a seat at the table again. "What of the heirs to the throne of Portus? How do you intend to remove them as well as the mighty Argos?" exclaimed Romus.

Mardok smiled, "You leave that to me as it is of no importance to you. The only people that know are those that are directly involved, and that is how it will remain. I fear that if too many of those involved know, that a tongue may slip and destroy a plan that has taken 2000 years to concoct."

A tiny creak was heard in the background. Mardok and Arsinian immediately turned and looked behind them and saw the eye of a man peering at them from behind the open front door. The eye quickly disappeared as soon as it was spotted. Romus did not have the physical abilities or discernment of the Adelphos, but could tell that something had gotten their attention, so he asked, “What’s wrong?”

Mardok yelled, “Catch him, Arsinian! He has overheard our plan!”

Arsinian jumped out of his chair and quickly made his way out the door. Romus asked, “What is happening, Mardok?”

Mardok said, “You must leave now! Take the secret passage out and let no one see you, Romus!”

Romus arose quickly, knocking his chair down as he made his way to the passage behind the bookcase. Meanwhile, Mardok ran towards the balcony which was several stories from the ground and jumped on the railing. He looked down to the ground to see if anyone was beneath him. Seeing no one, he jumped. Mardok landed on the ground with both feet, unsheathed his sword and then ran with all the speed he could conjure towards the entrance to the complex.

Arsinian was about 25 yards behind the man he was chasing down the hallway. He thought to himself, “Only a messenger of the king could run this quickly.” The messenger approached the stairwell and chose to run up the stairs without breaking his stride. As he made his way up he looked down and saw Arsinian closing in on him. He gasped, gritted his teeth and ran like wild game fleeing from a hungry predator. Arsinian taunted the messenger, “You can’t escape me, for I have already consumed your mind with terror. Here I come!”

The messenger made his way up to the roof and then fell as he tripped over the last step. Arsinian smiled and reached out and grabbed part of messenger’s tunic as he stood back up. The messenger gasped again, pulled out his dagger and sliced the piece of cloth Arsinian held, freeing him from his enemy’s clutches. Arsinian laughed and said, “You cannot escape me mortal. You are trapped, and I am hungry for your life.”

Meanwhile, Mardok made his way to the entrance. He looked all around. He turned and asked a food vendor that was located by the entrance, “Did you see a man come running out of the entrance to this complex?”

The vendor replied, “No, my lord. I have not seen any man.”

The messenger ran hastily to the eastern edge of the building overlooking the street. He had no place to go, so he ran to the northern edge. There he saw a building beneath him that was around a 10 foot drop. He looked behind him. Arsinian was running nearer. He took several steps back, ran, and then jumped off the roof. Mardok saw him fly to the next building. He waited to see if Arsinian was behind him. A few moments later he saw Arsinian make the jump down to the next building. Mardok ran looking up to the next roof attempting to track the man. As he took a quick glance ahead he saw that the messenger would not be able to jump to the next building. It was three stories taller and the alley between them was 30 feet wide.

Arsinian was closing in on the messenger as the roof of the building was about to run out. He knew that he had the messenger when he saw that the next building was much taller, so Arsinian then slowed down and began to walk. He crowed, “There is no place to go! Come, taste the steel of my sword!” The messenger did not even turn around when he heard Arsinian, but rather grunted, jumped onto the ledge and with his momentum jumped off the building. Arsinian’s brow furrowed while his mouth opened in shock as he witnessed the messenger jump. The messenger held his breathe like one jumping into the ocean from a ship as he helplessly descended downward to the street. Arsinian hurried over to the ledge, looked down and saw the man on a lower balcony on the next building. Mardok was already standing in the alley between these two buildings. “Get him!” he shouted to Arsinian.

The messenger struggled to his feet as he shook off the fall and went into the building. Arsinian jumped off the ledge down to the balcony, landing on his feet, while Mardok waited outside. The messenger made his way through the dwelling and into the hallway, but quickly sidestepped into another dwelling. He ran to the balcony and jumped on one of the giant tapestries, pulling it over the ledge with his momentum and slid down to the street. As he stepped away from the tapestry Mardok appeared from behind it, putting his hand on the messenger’s shoulder. The messenger unsheathed his dagger and pierced Mardok’s chest. Mardok struck the man in the face and then grabbed him and dragged him to a nearby alley. Mardok pulled the dagger out of his chest with a grimace. The wound immediately began to heal.

Arsinian leapt down from the balcony and quipped, "He was a shifty fellow."

Mardok replied, "All that matters is that he is caught. If word of our plan was leaked then my plans for Athanasia would be thwarted forever."

Arsinian walked up to the man who was on his hands and knees and kicked him in the stomach so hard that he flew up against the wall. He began coughing when Mardok grabbed him by the hair and said, "What were you doing in my quarters? How much did you hear?"

The messenger was able to blurt out between breaths, "I don't know what you are talking about." He took another breath and continued, "I was sent by the King to request your presence on the preparations for the journey to Methos."

Mardok replied, "We know you heard something, mortal. Speak up and tell me what you heard, messenger to the king!"

Arsinian drew his sword and put it up against the messenger's neck. The exhausted messenger was now catching his breath, but realizing that his end was near. He smirked, "You will never get away with usurping the throne of your king!"

Mardok smirked back and replied, "Arsinian, it looks as if we found a fellow conspirator that will be implicated with Romus in the insurrection that we have uncovered."

Arsinian replied, "However, I think he is one of the rebels that was killed when we uncovered the plot."

Mardok responded, "Yes, unfortunately, he was the only one that was killed."

The messenger shouted, "Treachery! King Argos will uncover your plot!"

The messenger then screamed hoping that someone would hear his cry, "Help! These men are seeking to usurp the King's throne!"

Mardok unsheathed his sword and ran it through the messenger, silencing him forever. Mardok then looked over to Arsinian. "My plan to take King Argos' throne must start now. Find Romus and tell him to implicate King Argos' messenger when you bring him into the throne room. I will bring this mortal's body to the castle."

Arsinian nodded, turned, and made haste to find Romus. As he made his way out of the alley he walked by some curious passers-by who witnessed the chase and heard the scream. One asked, "What is happening?"

Arsinian turned and said, "We have uncovered a plot to murder the king and now we must move quickly before these rebels carry out their plan. Please, move out of my way. It is urgent that I warn the king!"

Arsinian darted out of the alley while the people quickly moved out of his way so that he could warn the king and thwart this assassination. Mardok picked up the body and hung him over his shoulder as he carried it out of the alley and headed towards the royal palace.

2 - THE ISLAND OF TELEMICHA, METHOS

In Methos, King Justinian was preparing for the arrival of the other 20 kings to the Island of Telemicha. Justinian was selected as the chief mediator because he was well respected by the other kings (he was the architect behind the settling of grievances). Justinian had ruled for over 200 years in Methos and his mediation was the reason that there had not been a war between kingdoms during that time period. He constantly referenced the ancient writings for wisdom and guidance and read history to learn from the mistakes of others. There were those who felt it was because of his worship of Sophos, the creator of all things, and meditation on the ancient writings that Justinian was effective in settling disputes.

Justinian had erected the temple of Sophos which was an ivory cylinder tower 230 feet tall overlooking the Athanasian Ocean. On the gray and white marble rooftop terrace was the symbol of Sophos. It was a circle with a perfect triangle in the center. The whole surface of the circle was paved in gold. The very rare Lapis Lazuli outlined the circle while red rubies formed the triangle. Around the circle were situated 21 gold thrones decorated with purple amethysts for each of the kings. The circle represented Sophos' omnipotence as it was a symbol that has no beginning and no end. The triangle represented two attributes as it intersected the circle. First, the perfect triangle showed his power being unsurpassed. The top of any triangle was significant as it symbolized the highest point that one can ascend. The triangle is also a symbol used to show great wisdom. The circle represents eternal, having no beginning and no end. When this perfect triangle intersected with the circle it stated that Sophos is everlasting, all powerful, all perfect and all wise.

The temple had a large marble staircase that circled around the interior walls of the tower with numerous windows cascading all the way down. Anyone that ascended or descended the stairs would experience scenic views like none ever seen in Athanasia, from whales and dolphins swimming together in the ocean, to colorful sunsets or giant thunderstorms illuminating the sky with crooked streaks of lightning as they approached Telemicha from the east. On the interior of the temple were the guard's quarters from the first level to the tenth level. On the eleventh level was a beautiful marble floor with a gray vignette of the symbol for Sophos. At the center of the room was a podium made of gold, decorated with emeralds and rubies. It held a large ancient book that contained the ancient writings which were said to be penned by Sophos himself. The book was filled with wisdom for walking a righteous path, but its contents were infinite. There was no ending to the book as no matter how many pages were turned more wisdom revealed itself and the ending of the book never grew closer. Looking up from the podium was open air that stretched some 130 feet to the temple ceiling. Along the walls were a dozen lit torches on each level up to the ceiling.

The meeting would take place two hours before sunset for seven consecutive days as the sun setting symbolized the settling of grievances between each kingdom that day. Justinian derived this yearly ritual from a saying in the ancient writings that said, “Do not let the sun go down on a dispute, or bitterness and anger will grow and cause great harm.”

King Justinian had an olive complexion with shoulder length silver hair and emerald green eyes. His hair transformed from black to silver after his father’s passing. Yet, his facial hair was black with the exception of two small patches of gray.

King Justinian received the grievances for mediation in advance. He would often go up to the top of the Temple of Sophos and read through each grievance and ask Sophos for wisdom and discernment in each matter. As he sat on the temple terrace looking through this vast list he noticed a repeated grievance against him by three kingdoms. After reading the grievances he put his head in his hands and released a tired sigh.

The grievances by these three kingdoms had to do with Sprasian, King Justinian’s nephew. Justinian adopted Sprasian at the age of 11 after his father Fabian fell in the last great conflict before the time of peace. His mother had passed away while giving birth to him. (The relationship between Sprasian and his father was strained as Fabian never ceased to grieve over his wife. Yet, it was the fact that Sprasian had been walking a less than noble path that grieved his uncle).

Justinian stared off into the distance and watched pelicans diving into the ocean and bringing up fish, which they immediately gobbled.

This sight reminded him of the first time his father took him to the ocean and showed him the pelicans feeding. Justinian's shoulders relaxed and a smile formed as he looked down at the charges. "King Melmot, of the Island Kingdom of Parrus has the following grievances against Sprasian, the brigand nephew and adopted son of King Justinian. The crimes against the Kingdom of Parrus are as follows:

- The pirating of two Parrusian merchant ships carrying gold and spice.
- The pirating of a Parrusian slave ship of all its human cargo.
- The murder of two ship captains and one first officer.
- For accepting tribute in order to stop pirating in Parrusian waters and then reneging and continuing to pillage Parrusian vessels.

From King Meridian of Othos:

- The pirating of King Meridian's flag ship carrying gold from the king's treasury to buy grain from the Kingdom of Methos.
- For the destruction of an Othosian naval ship and the deaths of its 200 crew members.
- For accepting tribute in order to stop pirating in the waters of the kingdom of Othos. After having received the tribute, Sprasian continued to pillage Othosian vessels including the very messengers that delivered the tribute right after it was given. He even took all the messengers clothes so that they returned naked.

From King Spiegel of Ramsey:

- For the pillaging of two merchant fishing vessels in which all of their catch was stolen.
- For accepting tribute to not pillage in the waters of Ramsey and reneging on the terms of the treaty.
- For the commandeering of a royal battle cruiser in which the cruiser was then used to pillage 2 royal cargo ships carrying food and clothing for the kings royal court."

King Justinian knew after reading these grievances to himself that these three kings were going to want him to pay for the carnage that his nephew Sprasian had caused. At that very moment a memory was triggered where he was instructing young Sprasian after he was caught in the act of stealing at the age of 12. *They were sitting on a fountain in the royal courtyard and Justinian in a firm but soft voice said, "What prompted you to steal one of King Argos' royal horses?"*

Sprasian crossed his arms and replied, "I did not know that what I was doing was wrong?"

Justinian countered, "What do you mean by that?"

Sprasian stuck his chin in the air as he spoke as one who knew an answer to a mystifying question, "My father never taught me that stealing was wrong". His voice began to crescendo with every word, "My father never cared about me. He looked at me as a curse and spent his later days drunk. He blamed me for my mother's death!"

This was the first time that Sprasian had ever opened up to him about his life. Justinian nodded his head and waited a few moments before he answered back. He looked at the boy and smiled, "May I ask you a question?"

Sprasian tilted his head and hesitated in his response for a moment before replying, "Yes?"

Justinian looked down and grabbed Sprasian's dagger hanging on his belt. He held it in front of him and said, "How would you feel if a stranger or even one of your cousins took your dagger from you?"

Sprasian's face turned red as he replied, "I would be angry with them!"

Justinian replied, "Why?"

Sprasian replied, "Because it's mine!"

Justinian smiled at his nephew and said, "Then let us apply your answer to this situation with King Argos' horse. Did you not take something that did not belong to you?"

Sprasian paused before replying, "Yes."

Justinian continued, "How do you think that made King Argos feel?"

Sprasian dropped down to one knee and perched his chin on his right fist. He answered, "It probably made him angry."

Justinian continued, "Why did it make him angry?"

Sprasian put his hands over his face and then gently let them down.

He looked up to Justinian's glittering eyes and admitted, "Because it was something that was his possession. It did not belong to me."

Justinian grinned as he looked at Sprasian, "Well done! You have discerned the truth as one that solves a mathematical equation! Now let me ask you one more question. Did your father's neglect for you as a son force you to steal King Argos' horse?"

Sprasian's head and eyes fell as he replied, "No, it did not."

Justinian's face began to glow when he heard his nephew's answer. "Understand that you are responsible for your own actions. No one else, or anything else is responsible for your actions, because they do not make the decision for you. You are the one who has the final decision on whether to do wrong or right."

With tears in his eyes Sprasian looked to King Justinian, "Please forgive me for stealing the horse."

Justinian exhaled a deep breath in relief, "I am proud of you! Now, you must also apologize to King Argos for it was his horse. This brings us to the last piece of wisdom that I want you to understand. Your actions have consequences, not only on you, but also on those around you."

Sprasian scratched his head and asked, "How do others suffer the consequences for what I have done?

Justinian's face shined brightly as he said, "We bring people into our own storms. If a man has a gambling problem and casts lots with his daily wages and loses all that he has, then he brings his family into his own storm. Instead of providing food for his wife and children, they go hungry as a result of his gambling addiction. That is how other people suffer from someone else's folly. Now, I will go and make restitution to King Argos and hopefully that coupled with your apology will calm his wrath."

Sprasian lifted his head as tears streamed out of his eyes and down his face. "Uncle, please forgive me for rebelling against you and stealing from King Argos. I was wrong to do those things."

The memory then faded away and Justinian thought to himself as he looked at the grievances against him, "He has brought me and my kingdom into his storm of rebellion. Where did I go wrong?"

3 - PORT VERDES, REMAR

In Remar, Sprasian was in the throne room of the castle arguing with a man over the price to build a new ship. The man said, "Your offer does not even cover the wages that I would have to pay my laborers, let alone the materials to build the ship, my Lord."

Sprasian slammed his fist on the throne and then stood up, "Who is your king?"

The man fell to one knee and exclaimed, "You are, my Lord." The man's hands were shaking as he lifted his head and would not make eye contact with Sprasian. "My workers and I have barely scratched a living since you destroyed the Parrusian garrison and hung all of King Melmot's Remarian officials."

Sprasian smirked as he stroked his black beard and began walking in a slow circle around the man. "Do you believe that I have been unfair?" asked Sprasian.

The man trembled and kept his head low as he replied, "All the trade that we had with the kingdoms of Athanasia is gone because they will not support your brigand nation. The taxes you levy against a destitute people keep us from feeding our own families."

Sprasian laughed as he walked in front of the man, squatted down and made my eye contact. "If you are insolvent, then you can always come and work for me. I pay my men very generously."

The man looked away from Sprasian's face and stared down at the marble floor. He uttered, "Two of my sons and the sons of many other families have joined your army because there was no other work for them. We grieve because we do not recognize them anymore. They are not the boys that we raised to live above reproach."

Sprasian gritted his teeth and muttered, "Above reproach." Those words triggered a thought of his righteous uncle, King Justinian. He snarled, "Curse you. Stand up."

The man began to inch backward away from Sprasian. "You defy a command from your king? Stand up!"

The man stood up trembling, keeping his head low and holding his hands up in front of his face. Sprasian pronounced, "Today, I am going to reward you for your piety."

The man slowly dropped his hands and tilted his head and inquired, "My Lord?"

Sprasian unsheathed his sword and ran it through the man. He grinned as he watched the man gasp and fall to the floor dead.

Sprasian wiped off his sword and commanded, “Get this carcass out of my sight.”

Sprasian went back to his throne and took a seat as he had more business to tend to that day. A few minutes later a six foot tall man, burly in stature and pale in complexion entered the throne room. He walked up to the throne and bowed his head slightly. “My Lord, Sprasian.”

Sprasian smiled, “Bremus, is that another scar on your face?”

Bremus grunted, “Yes, it was a gift from an enemy I vanquished during our last raid.”

“You are starting to make a name for yourself as my second in command.” remarked Sprasian.

Bremus growled, “Can we stop with the pleasantries and get to the business at hand?”

Sprasian smirked as he answered, “By all means. What shall we do with the 20 soldiers that surrendered after we plundered Westphal?”

Bremus looked at Sprasian in the eyes and then quickly looked away as he replied, “We should just kill them. They are of no use to us."

Sprasian replied with a grin, "Is that your answer to everything?"

Bremus grunted and then replied, "Why not?"

Sprasian said, "Very well! Do as you judge best."

Bremus looked over to one of his messengers standing in the room and said, "Lead the prisoners to the city square for execution. Wait for me as I will be the one to commence with the executions." The pirate nodded and quickly left.

Sprasian saw a smudge on the hilt of his sword and began to wipe it off with part of his tunic while asking Bremus, "What is next on the agenda?"

Bremus replied, "One of my spies gave me some information. King Melmot is sending a large chest of gold to pay for sheep and wheat that he purchased from King Justinian. It is estimated to be around 10,000 gold coins. However, it did not come close to covering what your uncle gave him. My informant said that your uncle was very generous. He gave King Melmot a shipment worth hundreds of thousands of gold pieces. In return, he asked only for what King Melmot could pay."

Sprasian's eyes perked up as he stopped polishing the hilt of his sword and looked at Bremus. "Ah! This is great news my red-headed friend. My dear uncle's compassion for the people of Parrus who are suffering from the famine has clouded his judgment. He should have known better than to be so generous to King Melmot and the people of Parrus. My altruistic uncle would never care about receiving any payment. However, I think we need to teach King Melmot a lesson so that he understands about who controls these waters. When does the ship leave port, Bremus?"

"In two days." replied Bremus.

Sprasian ran his hand through his short black hair as he thought about what to do. "Let us make preparations for battle! The cargo ship will have a two ship naval escort."

Sprasian ordered, "Prepare my three best ships: The *Miranda*, *Velonova*, and the *Sea Serpent* for the raid."

Bremus replied, "My Lord, I have a little business to take care of first in the city square." Sprasian nodded and Bremus unsheathed his sword and walked out of the throne room.

Sprasian went to his private quarters after meeting with Bremus and wondered why his uncle's compassion had not led to his downfall. "How can such a powerful man be so concerned about people that are not even in his kingdom? He lets other weaker kingdoms take advantage of him. How can he not be setting up his kingdom to be conquered? I would never lead that way lest I desired to give up my power."

As he pondered pirating the ship carrying the gold, a vivid memory of his uncle leapt into his mind. Justinian was standing in the courtyard with a 14 year old Sprasian.

Justinian said, "I have never met anyone with your uncanny ability to inspire people with your words. You think very quickly on your feet and are decisive in your actions. This is a gift in which if you are not careful can be used for great evil rather than the greater good." Justinian came down to eye level with Sprasian and asked, "Why did you beat your classmate within an inch of his life when you sparred with the wooden swords?"

Sprasian roared, "Because he said that he was a better swordsman than me. He said evil things to me about my mother!"

Justinian looked down to the ground and sighed before looking back up at Sprasian and saying, "Understand that what this boy said to you was wrong and you have a right to be angry. The problem is that you let your anger cloud your better judgment. You became filled with great wrath and had it not been for the interference of others, you would have killed that boy. What you must understand is that a man's discretion makes him slow to anger. It is to his benefit to overlook an offense."

Sprasian rolled his eyes and replied, "Do you cite the ancient writings of Sophos for everything?"

Justinian looked at the boy more intently, elevated his voice and said, "It is a virtue called meekness."

Sprasian crossed his arms and bellowed back, "Meekness is weakness!"

Justinian gritted his teeth and his face started to turn pink. Then Justinian remembered, "Harsh words stir up anger, but a gentle response turns away wrath." Justinian's teeth unclenched and his face returned to its normal color as he said, "Meekness is not weakness. It is power under control."

Sprasian furrowed his brow and asked, "How is meekness power under control?"

"Let me explain." countered Justinian. "Do you wield the best sword of anyone in your class?"

Sprasian folded his arms and elevated his head. "There is no one in school that can wield a sword as well as I can!"

Justinian smiled and nodded his head as he responded, "Sprasian, knowing that you were the best swordsman in the school, why didn't you ignore the words of this boy that spoke foolishly?"

Sprasian barked, "Because I wanted to show him that he was a liar. I wanted to embarrass him in front of everyone so that they would see what I saw."

Justinian exclaimed, "Meekness, being power under control simply means that you, in this instance knowing that you were the best swordsman, could overlook his offense instead of putting him in his place. That you would absorb the transgression and not give him what he deserved. It takes more strength to absorb an offense than to repay one."

Sprasian promptly replied, "Why would I want to absorb his transgression? He should suffer for what he did, an eye for an eye, Uncle!"

Justinian locked eyes with his nephew, "Understand this, Sprasian! That law was instituted with the ancients because men's desire for revenge would supersede the transgression that was inflicted upon them by the other party. The injured party would want to inflict more suffering and pain than what was inflicted upon them. You demonstrated this by allowing the boy's transgression against you with words to overtake your emotions. He has two broken arms, and a fractured sternum. How does that equal an eye for an eye? You inflicted more pain and suffering on him, than he did with you!"

Sprasian looked away from his uncle and his face became red.

Then Justinian's voice softened. "Sprasian, your actions have made you a breaker of the law. You will not be required to be incarcerated, but will be taken to the city commons where punishment will be administered in front of all the people."

Sprasian cried out, "Why? Why would you humiliate me?"

Justinian continued, "You will receive 12 lashes for this abominable act. You must pay the consequences for your actions. Please understand that there are consequences for evil behavior. If you are ignorant of what an evil behavior is, then you will know it when you are punished."

Sprasian put his hands on his head and began pulling his hair. He started to cry and then growled. He clenched his fists and looked to the sky and then the ground. Seeing this, Justinian said, "You must overcome this anger and pride that dwells in your heart."

Sprasian shouted, "Never!"

Justinian's eyes shut upon hearing his nephew's response and he rested his head in his hands.

Sprasian said, "I will take my lashes and leave you and your wretched kingdom forever."

Sprasian went to the city commons and received his lashes.

Justinian sat down with the boy after his punishment and said, "When one is humiliated, they can go one of two ways. They will either gain humility and embrace it, or turn to pride and walk with great bitterness and hatred. With humility comes wisdom, but with pride comes destruction."

Shortly after his punishment, Sprasian left his privileged life and ran away from the land of Methos to the island kingdom of Parrus. It was there that he associated himself with some brigands. In time he became their leader and grew this group to the size of an army of 7,000 men. Thus, the feared pirate Sprasian was born.

As the vivid memory faded from Sprasian's mind he began wrestling with conviction for the evil acts he committed. Sprasian didn't know what was manifesting this conviction, but as always he fervently rejected it and justified to himself that there is no absolute truth, thus he is free to do whatever he wants. He walked over to his bed and laid down to get some rest before their next raid against King Melmot.

4 - SALEM, PORTUS

Mardok hastily entered the throne room of King Argos with the deceased royal messenger on his shoulders.

"My Lord!" Mardok said. "Arsinian is on his way and has uncovered a plot to assassinate you!"

King Argos' eyes opened wide and his face started to become pale. He asked, "What evidence do you have to support this claim? What happened to my messenger?"

At that moment Arsinian burst into the throne room with a host of royal guards. With them was bound a man that was one of the top lieutenants in the royal guard named Romus. As this mighty host brought him in they threw him to the ground in front of King Argos' throne. King Argos looked down at him and said, "Romus?"

At that moment Mardok threw the deceased messenger to the floor while looking down at Romus. He kicked him in the stomach and chided, "Tell the king what you have told me, traitor!"

Romus was trembling as tears filled his eyes. In his humiliation he slowly raised his head and looked up to the king, "I have conspired with some others to assassinate you, great king, and take your throne."

Arsinian was standing over him when these words were spoken

and cried, "Treason!"

King Argos took a deep breath as his face began to turn red. He bellowed out, "You plotted to take my throne?" He paused for a moment and began to clench his fists. "When and how was this treacherous act to take place?"

Romus exclaimed, "In your caravan as you returned from Methos from the meeting of kings." Romus dropped his head and looked down at the floor. He had a hidden nail in his hands that he pressed into the inner thigh of his left leg. He started sobbing before King Argos.

King Argos walked down and stood over Romus and drew his sword. Romus started sobbing even harder. King Argos hollered, "Who is conspiring with you? Speak to me, traitor!" At that moment Argos pointed his sword at his chest. "Answer me, traitor!"

Romus pressed the nail even harder into his thigh and sobbed violently, "One of your royal protectors. Spiros, of the Adelphos, your royal messenger, the captain of the royal guard and all of his lieutenants."

King Argos' eyes and mouth opened wide as he slowly turned from Romus to Spiros, one of his immortal protectors.

Mardok looked to the host of royal guards that had entered the room with him and roared, "Seize them!" The royal drew their swords and leapt forward to arrest those accused.

Tears began to form as he stared at his royal protector. "Spiros?"

quivered King Argos.

Spiros answered, “He is lying, great King! I would never commit a treasonous act against you! I was charged by Sophos to protect you!”

Spiros and all those accused were seized and brought before the king. Spiros was taken and placed next to Romus. The king continued to look at Spiros and said, “Why, Spiros? Why would you seek to supplant me? How could you betray me?”

Spiros’ eyes remained soft and warm despite the charge. He shook his head, looked at King Argos in the eyes, and calmly stated, “It is a lie. You know that I would never betray you, my Lord. You are my friend.”

As King Argos looked at Spiros he started to recall the event that began their friendship. King Argos was but a prince when he met Spiros. The Adelphos protected the King’s family, so it was easy for them to have close relationships. King Lorrent of Portus sent his son Argos to a mountainous region in the north eastern part of the kingdom. The villages and cities that were located in this area had been plagued by attacks from marauders. Prince Argos and Spiros were sent with 5,000 soldiers to bring order back to this area of their kingdom. When they reached this region Argos had his men set up camp. He cared for the citizens of the kingdom so he took a small detachment of about 50 men to visit one of the towns called Thieras.

“Spiros, please stay here while I travel to Thieras to survey the losses they have suffered for the last several months.” ordered Prince Argos.

Spiros protested, "I have sworn to protect your father, thus I am a protector of all that he loves and cherishes, including his family. I must insist that I travel with you."

Argos put his hand over his face, sighed, and said, "Spiros, I don't need your protection. I can take care of myself! I have never understood why the kings of Athanasia were given immortal protectors by Sophos. We mortals are all going to perish at some point from old age if some other peril doesn't claim our lives. I order you to stay here and set up the camp and prepare for an expedition tomorrow. I want you to send out scouts this afternoon to find the marauder hideaways and give us an accurate count of their numbers."

"With all due respect, my Lord, we don't know their positions, which leaves you open for attack as you travel to Thieras." pleaded Spiros.

"I have made up my mind, Spiros. Thieras is 10 miles away which will be a short jaunt for a small group. Do not question my decision any longer!"

"Please forgive me, my Lord." said Spiros. "These are dangerous lands. There is no order in this part of our kingdom. I thought it prudent to allow our scouts to scour the area so we can know our surroundings and potentially find where these thieves reside. It is unsafe to go blindly into the wilderness not knowing what may lie in wait for us."

"I do appreciate your concern Spiros," growled Argos. "Please trust my judgment. I do not need your help or counsel to make decisions. I am

a prince who is first in line to the throne. I consider myself much wiser than a protector. That is why I am in line to be king and you are not!"

Spiros' eyes opened wide immediately after Argos' cutting words. He slowly closed his eyes and bowed his head as he gently replied, "I will set up camp and send out the scouts immediately. I will await your successful return from Thieras, my Lord."

Argos then mounted his horse with 50 other men and said, "Good. I am glad that you see things my way." With that he galloped off with his men on the road to Thieras.

As Argos approached Thieras they headed down a pass with a dense forest. As they rode through this area Prince Argos heard a bird call come from the left side of the road from within the forest. Moments later Argos heard another bird call from the right side of the road in the forest. At that moment a rope that was camouflaged on the road extended up. It was tied to trees on each side of the road and stood four feet off the road. As soon as the horses hit the rope they tripped and fell unencumbered to the ground. All of their riders plunged to the ground screaming. Hundreds of armed men immediately emptied from the forest on both sides of the road.

The attackers walked up to Argos's injured men sprawled out over the ground and impaled every one of them as they lay helpless. They grabbed the young prince who lay semi-conscious from his hard fall and bound him. They took the horses and any other valuables they could gather and entered the forest.

The leader of the ambush had long blond hair and scars on his face. He walked up to the bound prince as they departed and laughed. "Look at the great fortune we have been given today. The life of a prince will fetch us quite a price. If the king wants his son back he will pay a price that will make us kings in our own right."

As the leader of this band of thieves gloated, a scout for Spiros stood hidden in the distance. He left his position and rode his horse hastily back to Spiros. As he reached the crest of a nearby hill he saw Spiros and the entire army gathered on their horses.

The scout rode in full stride all the way up to Spiros and then came to an abrupt stop. "My lord!" said the scout whose face was as pale as snow. "Prince Argos was ambushed by marauders on the trail that goes through the forest. He was taken captive, but none in his party were spared. They disappeared into the forest on the left hand side of the road."

"How many were in their party?" replied Spiros.

"It was less than a thousand men, my lord. They were all on foot," responded the scout.

Spiros looked to his top lieutenant on his right and barked, "Borus! The road to Mepos runs parallel to the road to Theiras on the western end of the forest. Take half the men with you and wait. We will take the road to Thieras and make our way through the forest. We will flush them out so that they retreat west to your position. When you hear the battle horn, rally your troops to that area and prepare to engage our enemies. We must save the prince!

Borus' voice erupted, "Yes, my lord! We will be ready for these anarchists. I cannot wait to repay them for the evil they have done this day!" Borus then blew his horn twice and made haste west with his soldiers to flank the marauders.

Spiros then blew his horn once and headed down the road to Thieras with the remaining soldiers in tow. When they reached the location of the ambush, Spiros and his men dismounted, surveyed the scene, and saw the fallen soldiers scattered on the ground. He said, "Many brave souls have given their lives in defense of their prince today. They should be honored with a proper burial and not left for the scavengers. I desire 50 volunteers that would honor these men by giving them a deserved proper burial."

A young sergeant stepped forward and said, "These men were from our unit and we loved them dearly. Rather than seeking vengeance, the soldiers under my command would like to honor our comrades with proper a burial. We would like you to exact punishment in our place for Prince Argos and our brothers."

Spiros replied, "Sergeant, you and your men are a ray of light in a dark hour. Please proceed. You have my gratitude."

Without hesitation the Sergeant and his men began digging a burial site to the right of the road.

Spiros then ordered all of his men to enter the forest to the left of the road. He sent two scouts to go ahead of the army to do some reconnaissance. Spiros broke his soldiers up into five units and sent them into the forest. He ordered two units to go to the northwest and two units to go to the southwest. His unit would head west.

The scouts went ahead of the force and tracked the path of this large host. They followed the trail of foot prints to a stream where they encountered a few of the marauders getting a drink. After a few moments the marauders crossed the stream while the scouts followed at a distance. When the marauders crossed the stream they headed to the right and went off the path into the forest. The scouts slowly made their way across the stream and followed the men's trail by examining broken twigs and disturbed branches left in their wake. After several minutes of slow and careful movement through the forest they found the camp and witnessed a bound Argos being ridiculed by his captors. The thieves were mocking him, spitting ale in his face and even struck him with their fists. The scouts were enraged when they saw this act of cruelty. Fueled by their anger they made their way back to Spiros at a feverish pace.

When they reached Spiros they informed him of what they saw immediately. "My lord!" said one of the scouts. "There were between six hundred and eight hundred men in their camp. They are positioned directly west of here. These men were insulting our future king, spitting ale in his face and striking him with their fists."

Spiros was incensed by this disgrace of Prince Argos. "Men of Portus! Our prince has been found, prepare for battle!" Word spread about Prince Argos and the poor treatment he was enduring. The soldiers marched forth with Spiros at a pace that was just short of running.

Spiros sent a dozen scouts ahead to clear the way of any enemy lookouts. The scouts were able to stealthily find six enemy watchmen on the perimeter. They broke up into groups of two and baited the look outs to their direction by throwing a rock or stick into the brush. As they approached to check on the noise, one of the Portusian's would uncloak and cover the guard's mouth from behind while the other would stab them with a dagger. The army marched forward unannounced and unnoticed. It was late in the evening, so Spiros' forces had the camouflage of darkness. When the men were ready, Spiros blew his horn for all to hear and his men charged the camp.

The marauders began to panic as they were caught off guard by this horn and the screams coming from the woods all around them. The marauders scrambled to grab their swords knocking things over and tripping over one another. The Portusian forces stormed out of the woods and clashed swords with their enemy. Spiros ran towards Argos. He belted the first marauder he met with a shield, knocking him unconscious. He engaged another and made quick work of him as his strike cut the marauder's sword in half and took his life. Eight more marauders charged Spiros, but several arrows came from behind him from the crossbows of Portusian soldiers. All eight men fell to the ground leaving an opening to the Prince.

Spiros made it to Argos' position and with a mighty swing struck one guard down. He then blocked the attack of another with his shield and impaled the guard with his sword. By this time his men reached

Argos' position and easily vanquished their outnumbered and outmatched foes.

Spiros cut Argos' binds as a smile beamed on his face. As he grabbed Prince Argos' hand he took a deep breath and then exhaled as if a huge weight was taken off his shoulders. "My Lord, I am so pleased to see that you are safe. Please forgive me for failing you as your royal protector."

The young Prince's eyes looked up at Spiros and began to well with tears. "No apology is necessary my faithful protector." He paused for a moment, then nodding his head he said, "You were right, Spiros. Thank you for coming to find me. Forgive me for my harsh words towards you. Please forgive me for not listening to your wise counsel. You only had my best interests at heart, not yours. I was blinded by my own arrogant pride. I shall never forget this act of faithfulness. I owe you my life and consider you my dearest friend."

The memory quickly faded as Argos' eyes had grown red as he fought back his emotions, but tears began to form. Argos looked at Spiros who was surrounded by the remaining three Adelphos charged to protect the king and several royal guards.

Argos' voice cracked as he said, "Give them your sword, old friend."

Spiros unsheathed his sword, laid it flat across the palms of his hands and dropped to his knees. He bowed his head and raised the sword with both hands above his head. Arsinian grabbed the sword by the handle and brought it to his side. The king then made a proclamation, "All of these men will be brought before the court in front of the entire kingdom to face these charges. If the evidence convicts them of these accusations, then they will all be executed immediately. Take them away!"

Spiros was grabbed and removed from the king's presence with Romus, the captain of the guard, and the rest of his lieutenants that stood accused. Arsinian and the two other Adelphos with 50 royal guards escorted them to the royal prison.

Mardok looked over at King Argos who was covering his eyes with his right forearm and quivering. "My Lord, there may be other conspirators that we have yet to discover. Allow me to assemble a contingent of soldiers and move all your family to a safe location until this treachery is fully uncovered."

King Argos looked at Mardok and said, "By all means, Mardok. Do what you judge best for my family." Mardok bowed and left the throne room. He signaled one of the guards to follow him as he went to gather King Argos' family.

At that time all the prisoners were being marched down the road that led to the royal prison after being put in shackles. The sound of chains could be heard clanging as many of the prisoners had drooping eyes and hanging heads gazing at the cobblestone road they walked. Buildings lined the street like a wall on both sides. There were some peasants that were in the streets walking by or tending to business in front of the buildings, but were very sparse.

Arsinian walked up next to Spiros as his head hung low. "How could you plot to kill the king whom you were created to serve?"

"You have to believe me when I say that I would never try to usurp the throne of our king," said Spiros.

Romus exclaimed, "How interesting, Spiros! Just last night we spoke about your plans for this rebellion. This was your idea, of which I foolishly embraced."

The other shackled men spoke up and supported Romus' statement. "I was a fool for listening to you, Spiros." said one prisoner. "This is your fault, Spiros." said another.

Arsinian commented, "It seems that your co-conspirator's think otherwise." Then looking at the Adelphos named Victus he said, "Wouldn't you agree, Victus?"

Victus turned to Arsinian and scowled. "I am not a judge, Arsinian. That decision is reserved for the king. Let King Argos weigh the facts and judge accordingly."

"Well said, Victus! I could not agree more." replied Arsinian.

As they approached a four way intersection which sat a half mile away from the prison, an ambush fell upon them as a flurry of arrows came from the sky and struck down many of the guards. Assassins disguised as citizens took off their peasant clothing and rushed toward this contingent from the left and right with swords drawn.

The prisoners huddled together off to the side to avoid the armed conflict unfolding beside them, but several of the attackers ran towards them. One freed Spiros and Romus, and the others struck down the lieutenants and the captain of the guard.

Romus screamed, “What are you doing? They were not supposed to be killed!”

Spiros raised his brow and exclaimed, “What did you say?” At that point Arsinian was making his way to the remaining prisoners. He and Victus cut down 10 of their attackers to get over to Romus and Spiros.

Arsinian was holding Spiros’ sword which he had surrendered to King Argos. He commanded, “Victus, retake Spiros and I will get Romus.”

Victus nodded and made his way quickly to Spiros. During the melee Victus’s back was turned towards Romus and Arsinian as he headed towards Spiros. Arsinian was then met by an assassin and inadvertently dropped Spiros’ sword in front of Romus. As Arsinian fought the attacker, Romus picked up Spiros’ sword and impaled Victus from behind. Victus fell face first to the ground and passed into eternity. He was the first Adelphos to have ever been killed.

Spiros, in anger, charged Romus and tackled him to the ground, knocking the sword from his hand. Romus quickly grabbed for a sword of one of the fallen royal guards that lay next to him and took a swipe at Spiros. Spiros rolled away from the strike, but was hit in the left arm. Spiros winced in pain as he rolled over to his sword, grabbed it, and stood back up on his feet. Looking down at the wound he knew that it would fully heal within the hour, however, this did not stop him from engaging Romus. Spiros dodged a thrust towards his abdomen which left Romus open. Spiros punched Romus in his face and he fell to the ground. Spiros swung his sword down at his foe, but Romus was able to come to his senses and block the death blow within the nick of time. Romus' eyes and mouth were wide open as he broke out into a heavy sweat. He then rolled to his right and blocked another blow from Spiros. Romus then jumped back to his feet, pulled back his sword behind him, and took a series of swings at Spiros that caused him to lose his balance from the force. Spiros was able to block each of the clumsy blows, then countered with some powerful swings at Romus' head causing him to stagger backwards. Spiros pursued him as he was determined to subdue his foe. It so happened that the skirmish abruptly ended with the remaining attackers retreating into the streets. Arsinian screamed out, "Do not give chase to the attackers!"

Arsinian then looked over towards the dueling prisoners and yelled, "Spiros has killed an Adelphos using his own sword! Seize them both!" Arsinian and the remaining guards made haste to capture both prisoners.

Spiros ran when he heard Arsinian's command. He was immediately confronted by two Portusian soldiers as he made his escape. He punched one in the face knocking him out and knocked the sword out of the others hand with a mighty swing. Spiros ran east and was pursued by several soldiers who were right behind him. As he fled, he ran into a peasant and fell down. He got back up quickly and ran into a pub with his pursuers' right behind him. As he made his way through the pub he kicked one patron out of his seat, took his chair, and hit a soldier in his face knocking him onto a table and then to the ground. He then swung the chair and broke it over the next soldier in pursuit knocking him into a table full of patrons. Spiros then rammed his way through the crowd in the pub and worked his way up a stairwell with several soldiers in pursuit. When he made his way to the top of the stairwell he saw a large open window with a long burgundy tapestry. He threw the tapestry out of the window and then drew his sword. He stepped onto the window sill and ran his sword through the tapestry severing it completely from its hooks so that his pursuers would not be able to follow him. He then jumped out of the window which stood 40 feet from the ground and landed safely on his feet. He found a horse tied to a feeding trough next to him, so he cut the rope holding the horse and jumped on the stallion, riding quickly out of the city.

Romus stayed and dropped his sword as the guards slowly surrounded him. With his hands raised in the air he exclaimed, "I watched Spiros try to escape with the attackers. They had come to rescue us, but I was resolved to stand trial for my transgressions against the king. I watched him grab his sword from the ground and impale the royal guardian from behind. That was when I picked up one of the swords that lay on the ground and tried to stop him from leaving with the attackers. They were coming to save us. I have a penitent heart and just seek to now protect our king."

The guards rebound Romus and made haste to the royal prison. Arsinian turned to a soldier by his side and said, "Sergeant, send a messenger to the city gate and have them close it immediately. Send another to the palace and have them lock it down. We must protect the king."

The sergeant nodded and then belted out the order to two of his soldiers who left rapidly to their assigned destinations.

Arsinian stayed back with two of the guards and investigated the area in hopes that they would find clues as to who attacked.

While they were searching Arsinian found the symbol for the kingdom of Methos underneath the right breastplate of an attacker's armor. They also discovered that the swords used in the battle were forged in the land of Methos. They too contained the Methosian insignia on the bottom of the hilt. If true, this would lead to a war between the two strongest kingdoms in Athanasia, and likely affect countless others as well.

Arsinian smiled and took the evidence back to the palace for King Argos to view.

A wounded Spiros rode through the city gate well before the guard that was dispatched by Arsinian was able to call for them to be closed. Yet, this didn't slow Spiros as he knew that the sooner he could get to safety the better chance he would have to understand what just happened.

He decided to hurry to the ocean as he would surely be captured if he tried to make his way to the nearest kingdom which was Methos. He was only 10 miles from the ocean, so he rode as hard and fast as he could to the port city of Phileus. He hoped to come across a freighter setting sail to a kingdom across the sea, perhaps Parrus. Parrus was mostly a lawless land with waters governed by no one and where fugitive was a title that most men could claim. If he could find a ship to take him there he would have the chance to regroup and find answers to his many questions.

5 - SALEM, PORTUS

The next day King Argos was gathered with his whole family in the palace courtyard as the sun began to rise. "My dearest ones, the reason we are gathered here today is that a plot against my life was discovered. My life is in danger, and if my life is in danger so too are all those in my family. I cannot risk losing any of you." Argos' throat started to tighten and his eyes softened as he observed the heads of his family beginning to hang. He continued, "If I were to fall prey to an assassin I would desire Portus to remain in your hands as it has since its boundaries were first drawn. You will all be taken to a safe location and protected by my most loyal soldiers. When this storm has passed I will bring you back. Pray that we root out the conspirators quickly so that your leave from me will not be long."

His beloved wife lay her head on his bosom and asked, "Must we all leave your side?"

King Argos replied, "This is not my wish. There are evil men that have infiltrated our ranks and seek to supplant me. No one in our family is safe."

The Queen's eyes closed as she tightened the embrace of her husband. Then the king's sons and daughters approached and began to hug their father. King Argos smiled and held his head high though his heart was fluttering rapidly. He took his sons aside and encouraged them. “You will be the men of the house while you are away. I want you to protect your mother and your sisters to ensure that no one harms them. Can you do that?” His four sons nodded and then backed away slowly with their heads slumped. “King Argos replied, “Hold your heads high my sons, for I will see you again.” Argos went and embraced each son again and they all wrapped their arms tightly around him.

King Argos then looked to his daughters who came up and gave him a long embrace. All the daughters tears cleared from their eyes and smiles began to crack through on their faces. Argos stepped aside and watched as his sons began to chase one another, while his daughters began to braid each other’s hair. The laughter from his children was like medicine to King Argos as his heart began to slow and the palms of his hands began to dry. The smile on his face was no longer manufactured.

The peace was quickly broken as Argos saw Mardok enter the courtyard. He called his wife and children over and gave them all one last embrace. Mardok bowed when he reached the king, “My Lord, it is time for us to depart.”

Argos nodded his head and said, “Yes, of course.” He went around and kissed each of his children on their heads before finishing with a caress of his bride’s hair and a kiss on her lips. “This will only be for a short time, my love. I will see you again.” said Argos.

The Queen smiled and put her hand on her husband’s face, “We will be fine. Do not worry about us.”

Mardok turned to the family and soldiers, “We will be departing within the hour. The caravan is awaiting our departure outside of the castle so let us make way as we have much ground to cover."

With that, the family began making their way out of the castle while King Argos looked on with sagging eyes and a lowered head.

Later in the day on the other side of the capital city of Salem marched the caravan with a great multitude of men prepared for battle. Mardok was leading five columns of fifty soldiers each in the rear, while there were five columns of 50 soldiers in the front of this contingent. Every soldier carried an ornate shield that had an eagle carved on the front, which represented the kingdom of Portus. They all wore heavy battle armor and carried swords. However, King Argos' entire family from his wife to their sons and daughters and siblings rode in open air carriages in the middle of the party. The number of King Argos' entire family stood at 147.

The streets they were traveling were cobblestone and were fairly narrow at about 100 feet wide. Buildings lined both sides of the streets like walls. The caravan was drawing nearer to a complex of three towers within the city that was easily defensible, and had many hidden escape routes if there was an attack. As they were marching up the final hill to their destination they started to approach an intersection. Atop the hill they were climbing, the sun was setting, blinding the host as they marched. Suddenly, they heard a faint rumbling sound in the distance that began to sound louder and louder. One soldier in the front was able to shield the sun enough to see several flaming wagons barreling down the hill at their position. The soldier cried out, "Brace yourselves!"

That was when the fiery, weighted-down wagons pummeled the front line soldiers. The impact sounded like a crashing of metal heard when two charging enemy forces meet in battle. Piercing screams started to multiply as the flaming pitch in the carts emptied all over the soldiers. These men began screaming and rolling around on the ground to extinguish their burning bodies. The front line of the caravan had been shattered as very few went unscathed by the attack.

Moments after the carts struck the soldiers, those in the caravan began to hear a "whoosh" in the air. A soldier cried out, "Take cover!" as arrows started raining down. They hit the remaining soldiers in the front line, but more specifically they seemed to be aimed at the king's family in the center. The soldiers guarding the queen and her children put their shields and even their bodies in the way of the arrows. They managed to absorb several volleys of arrows protecting the royal family, but the guards were now much fewer. As quickly as they began, the arrows stopped and a large force of men stormed down the hill onto their position and clashed with the few soldiers that remained in the front of the column. The soldiers guarding the rear came under attack from a group of heavily armed men. In total, they were ambushed by roughly 1000 enemies.

The attackers from the front easily overcame their targets, but Mardok made his way up with a small group of soldiers to defend the queen and the heirs to the throne.

Slowly, the attackers made their way to the middle where the King's family was being protected and began executing the few family members that had lived through the fiery carts and barrage of arrows.

The attackers were lightly armored and carried swords, axes, and spears. Not many of the attackers brandished shields as the attack seemed to be a quick strike.

With the front forces depleted the remnants of the royal family began to retreat away from the attackers in hopes of making it to the rear guard for protection, but were quickly overtaken.

However, Mardok and nine valiant warriors of Portus that accompanied him engaged the attackers that were executing what was left of the king's family. All that remained were the queen and two of her sons and her three daughters.

One assassin approached the queen who stood defenseless in front of her remaining children. As this attacker was about to impale her, Mardok's sword came down and cut off the head of the spear just before the tip reached her body. Then one of the valiant warriors cut the assassin down. Within seconds the attackers collapsed on the queen's position. Mardok screamed to the nine warriors with him, "Form a circle around the queen and her children! Defend them with every fiber of your being!"

The attackers in the front descended upon the circle of 10 soldiers protecting what was left of the king's family. Mardok blocked the ax of one attacker and punched him in the face. The assassin fell to the ground and Mardok struck him. Mardok then took the ax and flung it at an approaching attacker bringing him down before his feet. Mardok took this fallen attacker's sword and wielded two. As soon as this happened Mardok blocked a sword strike and went down to one knee and impaled his attacker with his other sword. Mardok stood back up and blocked a spear strike with one sword and impaled the attacker with his other sword. He then blocked a sword strike with the sword in his left hand and then blocked an axe strike with the sword in his right. He kicked the assassin with the axe in the chest and swung his free sword into the side of his other attacker. The attacker with the ax swung it at Mardok's head which he blocked, dropped to one knee, and impaled with his other sword.

The circle of soldiers around the royal family was working as they kept their enemies at bay. Many screams could be heard as they drove their swords into the several dozen men that surrounded them. The soldiers called out, "Watch my right!" or "Hold your positions!" The soldiers lay waste to so many enemies that they were starting to tire. It only got worse as the fighting shifted away from Mardok as he was eradicating any attackers that confronted him. The assassins tried to punch a hole to the right of the queen by having men fling their bodies into the shields, but the tiring soldiers never backed down. As the soldiers used their shields to fend off the push, one of the king's remaining sons said to the other, "Do you remember what father said?"

The other son nodded his head and replied, "We have to protect mother and our sisters."

The king's young sons then picked up swords of the fallen attackers and began to thrust at their legs incapacitating them. With this help the soldiers began to push back the attackers by striking them in the face with their shields thereby stunning them momentarily and then slashing them down with their swords. These soldiers yelled out words of encouragement with every foe that was struck down by the sons. They were liberal with their praise as they said, "Well done," or "Good stroke." However, Mardok remained silent, not uttering one word of praise to the boys.

Motivated by the valor of her two sons the queen picked up a spear from one of many fallen assassins. She looked around the circle and witnessed a man standing on the shoulders of one of his fellow assassins looking to jump over the protectors. She thrust her spear into the man and he fell to the ground. Then another man climbed on an enemy's shoulders and she ran him through. Her daughters who were mature women then grabbed for fallen weapons and began to fight these evil men. One prince struck an attacker on the foot with his sword and as he screamed in pain the queen impaled him with her spear. The three daughters had each picked up a spear and began thrusting them into the enemy as they were held at bay by the shields of their Portusian protectors. Many of their foes fell as a result. The other prince rotated around the circle thrusting his sword into the enemy and watching many of them fall. Their protectors, including Mardok were keeping the assassins at bay, but the deceased assassins that lay around them started to create another obstacle. These two barriers allowed the remnant of the royal family to stab and spear their attackers without being touched.

The carnage was so great that the assassins began to flee. Mardok turned his head to check the rear flank and saw that the Portusian soldiers were holding their attackers to a stalemate.

Mardok witnessed some of the Portusian soldiers in the rear make their way up to pursue the attackers. He then looked around the circle and saw that all of the attackers in the front broke away into full retreat. The queen and her family were so emboldened that they even gave chase to the fleeing assassins, cutting them down from behind as they fled. The queen turned and yelled out to her soldiers, "Soldiers of Portus, give chase to the enemy for the battle is ours!" Her words rang through the ears of her soldiers as they began to cheer and gave chase to the enemy.

The tide of the battle had turned and victory was at hand. The Portusian soldiers and royal family were catching their attackers and cutting them down. As the queen looked behind her, she saw the assassins in the rear begin to retreat. She then heard something cutting through the air from behind her. Her muscles tensed, her eyes opened wide, and she dropped her spear as she slowly turned her head to verify her fear. There were countless arrows raining down from the sky onto the royal family's position. The queen yelled, "Take cover!" and was hit by 3 arrows in her chest. Shrieks of pain were heard as the arrows bombarded everyone within a 50 foot diameter of the royal family, which included their attackers.

Mardok caught two arrows into his body, one into his right shoulder and the other into his torso. He crawled over to the family as both arrows still resided in his body and witnessed that they had all died. No member of King Argos' bloodline remained.

The remaining assassins, once seeing their work was complete, began to scatter and dissolve away from the carnage they created just as quickly as they had arrived. The remaining soldiers fell to their knees and began weeping because they had failed their king. Yet, this weeping was not out of fear for their lives, but rather out of love for their king as they fell prostrate in front of the bodies of the royal family.

Before Mardok stood, he looked one last time at the fallen royal household and smirked. It was brief, but there nonetheless, as he had to resume the role of a grief-stricken loyalist to the king.

Mardok rose and broke the arrows off that attempted to bring him to the same fate as the royal family. Yet, he like Arsinian looked around to find "evidence" of who might have committed these heinous acts. It was no surprise to Mardok when he found some men that had the emblem of Methos etched on their armor and he also brought forth an arrow that was Methosian. Everything was coming together as he picked up this false evidence to present to the king. Mardok's eyes began to well with tears as he dropped to his knees and put his hands over his face. He wept loudly, "Please forgive me for failing you, my king."

This ended the darkest day in Athanasian history, but was only the first step in an elaborate plan.

6 - THE ISLAND OF TELEMICHA, METHOS

King Justinian knelt on top of the temple of Sophos where he was meditating on a copy of the ancient writings originally penned by Sophos. There was a beautiful red sunset behind him that was starting to take shape as its beams created a burgundy sky amongst the clouds. As he was sitting there he bowed his head down to pray. No sooner had he done this did he hear the call of a dove in front of him. Startled, he looked up and saw a man surrounded by doves standing in the center of the symbol for Sophos amongst the 21 thrones. He saw a tall man with broad shoulders, but was dressed in nothing more than sackcloth. He looked like a man that was still in his youth with a cleanly shaven face, short-jet black hair, and piercing blue eyes.

This man of mystery began walking towards him. As he did so the doves began to form two lines on the marble rooftop, one on each side of him that stretched like a pathway to Justinian. Justinian had never seen a sight like this, yet he was not afraid as this stranger approached down the dove lined path.

As this man reached him Justinian asked, “Who are you?”

The man standing there replied, “Who do you think that I am?”

Justinian said, “I feel like I have known you for a very long time. I have never seen your face before, but you seem so familiar to me.”

The man smiled and replied, "I have known you your entire life, Justinian. I wove you together in your mother's womb."

"Lord Sophos!" replied Justinian. "Forgive me for not recognizing the creator of all things. No one has seen you in 2000 years."

"Quite true, no one has seen me in 2000 years, but I have still been very much at work. You can see the effects of the wind, but you cannot see the wind. So too, know that I have always been here at work. Is faith exercised by having sight first or when the object of your faith becomes sight? Remember when you desired a wife, but no woman would have you because of your ailments? You cried out for many years until one day you stumbled upon one that saw your heart as I do. When you were betrothed to Alexis on my temple, you recognized that faith is the assurance of things hoped for and the conviction of things not seen."

Justinian immediately fell to the ground, bowed his face and said, "Forgive me, Lord Sophos, for my unfaithfulness."

Sophos' voice resonated with the gentleness of a harp, "Arise." He continued, "Justinian, you have been one of my most faithful servants. You seek righteousness and you always call on my name for wisdom. You have led your people with the heart of a servant. That is the very foundation of leadership. Your obedience proves your love for me, and I consider you one of my dear friends."

Justinian's face shone as bright as the sun at its peak on a summer day. "Thank you, Lord Sophos." He paused for a moment. "Many people do not think of me the way that you do. Your words strengthen my spirit."

Sophos then placed his left arm around Justinian and led him to the ledge of the temple facing the sunset. "Justinian, I am here with you today to let you know that your faith is about to be tested to likes of which it has never been tested before. A great evil has finally revealed itself in Athanasia and you will hear of it in due time. It will be the darkest time this world has ever seen. I want to encourage you to be strong and courageous! Stand faithfully in my truths and you will weather this storm, emerging victorious. If your faith dwindles, so too will the hopes of overcoming this great evil. My visit to you today was to let your faith become sight, so that it may strengthen you as this tempest approaches."

Justinian opened his mouth as if to speak and then closed it and looked down at his feet. Sophos smiled, "All your questions will be answered in due time. Now you must be about my work. There will be a passenger on a cargo ship coming into the port of your capital city tomorrow. The ship will just be making a small delivery and will pick up a few provisions before heading to Parrus. Find this passenger and implore him to stay with you until the end of the settling of grievances. He will have many questions too. Together you will be able to answer some of these questions, however, you must listen to him as every word uttered from his mouth will be truth.

"When everyone is discharged from the settling of grievances you are to send him on his way to Parrus for I have work for him there."

Justinian asked, "My Lord, might I ask how we will be able to identify this man?"

"Indeed. He will be a man out of his position. Keep this in the forefront of your mind and you will recognize him," replied Sophos.

Justinian scratched his head and then gave a small nod and smile. "Yes, my Lord."

Sophos walked to the precipice of the tower and turned to give one last pearl of wisdom to Justinian. "What I am about to tell you, you already know and demonstrate faithfully. However, the truth always bears repeating because it is easy for man to forget. Mercy and grace are signs of humility that always lead to compassion. Keep alert for opportunities to demonstrate these virtues in the midst of this storm. However, keep in mind that this evil will deal ruthlessly with all that oppose it, so you too must deal ruthlessly with this evil. You cannot reason or treat with evil for it only seeks its own insatiable ends."

Justinian began to tremble as he cried out to Sophos who turned his back to leave. "Lord Sophos, why have you revealed this to me? Why are you leaving me alone to face it?"

Sophos turned towards Justinian and smiled. "I will be here by your side always. Be strong and courageous my dear friend!"

Those words immediately changed the countenance of Justinian as the trembling ceased and a warmth flowed through his body. The presence of Sophos brought a peace similar to that of his own father who had encouraged him in times of worry. Justinian said, "My Lord, I do not look forward to embracing this evil that you have spoken of, but I trust that you will strengthen me to endure it."

Sophos walked over and gave him an embrace, pulled back, and looking at Justinian in the eyes said, "I always keep my promises."

Justinian's head immediately arose and peaked like that of the sun during the height of day. "My Lord, will I ever see you again?"

Sophos responded, "Indeed, faithful servant." At that moment the doves that had accompanied Sophos flew off into the sunset. Justinian turned from Sophos and gazed at this majestic site, but when he turned back to Sophos, he had vanished. Justinian looked around the entire roof top terrace for Sophos and then refocused on the doves. As he gazed at the sunset, Justinian's face was illumined with a beaming smile and the stature of a servant eager to carry out his master's will.

7 - PHILEUS, PORTUS

In Portus, Spiros entered the harbor and dismounted his horse. He began looking around at the various ships to see which one's had their oars in the water and sails mounted. He reached his hand into his pocket and fumbled around for a moment, but found no coins to pay for his voyage. He turned to the horse and started to stroke its head and face, "The only thing of value that I have is you, my faithful steed. Come, let us see if we can find you a good master."

Spiros' solicitation of the horse was not well received. One sea merchant shouted, "Off you go!" while another barked, "I am a fisherman, not a seller of equine." After several rejections Spiros sighed and began to stroke the horse's neck with his hand. "Well, my faithful steed, it seems that we are stuck with each other. We will be fugitives together. How does that sound?" The horse began to nicker softly as Spiros continued to pet him. Then a voice from behind him said, "That is one magnificent horse you have, sir."

Spiros quickly turned around and saw a man and a boy admiring the horse. Spiros asked, "Have you some interest in my steed?"

The man was wearing tattered pants and a shirt made of sackcloth. He handed his fishing nets over to his son and walked over to Spiros. "That is a kingly horse that you ride, my lord, but we cannot afford to purchase it from you."

Spiros pried a little further, “You cannot afford to purchase my horse, but do you have some need for it?”

When Spiros said this, the little boy came up to the horse with a countenance reminiscent of a child that is given their first pet. He dropped his fish nets and began to gently pet the horse on the nose softly. “That’s it, boy. You are a good, boy. You are one of the most beautiful animal’s I have ever seen.”

The horse responded by burying his nose into the boys hair and sniffing around. The boy began to giggle, “Stop it. It tickles.” The horse then licked him on the head.

Spiros and the father both had a small chuckle as they witnessed the interactions between the boy and the horse. The father said, “This is the first horse that he has ever touched.” The boy then closed his eyes and laid his face on the horse’s furry nose and stretched his arms up to the horse’s neck and held him.

Spiros asked, “Would you be interested in buying him? I am not looking to make a profit with the sale. I just need enough money to pay my way to Parrus.”

The father said, “We do have some need for it. We are unable to carry our catch each day to the market which is 10 miles away. It takes us several hours on foot to haul a small amount of fish. By the time we reach the market it is towards the end of the day, so the fish begin to rot and most people are finished with their daily food purchases. We have a carriage we can use, but no horse to pull it.”

Spiros shook his head and said, "My mind is no longer on my plight, but rather on yours." Spiros walked up to the man and put his right hand on the father's left shoulder and looking him in the eyes said, "I would like you to have the horse. My need for money is but for a moment to travel to Parrus, but your need is daily to provide for your family. Please take my horse."

The father's face began to stream tears like a dam that had opened it gates. Spiros squatted down and looked at the boy in the eyes. "If I let you have my horse, do you promise to take good care of it?"

The boy nodded his head up and down wildly. "Very well then, the horse is yours to keep!" said Spiros.

The father hugged Spiros and said, "Bless you, friend! We will never forget this generosity. Please, we would be honored to have you stay with us."

Spiros replied, "I must decline your generous offer as I need to make my way to Parrus."

The man said, "We know of a ship headed to Parrus within the hour. Come! We will hurry you to the ship."

When they came to the ship Spiros found the captain and asked, "What would be the fee for my passage to the kingdom of Parrus?"

The captain replied, "20 pieces of gold."

Spiros exclaimed, "That is a large price you ask. Is there any work I could do on the ship in exchange for passage?"

"No, we have enough hired hands to maintain the ship. However, I would gladly take that beautiful sword that you have as payment," remarked the captain.

Spiros held the grip of the priceless sword tightly. The blade at his side was worth a fleet of ships, so the captain spoke true when he said it would pay for his passage. Spiros gazed at the captain and sensed that he was a shrewd man and that the captain saw his eagerness as a way to profit.

Spiros thought to himself, "This sword was given to me by Sophos. I was charged to never surrender my sword to anyone, but what good would the sword be to a dead man?" Spiros began to gnash his teeth under the cover of his lips as he unsheathed his sword and placed it flat into both hands of the ship's captain.

The captain held the sword up to his face and began to gaze at its workmanship. His gaze soon became a trance as he uttered softly, "Beautiful." The captain turned and walked away grinning.

Before Spiros went on board he turned and hugged the man and his young son. The man extended his hand and said, "My name is Jordan and this is my son Marcus. We owe you a great debt for what you have done for us today."

Spiros responded, "You owe me nothing. For if we only give to those that give back to us, what reward is there in that?"

Spiros turned to board the ship, but heard Jordan say, "What is your name benevolent servant of the king?"

Spiros spun to face the man once again. "How did you know that I serve the king?"

A smiling Jordan said, "We have seen a sword like that once before. Only an Adelphos would carry a sword of that caliber."

Spiros whispered, "My name is Spiros. I am a servant of the king who has been forced into exile."

Jordan asked, "Why are you going into exile?"

Spiros replied, "I am being chased by a lie, and that is all that I can say. Now, I must go, thank you for leading me to this ship."

Spiros then turned and boarded the ship and was greeted by the first mate who guided him down to his quarters.

Spiros stared and ran his hands over the woodwork of the ship. He asked, "Is this ship made from Megalos trees?"

The first mate answered, "Yes, but I do not know much about them."

Spiros said, "Well, let me enlighten you."

The first mate rolled his eyes and said, "Why not."

Spiros started, "The Megalos trees are the rarest trees in Athanasia. These trees could grow as tall as 300 feet with 30 foot trunks, but could only be found in a small section of forest of only a few hundred miles in both Parrus and Methos. This natural resource produced the sturdiest, most durable wood in all of Athanasia. As legend has it, the trees are eternal and do not die of disease or old age. The trees would only die if they were uprooted from the ground or transplanted into another environment. I firmly believe that it is the soil in which they are planted that gives them endless life and makes them colossal in stature. The ship was a world class ship built by the Parrusian's. The Parrusian's and Methosian's are master ship builders, and they build the strongest, most ornate seafaring ships in all of Athanasia because of the wood that they used from the Megalos trees. In fact, King Lorrent had received some of this wood from Methos and built a royal cruiser that had now been passed down to King Argos and was still in service over 600 years later."

The first mate replied, "Aren't you a bastion of useless knowledge."

Spiros replied, "When knowledge is internalized then it becomes wisdom, which is priceless."

The first mate shrugged, "Only gold is of any value to me."

Spiros did not utter another word, but just followed the man into the lower levels of the ship. The man escorted him into a room with three beds and a fireplace. Spiros walked over to the bed closest to the fireplace and sat down as he began to make himself comfortable. When the first mate left the room Spiros lay down and began to finally relax from the crackle and warmth of the fire. As Spiros lay in the bed his troubled thoughts slowly began to fade away. As it so happened, Spiros fell into a trance like state as the ship proceeded to leave the port.

In the Salem there were soldiers blocking every exit, and Mardok had declared the capital city to be put on lockdown so as to prevent any of these invaders from escaping. Skirmishes were reported all around the city where King Argos' soldiers were fighting these attackers and vanquishing them, but a few managed to escape. Yet, a few of these invaders were captured alive and brought to the royal palace for questioning.

Mardok stormed into the throne room with a host of soldiers. The king was surrounded by members of a personal guard by order of Mardok. King Argos voice shook as he said, "What is the meaning of this Mardok? Why has the palace been locked down and I placed under heavy guard?"

Mardok went to one of the king's ears and whispered, "My Lord, I have grave news. The assassination plot that we uncovered came to pass today. We were ambushed by a host of men." Mardok then told Argos the details of the ambushes, but did not tell him what happened to his family.

After hearing this King Argos stood silent. Then his eyes opened wide and he began to breathe heavily for a few moments before he screamed, "What happened to my wife? Where are my sons and daughters? Tell me, Mardok!"

The soldiers in the room with Mardok had tears in their eyes. King Argos witnessed this and became despondent as he yelled, "What happened to my family?"

Mardok was able to produce false tears and said, "They fell."

King Argos became weak and fell to his knees. He began to cry out for some time, with his hurt echoing off the walls. However, his cries began to turn to angry wails and the king arose with his eyes wide and nostrils flared, "Who did this?"

Mardok handed the king a few arrows and two pieces of armor with the Methosian insignia of the triangle within a circle engraved on them.

"They were Methosian, my Lord. Justinian was behind this. These are what we found on the attackers that we vanquished."

The king snapped the arrows in rage and yelled, "Justinian did this? No. Justinian was responsible for this?"

Mardok softly replied, "The evidence most certainly suggests that it was."

Argos screamed, "Why? Why would he do such evil?"

Mardok signaled to one of the soldiers and three men who were bound were brought up before the king.

Mardok said, "We have captured or killed almost all of the attackers. A few escaped including Spiros, but we managed to capture three of their men."

The king turned to the men.

Mardok raised his voice, "Tell Lord Argos what you told me!"

As there was silence from all three he proceeded to strike them on their knees with a metal rod. The men screamed in agony as he then began to strike them across the face with his fists as they were kneeling down. Then Mardok picked one of the men up by the hair and screamed, “Tell King Argos who sent you!”

The man gasped in pain and belted out, “King Justinian! He is the one who sent us. He wants your kingdom!”

Mardok then dropped the prisoner on the ground. King Argos clenched his teeth and his face began to turn a dark red. He screamed so loud that the people began to tremble. He drew his sword and roared like a hungry lion ready to devour its prey. He approached the assassins and ran his sword through all three of the men. King Argos dropped his sword after he killed the last man and fell to his hands and knees screaming once again. He bellowed, “Why do I not feel any better. Is not revenge supposed to quench the pain?”

A close vizier came to Argos’ aid. He helped Argos to his feet and took the king aside, “My Lord, is not Sophos the one who heals the pain from loss. Revenge only intensifies bitterness, it does not relieve it.”

King Argos said, “I cannot do this. It is Sophos’s fault that this happened.”

The vizier responded, “Oh great King, please understand that Sophos gives and takes away. We live in a flawed world, thus we can expect to have our bells rung by suffering. I cannot attest that I know why Sophos allows these things to happen. In truth, as the creator of everything he can take away those things that we love dearest and not tell us why. They are his gifts that he chooses to bestow on us and can at any moment take them away."

Mardok had positioned himself closer to the king and with a turned ear heard every word the vizier spoke. He walked quickly over to Argos and interrupted, "My Lord, we have all the evidence we need. I believe it is best that we go forward and avenge you of this treacherous act. There must be justice for this wrong."

The vizier furrowed his brow and said, "Don't you know that revenge doesn't heal wounds, but only exasperates them. It devours your soul until there is no joy or happiness left. You become a bitter, pessimistic, judgmental person full of hatred and devoid of all virtue."

Mardok looked at him and said, "You unjust man. Your king has lost all that is dearest to him and you counsel him to not seek justice? Were you too part of this insurrection? To not take revenge is to let Justinian escape his act of treachery without consequences." Mardok then yelled, "Guards seize him and take him away to be questioned."

The vizier exclaimed, "My Lord, please do not listen to this foolishness. He is the head of the order of the Adelphos and knows all the writings and ways of Sophos, yet his words and actions suggest that he has diverted away from them. Sophos abhors vengeance."

King Argos was pale and dark circles under his eyes had suddenly made him look like a man who had gone days without rest. He looked at this vizier and said, "Mardok is the only person I trust now. He has been the only one trying to protect me. Take my vizier away to be questioned! If you find that he does indeed have a hand in this insurrection, then he is to be executed immediately."

Arsinian grabbed the vizier and bound him before taking him away.

Mardok then ordered, "Everyone must leave the throne now. "The king needs time alone to grieve." As everyone was leaving Mardok thought, "I wonder how much time a deeply wounded man in solitude will need to lose hope and take his life?"

8 - THE WATERS OF NORTHWEST PARRUS

It was a foggy day on the waters of Parrus as three battle ships sailed on what would be a long voyage to Methos. One of the ships had 10,000 gold pieces to pay for the provisions that King Justinian sent to Parrus, but each ship was heavily armed and had 300 soldiers ready for battle. Hours after their departure the fog began to lift. The ships were sailing in a triangle formation when the soldier in the crow's nest of the lead ship noticed a vessel heading towards the right flank of their formation. He called out "To arms! To arms!"

The captain yelled to the soldier, "Is it Sprasian?

The soldier exclaimed, "Yes, it is the bane of our existence!"

When the crew heard this they became quiet and their faces began to turn pale. The captain seeing that his men's courage began to waiver broke the silence, "Very well! Soldiers of Parrus, too long have we been made a fool by the brigand nation! Too long have we cowered before evil men! I am tired of kissing the feet of these serpents. Today is the day that we fight for each other, for our loved ones and for ourselves. Let this be the day that we show this monster that we are not afraid! Men of Parrus, prepare for battle!"

The countenance changed on the crews face as their natural color returned and they began to grit their teeth. A voice from the crew shouted, "Kill the lot of them!" All the men on the ship began yelling in agreeance. The captain ordered, "To the armory! Archers, be on the ready!"

As the Parrusian troops were preparing for battle the soldier in the crow's nest pointed to two ships coming fast onto their left flank. The captain had the other two battleships come up to their left and right flank in a tight formation. They decreased their speed because a battle was inevitable. Archers lined the decks off all three ships. Some had long bows to fire at a distance, while others had crossbows for short range fighting, but both had arrows dipped in tar ready to light and set the ships ablaze.

As Sprasian's ship, the *Sea Serpent*, approached from the Parrusian right flank, he didn't slow his pace. The first mate inquired, "Should we slow our approach and engage the center ship?"

Sprasian replied, "No, hold your speed. The middle ship is a decoy. They are playing a game of hide the treasure. They must think me a fool."

As the ship swiftly approached the Parrusians, Sprasian called out to his crew, "Men of the *Sea Serpent*, we are about to endure a fierce battle for a king's ransom. First Mate, make haste to the closest ship on the right flank. On that ship will be where our treasure lies. I will need a boarding party of 100 men to take this precious cargo. Those that choose to board the enemy ship and retrieve the gold shall receive a sum of three times greater than any other bandit fighting today."

In only moments he had the 100 volunteers he needed.

He then yelled above the clamor, “Men of the *Sea Serpent*, today we make history. We have never plundered an amount of gold this large. Today we seek to strike fear in our enemies and make known to them who rules these seas. How dare they sail through our waters without paying tribute? How dare they think we will allow their offense to go unpunished? Today we will chasten the kingdom of Parrus for their blatant disrespect against our pirate nation!”

There then arose a great cheer from all the men on the *Sea Serpent* as they raised their swords in the air. As the *Sea Serpent* closed in on their target they began to see volleys of arrows fired in their direction. Sprasian yelled, “Take cover! Extinguish any fire you see!”

The brigands immediately hid underneath their shields which were covered with damp leather. As the arrows hit the ship and shields they made a “thunk” sound. The flaming arrows that hit the shields were extinguished, but those that hit the pirate crew and the ship started small blazes. Crewman frantically took buckets of water to extinguish their comrades and the areas of the ship that were hit. The pirates were only 100 yards from their target when a second volley of arrows began to whoosh by the brigands, striking several without shields dead. At this point Sprasian hit a lever that lowered the head of the sea serpent on the front of the ship. A giant spike began to protrude from the serpent’s mouth. Sprasian then yelled, “Brace yourselves!”

Within a few seconds the spike and the serpents head smashed into the battleship and pierced through it. The impact knocked most of the men on the opposing ship to the floor while others fell overboard. The pirates were braced and ready so that after the impact some swung across onto the ship, while the majority boarded by laying a bridge across onto the opposing ship's deck. The pirates flooded over and a battle ensued.

Sprasian made his way over and jumped into the thick of the battle. He was greeted by three Parrusian soldiers as soon as he set foot on their vessel. He struck one down and took his sword as he began to defend himself against the other two soldiers. Sprasian was able to slay one soldier with the sword in his right hand and impale the second with the sword in his left hand.

Sprasian then yelled out to some of his men boarding the Parrusian ship, "Follow me into the depths of the ship! Show no mercy!"

Sprasian charged to the door that would lead them down to the gold, which was defended by several soldiers. Sprasian charged the soldiers and threw one sword end over end impaling one guard. Being aware of his surroundings he noticed a loaded crossbow laying on the ground in front of him. With one foot he kicked the crossbow up to his right hand and then discharged an arrow into another of the soldiers guarding the door. He then engaged another soldier by blocking his strike and then punching him in the face and knocking him to the deck of the ship. The remaining soldiers charged Sprasian, but their fixation turned deadly as his companions flanked them, slaying them all.

Sprasian then yelled to his companions, "Good work, men! You are some of the bravest souls that I have ever had the pleasure to pillage with. Let us make way to the gold!"

Sprasian made his way with this group of pirates into the lower level of the ship. Most of the fighting was taking place on the deck of the ship but there was still some resistance as they got closer to their goal, the gold.

When they had reached the bowels of the ship they could see where the serpent had breached the hull and water was beginning to make its way in.

The soldiers guarding the treasure outnumbered the pirates. They took up a defensive position using the confined space to their advantage and formed a wall. Sprasian and his men engaged them, but were unable to break their ranks as the small space made it hard to wield swords. Behind this line of men were other guards with daggers and they would stab the pirates from behind the line causing many to fall to the ground creating another obstacle. Sprasian's men began to lose heart and back up from the line of soldiers who did not give chase. Sprasian screamed, "Men, hold your positions!" When his men held their positions, he yelled, "Reform the line!" His men quickly lined back up and waited for the next command.

Sprasian just waited as the two opposing forces just stared at each other from a distance. The Parrusian soldiers began to look to the left and to the right frantically, while sweat began to bead down their face. A young sergeant was heard saying, "Why are they not engaging?"

Sprasian looked over to the serpent's mouth which had breached the hull and was directly behind the Parrusians. Within a few moments pirates came funneling out of the serpent's mouth and engaged the soldiers from behind. Sprasian yelled, "Charge!" The Parrusians were now surrounded and outnumbered.

The close quarters still made it challenging to fight even though Sprasian's pirates now outnumbered and outflanked the Parrusians. Sprasian yelled, amongst all the commotion to the few pirates next to him, "Follow my lead."

Sprasian found the weakest point in the surrounded Parrusian defense and exploited it by cutting the soldiers down in his way. When he and his men were able to clear out a gap amongst the fighting, he yelled out, "Do not let fear grip your hearts, men. Victory is within our grasp!"

Sprasian's words and actions reinvigorated the pirates and they stormed forward towards the gold. The screams in the bowels of the ship were almost deafening as Parrusian soldiers and pirates were slain. This skirmish became more complicated as water rushing into the ship was almost up to their knees. Sprasian had the treasure in his sight and began make his way to it, but tripped over some of the dead bodies that began to float. The soldiers seeing Sprasian on the floor went in for the kill. One soldier thrust his sword at Sprasian who dodged to the right and then pulled out his dagger and cut the man's arms. The man cried out, dropped his sword and fell to his knees. Sprasian continued as the confined space made it hard to wield a sword, but not a dagger. He gashed soldier after soldier and very quickly his pirates followed suit, pulling out their daggers and incapacitating the enemy. Within moments there was no more enemy obstruction to the gold. Sprasian yelled to his men, "Check the chest!"

Very quickly two of his men broke the lock and opened it, revealing its contents. The sparkle caught Sprasian's eye as he grinned. "It is time to go home boys! Our work here is done!" The pirates quickly grabbed the chest and then started their retreat through the serpent's mouth with the treasure.

The message of the gold's procurement quickly reached the first mate's ears and he blew a horn to signal the pirates to disengage, and as best they could the attackers began flooding back onto their ship. Sprasian went top side after boarding through the serpent's mouth and he saw the fighting remained intense on the other two battleships as the *Miranda* and *Velonova* pulled alongside them.

The pirates started making their way back to the *Miranda* and *Velonova* as the horn of retreat was blown. On the *Sea Serpent*, Sprasian made his way to the wheel on the ship, oars descended from the inside of the pirate vessel and started rowing backwards. Sprasian took the wheel after the serpent's head had pulled out of the enemy ship, pulling away more of the hull as they went. He started turning the wheel of the ship to the right.

During this stage the other two pirate ships fired flaming arrows of their own into the sails and onto the deck of the wounded ships. The fire soon spread forcing the battleship crews to stop their pursuit of Sprasian and the other two ships and address the more immediate issue of their safety.

Sprasian smirked while he said, “I am the greatest pirate that has ever lived in Athanasia! No kingdom can stop me from taking what I desire!”

The young captain on the ship that had just been robbed yelled, “Archers, on the ready!”

One of the archers responded, “But sir, our ship is ablaze.”

The captain picked up a bow and looked at the man and said, “Drop your bucket and pick up your bow!” The archer dropped his bucket and found his bow. Others seeing this began to do the same.

The captain picked up an arrow and readied it on his bow. He yelled, “Make ready!” The archers loaded their bows. The captain shouted, “Aim!” The captain smirked as he aimed at Sprasian, “Fire.” All the bows discharged their arrows.

Sprasian was in a daze smiling as he thought to himself, “What is stopping me from overtaking Parrus and becoming the King of Parrus? Is there anything too great for me?” No sooner had this thought crossed Sprasian’s mind did the arrows begin to whoosh onto the ship. The arrows started hitting around him while dozens of his men began falling to the deck pierced by arrows. That was when Sprasian was pierced in his upper left thigh and screamed. Intense pain radiated from his leg and traveled from his spine to his head.

Sprasian dropped to his knees in front of the ship’s wheel holding his left thigh and wincing from the excruciating pain. No sooner had he fallen to the deck on his knees was he pierced in his left upper chest. The pain was intense initially, but then his body went numb as he fell backward like a tree that had just been cut down. He had glazed eyes and a blank stare on his face as he looked up to the heavens. Immediately after being hit, his first mate took the wheel and barked, "Get Sprasian into his cabin!"

As Sprasian bled, he thought, "Never have I encountered such opposition in a raid. No one has ever touched me until now. I was indestructible." Then he thought, "What if I die? Then everything I pillaged was for nothing." Sprasian started to break into a cold sweat and began to turn pale. His eye lids started to become heavy and the light started to fade into dark. The last thought that crossed his mind before he lost consciousness was, "Am I being punished for my crimes?"

The men began to treat his injuries by taking salt water and pouring it onto the wounds as a way to clean them. Then another pirate brought out a bottle of clear liquor and poured it onto Sprasian's wounds. His face turned dark red as he lay down, his upper torso thrust to the upright position as he cried out until his breath had run out, then fell back to the table motionless. The men then took clean rags and placed them over his injuries and applied pressure to slow the bleeding.

The pirate ships sailed hastily to their home in Port Verdes. As they reached the docks a pale Sprasian was rushed off the ship and to a physician in the city. The physician inspected the wounds and then dislodged the arrows with a gripping tool. Sprasian began to scream and writhe in pain, but was restrained by bonds on his arms and legs. The doctor then walked to a fireplace and pulled out a rod that was dark orange at the tip. A nurse came over with a short but thick stick and placed it in Sprasian's mouth. The doctor said, "Biting down will help with the pain." Sprasian's eyes opened wide as the doctor took the red hot iron and placed it on his wounds. Long stretches of screams came from the physician's home, but there came a point where silence returned as the physician sat next to the wounded pirate leader and smiled, "Sprasian, your wounds have been cauterized and you should have a full recovery in several months. Do you realize that had the arrow in your chest landed two inches lower it would have struck your heart and killed you instantly? Now, the arrow that hit you in the leg was ¼ inch away from hitting the artery in your leg. Had that happened you would have bled out and died."

The physician laughed and shook his head in disbelief of Sprasian's great fortune. "You are a lucky man, Sprasian. You will live to plunder another day. The luck of the gods must have been with you."

With that, the physician went out of the room and left Sprasian as he stared out of the window by his bed. His men came in and took him from the physician's home and placed him on a cart filled with straw and headed toward the palace. During the bumpy journey Sprasian kept thinking of the stinging pain in his chest and leg when the arrows hit. The fear of uncertainty washed over him in those moments as well as the words of the physician. He thought to himself, "Why am I still alive? Have I been given a second chance? Should I continue or cease in my ways?

Accompanying Sprasian was Bremus who had taken count of the men that were lost and wounded. He counted 295 men that were killed in the fighting and another 170 that were wounded; over 1/2 of their men.

The battle had left many of the men somber and sitting either alone or in small groups, wide-eyed, retelling what had happened to them. The shaken feeling the men had could be felt in the air, but Bremus seemed to be the only one who was exuberant over the battle. He was talking to himself as he walked by groups and was overheard by some of the men saying, "Well done, Bremus. You killed 31 men today." He continued, "There should be a day in my honor for my many conquests." One of the pirates that heard him remarked, "Aren't you going to honor our dead and not yourself?"

Bremus' eyes opened as if they were on the verge of popping out of his face and his pale complexion turned red. He unsheathed his sword, pointed it at the man, and ordered, "What did you say?"

The pirate opened his mouth to speak, but Bremus grabbed him by the neck and began choking him with one hand. Bremus put his face right over that of his victim and said, "I care nothing of the dead. They are nothing more than a means to an end. I care for no one but myself, and that includes Sprasian who was foolish enough to get hit by two arrows. One day I will be your leader."

Bremus took his hand off the throat of the pirate who began to cough and gasp for air. Bremus stood over the man and said, "I should kill you for your insolence."

The man dropped to his knees and put his hands into the air. "Please do not kill me, my lord."

Bremus said, "I will spare your life, but will give you a token to remember the day that you spoke out of turn." Bremus took his dagger and jammed it into the man's left arm. He looked to all the men around him, "Let this be a warning to you all. If anyone speaks out of line to me ever again, I will take their life."

The men all looked down to the ground as Bremus stared at them. He barked, "Good."

As Bremus walked toward the ships that executed the raid his eyes glazed over as he fantasized about killing people and stealing their wealth. He wondered, "It would not take much to finish Sprasian in his weakened state, making me the leader. Sprasian might be ripe for the plucking."

As the pirates were unloading the bodies of their dead comrades off the ships Bremus ordered, "Take them to the incinerator."

One of the pirates asked, "Should we try to identify them first?

Bremus replied, "They are useless. I don't want to waste time to see if they had any family. It will only take resources away from our pillaging. Burn them."

Bremus made his way to the *Sea Serpent* to take tally of the spoils for the day, and smiling as he did so. He counted 10,077 gold pieces, skimmed 77 gold pieces from the top and put them in his satchel to make it an even 10,000 as was expected.

After counting the gold Bremus started his way back to the palace to check on the condition of Sprasian. As he walked from the docks up the cobblestone roads to the palace he had a thought from his past manifest. It quickly consumed his mind as he began to meditate on it.

"Bremus! Bremus!" yelled his father, Braedon. "Do you have the tent ready for our customer?"

The 18 year old Bremus had just finished rolling a new tent that he and his father worked on. He and his two younger brothers carried the tent from the back of their home to the front. Waiting there was his father and a man dressed in fine clothes and wearing several rings.

"Good job, Bremus! Now please load our customer's tent into his carriage," said his father.

Bremus loaded the tent into a large carriage that was drawn by four horses. When he finished he went to his father who patted him on the back and said, "Thank you, my son, for your help making this tent."

Braedon's family was quite poor and could barely afford to keep food on the table. When Bremus saw the wealthy customer of his father's pull out a large satchel of gold to pay his father's fee, he began to gaze at it. This initiated a day dream of living in a large home with many servants and animals. He thought about having chests of gold in a large room where he played with, and counted the coins. The dream quickly passed and Bremus immediately hated this wealthy man because he possessed what Bremus did not have.

The wealthy customer gave Braedon more than his asking price for the tent. Braedon responded, Thank you for your altruism. I am grateful for this grace. This will help me to feed my family for a month."

All the man said in reply was, "You are most welcome. You are a hard worker and a man of integrity. Thank you for making a tent of this fine quality for me."

The man then took his right arm and grabbed Braedon's left shoulder as an embrace. His eyes were very soft and he cracked a small smile as he looked at Braedon. He then turned and boarded his large wagon and the two servants with him began to conduct the horses forward to take them all home.

As the man rode off Bremus asked his father a question. "Do you ever desire to be wealthy like that man?"

Braedon was caught off guard by Bremus' comment. He raised his eyes and then let out a laugh. "I think everyone desires to be wealthy like that man, but we must first learn to be content with the blessings we have been given. If we are not content with even the little we have, then we will grow envious and covetous. Those are signs of ungrateful hearts. We must be content in all things we have been given my son, no matter how small they are when compared to others. If we do not, then lust will set in and we will do the vilest of things in order to attain wealth."

Bremus replied, "Are you saying that I am ungrateful and lack contentment?"

Braedon shook his head and responded, "Why does a thief steal? Why does a man use dishonest scales when calculating the price for a customer? It is because he has greed in his heart. That greed is what directs his actions. That is why I am telling you to not covet what that man has or you will become a greedy man. Rather, be content with what Sophos has given us. I am to be a steward over what Sophos has given me, not over what others have."

Bremus scowled at his father. "So you are saying that I am greedy because I covet my neighbor's possessions?"

Bremus began to grit his teeth while his face began to turn red, and after a few moments of silence he yelled back at his father, "It is not fair that we are poor and that he is rich. Is it wrong to desire what he has? Why can't I have what he has?"

Braedon countered, "It is not wrong to be wealthy. It is wrong to covet what someone else has, which seems to me what you are doing now. Greed tempts every person no matter how high or how low your social class is. Do not give into this evil temptation for it will take you places that you never would have imagined going, my son. You must fight it for it is crouching at your door. Be content with what Sophos has given us and you will have a life filled with joy which is far greater than any material possession."

Bremus shook his head and pointed his finger in his father's face. "No, I don't agree, father. One day I will be rich and will be able to buy and do whatever I please." He then stormed off into the house.

Braedon was greatly concerned for he had seen hints of this in Bremus' life before, but never had it manifested like this. "My son's true heart is now revealing itself," he murmured to himself. "I cannot and must not give up on him."

In time, Bremus continued making tents for his father, but started to cut corners which affected the tents quality. He did this thinking that he was saving his family money by using less material and spending less time on their creation so as to turn around tents more quickly. His father began receiving bad reports from customers about their quality. They demanded their money back or that the tents be fixed properly to the standard that they had agreed to. Braedon was now marked with a bad reputation which affected his already struggling business. When he confronted his son, he responded with a lie saying, "I used all the materials necessary and did not withhold any effort in their creation."

Braedon then showed him an example where Bremus neglected to stitch the tent and even used a cheaper material that the customer never wanted. Bremus started to growl when his father showed him to be liar.

"How could you do this, my son? You have destroyed my reputation and our family starves as a result," said Braedon with tears in his eyes.

"I was only trying to bring more money into to our family so that we could have a better life," screamed Bremus.

Braedon raised his voice to rebuke Bremus, but his eyes began to cloud with tears. "You have brought great shame upon our family. Your lack of contentment has caused you to be greedy. Your greed has caused you to become lazy, to lie and to steal. It has destroyed our family business, but most importantly, our name. I have taught you to be better than this, but you have ignored my wisdom. You have no contrition for what you have done. You are a 20 year old man which makes you old enough to leave the house. Please gather your things and leave our home. Your mother, brothers and I love you very much, but your actions have given me no choice."

As Braedon looked at his son in the eyes, he pointed out to the road and said, "Leave."

Bremus began to cry as his father's words left a gaping wound in his heart. His mother, brothers and father were all crying as they hugged him. Bremus then became incensed with rage. "How dare you force me to leave when all I tried to do is help our family!" He pushed his family away and stood alone.

Braedon then extended his hand to his son with a small pouch that contained all the money they had. "Bremus, please take this money."

Bremus fell prostrate to the ground as he cried at his father's feet and covered his head with his hands. He then began pulling his hair and thinking to himself, "My family is willing to starve so that I may eat? They choose to suffer on my behalf?" This act of mercy and grace was heaping what felt like burning coals on his head. Bremus stood up with tears still streaming from his eyes, and in anger he grabbed his father's money and said, "I hate you all!" He then ran down the road in front of his parent's house never to be seen by his family again.

As the memory faded Bremus gnashed his teeth to the thought of what his father did. As he approached the palace to see Sprasian he began to scowl while squeezing the hilt of his sword. Finally, Bremus erupted with a scream, unsheathed his sword and struck a feeding trough, which he split in half. He started breathing heavy as sweat poured down his face after the strike. Bystanders were looking at him with wide eyes and began to step away from him. With his mouth wide open he continued to breathe heavily and grunt. Bremus then looked up and saw the people around him staring, which prompted the return of his senses. His face went from a dark red back to its pale complexion. Bremus sheathed his sword and then walked up to the entrance of the palace to Sprasian's quarters to check on his health.

While Bremus was on his way, Sprasian was awakened in his royal quarters and was attended by a beautiful nurse that lived under his rule on the island. Sprasian was enamored by her gentleness as she removed the bandages and cleaned his wounds. This seemingly inconsolable man's heartbeat began to slow and he fell into a blank stare from her soothing touch.

Sprasian broke the silence, "What do you think about a man like me?"

She responded to his question. "You seem like a man that has lost his way."

Sprasian smirked as he replied, "Ha! A woman that is direct is so refreshing. Explain to me how I have lost my way?"

The nurse responded as she continued tending to him, "You do things that are morally wrong. You have a gaping hole in your life that you cannot seem to fill. You try to fill it with money and countless other things, but no matter how much you get you are never satisfied. It seems you think these actions will make you whole but your wounds don't heal."

She sighed and then continued.

"Since when did gold become more valuable than human life?

Sprasian opened his mouth and just stared at her. After a few moments he said, "You have just overwhelmed me with your response. I am not quite sure how to respond." He pondered the question in silence as she began dipping more clean rags in fresh water.

Katherine continued, "Deep is the pit of despair to those who lose loved ones to the sword, as the emptiness that remains will only yield painful memories."

Katherine paused, then looking at Sprasian in the eyes said, "I believe you should do to others just as you would want them to do to you. What do you think?"

The room became silent as the only sounds that could be heard was that of the water being wrung from the cloth back into the bowl.

Sprasian replied, "You speak very boldly for a person whose life I could end with one command or a swing of my sword."

Katherine replied, "You asked for the truth, so I gave it to you. Do not ask me the question if you do not want to know the answer."

Sprasian stared at her with his cheeks raised so that his teeth flashed like a wolf posturing for a fight against its adversary. He replied, "It would be wise to bridle your tongue before I cut it out."

Katherine was paralyzed by his words, while her face started to turn pink and her head dropped, not looking over to Sprasian. Her voice quivered as she replied, "Forgive me for being so sharp with my words, my Lord. I meant you no malice by them. I just wanted to convey to you how your actions have hurt others and for you to reflect on that sentiment. I should have been gentler with my tongue."

Sprasian's countenance changed as his eyes softened and he laid back on his pillow looking up at the ceiling. After a moment of reflection he replied, "I never looked at the things I did or decisions I made from the standpoint of how my actions would affect the lives of others. This is the first time my heart has felt heavy after a raid. Yet, you are wrong if you think I am not aware of that hollow feeling."

The nurse smiled and put the covers to the bed back on Sprasian and tucked them slightly. She said, "You are a walking miracle. You should have never survived these wounds. Every life is precious. Today your life was spared for a greater reason than either you or I know. Only in time will you be able to discern your greater purpose. Our creator must have an amazing plan for your life."

The nurse turned and began to walk out the room when Sprasian asked, "What is your name?"

The nurse replied, “Katherine.”

Sprasian replied, “Of course. Your name means, ‘purity’.”

She smiled at Sprasian and left the room. Sprasian thought, “What would a pure one have to do with a wretch like me?” I could take anything I wanted but I can never force anything to want me.” As she left Sprasian’s eyes began to fill with tears as the faces of many of the people he killed began rushing through his mind. He never realized how many wives he had widowed or children he had orphaned. He never contemplated about the cargo he stole over many years as preventing people from eating or being clothed. He imagined how he would feel if he had a wife or children that were taken away from him. The exhaustion from the day began to take him, so he closed his eyes and quickly fell asleep.

9 - THE WATERS OF WESTERN ATHANASIA

Spiros was in a deep trance in his quarters on the cargo ship heading to Parrus. His body lay completely still, but in this trance his spirit began to float. He felt wind blowing against his face, but saw nothing but total darkness. He put his hand in front of his face, yet he could not see it. Within a few moments a light started to shine beneath him. It began to shine brighter and brighter until it illumined the entire continent of Athanasia. Within the continent he was able to see all 21 kingdoms. As he floated he began to hear the faint sound of a woman weeping. The weeping gradually got louder as more people seemed to join the woman.

As Spiros floated over Athanasia he was able to hear the cries coming from the kingdom of Portus. The weeping became so loud that it sounded as if myriads upon myriads were mourning. Spiros thought to himself, "Did someone of renown pass into eternity in Portus?" Yet, the more he heard the more the wailing and weeping seemed to turn to bitterness and anger. He heard growls and yells as if this possible procession turned into a violent mob bent on vengeance. His spirit could feel this malice gripping his heart as if it were trying to turn him too. This contempt began dragging Spiros down from the sky towards Portus. Spiros tried to twist and turn his body and flail his arms and legs away from Portus, but it was no use.

As Spiros continued to struggle he witnessed a darkness that spawned in Portus. It started in the city of Salem and quickly enveloped the kingdom like a wild brush fire. This darkness spread to every kingdom in Athanasia until it enveloped the entire continent and its neighboring islands.

Spiros mumbled to himself, “What is this darkness and from where did it come?”

His chest began to tighten and panic rose in his throat as he was continuing to be drawn down towards the black landscape against his will, but suddenly Spiros awoke. He sat up and screamed, “No!” while beads of sweat poured down his face. For the moment he breathed heavily until he was aware of his surroundings.

Drenched in sweat Spiros decided to go topside to get some fresh air. As he reached the deck he immediately saw the tower of Sophos on the Island of Telemicha. He was surprised at what he saw as he knew that it would take a full two days voyage on the ocean to get from the dock at Portus to the dock in Methos. The two kingdoms were neighbors, but both had a great deal of land. Spiros just leaned on the deck and gazed at the temple of Sophos admiring the beautiful white aura that formed as a result of the rays of the sun reflecting off its surface. Seeing the temple had a calming effect on Spiros as the burden on his shoulders seemed to start dissipating. Spiros cracked a smile and took a deep breath through his nose and exhaled through his mouth as he began to relax. In the background, he could hear seagulls cawing from a distance. As he looked to the mainland he saw the capital city of Methos, called Patras. The city was made of white stone with rooftop terraces and an occasional burgundy roof that dotted the city scape. These sites and sounds brought great joy to his troubled heart.

Before he realized that he was no longer alone, the captain of the ship spoke, “How is our ship’s reclusive passenger?”

Spiros looked at him, and then looked off into the distance and said, “Is it just me or did we make it to Methos in astounding time?”

The captain replied emphatically, “Yes indeed! This voyage took only one day as we were expedited by a gale force wind that propelled us until an hour ago. I have never seen anything like it in all my years on the sea.”

The captain slapped Spiros on the back and said, “We will dock in just a few minutes to pick up some supplies. I am going to head down to the auction house on the square and sell this precious sword of yours.” The captain smiled at Spiros and began humming as he walked away.

Spiros shook his head and thought to himself, “This crooked captain extorted me, what else could I have done to escape?”

After the ship docked the captain headed directly for the auction house in the market square. This was where rare and exotic items were sold for large sums to wealthy collectors. Spiros followed the captain at a distance, and when he came upon the auction house in the center of the market square he mingled in with the crowd. The auction house was actually an open-air building behind a large stage. That was where the final business was conducted to finish the transaction. The stage was open for all in the square to see the items being auctioned and it was where the bidding would always take place. Spiros just hung his head and waited for the sword that he had carried since he was created to be sold.

At the same time Spiros was waiting, two of King Justinian’s Adelphos came into the area with a few hundred soldiers. These two Adelphos were named Brackus and Petros. King Justinian told them to look for a man that was out of his position. They dispersed the soldiers throughout the square and docks to question everyone they could find and see if they could stumble upon the answer to this ambiguous clue.

Meanwhile, the bidding had started on Spiros’ sword. The

price was already up to 1500 gold pieces and with each bid the captain's grin seemed to grow larger and his eyes wider. If the pace of the bidding continued he was going to become a wealthy man.

The bids continued to ascend as the potential buyers saw quality that could never be replicated by human hands. "Sixteen Hundred!" yelled one man.

"Seventeen Hundred!" yelled another man.

"Two thousand!" yelled another.

Spiros was watching a piece of himself being auctioned off. He sighed and then mumbled, "This is more than I can bear," as he turned and headed back to his quarters on the ship.

Petros entered the square with some soldiers only seconds after Spiros had left. He began questioning people all throughout the market to try to find some sort of lead. It was comparable to searching for a grain of salt on a sandy beach. Petros decided to stand back and observe what was going on in the square to see if anything would catch his attention. As he looked around he heard "10,000 gold pieces!" come from the auction area. His eyebrow raised, "What would fetch such a hefty price?" he muttered. He beckoned his soldiers and ordered, "Follow me to the auction stage."

As he and his men made their way up to the stage, Petros' eyes opened wide. "That is a sword just like mine!" he shouted. He quickly made way with several guards and stormed the stage to the shock of the bidders.

"I am confiscating this sword as it has been stolen!" yelled Petros as his voice carried through the market for all to hear.

Gasps could be heard as silence fell over the crowd. Petros barked, "Who is responsible for selling this sword?"

The auctioneer pointed directly at the captain. The soldiers immediately surrounded him and placed his wrists and ankles in chains.

Petros looked at one of the soldiers, "We will take this thief for questioning!"

The captain stammered out his plea, "I am innocent. I acquired the sword fairly in a business deal," as he was dragged away.

When they had reached a spot where the commotion had died down Petros plainly asked the captain, "How did you procure this sword?"

The captain's voice trembled as he replied, "A traveler from Portus used it as payment to sail to the kingdom of Parrus."

Petros snapped, “Take me to this traveler.” He then seized the captain and placed him on the back of a horse. Both he and the royal guards with him mounted theirs to follow.

Petros held the reigns to the captain’s horse and ordered, “Take me to your ship.”

The captain just pointed in the direction of the docks, but said nothing.

As they rode, Petros asked, “What is your name?”

The captain stuttered, “Korah.”

“Where is your ship, Korah?” asked Petros.

Korah began to lift his nose at Petros, “On the southern docks.”

“What is the name of your ship on the southern docks?” grilled Petros.

Korah replied, “It is called the Voyager.”

“Very well then, we ride for the Voyager.” Petros then raised his voice, “We should be coming upon the southern docks any moment now. Men, we will enter the ship with swords drawn, and you, Korah, will point us to this man that gave you the sword!”

As Petros reached the ship he unsheathed his sword and grabbed Korah by the neck and drug him onto the Voyager. With soldiers in tow they boarded the ship, but Korah's men saw their captain in bonds and his captors with unsheathed swords. They thought that the ship was being seized, so they grabbed their swords and a fight ensued.

As they engaged in battle, Petros' men spread across the length of the ship so as not to be flanked by its defenders.

Petros started by blocking a strike from an attacker with his sword and then punched the man in the face so hard that he left the ground and landed on his back unconscious. Two more attackers descended on his position. He blocked the strike of one attacker with his sword in his left hand and grabbed the wrist of the other attacker with his right hand preventing him from bringing his sword down for an overhead strike. Using the leverage that he gained from holding the wrist of the one attacker, he kicked the other in the stomach, which freed up his sword and allowed him to cut down the man whose wrist he was holding.

Petros looked over to the bow of the ship and saw Brackus throw a man overboard into the ocean. He then looked to the stern of the ship and saw the heaviest fighting and made his way over quickly.

While Petros made his move Korah was yelling, “Stop! Stop! Stop! They are not trying to steal the ship or cargo!” However, his words were drowned out by the clashing of swords and the screaming of all the combatants.

As the battle raged one of the Methosian soldiers impaled a defender with his sword, but could not pull it out. Another of the ship’s defenders saw this and came over to strike the soldier down. Petros extended his sword and blocked the blow, and with his right foot kicked up the sword of a fallen defender nearby into the hands of the soldier, who then struck down the defender. The soldier gave Petros a nod of gratitude and jumped back into the fray.

On the bow of the ship a defender lunged at Brackus with his sword. Brackus spun to his right and struck the man down. As he continued to engage the enemy he saw two men with crossbows emerge and they took aim at two of his soldiers. Brackus quickly went to the rescue of his unsuspecting soldiers and jumped in the way of the arrows, absorbing one in his left shoulder and grabbing the other with his right hand from the air. The two crossbowmen’s eyes and mouths opened wide as they marveled at the feat. The two Methosian soldiers went and engaged these two men and struck them both down.

Meanwhile, an unattended Brackus was descended upon by

four more defenders of the ship. Brackus stood up and stabbed one attacker in his shoulder with the arrow and cut the other down with his sword. He then pulled the arrow out of his left shoulder and blocked a strike from the third attacker with his sword, while simultaneously planting the arrow into the aggressor's thigh leaving him to writhe in pain. Seeing this, the fourth attacker dropped his sword, ran away, and jumped overboard into the ocean.

Brackus looked over to the stern of the ship and saw Korah laying in the fetal position with his face buried into the deck. When he gazed up from the ground he saw two Methosian soldiers fend off an attack on Petros' flank, while Petros was engaged with two of the ships defenders.

Petros yelled to one of his Methosian soldiers fighting nearby, "Sword!" The soldier immediately threw an enemy sword to Petros who caught it at the hilt. He was able to block two strikes from his attackers with his swords and then struck them down quickly with a blow from each sword. Petros then spun and blocked two more attackers' strikes and planted one sword into the right foot of the man on his left sticking him to the ship. He then struck the other attacker down. The man whose foot was stuck into the ship stopped screaming and eventually passed out from the pain.

The ship's defenders were now very few, so they dropped their weapons and surrendered to the Methosian soldiers.

Spiros heard the chaos from the lower deck and rushed to the top to see what was happening. Realizing the ship was being taken by soldiers of Methos, Spiros fell to his knees and put his hands behind his back. While Petros and his soldiers secured the top deck they found the unarmed Spiros surrendered with Korah's men. Petros saw Spiros and said, "You are the one out of his position. Spiros? What are you doing here?"

"You wouldn't believe me if I told you," answered Spiros.

Petros reached down and lifted up his brother. "Lord Sophos told King Justinian to find a man that was out of place. He told us to accept as truth everything that you say. Come, let us take you to the king."

Spiros descended off the ship with a couple of soldiers, while Petros held back and ordered the ship to be searched. He looked at Korah in the eyes and said, "Your men were quick to defend their ship with their lives for you and the cargo. There are no pirates docked in Methos or scavenging our seas. We did not attack any of your men, but they chose to attack the king's royal guard which you most certainly cannot mistake as brigands. Something has to be amiss here."

Petros called for one of his lieutenants to start scouring the ship to look for anything illegal that they may be carrying. They went through the quarters for the ship's crew and all the cargo, but found nothing, so Petros decided to check one last place. He looked at the food rations they were carrying and when he broke open one crate labeled "fruit". He found something very odd.

At the bottom of the crate underneath the fruit was a compartment that contained a pouch that had 100 gold pieces. He ordered all of the ships provisions to be opened, and once this had been completed they had found a total of 2,000 gold pieces stashed away.

Petros knew that having gold is not illegal, but wondered, "Why is it being hidden as if it is being smuggled?" Petros brought Korah in and questioned him again, "Why are you hiding this gold?"

Korah said, "We are going through the pirate infested waters of Parrus and do not want each individual to lose their gold if we are overtaken."

Petros replied, "Of course! Pirates would never steal provisions. You must think I am fool. That is an exact amount of gold."

"I speak the truth, sir." replied Korah.

Petros slammed his fist on a table next to him. "Give me the manifest for each crew member and how the gold would break down to each."

Korah answered, "Everything is in my head."

Petros responded, "Of course it is. Someone bring this man a quill and paper so that he can write it down."

Korah refused, "That is private information that I am not at liberty to discuss or reveal."

Petros gritted his teeth and ordered, "Men, check every inch of this boat again and look for hollowed out walls or compartments! There are things being hidden and it wreaks of something sinister!"

Petros and his soldiers used the hilts of their swords against the ships interior walls as they listened for a hollow sound. Others used poles or stomped their feet against the floors of the ship. On the lowest level of the ship a soldier found what sounded like a hollow wall and called for Petros.

Petros with Korah in tow asked him, "What is behind this wall and how do we open it?"

Korah replied, "I don't know what you are talking about. We are only taking a shipment of grain to the island Kingdom of

Parrus."

The soldier struck the pronounced hollow wall twice more and it seemed as if there may be a hidden room judging from the sound. Petros ordered that the depths of this lower level be scoured to find a mechanism that would trigger the wall to open. Nothing was found.

Petros ordered, "Bring me axes to chop this wall down."

Within a few moments soldiers began cutting away at this hollow sounding wall. In no time, a hole about twice the size of a human head was cut and a strong stench emanated from this hole. Petros grabbed for a lamp to chase away the darkness. Affixing the lamp to his sword he extended it into the hole and saw there was indeed a room on the other side.

He sheathed his sword, picked up an axe, and began to cut away at the wall with speed and ferocity, exclaiming, "There are children in this room! Help me to cut away this wall."

With the help of several soldiers they were able to cut away a four foot by four foot opening. In a voice like that of a father comforting his son after a nightmare, Petros said, "Children, please come out. We are not going to hurt you. We are here to save you. We want to protect you from these evil men. Come, you are safe now."

One by one, children of all different ages and sizes came out hesitantly until this room was emptied. There were 60 in all with their ages ranging from 5-14 years of age. Petros looked at Korah and yelled, "You were taking these children to Parrus to sell them as slaves."

Korah lowered his head and just stared at the floor.

The children were hurried to deck of the ship, but stood silently, squinting as their eyes adjusted to the light. Petros noticed bruises and scratches on the children's faces. He asked one child, "Did they beat you?"

The child nodded his head up and down slowly.

Petros asked, "How did they capture you?"

The child answered, "I lost my parents at a celebration. A man said he would help me to find them, but he led me outside the celebration, bound my mouth, tied me up and put me in a wagon."

Petros' eyes softened from the child's story and he looked to a child that looked to be a four year old girl. He gave her some water which she gulped down until the cup was empty. Petros commented, "You are safe now. These evil men will never hurt you again." He paused. "Did anyone on this ship take your from your parents?"

The little girl nodded her head up and down.

Petros asked, “Can you point to the man who did this to you?”

The little girl pointed at Korah.

Petros asked, “Did he hurt your mother and father?”

The little girl just nodded her head up and down as a tear fell from one of her eyes. Petros gave her a long hug and kissed her on the forehead as she nuzzled her head into his neck. He was silent for a few moments before he commanded, “Take these precious little ones to the king’s palace and have them fed, bathed, and given new clothes. They will be our guests until we find their parents or find them new homes.”

When all of the children had finally left the ship Petros dropped down to one knee and began to clench his fists. He then struck the deck with his fist so hard that a snapping of wood could be heard. Petros fist had almost punched a hole through the deck. He stood up and ordered, “Brackus, arrest every crew member on this ship and take them immediately to the royal prison where they are to be held until further notice. I seek to ask King Justinian to convene the royal court tomorrow and pronounce judgment for these crimes against their creator and against humanity.”

Brackus nodded and ordered, “Get these men to the prison,

spare none that try to escape."

Petros exited the ship, mounted his horse, and headed hastily to the royal palace to inform the king of what just happened.

10 - SALEM, PORTUS

In Portus, Mardok entered King Argos' chambers where he had been left alone for an entire day. He did not allow anyone to approach the king. As Mardok surveyed the room for Argos, he found him lying on the floor of the balcony with his face buried into the tile. His hair was disheveled like a beggar, his eyes were swollen from constant tears, and his face was pale.

Mardok approached the king, dropped to one knee and said, "My Lord, we must leave for Methos and confront Justinian at the settling of grievances on Telemicha."

King Argos, turned his head towards Mardok and in words just above the sound of a whisper said, "I cannot go Mardok, for I have no desire to live."

Mardok responded, "My Lord, we have insurmountable evidence that Justinian murdered your family and plotted to take your life. This is inexcusable, we must exact justice for this treachery."

Argos looked over at Mardok again and said, "Can't you see that I have nothing left?"

"Forgive me my king, I don't mean to add more of a burden onto your troubled soul. I am zealous for justice. I have an edict here which would empower me to assemble the military and lead them against

Methos in your place temporarily."

King Argos slowly nodded his head and lifted his right hand with his signet ring. Mardok dropped down to both knees, his heart began beating faster, but his face remained downcast.

Mardok took the king's hand with his signet ring and pressed it hard into the wax on this thick paper for a few seconds. He pulled King Argos' hand off the edict and a distinct pop could be heard from where the ring pulled free from the wax. Mardok beamed as one fulfilling a desire that has never been experienced.

Mardok stood up and said, "Is there anything I can do for you, my Lord?"

A faint, "No" proceeded from his mouth as he stared blankly into the tile.

"You will have justice, my Lord, if it is the last thing I ever do." Mardok bowed and left the king's quarters leaving Argos to suffer alone.

As Mardok left he met Arsinian just outside the threshold of the king's quarters. Mardok's smile covered his whole face as he met his fellow conspirator.

"The king is ready to fall. He signed the edict making me the king of Portus if he dies. His anguish has put him into depression to the point where I knew that he would never read the document."

Mardok looked at the paper in his hands and thought of what it meant for him and his life from that point onward. He whispered, "I will be the eternal heir to Portus and eventually Athanasia, because I will not leave myself open to the weakness of love. Look at our mighty king crawling on the floor like a wounded deer that is helpless to escape the jaws of the lion. All love and compassion do is make one ripe for a fall."

Arsinian reverenced Mardok with a bow of his head and said, "I have executed the vizier. He was too dangerous to keep alive as others including King Argos might listen to his counsel and find out our true intentions."

"Excellent work, Arsinian. You shall be my second in command when King Argos passes." As Mardok had just finished speaking those words, he heard a shout. They rushed into the king's quarters and found Argos standing on the marble railing of the balcony.

"I cannot live with this pain any longer! It is just too great!"

As King Argos stood on the railing he was wrestling with continuing the fight through all this loss. He thought to himself as he wept openly, "All that I have cherished has been taken away from me. What reason is there to live?"

As he sobbed for a few moments he countered his last thought. "There have been citizens in my kingdom that have lost their entire families from tragedy. Am I so different than they that I cannot suffer the same tragedies?" As he pondered this thought he covered his face with his right hand and started to sob uncontrollably.

King Argos screamed out, "How do frail mortal men persevere through life when all that they value is taken away?"

Mardok saw this as the perfect opportunity to heap more fuel onto the flame of King Argos' grief, so he walked briskly to the balcony where the grieving king stood. "My Lord, what are you doing?"

King Argos turned his head to the side and saw Mardok standing behind him. "I am grieving, Mardok."

Mardok replied, "My Lord, perhaps if you stepped down from the balcony it would be easier for us to converse?"

King Argos replied, "We can converse from here, Mardok! What is it that you want?"

Mardok replied, "I know that you have been bereaved of your family. I was there when the flaming carts crushed and set ablaze many of your kin. I cannot erase the images of them screaming and crying for help as they were cut down mercilessly by King Justinian's soldiers."

Hearing these words from Mardok made King Argos' heart even heavier as he pictured his beloved kin, standing helplessly in the wake of the attack. Mardok saw tears starting to stream down the right side of Argos' face, which was turned in his direction. Seeing this, he decided to embellish the story to further hurt his king.

"My Lord, your children were crying out for their father to save them. I heard cries of, *'Father, save us! Father, where are you?'* The very thought of these words stills brings anguish to my heart."

King Argos started to convulse upon hearing this as he tried to hold back the cries that wanted to surface. Mardok continued as he started to manufacture tears as if this were some harrowing event in his life, "The queen cried out aloud, *'My love, where are you!'* Then the arrows fell from the sky, and many struck her body. As she fell to the ground and the life in her body started to wane, she said, *'My love, where are you? I am so afraid.'* After she said those words, the light in her eyes faded away."

Argos could hold his tears back no more. He began to wail as his body trembled uncontrollably. He yelled out, "What have I done?" He began to weep for a few seconds and then said, "I deserve to die! I wish I had taken their place!"

The king then turned away from Mardok and put his hands over his face as he continued to weep. Mardok replied, "My Lord, it is not your fault."

The king turned towards Mardok with gritted teeth and a red face, "Get away from me, Mardok!"

Mardok bowed, walked over to Arsinian and the two stood back together at a distance to observe what would happen next. Mardok whispered while he looked at King Argos, "The hour may have finally come."

Arsinian responded, "Whatever you said seems to have brought more grief to the king."

As they both glared at King Argos with eager anticipation of his suicide, Arsinian began to fidget. "Why don't we go and throw him off now? You are but inches away from being king," muttered Arsinian.

Mardok kept his gaze on King Argos while he responded to Arsinian in a hushed voice. "Have patience my faithful, Arsinian. I am on the brink of kingship and do not want to jeopardize it from becoming a reality."

Mardok paused for a moment as he continued to glare at Argos. He started to bite his lower lip with his teeth while squeezing the hilt of his sheathed sword. He continued, "If we push him or throw him off the balcony, then there would be many witnesses to that effect. Many questions would be raised and much doubt would be cast on the edict that would make me king. I have studied Argos since he was a child and have learned his greatest fears. He confided in me on more than one occasion that his greatest fear was to lose the family that he loved so dearly. He said that if he lost them that there would be no one to love him, so he would not be able to continue in this life."

Arsinian spoke in a low voice to Mardok as King Argos began to scream. "Are you positive that he will take his own life?"

Mardok responded, "Yes," as his eyes continued to fixate on Argos. "I have tempted him with his greatest fear by bringing it to reality. He is weak and feeble. He knows that he cannot overcome this grief and that is why hopelessness is setting in his heart."

King Argos stood a little more erect on the railing as he seemed to be finding resolve in what he was about to do. He thought to himself, "Why should I continue to go on living? If I take my own life then I will be freed from this bondage of anguish. No one can save me from this misery, for all those that could are now dead."

At that moment King Argos recalled what his father, King Lorrent, said to him on his death bed. He wanted to convey one last pearl of wisdom to his son, Argos, before he died.

"My son, always remember that the citizens of Portus do not exist to provide you with your position, rather your position exists to serve the citizens of Portus. The ancient writings speak a great deal about this. I encourage you to read them and take them to heart as they will give you wisdom that will guide you through the worst of trials."

The memory then faded and the king now stood fully erect on the railing as the tears cleared from his eyes. He seemed as though he made a decision.

"I am not strong enough to continue in this life! I pray that whomever your next king is, that he will serve you better than I!"

King Argos then stretched out his arms and leapt from the balcony. As King Argos fell to his death, he now had regret for jumping off the balcony. He just realized before it was too late that he had made a mistake in taking his life. He yelled out during his fall, "No!"

Mardok and Arsinian heard a thud and noticed that the screaming had stopped. The next sound they heard was weeping in the streets that grew louder and louder. Mardok, with the realization of his desire coming to fruition flashed a quick smirk to Arsinian and said, "So passes King Argos the last remaining heir of the throne of Portus."

Arsinian looked up at Mardok and said, "Since Argos has abdicated his throne, what is your first command, my king?"

A grin immediately sprung onto Mardok's face as he exclaimed, "Send word that Portus' new king will speak at sunrise tomorrow morning on the balcony overlooking the city square. Prepare my royal caravan for departure after the speech, for we are headed to Telemicha to start a war. Now begins our campaign to take Athanasia."

"Yes, King Mardok," responded Arsinian.

With that, Arsinian and Mardok made their way to the street with wide open eyes and mouths and a paler facial complexion. They fell down to their knees and wept as a father would for the loss of a young son. They were the loudest of the mourners and falsely grief-stricken as Mardok went so far as to hold King Argos' lifeless body close to his chest while he wept. Mardok ordered King Argos' body to be moved and prepared for burial with the rest of his family when he returns from the island of Telemicha.

The next morning as the sun arose Mardok made his way to the royal balcony overlooking the square with several royal viziers, a host of guards, and Arsinian. As Mardok approached the balcony several horns sounded in unison. Everyone in the city square stopped talking and looked to the balcony. The people had heard of the attack through rumors that were spread by Mardok's men, and they were angry at this treachery that had fallen on their king, causing him to take his own life.

As Mardok stood at the edge of this massive balcony that could entertain around 200 people, his countenance changed from that of a stoic to one of elation. As he looked at the crowd, goose bumps began to form all over his body, while his heart began to race with excitement.

His face blushed a light pink color as he closed his eyes, held his head up to the sky and took a deep breathe through his nostrils. Pleasure is not just derived from experience, but more so when you experience your desires becoming reality.

As he looked down from the balcony he saw a city square that held 100,000 people filled to its capacity. He grinned while beckoning the head vizier to start the ceremony as he was ready to be crowned king. This chief vizier stepped forward and addressed the crowd.

"My brethren, our land has been ravaged by a great scandal that claimed the lives of our king and his entire family. Our land has been stricken by a plague of hatred of which no Portusian in any generation has experienced. Having lost our hope we turn to another to restore it. King Argos asked for this man to take his place should he die and have no heir to the throne of Portus. We have the document here with his royal signet stamp making this law.

"Today, we will be crowning a king who is not fragile like us, but is the head of the Adelphos and blessed with eternal life. It gives me great pleasure by royal decree of our great King Argos that I crown our new king."

Mardok then stepped forward and bowed on one knee so that the crown could be placed on his head. "King Mardok, do you swear to serve selflessly and protect vigorously the people of Portus?"

Mardok replied, "I do!"

The chief vizier then lifted King Argos' crown and placed it on a jubilant King Mardok's head.

"As the new king of Portus we bestow upon you King Argos' sword. I exhort you to use this sword to rule justly and protect the people that you have been called to serve. Use it to bring justice and healing to our land."

The vizier stepped aside as the massive crowd then roared in agreement. Mardok stood basking in this moment absorbing all the glory as he held his arms up and nodded in agreement with the crowd.

Mardok then stepped forward and spoke. His words thundered for all in the square to hear, "Citizens of Portus, a grievous evil has been committed in our lands as you are well aware. You may have also heard that the evidence points to King Justinian as being behind this insidious plot. Know this, he and his people will suffer for this treachery. As king, I will avenge the death of King Argos and his family. Justinian is no longer deserving of his kingdom and I will remove him from his throne and annex Methos into the kingdom of Portus.

"Any other kingdom that takes allegiance with Methos or is neutral in this treachery against us will be deemed co-conspirators. I will remove any king and annex their land into Portus that does not ally with us in the war that will be waged against Methos!"

The people threw their fists in the air and screamed like an angry mob in agreement.

When the crowd quieted Mardok spoke again. "Today we will wage war against Methos and will need the help of all Portusian citizens. We will need men to enlist in the army. We will need builders, engineers, and blacksmith's to forge weapons, armor, shields, and to build catapults, ships, and siege towers. We will impose a 10% war tax on goods to gather revenue to fund the war so as to see it out to victory. We will need every natural resource and every man, woman, and child to contribute to our effort. Who will stand with their king to see us to victory over our enemies?"

With a deafening roar the crowd yelled and gave the king their approval. As King Mardok reveled in the adoration he mouthed something that no one would have been able to see unless they were right in front of him. "My will is now their will."

Mardok turned and walked away as the people started cheering his name.

Mardok looked over to Arsinian with his head held high as a smile slowly began growing and said, "Set up a time where I may speak to the people again after we return from Methos. I am going to dispose of the moral code that Portus and most of Athanasia have followed since the beginning. Prepare an edict as I seek to destroy anything that mentions Sophos. It will be illegal to own a book, worship or even speak about him. In his place I want temples to be erected in my name for my glory. I want books written about my wisdom and my strength. I want people to worship me and no other. I will be their God."

A smiling Arsinian said, "I will draw up the edict before we leave for Methos, my King. I will ensure that the work will be started while we are away."

As Mardok walked to the throne room with Arsinian in tow, his hatred toward Sophos began to stir an old memory.

It was the early years of Athanasia when Sophos dwelled with the people in his creation. He was sitting on his throne as every nation approached Sophos to give praise and tribute. Sophos sat on an ornate throne of gold with his symbol etched on the back of the chair. On each side of the throne atop the armrests was a lion's head, ornately carved, with red rubies for eyes. More so than this were the pride of lions that rested by Sophos' throne. He would walk up to these intimidating creatures which were as gentle as lambs in his presence and pet them. They would most often lick him in the face when he did this, bringing about a smile.

Sophos' throne stood on the top of a ziggurat. The people that represented the nations would climb to the top and offer Sophos the best of their clothing, animals, and food once a month. Even the poorest nations offered their best to Sophos.

Mardok would approach the throne every month with his king, Arsinian, Victus, Spiros and others of the king's court to pay tribute. Mardok watched as his king bowed before Sophos' throne and praised him for all the blessings he had given their kingdom. He also praised him for all the adversity and suffering that had faced their kingdom, thanking him for the good it brings about.

As his king did this, Mardok was caught up by all the praise and glory that Sophos was receiving. A thought trickled into his mind where he saw himself in Sophos' place. He began to imagine people bowing before him and paying him tribute. This thought continued to grow as he began to imagine himself being praised and honored. As he embraced this thought he began to feel something that he never experienced before: Hatred towards Sophos his creator.

As Mardok meditated on these thoughts, Sophos looked over towards him as if he sensed something. Sophos' countenance changed. His smile had departed and his eyes drooped. Mardok caught Sophos' gaze and was so pierced by it that he immediately looked away feeling convicted of desiring a position that would never be his to have.

Mardok's insides began to burn with rage, he clenched his fists so tightly that they began to turn white. He looked at the Athanasians around him and had thoughts of murder. He thought to himself "I am immortal and they are mortal. Why should they rule over me?"

Mardok hurried away from Sophos and descended down the steps of the ziggurat until he found a remote ledge. He pulled out a dagger that he carried and pricked his finger. Mardok then began to recite over and over, "Do not heal." The wound quickly healed against his will and looked as if nothing had ever happened to his finger. Mardok became incensed because he had no control over his being. In his wrath he broke the blade off the hilt of the dagger and threw it on the ground. He shook his head and murmured, "I am not my own."

Mardok sat down on a stair and put his face in his hands. He mumbled, "What have I done?" He removed his hands from his face, gnashed his teeth and began scraping the stone where he sat on the ziggurat so hard that he left a trail of nail marks. As the king of Portus descended down the steps of the ziggurat, Mardok regained his composure and rejoined him. Mardok's eyes began to glaze over as he pictured himself sitting in Sophos' throne. That fantasy planted an idea, "I can eliminate the line of kings and make my own throne." Mardok's eyes opened wide as he spoke under his breath, "That's it."

As the memory faded a soldier appeared. He approached Mardok and bowed. "My Lord, your ship is ready to set sail for Methos."

"Very well, take me to my royal steed and let us set sail for Telemicha."

As he and Arsinian walked to their horses, King Mardok had an idea. "Arsinian, I desire for you to contact the pirates that rule the waters of Parrus. I believe Justinian's nephew Sprasian rules those brigands. We could use them to disrupt their supply chain and throw their warships into chaos."

"Lord Mardok, you can't believe that these thieves would willingly serve you? These filthy rags idolize money. They have no sanctuary on this side of Athanasia and could not possibly survive so far away from their colony in Parrus. It would take an insurmountable amount of money and a sanctuary city for them to call home before they would even think about this undertaking."

Mardok's face turned dark red as he said, "You dare question your king, Arsinian? I am your sovereign. I don't need your advice, vizier. I need you to follow my commands. Is there a vizier that desires to carry out his king's commands?"

"Forgive me, Lord Mardok", said Arsinian in a quiet voice. "What authority will be given to me to negotiate with these brigands?"

"That is much better," said King Mardok as he held his nose up. "For the last 200 years I have been raising money through the slave trade so as to finance the war when I became king. For 200 years I have taken orphans and children from their homes in most of the Athanasian kingdoms. I have given these men a percentage of the proceeds from the auction blocks in the kingdoms of Parrus, Othos, and Ramsey. The slave trade is very profitable for I have earned over 10,000,000 gold pieces a year for 200 years. I have amassed the wealth of a mighty kingdom for myself."

Arsinian asked, "Lord Mardok, what are your plans with this great wealth that you have accumulated?"

Mardok replied, "I now seek to use my wealth to wage war and conquer all of Athanasia. I'll fund the war through the Portusian treasury, but will use my wealth to buy mercenaries and fund allies that have smaller war chests. Take 1,000,000 gold pieces with you to Sprasian. He is a shrewd negotiator, so you must be even shrewder than he. Knowing his corrupt heart, he will do whatever we want for 1,000,000 pieces of gold. However, try to negotiate less as I discern that we could buy his brigand army for a smaller amount. We are allowing him to keep all of the spoils from his plundering of Methos." He paused, "There is one more matter to discuss about Sprasian. After we have conquered Athanasia I want you to put him to the sword. I cannot allow any heir to any throne in Athanasia to live, even if one is beyond redemption. The line of kings must be completely severed if I am to reign.

Arsinian replied, “It would be my pleasure to cut Sprasian down. Now, please tell me how to procure this gold, sire?”

King Mardok lifted his nose again, “I have already sent a trusted messenger to where it is hidden. He will inform the steward that is protecting it of the need. It will be delivered to Methos when we arrive so that you can travel immediately to Remar.”

Arsinian responded, “My Lord, I see that you indeed are wise and have forged a plan that is beyond my comprehension. I look forward to seeing how your will unfolds and glorifies you as the future King of all Kings.”

11 - PATRAS, METHOS

It was mid-morning in Methos and King Justinian was sitting on his throne judging crimes that have been committed in his kingdom. Before him knelt a man with the tattered clothes of a beggar that owed several thousand gold pieces in taxes to Methos.

“My king, forgive me for stealing from you,” he said, “I worshipped money and lived my life for it. So much so, that I put it in front of my wife and children, friends, and business associates. It was my god. Now.....I have no one......my wife has deserted me and my children want nothing to do with me as I had chosen to have nothing to do with them. I have lost my business and I stand before you now a scourge and an eyesore to all humanity. I have lost everything that I held dear. Most importantly, I have lost everything that I should have held dear. I kneel before you a man who is broken.”

The man sighed before continuing.

“I will accept whatever punishment that you deem worthy of my crimes. I want to have peace with you, my king. If it takes the rest of my life to pay you back my lord, then I am willing. My life is in your hands.”

King Justinian’s face held a small, kind smile and his eyes were shimmering as he looked on the broken man. Justinian said, “Admitting one’s folly is a sign of true contrition, but I want to test your heart. Arise! Tell me, what have you learned from being in this fallen state?”

The man began to sweat and his hands began to shake upon hearing this. He stood up on his feet with tears beginning to well in his eyes and said, “I was a filthy pig in my heart sire.”

The king continued to gaze at the man, examining him like a jeweler would a diamond, looking for even the slightest flaw.

The man continued, “My heart is corrupt! No matter how hard I tried I just couldn’t change who I was. I saw how my obsession with money pushed everything that I once held dear away, including my king. I still proceeded after money knowing that I would suffer great consequences for my actions. I have learned from this that gold is amoral. It is not evil. You can either choose to do good with it or choose to do evil. I chose evil and have reaped what I have sown. As I sat in prison awaiting my trial I was struck by something that I read from the ancient writings.

“It said, *‘You may cleanse a swine, you may dress it in fine linen and spray it with fine perfume, but it will still remain a swine. The swine will always go back into the mud and feces because the heart of the swine was not changed.’*

King Justinian interrupted, “I know the ancient writings which you have quoted. What message do you wish to convey in your defense by their quotation?”

“Forgive me, my Lord.” said the man with his eyes wide open from being caught off guard by the interruption.

“I realized that I could not make this change and would continue to go back to my vices. This was when I was visited by a man wearing a light gray sackcloth cloak. He appeared in the evening as I was lamenting my inability to change. He said that he had been watching me all of my life and that now was the time he would change my heart. He touched me on the shoulder and I felt an amazing power course through my body as the weight I was carrying departed. I will never forget his words. He said, 'You are a new creation. Your days of wallowing in the mud are over.' Before he departed he said that he would call on me for a great task in the future. He vanished in the blink of an eye as did the weight of my transgressions."

The people that observed the trials in the king's court thought that this man was lying and began to murmur against him. Yet, above the chatter of the crowd Justinian spoke up and asked, "Did the visitor tell you his name?"

The man hesitantly replied, "Yes, my Lord. He said he was Sophos."

An uproar from the observers ensued in reaction to this statement. People blurted out, "No one has seen Sophos in 2000 years! Impossible!"

Justinian took charge promptly as he roared, "Silence!"

A hush fell over the crowd while the man under trial began to shrink back from Justinian. "Sophos does not just reveal himself to kings, but even to the lowliest of men. I am a man just like you. I was visited by Sophos recently and he fits the exact description that this man has given me. I do not believe that this man is lying."

The people stood in silence as Justinian arose from his throne and approached the man. Justinian pronounced his judgment. "I pardon this man of all charges. If Lord Sophos can forgive him of his transgressions, than I too can forgive him. Your debt to the kingdom of Methos has been forgiven. You may go in peace."

The man leapt up and began jumping around and hugging everyone around him. Justinian was even the recipient of a hug. The man was so joyful that he began to dance in Justinian's presence and the people began to clap. Justinian began to laugh and clap his hands with the crowd. The man looked over to Justinian and kept repeating, "Thank you! Thank you! Thank you, my Lord!" He was then ushered out as the people erupted into cheers.

As the crowd began to calm the herald announced the next case. "Next on the docket is the kingdom of Methos versus Korah Meridius. He is accused by Petros of the Adelphos of abducting children with the intention to sell them as slaves."

Petros brought Korah before the king in shackles. Where others had approached the king with downcast eyes, Korah looked directly at Justinian as he walked, and when he stood at the threshold of the throne he refused to kneel.

Petros exclaimed, "You refuse to bow to the king who holds your life in his hands?"

Korah replied, "I refuse to bow to this puppet king. He is the lesser son of greater kings. I will not bow to a fool bereft of wisdom and courage."

When Petros heard this he was enraged and said in a louder voice, "Do you realize that a curse levied against the king is punishable by death?"

King Justinian's countenance began to change as his eyes squinted, and his nose scrunched as he peered down at Korah. The wrath welling up inside Justinian began to turn his face pink. As his rage was ready to overflow onto Korah, he realized he was being tempted to anger. It was at that moment that Justinian's eyes softened and the muscles in his face relaxed. The color in his face went from pink back to olive immediately. Justinian stood up and said, "I forgive you for your hurtful and untrue words."

Petros immediately replied, "But Sire, he committed a crime that gives you the right to take his life."

Justinian spoke for all to hear. "Yes, Petros, I have the right to take his life, but I chose to spare it. If I chose to seek justice every time that I have been wronged, then everyone will live in terror. If I never exercise mercy or forgiveness, then what example would I be setting for the people to emulate?"

Petros locked eyes with Korah for a moment and then leaned forward to whisper in his ear, "Good try."

Korah was caught off guard by Justinian's answer. He began to inch backward and then dropped his head. Korah murmured, "I thought, I thought" but never finished his sentence.

Justinian turned to Korah and said, “The charges brought against you are severe. You have been caught abducting and trying to sell children into slavery. We have for hundreds of years tried to find and stop those responsible for this most detestable of evils. I find it no coincidence that we caught the main conspirator. We were looking for a man that Sophos had revealed that I must find. We found this man on your ship. In finding him, we also found the incubus of the slave trade that has ravaged almost every kingdom in Athanasia. For hundreds of years you docked on our shores and ravaged our land, but your dark secret eluded us. Today, your evil empire comes crashing down. Do you have anything to say for yourself?”

Korah lifted his head and raised his nose, “Yes, I do, King Justinian. Business is business. I did nothing wrong. What someone else might see as wrong, I see as a business that puts food on the table for my family. The truth is relative, free of absolutes. I did nothing wrong.”

Justinian stood speechless for a moment at Korah’s justification. He tilted his head as he stared at Korah, and finding his voice said, “Interesting, so if I abducted your family and put them to work in the salt mines 18 hours a day, you would have no issue?”

The smiling Korah opened his mouth to reply, but his eyes strangely opened wide for a brief moment before closing shut. He closed his mouth, dropped his head, and began staring at his shackles.

Justinian replied, “Ah! You do see the foolishness in your logic. Your silence convicts you of your transgression. It appears that you hold to the same truth that I hold to. The truth that governs us all.”

Justinian paused and began to walk around Korah, but looked out to the crowd to speak. “I believe this is one instance where it was right to answer a fool according to his folly, so I will continue to shred your faulty logic.” If “truth” is relative and not absolute, then why are you making an absolute statement by saying that all truth is relative? It is a contradiction. You, Korah, are a walking contradiction. I have heard enough! It is time to render my judgement.”

Korah began to tremble and breathe heavily.

Justinian continued, “Korah, I rule as a king by showing grace. Your life was spared after your audacious remark. With this being said, I will continue to show you mercy and grace as it can never be merited. My hope is that your eyes will one day open to the foolish things you have done. The law of Methos states that any man found guilty of involvement in the slave trade shall be put to death. Today, I will spare Korah’s life for a second time. I will invoke the law of the ancients. ‘An eye for an eye and tooth for a tooth.’

Justinian paused and then continued with his judgment against Korah, but this time by looking out to the crowd and addressing the people.

“We do this so that people will not inflict more pain or punishment than was inflicted on them. If given the opportunity to avenge an egregious act against us, as a judge we would inflict more punishment than the crime deserved. It is in our human nature.”

Justinian now turned and looked at Korah in the eyes, “The

evidence against you is overwhelming. That is why I find you guilty of the acts of abduction and engaging in the slave trade. Your punishment will fit your crime.

"We have had many families that had their children abducted by you in our kingdom. Tomorrow in the King's Square you and your men will be auctioned off to only the families of those that have lost their children as a result of abduction and were sold into slavery. My one stipulation is that they may not kill you nor flog you to the point of losing your life. They may flog you reasonably for disobedience, but it would have to be administered in the King's Square for all the people to see. You will be their slaves for the rest of your lives and can never earn your freedom."

Korah was wide eyed and gently shaking his head as sweat drops began to form and run down his face. He shouted, "No!"

Justinian screamed, "Silence, Korah!" He then finished his judgment saying, "I am sure that these people will be better master's than the ones you sold their children to. If you try to escape or hurt these people, then your very lives will be taken from you! My hope is that you will get a small taste of what it feels like to actually be a slave and someday repent of your evil deeds."

Justinian turned to Petros. "Take these filthy rags out of my sight and notify the families that have lost their children to slavery of my decree. It will be enforced starting tomorrow at the auction."

Korah shouted, "No!"

Petros looked Korah in the eyes and said, “Your arrogance and pride has now brought you even greater humiliation. I pray that these families will show you more mercy than you have shown them.”

Korah began weeping uncontrollably and had to be dragged out of Justinian’s court.

The king adjourned to his quarters with his wife Queen Alexis and all four of his Adelphos in tow. Waiting in his quarters was Spiros with two of the royal guard. Spiros was staring at the floor shaking his left foot up and down repetitively as a few drops of sweat trickled down his face.

Spiros jumped to his feet when King Justinian and Queen Alexis entered the room. He bowed and said, “My Lord and Lady, the sight of you brings relief to the anguish in my soul.”

Justinian replied, “Arise, Spiros. Come, sit with us.” They all sat down together on a large lavender couch as the guards crowded close to them.

“Spiros, one day ago Sophos visited me and told me to look for someone that was out of place on some sort of cargo ship. We had no idea where to look, but as it happened Petros found this wicked fiend Korah auctioning off your sword. This is what inevitably led us to you. Sophos warned me of a great evil entering Athanasia and said that you would have some information to help assemble this complicated puzzle. He said to believe everything that you speak as it is all truth.”

Spiros responded immediately, “My Lord, it gives me great comfort to know that I can speak freely and openly to you without condemnation. I have seen a glimpse of this evil and it is blinding people to the truth."

Queen Alexis' voice quivered, "Please, noble Spiros, enlighten us as to what you have witnessed. Your wisdom in this matter is of great importance."

Spiros took a deep breath and then began to recount the whole series of events starting with his arrest. Everyone in the room put their eyes on Spiros and remained silent the entire time he spoke. As Spiros finished he exclaimed, "I had to escape otherwise I would have been falsely accused of treason and executed. I did not do these treacherous things of which I was charged. I am innocent!"

Petros broke the silence, "If we are to take Sophos at his infallible word that you are telling the whole truth, then this would be an indictment upon someone close to King Argos. If Arsinian had your sword, Spiros, then he either lost track of it in the heat of the battle or allowed it to fall into the wrong hands purposely. I cannot believe that one of our brothers would be involved in such a treacherous act."

"Well said, Petros." responded the king. Justinian then asked, "Why did you surrender your sword to this savage, Korah?"

Spiros looked at Justinian, "My Lord, what other choice did I have? I chose to go to Parrus because it is a lawless kingdom where a fugitive would be hard to find. It would have given me time to think through things and figure out what steps I should make next. Korah refused to allow me passage on the ship as a deckhand. He could tell that I was desperate, so he asked for my sword. I had nothing else to give him to pay for passage, so I surrendered my sword. Had I not, I would have been captured and executed for an egregious crime that I did not commit."

Queen Alexis stopped Spiros and asked, "Did you know that this was a slave ship in disguise?"

"No, my lady! There were no signs that revealed the heart of this captain other than that he loved money."

Queen Alexis responded, "Was there anything else that happened before you arrived in Methos?"

Spiros looked down at the floor and said, "What I will tell you now brought great fear to my heart as something wicked is manifesting itself in Athanasia."

The queen put her hand on Spiros' shoulder, prompting him to look up. She asked, "What is this restless evil that you speak of? Is it headed towards Methos?"

"My lady, I fell into a trance on the ship for 24 hours. It was this deep trance that allowed me to have a prophetic dream."

Justinian asked, "How did you fall into this trance? Those in your order are not often known to be prophetic. How can this be?"

Spiros then stood up and said, "You are correct, rarely do we ever have visions nor do we ever sleep. This only happens when Sophos seeks to convey a message."

Spiros paused, shook his head as if to clear some thought, and continued, "I cannot explain it." He put his hands on his forehead and then ran them down his face.

Spiros went on to convey the vision in its entirety to everyone in the room. When Spiros had finished conveying what he saw, King Justinian was embraced by his wife as she buried her head in his chest. All the others in the room hung their heads low with the exception of Petros.

"That is enough, Spiros," said King Justinian gently. "You have given us much to ponder. We will reconvene tomorrow to discuss this in greater depth. Do not fear Spiros, you have come to a safe haven and can take rest in the borders of Methos. You may all take your leave."

As Spiros stood up King Justinian called out to him, "Oh! There is one more issue."

Justinian signaled to a soldier who brought forth Spiros' sword of Helios and gave it to Spiros.

Spiros' eyes and mouth opened wide as he gazed at his prized possession and exclaimed, "My sword!"

Justinian responded, "Whatever you do, never surrender your sword. You are a protector."

Spiros said, "Thank you, my Lord. It will never leave my side ever again."

Petros asked Spiros as they exited the room, "Do you think King Argos' life is in danger?"

Spiros replied, "I believe so."

When everyone left, the queen began to weep in her husband's arms. "Does this mean that we are going to be destroyed by this great evil? What will happen to our children and to our people?"

Justinian replied, "This evil has not overtaken us yet. Maybe this is a warning for us to prepare for the wickedness that looms over Athanasia? Whatever it means we cannot become fearful, for it may be that it is fear that allows Methos and the rest of the Athanasian kingdoms to fall to this darkness. If we stand strong with courage and confront this evil, then it may inspire others to do the same. We cannot acquiesce to this evil. All we can do is prepare for the day we finally meet it. I love you very much, Alexis. Know that I will give my life to protect you, our children, and our people from this threat."

12 - Port Verdes, Remar

In Port Verdes, on the Island of Remar that was part of the outlaw kingdom of Parrus, Sprasian awoke from a long night's sleep. It was the afternoon and Katherine had entered the room to change his bandages. As she entered, so too did Bremus and as Katherine was changing Sprasian's bandages Bremus asked, "How are you doing, my Lord?"

"How do you think I am doing, Bremus?"

Bremus chuckled, "I guess you are not doing that well, but it is better than being dead."

Sprasian just looked at him and shook his head. "What do you want Bremus?"

Bremus smiled, "Well, my Lord, I have used some of our money to recruit more men to join our ranks. I was able to recruit 500 more able-bodied men. Our army continues to grow by leaps and bounds each day. The spoils were well worth the loss of some our soldiers."

Sprasian replied, "Indeed."

Bremus responded, "I have another bit of good news."

Sprasian put his hand over his face and replied, "Speak."

Bremus said, "I have received word of a shipment of livestock and some spices that will be landing at the Port of Westphal tomorrow. Knowing that you cannot make the voyage because of your injuries I would like to take a few of our ships for a little stroll. We need the livestock to feed our men. We can sell the spice."

Sprasian looked up at him and said, "Very well, do as you judge best."

As Bremus bowed and walked out, Sprasian yelled out to him, "Bremus, are you really satisfied by the lifestyle that we lead?" Bremus tilted his head and squinted as he looked at Sprasian and said, "I am never satisfied, that is why I must keep doing it."

Bremus paused for a moment and stared at Sprasian who had turned his attention to something outside his window. Bremus thought, "Is he getting soft because of his wounds?" Bremus turned swiftly and exited the room, leaving Sprasian and Katherine alone.

Katherine only left Sprasian alone to his thoughts for a moment before she said, "Are you not satisfied with the life you are leading Sprasian?"

Sprasian replied promptly, "I have been a pirate for 200 years and leader of this band for 150 of those years. Everyone longs to have what I have. I will not feel guilty for my lifestyle. I will not feel guilt for the people I have killed or money and goods that I have taken. That is how I will always live!"

Katherine responded, "And what of those you have wronged?"

Sprasian waved his hand, “I have ‘wronged’ no one. There is no right and wrong. I took from the weaker; that is the right of the strong. If I can get away with it then it is right by me.”

Katherine bowed her head and said, “My Lord contradicts himself.”

Sprasian rolled his eyes and turned his head away from Katherine while she continued to clean his wounds. Neither said a word for a short length of time as she continued to work on his wounds and replace bandages. Finally, Sprasian broke the silence.

“No...No. What is right by one man is right by him. It doesn’t have to be right by another.”

Katherine replied, “So, if I take your gold you will not feel wronged?”

Sprasian’s neck grew red but he said nothing as he remembered the lecture from Justinian about stealing King Argos’ horse as a child.

She looked down at him and spoke gently again. “Sprasian, we see these absolutes in the physical sense as well.”

Sprasian clenched his teeth and said, “Please enlighten me, Katherine.”

Seeing Sprasian’s frustration and knowing the harm that Sprasian was capable of inflicting, Katherine chose to speak softly in her response. “If you jump off the top of your 100 foot tower to the city street, you will die. If by some miracle you manage to live, then your body will be broken beyond repair. It is the law of gravity which no man can violate."

"Of course Katherine, I understand the law of gravity, so what is your reasoning?" said a more frustrated Sprasian whose face began to turn red and body began to fidget.

Witnessing Sprasian's demeanor she continued to speak gently, "It is an absolute truth that if you violate this law, that you will hurt or destroy your body every time. If we have laws in our physical realm then we most assuredly have laws that guide us in the moral realm. When you violate moral laws that are absolute, then there are consequences just like in the physical sense. If you murder someone, then you are poisoning your soul and setting yourself up for judgment under the law. It does not surprise me that you have been grappling with the transgressions you have committed over the years. Your conscience has these moral laws that you chose to violate etched on your heart. That is why you feel guilt when you do something wrong. They have added up over the years and you cannot bear their burden any longer."

Sprasian shook his head and raised his voice louder, "What about men like Bremus? He is a man devoid of any good. He revels in doing what you call evil and feels no guilt for it."

Katherine replied, "He has made a willful decision to bury his transgressions and silence his conscience. He has deadened himself to them for committing the same evil acts over and over again. However, just because they are buried does not mean they are dead. One day he, like you, will have to stand trial for the evil acts that you both have committed. When you are confronted by the judge and the truth of the crimes that were committed are brought back to life, then your consciences will revive and remind you of your guilt. Your consciences will convict you, find you guilty just as the judge will, and you will both pay the ultimate price."

Sprasian didn't know how to respond so he looked out the window and did not utter a word in defense. He reasoned in his mind, "If I was taken before any king of Athanasia, then I would most certainly be executed for my crimes."

Sprasian turned and looked back up at Katherine, "As much as it pains me to say this, I cannot argue with what you have stated. If I do, then I would be painted a fool in light of the truth. Katherine, how does one make things right?"

She spoke slowly as she responded. "You would need a change of heart. If your heart changed then you would not be subject to carrying out these transgressions any longer."

Sprasian countered, "How does one's heart change?"

Katherine smiled and said, "Well, that is between the man and his creator."

Sprasian began to gnash his teeth and clench his fists, "You are telling me that Sophos is the one who can change my heart. I hate Sophos and I hate my Uncle Justinian who worshipped him. He held to Sophos' foolish and antiquated writings."

"My Lord, it appears that this bitterness between you and your creator is poisoning your soul."

Sprasian's face turned a dark red as he screamed out, "You refer to Sophos! He has done nothing for me just as you are doing nothing for me now! He is worthless, just as you are worthless! He is a tormentor, just like you are a tormentor!"

He snatched the remaining bandages from her hands and said, "You are no longer needed today."

Katherine quickly exited the room with her head down.

Sprasian yelled out to one of his guards, "Find Bremus and bring him here!"

The servant quickly exited the room and a few moments later returned with Bremus.

Bremus saw the red faced Sprasian and quipped, "Who ruffled your feathers, Sprasian? Was it the nurse? She is a pious one, isn't she?"

Sprasian responded, "Yes, it was the nurse." He paused for a moment and then continued, "Bremus, it has come to my attention that we have allowed far too many boats to roam these waters uninhibited. Over the next month I want you on the sea at all times, plundering every boat that you see enter the waters of Parrus, Ramsey and Othos. Take as many ships as you need. If you face resistance, then you know what to do."

Slowly, a smile crept its way across the face of Bremus as he replied, “You have just made my month, Sprasian. I promise that I won’t disappoint you. I think that before I come to see you next, I will have the nurse come in before me just to make you angry. Then you might let me pillage for 2 months.” Bremus began to laugh, but was the only one laughing in the room. Sprasian just put a pillow over his face and turned away. Bremus then turned and walked out shaking his head and muttering, “I can use this feisty wench to my advantage.”

When the door closed behind Bremus, Sprasian began to delight in the fact that this would spite Katherine and Sophos. “I hate Sophos and his righteous ways. I hope all the pillaging and murder we do will send a stench so high to his throne that he and his followers will weep.”

13 - The Island of Telemicha, Methos

It was the first day of the settling of grievances. King Justinian was presiding on the top of the temple of Sophos with a beautiful sun in the background beginning its two hour descent. Every king in Athanasia was present with the exception of Portus, however the ritual had to begin without him.

Justinian called forth the first grievance to be settled. "I now call King Bastian of the Kingdom of Corpus and King Drajian of the Kingdom of Grekland." Justinian read the grievances aloud as they stood in the center of this circle.

"King Drajian has brought forth an issue in which his kingdom paid for 14,000 tons of grain and only received 10,000 tons. King Bastian has countered that he has not fulfilled the remaining 4,000 tons because of marauders in Grekland that attack the border towns of Corpus. King Bastian has reported that in the past year 75 people have died at the hands of these marauders when they commit their thievery and destruction. Over 350 homes and businesses have been burned to the ground in these attacks. He is withholding the additional 4,000 tons of grain and any further contracts until King Drajian handles this issue within his borders."

He turned to look at Drajian, "King Drajian, what say you to these charges?"

King Drajian stood and immediately addressed this accusation loudly, “Kings of Athanasia! When has it become lawful to steal? Where in the ancient writings does it say that it is appropriate to steal? I agree that these marauders are a curse. They rob and destroy my people as well. I cannot control them or the evil acts that they carry out. We have tried to hunt them down, but have been unsuccessful. We have lost many men in skirmishes in which we were trying to rid our kingdom of this plague! We are doing all that we can. How do the actions of these wicked men translate to stealing from our kingdom? This hideous act has taken food from the mouths of my people. We are in the midst of a famine just as some of the other Athanasian kingdoms. We have people dying of starvation, so in the same way that King Bastian complains of his people being destroyed, he blatantly does the same thing to my people by withholding the food that we have purchased!”

Drajian paused as the other kings clapped and said, “Here, here.” Drajian closed, “The eastern side of Athanasia has been experiencing a great drought and this was not something that has ever been recorded in Athanasian history. Being the first of its kind it has perplexed me to the point of despair. I just want the food so that I can feed my people.”

King Drajian was applauded for his valiant speech.

However, King Justinian spoke up, “My fellow kings, as you know there are always two sides to the story. Please let us listen to what King Bastian has to say.”

King Bastian scowled over at Drajian as he walked into position to state his case.

"Kings of Athanasia!" he said. "Yes, it is true that we have withheld 4,000 tons of grain owed to King Drajian. It is true that we withhold it because of the lawless borders of Grekland! However, King Drajian has painted an unfair picture. The general of my army sent scouts to infiltrate the ranks of these marauders. These scouts have reported back the locations from which these marauders operate. We have given this information to King Drajian, and he has done nothing! He refuses to address these issues in his own kingdom. I have even gone so far as to offer Corpusian troops to assist his army in destroying these dredges of society for the sake of both our kingdoms. He has refused every time. In my judgment, King Drajian either doesn't care about what happens in his kingdom and how it affects other kingdoms, or he is colluding with these scoundrels. Which is it, King Drajian?"

King Drajian's face turned dark red as his clenched fists began to tremble. He bellowed, "How dare you? You insolent fool!"

King Bastian promptly replied, "If allowing my kingdom to fall into lawlessness constitutes wisdom, then I will gladly accept being a fool."

That insult influenced a yelling match between the two kings in which Justinian inserted himself, imploring them to calm down. Once they had quieted, he addressed the issues based on the two stories.

"King Drajian and Bastian! After hearing your valid arguments against one another I believe there is a way to bring peace to your two kingdoms. It appears to me that both kings have paid back one wrong with another wrong. As you can plainly see, repaying a wrong with another wrong does not settle the situation, but rather allows it to escalate."

"With this being said, I would like to propose a solution to bring an end to this dispute in which both offended parties may walk away with hearts of satisfaction and contrition. King Bastian, you must give King Drajian the grain that he has rightfully purchased. You have broken your word and have stolen from King Drajian. You must always fulfill your obligations and commitments even when it hurts to do so."

Drajian was donning a smile on his face when Justinian turned to him.

Justinian continued, "King Drajian, you have allowed lawless men to take refuge in your kingdom. In doing so, they wreak havoc on the Kingdom of Corpus and all of its people living in the border region. As king it is your responsibility to maintain law and order within your borders. If it spills out, then it becomes a reflection of the king and his leadership. This gives King Bastian a reason to declare war because he has to protect his people. King Drajian, you cannot be forced to deal with these marauders, but I will give you two options that will prevent war. The first is to combine your forces and search these lawless men out and destroy them completely. That will end the issue at hand. However, after destroying these marauders you must maintain order behind your border so that this doesn't happen again. The second is that you will pay damages for any destruction these marauders cause when they attack. King Bastian also will have the authority to go into your lands with his army and crush these marauders. Do these sound like alternatives that will keep your kingdoms at peace and address the issues at hand? Our desire is for you to have reconciliation. What say you both?"

King Bastian's eyes softened as he responded tenderly, "I will pay back King Drajian what he is owed. It was wrong of me to withhold food as it was an act of retaliation and manipulation. I will also accept the terms of whatever of the two options King Drajian chooses to accept. Please forgive me for not honoring my word."

King Drajian chewed his bottom lip as he stared at the men. He let out a sigh and began to nod his head as he replied, "As I think about what was said," he began, "I would like to accept option two. I should have taken the intelligence that was given me and acted upon it. I will admit my failure to protect my people and allowing lawlessness to spill over into another kingdom. They are suffering from my inability to act wisely. Please accept my apologies, King Bastian. You have my permission to enter my lands and eliminate these vermin."

King Justinian smiled and said, "In the ancient writings it says, 'A harsh word stirs up great ire, but an answer of gentleness turns wrath away.' It is most refreshing to see this truth demonstrated today. With that, I now consider this matter settled."

All the kings and those that stood by their side cheered and applauded that reconciliation was found between their two kingdoms.

Justinian then brought the next grievance to the council. It happened that these were the grievances against him from King's Melmot, Meridian, and Spiegel. Justinian called them forward to the center of the circle to address the grievances against him. King Melmot agreed to speak about all their grievances as a whole and then address them individually.

Melmot was quirky to say the least. He had no heirs to his throne nor did he have a queen. He spent most of his time throwing lavish parties for his animals in which they were well fed, but his people were dying as a result of the kingdom's famine.

King Melmot approached his position with his nose pointed up to the sky and eyes which would not even glance at Justinian, and began his diatribe.

"Kings of Athanasia, today our three kingdoms come with many grievances against King Justinian for his pirate nephew who is also an adopted son has wreaked great havoc across our three kingdoms. He has robbed us of treasure, slaves, food, and clothing. He has stolen a battle cruiser and used it to destroy our own naval vessels and to pirate merchant ships. We gave him tribute to stop his attacks on the ships in our waters and he reneged on his promise immediately. We have done all that we can do for the Island of Remar and its 100,000 inhabitants under his tyrannical rule for the last 50 years."

"He destroyed the garrison stationed at Remar and killed the regent that ruled the island. We three kings find Justinian liable for Sprasian's tyrannical rule of our waters. Sprasian is bankrupting our kingdoms. We have sought peace with this brigand and he has rejected it. We have attempted all that we can do to find peace."

King Justinian spoke up. “What are you suggesting needs to be done in order to reconcile our four kingdoms?”

King Melmot replied, “He is your kin, thus he is your problem. Deal with him in whatever manner you deem best. One caveat to this is that we also demand payment for all that Sprasian has pillaged from our three kingdoms for the last 50 years.”

The frown on Justinian’s face grew deeper all the while Melmot spoke. Upon hearing the conclusion of King Melmot’s words, his face turned a dark red.

Seeing this Melmot broke eye contact with him and began to look down.

Justinian said, “King’s Melmot, Meridian, and Spiegel, have you ever reasoned that the only way to get rid of an evil person is to not bargain with him, but to fight back against him?

“For 50 years Sprasian has ruled the Island of Remar under your watch, King Melmot! He took the island while you sat and did nothing to liberate it from his clutches! Like a malignant growth his hold grew stronger, and still its people suffered as you sent no force to liberate it. There are times King Melmot in which peace can only be found on the other side of war! You are a coward who is afraid to fight a just war. You cannot bargain with evil people as they only seek to continue to propagate their evil desires.”

Justinian began to pace and to speak faster.

"My nephew made a conscious decision of his own to run away from Methos and join this pirate nation. It is under his leadership that it flourished and has become the strongest and most organized group of brigands to ever exist in Athanasia. He has made himself into a king in your own lands and waters. He is sovereign over them, not you. Sprasian chose the life of a transgressor. Not I. Sprasian chose to lie, pillage and destroy. Not I. I did not bring him up in these ways. I taught him the right path to take and he chose to reject the teachings of the ancient writings.

"No, Lord Melmot, it is not I who am at fault. It is you who are at fault for not confronting this problem. It is you who are at fault for watching these things take place and choosing to sit back and do nothing. King Meridian and Spiegel should be angry at you for allowing this evil to fester and operate out of your lands. Couldn't your three kingdoms have come together to confront the terror of the seas and destroy him?"

With that last word was a great hush. King's Spiegel and Meridian started to shrink away slowly from King Melmot until he was left alone in the center of the circle by himself.

Then King Justinian addressed another issue. "King Melmot, you do realize that two days ago we captured a slave vessel headed to your lands that had children from different kingdoms being sent to Parrus to be sold as slaves? No kingdom should ever be built on the backs of slaves. No child should ever be taken away from their mother and father. Unfortunately, your kingdom is one that has made slavery lawful. In doing so, you and the other kingdom's have created a new trade from this filth. Maybe I should seek restitution from you for all of the Methosian parents that have had their children abducted and sold into slavery?"

With this, King Melmot recoiled back to his throne to be consoled by his entourage.

King Justinian went back to his throne and spoke to Petros who was accompanied by a cloaked Spiros. "Well said, sire! Hopefully, this rebuke will help him to see things more clearly, so that he can finally do what is noble."

King Justinian sighed and said, "I hope so, my dear friend."

Justinian then called Spiros over to him. "Today we will see what has happened with King Argos. Keep yourself cloaked so that he does not know that you are here. I am certain that your name will be mentioned and that we will learn more about this great conspiracy."

As Justinian leaned back in his throne he witnessed a vast entourage entering the top of the temple. It looked as if King Argos had finally arrived.

As everyone watched the entourage head towards the throne for Portus, it appeared as if the king was walking in the middle of this group. As they came to the throne Arsinian took on the role of a herald and announced the king.

"Kings of Athanasia, I present to you the ruler of Portus.... King

Mardok!"

When these words were uttered every person on the top of the temple began talking one to another.

In the midst of the confusion King Mardok stepped forward and sat on his designated throne. After a few seconds of reveling in this achievement he stood up and made his way to the center of the circle smiling like a murderer set free by a corrupt judge.

"Kings of Athanasia! I bring you discouraging news. My Lord, King Argos, has died. We uncovered a plot of insurrection to take his life and usurp his throne. However, we discovered it too late. The plan was already set in motion and every family member of King Argos has perished as they were killed in an ambush by a foreign group of soldiers. King Argos languished in great despair and asked that if anything happen to him that I would be made King of Portus and bring justice against these conspirators. To my great misfortune and the misfortune of the Portusian people, King Argos chose to take his life. I hold before you the edict that was signed to make me king if he perished."

He held up the paper with the royal signet stamp of Argos and had Arsinian hand it to the scribe over the ceremony as proof.

"My fellow kings, today I come to you with the evidence of who committed these evil crimes against Portus. I come here today to seek justice for murder and the attempted insurrection. We have found that Spiros of the Adelphos was one of these conspirators. Unfortunately, he was set free as he was being marched to the royal prison by a large group of attackers. They freed him from his binds. He was also able to retrieve his sword which he used to kill Victus, one of the king's royal protectors."

Every person on top of the tower gasped at the mountain of ill news that was just spoken. King Justinian looked over to Spiros who was holding a clenched fist up to his lips, tapping them. "I should have known." muttered Spiros.

Mardok exclaimed, "Spiros has escaped Portus and we do not know where he has gone. However, we were able to find evidence of who was behind this attack."

Mardok then signaled to Arsinian. Arsinian came forward with some armor that had been taken off the attackers and presented it to Mardok. "I hold before you armor bearing the insignia of Sophos, which is the insignia we are gathered around at the top of this temple, and happens to be the royal insignia of Methos! King Justinian was behind this attack as all the evidence has pointed out!"

Mardok threw the armor down on the gold covered floor towards King Justinian. Justinian surveyed it with a quick glance and saw that it was Methosian armor.

Spiros uncloaked himself and walked briskly towards Mardok.

"Liar! Liar! You killed King Argos!"

Mardok's eyes opened wide and a sneer appeared for less than a blink of an eye. Mardok shouted, "Traitor! Traitor! Further proof that

Justinian was behind this! The escaped conspirator stands in our midst with the mastermind King Justinian! No more proof is necessary!"

Petros and a Methosian soldier under his command named Tiberius ran and grabbed Spiros from behind and drew him back to Justinian for protection. Arsinian yelled, "What manner of treachery is this?" which sparked the ire of all the kings.

The kings and their courts started yelling at Justinian, "Traitor!" "Murderer!" "Coward!" "Usurper!"

King Drajian pulled his sword and marched with his royal protectors and several guards towards Justinian. "Arrest this murderer!" yelled Drajian as he pointed his sword at Justinian.

Petros, Brackus, Elias, and Lucian all stepped in front of their king and blocked the advance towards Justinian. Tiberius yelled out to the Methosian soldiers around him, "Soldiers of Methos, protect your king!" All the soldiers drew their swords and encircled Justinian's position.

King Bastian stepped forward with his sword drawn and proceeded to be involved in a yelling match with King Mardok in Justinian's defense. Kings that wanted more evidence and were not ready to condemn were locked in heated verbal exchanges with those that wanted Justinian's arrest. Their entourages were pushing each other back and forth while shouting and spitting in each other's faces.

King Melmot crouched down to his knees and put his hands over his ears and started screaming. He then laid down on the ground and began flailing his arms and kicking his feet as he yelled. Chaos had truly manifested itself on top of the Temple of Sophos and to the point where a battle could break out at any moment.

Mardok had taken the shocking news of his being crowned king, which was forbidden, and turned the focus to murder and treachery from a righteous king. Mardok signaled to Arsinian, who blew a horn so as to regain everyone's attention.

As everyone quieted down, Mardok stated, "Based on the facts that we have uncovered, which beyond a shadow of a doubt indict King Justinian as trying to usurp the throne of Portus. I have no other choice but to make a declaration of war against Methos. Who knows what other schemes he has concocted in hopes of taking over all of Athanasia?"

The uproar amongst the kings began again. One king yelled, "I would declare war before I would let a filthy usurper take my throne."

Justinian responded boldly to Mardok's accusations. "Put your forked tongue behind your teeth! Lies are your native tongue! The job of the Adelphos is to protect the kings of Athanasia. They were not created to rule kingdoms. This traitor has proven that he is a liar by going outside of the design that Sophos created for them. He is the usurper! His very acts have proven that he is the one behind this scheme!"

With gnashed teeth Mardok countered, "I speak the truth! The evidence does not lie and it has pointed you out as the conspirator! King Argos made me the king in line after all his heirs were murdered. I can only be obedient to his decision as his most trusted servant.

Mardok then directed his fury towards Sophos as he addressed everyone on the temple, “What kind of God hides behind his creation and refuses to show himself? Certainly, not a God that is in control of things!”

Mardok looked to the sky and raised his sword straight up and continued his tirade. “I have a message for you, Sophos. How dare you put a liar, murderer and usurper over the throne of Methos to persecute the innocent people of Athanasia! I will ascend to your throne. I will ascend to your throne and rule more justly than you have! If you are all powerful then strike me down now as I stand on top of your temple. If I am a liar, then strike me down now if you are so powerful!”

There was a hush that came over everyone on top of the temple. Everyone was waiting to see what would happen as a result of this blasphemy. Sophos had just been challenged and cursed by Mardok who said that he would take His throne. Not a word was spoken after Mardok’s blasphemy as everyone waited and looked around.

The heavens remained silent.

After several moments Mardok broke the silence. “You see, Sophos is not all powerful! He has been challenged and refuses to face me! He is a coward and not a God worth serving!”

Then Mardok looked to all that were in attendance. “If Sophos was all powerful would he not seek justice on the forces behind this evil act?

Look at king's Melmot, Meridian and Spiegel who have been terrorized by the ruthless pirate Sprasian, who is Justinian's adopted son. Sophos has allowed Sprasian to pillage and murder the people of these lands."

Mardok scowled, and then looked over at Justinian while addressing the crowd, "King Justinian, who seeks to invoke the wisdom of Sophos to settle disputes has done nothing to resolve the chaos that Sprasian has caused. Justinian is Sophos' chief servant in all of Athanasia and shows the hypocrisy of both he and Sophos to not bring justice to his vile nephew! Since Sophos doesn't seem to care about the evil that has happened in Portus, or anywhere else that Justinian allows his wickedness to thrive, then I will seek justice for Portus and Athanasia! Who will join me? I will also protect any kingdom that fears retribution from Methos if they align with me. What say you kings of Athanasia?"

With that said, the kings of Parrus, Othos, and Ramsey immediately joined Mardok as they already had great disdain for Justinian. Then the kings of Grekland, Thessoli, Solas, Astoria, Melos, Storgos, Corpus, and Kalipso followed suit and joined Mardok. Only the king of Solcis followed Justinian as he thought everyone was acting rashly and wanted things to slow down so as to investigate all that has happened. The other seven kingdoms of Brispar, Praxis, Talis, Goresh, Zerastos, Wrestrum, and Dulum all stated that they would remain neutral.

These seven kings wanted peace like most Athanasians desired, but sometimes war is thrust upon a nation regardless of what they desire.

However, in a broken world where people transgress others and evil men are born every day, peace is a noble idea, but it could never be a constant. In most instances these kings have always chosen not to fight whether for bad or good. They scaled back their armies in hopes of avoiding war with the other kingdoms of Athanasia. They were ripe for Mardok's picking.

Mardok exclaimed, "Since you chose to abstain from fighting against a king that seeks to seize all the kingdoms of Athanasia, then I declare you enemies of Athanasia. Your indecision is your decision. By choosing not to fight, you are giving Methos approval for their evil acts. By not standing up to fight against tyranny, you kings are giving Justinian approval to usurp the whole of Athanasia. You are nodding your heads in cowardice to the spread of tyranny. Therefore, if you are not with us, you are against us!"

Justinian walked up to Mardok and looked at him in the eyes. "You are no king! My country will not recognize you as a legitimate heir to the kingdom of Portus. You are nothing more than a filthy usurper not worthy enough to oversee the lands where we dump our kingdom's refuse. By lies and accusations you seek to turn the whole of Athanasia against Methos. You do this because you are not strong enough to take our kingdom yourself, so you solicit allies in order to carry out your wicked scheme."

Justinian then broke eye contact with Mardok and turned his head to address the kings. "Kings of Athanasia! Listen closely, for Mardok seeks to overthrow you and rule Athanasia as the one and only king! He is using you!"

Mardok's nostrils flared and his eyes were wide watching Justinian.

"Very well, murderer!"

Then in a whispered voice that only Justinian could hear Mardok said, "We will settle this on the battlefield and I will show you, your family, and your citizens no mercy."

Mardok then walked to the throne reserved for the king of Portus. Arsinian approached Mardok with a similar look of outrage. Mardok whispered to his accomplice, "Arsinian, leave for Parrus immediately to make the offer to Sprasian, and I will begin our campaign against these seven neutral kingdoms once I return to Portus. I should be able to overthrow these cowardly kings by the time you return from Parrus. Make haste."

Arsinian bowed and said, "As you command, my sovereign king." He then left the top of the Temple of Sophos amongst all the chaos.

Mardok called his new allies over and implored them to come back to Portus to plan their offensive. All agreed, and with that Mardok's plan was in full bloom. War was being planned on the very temple that ended many wars and diffused many situations that could have led to war.

King Justinian saw this terrible sight on this hallowed temple as an atrocity. He said to those around him, "The temple has been defiled." He shook his head, looked down, and closed his eyes. "Lord Sophos, the evil that you have spoken of has revealed itself. Give me strength to cling to your promises."

Justinian lifted his head and began walking towards Mardok with his Adelphos in tow. Justinian came to within a foot of Mardok as both adversaries began to stare at each other.

Justinian spoke first. “An undeserved curse will not come to rest. Your lies will be exposed and will never stick to me warmonger! We will never bow to tyranny as it would be better to die fighting for freedom than living in bondage!”

Mardok smirked, “I am glad to know that you are aware that your life, as well as the lives of all those in your line will be extinguished!”

King Justinian countered, “I do not fear you, usurper! You are to leave my lands immediately otherwise you will be arrested and stand trial for treason.” With that, Justinian turned and walked away, but Mardok watched him closely as he left.

As Justinian walked away, he called Petros to walk beside him.

“Petros, I want you to set sail to Parrus with five ships. Spiros is to accompany you. Sophos mentioned that Spiros should continue on his voyage to Parrus, so I want to ensure that he gets there. I do not know why, but I do know that you will run into Sprasian and his pirates. Stay there with Spiros until whatever he is looking for finds him. I want you to take Elias with you as well. If something happens to you or Spiros I know that Elias will be able to take command.”

Petros bowed and said, “Yes, my Lord.” He then motioned for Elias and Spiros to accompany him, and they made way their way quickly out of the temple.

14 - Salem, Portus

It had been two days since Mardok shocked Athanasia with his announcement as king of Portus and declaration of war on Methos. He was standing in his war room in his palace with the other 11 kings that allied themselves to him.

"My Lords, we are united today because of a common enemy. King Justinian is the greatest evil that our world has ever seen. We must remove him as king and make sure that none of his heirs will be allowed to ever reign. However, in order to do that we must eliminate the neutral countries that would rather allow a criminal to succeed in his evil and prosper. Does this sound reasonable?"

All the kings replied, "Yes!"

Mardok then posed another question once he received their consent. "My fellow kings, being that we have so large and spread out a force, I would like to lead all of our armies with your approval. We need to be united if we are to succeed. If we have 12 kings with 12 different strategies for war, then we will most certainly fall in defeat. With your permission I would like to plan the strategy and lead the armies until our foes are vanquished?"

Every king accepted this as reasonable with the exception of the kings of Grekland and Solas. King Drajian explained why he dissented. "My military is what makes me powerful and gives my kingdom strength. Turning it over to the control of another would make me a lion without any teeth."

Mardok began to clench his fists and every muscle in his body tightened as his heart began to burn with rage. He thought to himself, "How dare they defy me." Mardok slammed his fist against the table and said, "This is exactly what Justinian would want!" He paused and glanced at every king in the room before continuing, "A house divided against itself will not stand."

Mardok then turned his back and walked away from the table waiting to see how the kings would react. After a few moments of silence the King of Solas responded, "Mardok is right, if we do not unite our full strength against the tyranny of Justinian, then our alliance will fall apart and Methos will be victorious."

Mardok smiled when he heard this, but then glanced over at the king of Grekland to see his reaction. King Drajian of Grekland was staring down at the table with his hand partially covering his mouth and holding his chin. As the silence continued, King Drajian covered his eyes with his hand and took a deep breath. Mardok sensed that the king was wavering, so he decided to add some incentive.

Mardok asked, "King Drajian, would you accompany me to the hallway for a private discussion?"

King Drajian nodded his head in agreement and followed Mardok out of the room into the hallway. When the doors closed Mardok said, "King Drajian, I know how extremely hard this must be for you to join your armies under one banner. You must understand that the only way to win is to unite as one. I will only command them until we defeat Methos and Solcis. You have my word."

King Drajian shook his head and replied, "King Mardok, you are undertaking a noble cause by uniting our nations to avenge the death of King Argos and his family. I am struggling with the fact that too much has happened in such a short span of time. I believe we need to proceed slowly and cautiously so that we don't make any rash decisions."

Mardok replied, "The evidence is clear that Justinian committed these heinous acts. What more evidence do you need?"

King Drajian replied, "I am very confused as my better judgment is telling me to not make rash decisions."

Mardok reached into his pocket and brought out several pieces of parchment and began looking through them as if there were a specific one he desired to find. All the parchments were the same, but he did not want King Drajian to know this fact. "Ah, here it is!" replied Mardok as he handed it over to Drajian to read.

Drajian read through the parchment quickly as it wasn't very long and replied, "You are promising me 10,000,000 pieces of gold just to use my armies until Justinian is vanquished?"

Mardok replied, "Yes."

Drajian continued, "You are also offering me 1/10 of the lands of Methos and Solcis?"

Mardok replied, “Yes, I am. You will have the first choice when we divide up their lands, so that you can choose the very best.”

King Drajian’s countenance changed as his eyes softened and he began to smile. “I accept the terms of this agreement, Mardok.”

Mardok smiled and walked over to a wall with a large candle that was lit. He extinguished the flame and dipped his signet ring in the wax, then he applied it to the parchment. King Drajian dipped his signet ring into the wax and then applied it to the contract as well. Both men then pulled their rings off the parchment and a distinct pop could be heard. Mardok looked over to one of his top lieutenants standing nearby and said, “Sinjin, bring the gold over for King Drajian to see.”

Sinjin commanded the soldiers at his disposal, “Bring in the chests.”

The soldiers made haste to a door on another hall and began pulling out chests of gold. There were 20 chests of gold carried by four soldiers each that were brought to the feet of King Drajian and Mardok.

Sinjin ordered, “Open the chests.”

The soldiers opened the chests and revealed the contents. “Mardok responded, “10,000,000 gold pieces as was agreed, King Drajian.”

Drajian’s smile beamed like the sun on a cloudless day as he watched the gold gleam in the light.

Mardok asked, “Does everything appear in order?”

King Drajian replied, “Yes, it does.”

Mardok looked over at Sinjin and said, “Have all of these chests taken down to King Drajian’s caravan and loaded onto his wagons.”

Sinjin replied, “Yes, my Lord.” After he turned away, he clenched his fist and gritted his teeth. When he looked up he saw Romus staring at him with wide eyes, while holding his hand open in a downward position. Sinjin nodded his head and looked away from Romus as he ordered the men to close the chests and take them to King Drajian’s royal caravan.

Romus walked up to Sinjin and took him aside while Mardok was finishing up his conversation with Drajian. Romus grabbed Sinjin’s arm and looked to the left and then right to make sure no one was watching them. “What are you doing, Sinjin?”

Sinjin had shoulder length blond hair, but had two different color eyes. The left eye was a light blue while the right was albino with a red tint. Sinjin pulled his arm away from Romus and stared into his eyes as if he was searching into his soul. He replied, “You betrayed me. You told me that if my men went along with your plan that they would not die.”

Beads of sweat began rolling down Romus’ face as he replied, “I communicated to Mardok not to harm any of our loyal men. They were not supposed to die when Spiros was freed on the way to the prison. I dare not ask Mardok why he had them killed for fear that he will take my life.”

Sinjin turned his head so that his albino eye was staring into the eyes of Romus. He replied, "Remember who put you into your new position, General."

Romus nodded his head as he looked at Sinjin in his albino eye and then gazed down. Sinjin turned and walked over to the soldiers preparing the chests and picked up one by himself and carried it down to Drajian's caravan.

As the conversation with Sinjin and Romus was finished, Drajian tucked the contract into his cloak and re-entered the room with Mardok. The kings immediately turned to inquire what the king of Grekland had decided.

Seeing the curiosity on their faces King Drajian replied, "King Mardok is very persuasive. He opened my eyes to see that I must demonstrate my integrity and not sit idly by in the face of grievous evil. I hear by lend my forces to King Mardok, so that all of our kingdoms will be united against the tyranny of Methos."

The kings began to cheer that Grekland had decided to join them. Mardok grinned, "Thank you my fellow kings! When this war is over I promise to return control of your armies back to you, so that Athanasians can all be at peace once more."

One of King Mardok's top vizier's walked into the room and found his king. "King Mardok! The people are gathered to hear your speech."

Mardok still smiled when addressed as king.

King Mardok stood out on his royal balcony where King Argos, in grief, signed Mardok's edict to be king before hurling himself off the balcony to his death.

"People of Portus, two days ago I declared war on the Kingdom of Methos on the Temple of Sophos. Spiros, the key conspirator who escaped our grasp after being found guilty of trying to murder our king and his family was found standing next to King Justinian at the temple when I arrived. That was all the evidence I needed to declare war on these usurpers. Eleven kingdoms have allied themselves with our cause of which I was made the chief overseer of all our armies. However, seven kingdoms have chosen to remain neutral and allow Justinian to continue to reign in terror over Athanasia. Their indecision was their decision of support for Justinian. Therefore I have declared war on the seven cowardly kingdoms of Brispar, Praxis, Talis, Goresh, Zerastos, Wrestrum, and Dulum. We will defeat these kingdoms before we defeat Methos and its ally Solcis."

The people then gave a great roar of approval to Mardok's words.

"Citizens of Portus, I have some good news to add about my rule of Portus. Today, I have signed an edict that will ban all worship of Sophos. We will no longer live under the laws of the ancients. They are archaic and not necessary or relevant to our time. Therefore, 'Forgive those that transgress against you' will be replaced with 'Seek revenge against those who wrong you'. Whatever you think is right in your own eyes will be considered right. You have the liberty to do whatever you want and no laws to inhibit you from seeking out your desires. In order to do this, all the ancient writings in Portus will be destroyed, all books referring to them or Sophos will be destroyed. All worship of Sophos will be banned and the temples will be either torn down or reconditioned to suit other purposes. Today, I hereby remove the moral code that has enslaved our people since the dawn of time. Too long have we been subject to these standards of which we could never attain. If we cannot attain them, then why have them? Believe me when I say that I will be giving you freedom by doing this.

"The only laws that you will be required to keep are the governmental laws such as paying taxes or worshipping your king. King Justinian, the murderer pledges to live by these so-called truths from Sophos and these ancient writings. Look what that has done to our kingdom. If the fruit of murder and deceit are what is born by walking in these ways, then I choose to expel them all from my life and the lives of my citizens!"

The people erupted in cheers as Mardok turned to walk back inside after his speech with a chiseled smile and glowing face. Everything that he and Arsinian had planned was coming to pass.

Meanwhile, Arsinian was sailing towards Parrus with chests of gold amounting to one million pieces.

"Captain Rolos, are we making good time towards Remar?" asked Arsinian.

"Yes, my Lord! We have caught a good wind and the ocean current is with us. We are making better time than expected," replied the sea captain.

“Excellent!” responded Arsinian. “The sooner that we work out this agreement, the sooner we will be able to stick a thorn into the side of Justinian using his own kin against him.”

“What do you hope to accomplish by employing this brigand?” asked Rolos.

Arsinian pulled out his sword and very oddly held it in front of his face gazing at its magnificence. While staring at the sword he began his reply. “We intend to cause internal strife in Methos. We want to take away Methosian resources and cut off their supply routes. What better than to have a group of brigands who would give their lives for gold and other material possessions to do our will. Pirates are expendable, no one cares if they live or die. We just desire them to be a thorn in the side of Methos to divert their attention and resources from our advances.”

Sailing hours ahead of Arsinian were five Methosian warships with 400 soldiers on each boat. The lead ship was a state of the art warship. It had a large catapult on the bow used to hurl large flaming balls of tar at ships or on the shores where opposing armies or structures are located. These balls were ignited before they were hurled and would impact an opposing ship with a crushing blow. The flaming ball would splatter sending flames everywhere and set an entire ship ablaze.

Petros, Spiros, and Elias were ready for a war either against the kingdom of Parrus or Sprasian. They had discussed this exploit in length over the two days they were at sea. They had no idea why Sophos wanted Spiros to go to Parrus. However, they reasoned that since they are now officially at war with Parrus that they would not accomplish much there. It would have to be in an area where the Parrusian army would have no control. They believed that the Island of Remar which was controlled by Sprasian would be the most logical place to dock and figure out their purpose. Either way they knew there was going to be conflict. Fighting Sprasian would be easier than fighting the entire Parrusian navy and army.

Petros was in the captain's quarters with Spiros, Elias, and Captain Broshius mapping out their strategy. It was beautifully decorated with wood furnishings which included an ornate dinner table that sat 16 people. It had many windows that brought light into the quarters and gave a beautiful ocean view. By the fire place were several stationary couches with purple cushions. The bed was located near the fireplace. Petros was sitting at the captain's table speaking.

"Sprasian has 12 ships under his command. Two of the twelve are warships that they captured, and each ship can hold between 300-350 men," said Petros.

Then Spiros, shaking his head said, "Are we going to commence a nautical assault against 7,000 brigands and then storm their shores?"

Petros replied, "Yes."

Spiros burst out in laughter.

"What do you find so humorous?" replied a stone faced Petros.

He continued, "You do realize that Sprasian will not allow us to dock on Remar? You do realize that his ships will attack us as soon as we are spotted? We have to take the island in order to be able to dock anywhere. Therefore we must plan an assault."

Captain Broshius echoed the sentiment of Petros. "The only way to land our ships is to attack Sprasian and take his island. His forces are divided between Port Verdes and Port Caprica. His capital is Port Verdes. If we are to take Remar we must cut off the head of the snake. When we take Sprasian the brigand nation falls."

Captain Broshius was a naval officer and warrior who had seen many campaigns and battles. He was well over six feet tall and broad shouldered and spoke with an eloquent voice that enunciated every word to perfection.

Elias stood next to the captain. He was a man with a dark complexion that was almost black. He was very ruddy and handsome like all of the Adelphos, and he had a shaved head and black facial hair only on his chin. He agreed with Petros and with Captain Broshius. "If we retake the island, the people that have been enslaved for the last 50 years would be quick to join our ranks and unseat Sprasian as their ruler. I have no idea why Sophos would want Spiros to head to Parrus. I would have to believe that the smartest option is to confront Sprasian, and not King Melmot, for we are not equipped to overtake his kingdom. It is through this planning that we can discern the best path to take which will inevitably lead us to why we are going to Parrus in the first place."

With that, all agreed that they would start planning an assault on

Port Verdes.

As they were sitting down at the captain's table a young man brought in a beautiful roasted turkey, some bread, fruit, and ale. Following soon after the boy was the captain's next in command. His name was Lieutenant Lorian.

He had a very dark complexion like Elias, but had short hair and green eyes. He was somewhat of a portly man that was clean shaven. He wore his officer's uniform with great pride which was apparent because there was not one blemish on it. Before he sat down he introduced himself to everyone at the table.

He nodded at Captain Broshius, "Sir."

Then he addressed the Adelphos. "My name is Lieutenant Lorian. I am second in command under our Captain Broshius and as you can tell by my exterior, I have a very deep appreciation for food."

Everyone at the table began to laugh.

As he sat down they all gave thanks for the food and began to eat. During the meal the young lieutenant directly asked the three Adelphos in the room, "How did this happen and why did Mardok abandon his post as protector to become King of Portus?"

All three Adelphos opened their mouths as if to speak, then looked at each other and said nothing. Captain Broshius tilted his head and furrowed his brow as he looked at Lorian. Spiros threw his hands in the air and replied, "That is a very hard question to answer. We were created from a diamond in Lord Sophos' court. All 84 of the Adelphos were drawn from it. This is what unites us as brothers. The diamond is a very beautiful stone that is strong, sharp, and reflects light. We were created to be eternal, and are virtually indestructible. We were also given great wisdom that no man could ever possess, while at the same time reflecting the glory of Sophos. We are only allowed to protect and use our wisdom to advise. We were not allowed to carry out an evil king's desires, but rather try to encourage them back to goodness. Obedience is a sign of love and devotion to our creator. We did exactly as we were commanded."

Petros pursed his lips and began tapping his fingers on the table. Seeing this, Spiros stopped talking and extended his arm towards Petros. "Would you like to add something, Petros?"

Petros nodded and said, "It is obvious that Mardok chose this path. Instead of accepting the role he was created for he has chosen disobedience, which is insurrection. He has usurped the throne of Portus as he desires to be a god and now wants the throne of every kingdom in Athanasia. He thought that he was better than the job he was given, and in his pride he became jealous for kingship and coveted it. In his lust for power and glory followed deceit, murder, and now war. He is the scourge of Athanasia deserving only death!"

Lt. Lorian countered, "If you knew he was this way, then why did you not stop him?"

Elias replied before Petros could respond, "We did not know. It was hidden from us. Who knows how many of our order have chosen to follow him? As far as we know every one of the Adelphos could have been swayed by him. All we know is that we are all loyal to our kings. We must assume the worst of our brethren that they have fallen under the tentacles of Mardok."

Spiros started to think about how this was not discovered beforehand. He remembered something that Arsinian did that never tipped him off. He interjected, "There was a time when Arsinian came up to me and asked me a hypothetical question. He said, 'Do you think that we are doing a job that is beneath our talents? That maybe we are deserving of something greater?' I remember responding to him and telling him that our talents were perfectly fashioned to the positions that we served. That our talents would be out of place and not used well if we used them outside of the responsibilities given to us. We were made and our talents were given to us to serve in the position we were entrusted with. The position we serve was not created for us, but rather we were created for it. To do anything outside of these parameters would cause us to not flourish."

The insightful lieutenant then asked, "How did Arsinian respond to what you told him?"

Spiros just nodded his head and looked down at his ale. After a few moments of silence in the room he looked up and replied, "Arsinian said," 'Great answer! As always you speak the truth and know the correct answer, Spiros.'

"Arsinian then grinned and said," 'I was just testing you to see what your answer would be.'"

Spiros turned his attention back to the men in the room. "I was such a fool. How could I have missed it?"

Petros interrupted, "Then this proves that we cannot trust any of our brethren without testing them. We may have to find one that is corrupt and interrogate him to find out what he knows."

Everyone nodded and the conversation lightened with less vexing issues. At the end of the meal they all relaxed at the table and enjoyed their ale while their stresses were melting away. This was when Lieutenant Lorian exuding a big grin on his face asked how the king's nephew became a brigand?

Elias pointed over to Petros. Petros exclaimed, "You are an inquisitive man, Lorian. So much so, that part of me thinks that you are a Portusian spy." Petros scowled at Lorian while all those present in the room turned their heads and put their hands on the hilt of their swords.

Lorian's eyes and mouth opened wide, but not a sound was uttered by him or anyone else in the room. Petros began to laugh while pounding his fist on the table. "I am only jesting, young one."

Everyone in the room dropped their hands from the hilts of their swords and began to laugh. Lorian exhaled and began to laugh when he realized Petros accusation was false.

When everyone had regained their composure Petros began answering Lorian's question. "Sprasian's father, Fabian, lost his wife to complications during birth. She died minutes after he was born. Fabian to this point was a valiant warrior and noble man. However, he did not handle this trial well. He blamed Sprasian for the death of his beloved wife. If anything it was the trial that exposed Fabian's heart."

The lieutenant inquired, "How so?"

Petros took a sip of his ale and leaned forward on the table. "On the outside he obeyed. He looked as if he had everything together and was a perfect man before his beloved died. It was once said that, 'Trials are meant to expose the true character of our hearts and can either refine us or destroy us.'

The lieutenant asked, "How did Sprasian's father die?"

"Do you remember the war with Solcis just over 200 years ago?" asked Petros.

Lt. Lorian replied, "I was not alive when the war took place, but read about it in school as a young boy."

Petros explained, "Then you will remember when the tyrant King Agios abducted Queen Alexis while she was on a peaceful mission in his kingdom. She was taking food to the starving people of his country because he stored all of the nation's crops. He forced the people to pay a premium price because of his monopoly. The starving people were fleeing Solcis and became refugees in Methos. Queen Alexis was outraged that a king would treat his people so badly, so she asked King Justinian if she could take food into Solcis. The king agreed as he shared her sentiment of helping these starving people.

"Queen Alexis left for Solcis with 20 tons of grain, 2000 sheep, 300 cows, and 100 bulls. As they entered into the land of Solcis, she and the Methosian people and soldiers with her began giving food to all of the border villages. Word spread quickly to the starving people of Solcis, but also to King Agios."

Lieutenant Lorian interjected, "I remember reading about this now. If memory serves me correctly didn't Agios send 50,000 soldiers to the border to capture the food? He captured Queen Alexis and made her his prisoner. When King Justinian heard of this, he did what any loving husband would do. He went after his wife. He launched a campaign against Solcis in two forces. Justinian marched from the east with 250,000 soldiers, while Fabian marched from the north with the same number in tow. They decimated any opposing force that got in their way. They finally descended upon the capital city and laid siege to it for seven days."

Petros responded, "That is correct, but that isn't the end of the story. Fabian was able to breach the wall in the north and with a large contingent of men, they invaded the city and stormed the royal palace. As Fabian valiantly led his soldiers through the palace for the sake of his brother and sister-in-law, he made his way into the throne room. Unfortunately, when we broke through the doors of King Agios' throne room we were greeted with a volley of arrows from crossbows. Everyone in the front fell to the ground and had no fewer than three arrows lodged in their bodies. Fabian was in the front. He led the charge with great courage, but fell that day as six arrows pierced his body."

Petros paused for a moment as his countenance began to fall with every word he spoke.

He continued, “I was in the second group of men to cross the threshold of King Agios’ hall. When I spotted Fabian on the ground with six arrows in his body I became enraged as did all the soldiers with me that day. We took no prisoners and cut down every soldier that protected King Agios.”

“We captured King Agios and freed Queen Alexis who was unharmed. It was a bittersweet day. We freed our queen, but lost the king’s beloved brother. In the end, Fabian may have failed as a father, but I think his true heart showed during this ordeal. Had he survived that battle I think he would have been a better father.”

The lieutenant asked, “How do you know that he would be a better father?”

“He was indeed a selfish man that blamed his son for something his son had no control over, however, when Justinian told him what happened to his beloved queen, it was almost as if a transformation had occurred instantly. When humility is present, courage always follows.”

Petros continued, “Judging by my interactions with him and his actions over the weeks it took to save the queen, I could tell that he was a changed man. He even confided to me about reconciling with his son for the way that he treated him the last 11 years. Had he survived, he would have been a father to Sprasian. When put to the test he realized what really mattered. His heart supernaturally changed from where it once stood, though it was too late for him to make amends with his son.

I often wonder why your kind is not mindful that no one is promised tomorrow."

Petros paused as silence permeated the room. Everyone began nodding their heads having given thought to the truth of not being promised tomorrow. Petros continued, "As it so happened, when we deposed the tyrant King Agios, we freed his nephew from prison who was the actual heir to the throne of Solcis. Agios usurped the throne from his brother and put his family into prison for the rest of their lives. That man we freed is the current king of Solcis, who is our lone ally against Mardok."

Elias responded, "Well said, Petros," He continued, "Now what do we do with the unredeemable Sprasian? He is the epitome of all that is evil is this world."

Spiros decided to interject some words of encouragement. "These things that you say, Elias, are undoubtedly true in regards to his character. However, I hold the belief that Sprasian can change despite the wounds of his past and the poor choices he has made. I hold out hope that the wisdom he was taught by Justinian is still there buried deep in his heart and just need to be unearthed."

Elias laughed, "Always the optimist, Spiros. That is what I like about you. Nothing discourages you. Even being falsely accused and set up as a scapegoat for usurping the throne of Portus."

Everyone laughed including Spiros. They all then emptied out of the room onto the ship's deck where the soldiers on board were sipping on a little ale and sparing with wooden sticks for entertainment. These soldiers had not seen military action in over 200 years, so they were excited. Morale was high and they needed to work off some of the energy.

15 - The Waters South of Port Verdes, Remar

It was day 17 of the Voyage for the Methosian expedition heading to Remar. Unbeknownst to them Arsinian was several hours behind as they entered the Parrusian waters. On the other side of Athanasia a federation of kingdoms was being led by King Mardok looking to destroy Methos, Solcis, and the neutral kingdoms. All of the kings of this federation left Portus and were headed back to their kingdoms to alert their people and prepare for war.

On the lead ship Elias, Spiros, Petros, Lt. Lorian, and Captain Broshius were mapping out their plan of attack in the presence of some of the soldiers. “If we are going to destroy the brigand nation we must attack the stronghold of Port Verdes,” said Petros in his typical direct manner. “They have eight ships in Port Verdes, but I am not aware of how many will be docked there as I am sure they will be carrying out raids on ships and cities. We must catch them by surprise, they would never expect a direct assault upon their capital. That is why I am suggesting a threefold attack.”

Elias interrupted, “I agree with your point Petros, the element of surprise is the best way to proceed. However, it can only work if we are able to camouflage at least part of our presence. Bearing this in mind, what would you propose?”

Petros smiled, “I am glad that you asked, Elias. We should have a ship come about to the east side of the city and send ground forces ashore. We should send one ship to the west of the city and send ground forces ashore there as well. This way we will be able to flank them when we make a direct assault on the ground. The major fighting does not need to take place at sea, but rather on land. The remaining three ships will plow through any blockades and will send troops to shore from the middle. The focus of the enemy forces will be squarely upon our assault, which will keep our troops cloaked as they come from the east and west. Our catapult should be able to destroy any ship that comes into range and pound any defensive positions on the ground that will obstruct our landing party. We also will have covering fire from our longbow archers as we send men to shore. Once we take the shore our group will head straight to the palace to take Sprasian while our soldiers that have flanked the enemy from the east and west will make a circular ascension up the hill to surround the palace and secure the area so that no one escapes."

Captain Broshius had their plan taken to the other ships captains as they prepared for battle. There was a nervous excitement that could be felt on each ship as soldiers were gathering their armor and swords from the armory and archers were bringing out their longbows. The men assigned to the catapult were preparing massive balls of tar on the deck. The battle was less than two hours away and all the preparations were just about complete.

Petros was on the deck instructing some of the soldiers on how to cut down their soon-to-be enemies by showing them defensive and offensive moves with the sword.

Elias gazed at his sword. He was focusing on it and picturing himself in battle. This method was used by great warriors in preparation for a conflict because it made them focused for battle. It gave them great awareness of what was around them when the fighting began.

Spiros went to the front of the ship where no one stood seeking solitude. It gave him time to meditate and ponder the great struggle that they would soon encounter.

As the time ticked away they had full view of the island. Two ships had broken off some time ago and made for their flanking positions while the lead ship was followed by the remaining two. Finally, the soldier in the crow's nest saw a ship approaching rapidly as they closed in on the harbor.

The sail of the ship was white, but on it was painted the head of a mythical dragon that had fire in place of its eyes. Most people would have been struck by terror at this sight, but soldiers scowled and gritted their teeth.

As the boat approached, Captain Broshius called out, "Prepare for battle!" The men began to scramble to their positions. Broshius ordered, "Catapult, fire when ready!"

The catapult team yelled in unison, "Yes, sir!"

The catapult had been loaded as one member of the team lit the large mass of tar. A lever was pulled and the catapult was fired. No sooner had the shot been fired did they lift the next tar ball into the scoop, they adjusted the trajectory and tension and then fired again.

Captain Broshius watched from the ships steering column and saw the first shot strike the back of the ship, setting it ablaze. Seconds later the next shot hit the center of the ship setting fire to it as well as the mast and sail. Those blasts slew many of the ship's sailors, yet others jumped overboard to put out the flames.

The fire was spreading through the ship at a rapid pace and the ship came to a complete stop as its sail disintegrated. The men underneath looked like they decided not to row, but rather made their way to the top of the ship to escape.

One of the Methosian battlecruisers pulled up to collect anyone that wanted to surrender as the lead ship continued towards the port with the other battlecruiser following on the right. The pirates refused to surrender and even started firing random arrows at the cruiser so Captain Broshius had his ships archers fire at the pirates. These archers fired with great precision and killed many of those remaining on the blazing ship.

Those that jumped overboard refused to be rescued. One pirate was heard saying, "I would rather die than be saved and live in captivity!"

The ship was completely engulfed in flames as the captain of the ship chose to sink with his vessel. As the Methosian battlecruiser was about to depart to catch up with the lead ship a few of the drowning pirates changed their minds and cried out for help. Quickly, wooden poles and a lift were inserted into the water and these men clung to them. They were lifted into the ship and immediately shackled.

The lead ship was approaching the harbor and saw five catapults being lined up and prepared.

Captain Broshius screamed. "Destroy the catapults! Make ready the landing crafts for the invasion! Long bowmen, prepare to fire onto the shore!"

With this command fiery tar balls were hurled at the shore and within moments had destroyed three catapults and their crews. Three hundred warriors filled 12 boats and were lowered into the water. They made great haste rowing towards the shore.

Captain Broshius screamed to the archers, "Let's give them some cover!" With that, 75 long bowmen began firing at the shore striking down those manning the catapults and those taking position for battle. Behind them were 24 more boats with 600 men. One hundred fifty additional long bowmen from the other two ships began firing at the shore giving these boats covering fire so that they would land safely. On each boat was a soldier screaming out the pace, "Stroke! Stroke! Stroke! Stroke!" The adrenalin of the men rowing on some of the boats was so strong that they went faster than the pace, and pulled ahead of the other boats. They were ready to meet the enemy.

In a matter of moments they landed on shore, were able to exit their boats, and engage the enemy that had been held in check by the arrows. A great collision of steel on steel could be heard as the Methosian troops clashed with Sprasian's pirates.

The invading soldiers were outnumbered two to one, but they

rushed up the beach to meet their enemy as if they were defending their own lands.

In the front were Elias, Spiros and Petros cutting down pirates without being touched. As they held their position they noticed 300 Methosian soldiers coming from the west led by Lt. Lorian. They flanked the pirates which proved to be the surprise they had hoped it would be. Moments later another invasion force came from the east and almost had the pirates completely encircled.

Lieutenant Lorian led the charge into battle yelling, "For Methos!"

A violent "clang" was heard as Lt. Lorian's men collided with the pirate forces. Lorian struck the first pirate he encountered with his shield, knocking him unconscious to the ground. He then thrust his sword into the next enemy and pulled it out quickly to engage another. Lorian's men were in a tight formation fighting side by side. As the battle raged, he screamed out to the men during the thick of the fight, "Tighten your ranks, men!" We must hold the flank."

Lorian stepped back to survey the fight and saw that his men had the pirates contained. As he looked to the north away from the dock he observed that the pirates were trying to outflank the line. He grabbed several soldiers and ordered, "Follow me." He took his men to this area and got a better perspective of the battle. He saw that the Methosian forces on the east and south were pushing the pirates back, which put pressure on the western line.

Lorian pointed to the line and shouted out to the soldiers with him,

"Fill in the gaps! Push the enemy back!" The soldiers rushed to the line and began slashing down pirates. Lieutenant Lorian joined the charge screaming as he tackled the first pirate he encountered. He buried his sword into his foe and rose to his feet shouting. His eyes and mouth were wide open like that of a deranged lunatic as every pirate he engaged was overcome with fear with every shriek of his voice. He cut them down one after another as the Methosian line began to hold.

Lorian then yelled to his forces, "Encircle the enemy to cut off any route of escape. If we box them in, then they will be unable to flee."

Lorian and his forces began to encircle the enemy way of escape on the northern front of the battle. When this happened the pirates began to panic and tried to retreat which lead to a fiercer exchange as men fought to avoid losing to their enemy and others fought to avoid losing their lives. A great melee ensued in which the pirates were able to cut through the line of Methosian troops to the north, so as to escape.

As the pirates fled, Lt. Lorian took his troops to the north and headed for the palace. The Methosian plan was to take their forces and surround the palace so as to lay siege. Lt. Lorian's men made haste to the northern wall while the force that flanked the pirates from the east hurried to the western wall. The main attack force of 900 men made their way to cover the east and southern walls.

The Methosian soldiers met small pockets of resistance along the way, but the sheer number of their force allowed them to roll over their opponents without stopping their momentum. The pirates were leaderless and could not get re-organized enough to stop the advance.

The Methosian force cut down any that stood in their way.

The people of Port Verdes in light of this hope of freedom came out of their homes with great boldness. They carried cast iron pans, brooms, knives, metal bars, and swords and went after the pirates as well. This unexpected blessing was fueled by the people's desire to be free from the tyranny of Sprasian.

It came about that the Methosian soldiers did not have to worry about opposition as they made their way to Sprasian's palace because the people were doing the rest of the work for them. By the time they had gotten to the palace to surround it, it had already been surrounded by the citizens for Port Verdes.

There were slain pirates in the streets and others that had surrendered or been overcome and bound in the front of the palace. The people were yelling, "Freedom!" and "Death to Sprasian and Bremus!"

With their adrenalin pumping from this trouncing Petros, Spiros, and Elias attempted to breach the palace wall. The castle was surrounded, so there was no way for its inhabitants to escape.

Making its way up the hill was a team of men carrying several ladders that were 35 feet in length. It was more than enough to breach the 30 foot walls. Petros did not want to wait so he took his Sword of Helios and stabbed the palace wall which yielded to his indestructible sword. Sparks flew from the strike.

"Elias, give me your sword!" yelled Petros.

Elias immediately handed Petros his sword. Petros, while grasping the one sword in the wall with his left hand took Elias' sword with his right hand and stabbed it into the wall. Immediately, Petros pulled out the sword on his left while pulling himself up with his right arm and planted it into the wall. Petros was scaling the wall with brute force. Every soldier and citizen looked up in awe as they watched him climb the wall in this fashion.

Elias and Spiros gazed upward grinning at Petros as he ascended with sparks flying from each strike. "I presumed that over the course of the many millennia that we have lived that I had witnessed all there was to see in Athanasia," said Spiros.

"Petros proves that theory wrong whenever I spend any time with him," added Elias.

Petros made the climb look easy, free from any strain. His movements were calculated and his rhythm was graceful like a horse in full stride. When he reached the top the pirates just stared with wide eyes and open mouths. Some became so overcome with fear that their body froze and they dropped their weapons. The pirate in charge yelled, "What are you waiting for lads! Knock him down to the ground. Do not let him get over the parapet onto the wall-walk."

Petros pulled the sword in his right hand out of the wall and blocked several strikes from the pirates. He then countered with a thrust and slayed one pirate. Two more pirates took swings at Petros while he was hanging. He blocked one and dodged another before slashing them both down. He then began to swing back and forth on the sword planted in the wall until he was able to fling himself over the parapet and onto the walkway. With two swings of his sword he vanquished two more attackers.

Petros then reached down, pulled the sword out of the wall, and proceeded into battle with six pirates coming from his front and six coming from behind him. His advantage was that the walkway on the wall was fairly narrow and would only allow one person on each side of him to be involved in the confrontation at a time.

With a quick strike he impaled a pirate in front of him with the sword in his right hand, he then pulled his sword out of the man and spun around striking the next attacker down. Petros then extended the sword in his left hand, impaling the next advancing pirate. Petros then pulled his sword from the impaled pirate, brought it around as he blocked an attack with it and then used the sword in his right hand to vanquish his opponent.

From behind a pirate thrust at Petros' back, but Petros immediately turned his body towards the wall dodging the blow. However, the next pirate that was directly in front of him became the recipient of this strike. Petros took advantage of the opportunity and struck down this pirate who was now wide open with no defense. Two more pirates then advanced from either side. Petros blocked both of their attacks with a sword in each of his arms. A third pirate tried to take a thrust at Petros while he blocked the attacks, but Petros dodged it by moving away from the wall. When Petros made this move he came too close to the edge and began to lose his balance. As he was teetering backward he dropped his swords and grabbed the beard of one pirate and the arm of another and pulled them towards him to gain his balance. In doing so, these two men fell off the edge of the wall to the ground.

The remaining pirates dropped their swords and ran swiftly away from Petros. Petros began to whistle while walking casually to the mechanism that barred the doors shut. He flipped the lever and the gate began to open. He then made his way nonchalantly down the stairs, picked up the swords and greeted Elias by handing him his sword back.

"Thank you, Elias!" said Petros.

Elias smiled and said, "I am glad I could be of service to you."

The peasants began to storm into the palace behind the Methosian troops. This now mighty host made its way through the courtyard to the throne room where Sprasian was certain to be.

Sprasian could see from the palace window that the Methosian's were on their way.

"Bar the doors now!" yelled Sprasian.

His men took defensive positions in the throne room. There were only 60 pirates, but they were well armed. They had crossbows for the initial surge when the doors would eventually fall and then swords and shields for the hand to hand combat.

The Methosian soldiers followed Petros up to the doors which were barred from the other side, so Petros called out for a battering ram. Within minutes some soldiers brought up a small battering ram to the door. Eight soldiers manned the ram and started pounding the door.

Petros then called out to the soldiers, "I need twenty soldiers with their shields to initiate the assault when the doors open."

The citizens of Remar were angry and were lined up at the door wanting to get in at Sprasian. Petros yelled out to them, "Citizens of Remar, let our forces handle the capture of Sprasian. When we have secured the room and captured him, he will be arrested and will stand trial for his crimes."

The citizens reluctantly honored Petros' request and slowly backed away from the entrance. Meanwhile, the battering ram was just a few strikes away from breaching the door.

On the other side of the doors Sprasian paced like an animal that had been cornered with nowhere to go. He yelled, "When those doors open commence firing."

In the hallway the ram hit the door and a great snap of wood could be heard. As the door broke open the battering ram team immediately fell back and 20 soldiers emerged to initiate the assault. However, the peasants disobeyed Petros command and stormed the door when they heard the snap of the wood. As they burst into the throne room the pirates began to discharge their crossbows. Within just a few seconds dozens of peasants had been killed by arrows. They stopped their advance and withdrew behind the Methosian soldiers.

Petros yelled, "You fools! Stand back!"

He then turned to the Methosian soldiers. “Soldiers of Methos, commence the attack! Spiros and Elias take your soldiers to the left, while I will take my contingent to the right.”

They nodded their heads as the twenty soldiers made their advance. As soon as they entered the room the pirates began firing their crossbows. The first ten soldiers dropped to their knees and hid behind their shields as the ten soldiers in the back placed their shields over the top of the shields of the front line. The arrows bounced and ricocheted off this metallic wall. They then got up from their positions and charged the center as Spiros and Elias covered their left flank and Petros covered the right flank. One hundred Methosian soldiers entered the room followed by an angry mob of peasants.

The pirates fought ferociously to repel the Methosian advance. Spiros slayed a pirate and grabbed his fallen enemy’s sword so that he could fight with two. He engaged two pirates, chopping down one enemy, while blocking the attack of another. He quickly slew the second pirate and engaged two more pirates. The sword of Helios was in his right hand and he swung it at his approaching enemies, cutting through both of their swords and striking them both down. Another pirate picked up a crossbow and fired it at Spiros’ head. Spiros immediately dropped the sword in his left hand and caught the arrow as he leaned back. He then charged the pirate that shot the arrow and planted it into the pirate’s upper torso.

Spiros looked to the left and saw Elias close by striking down a pirate. He then looked right and saw Petros body slamming an enemy to the ground.

It was an amazing sight as the peasants in confidence now made their way to Sprasian. Sprasian was still injured from his wounds, but found the strength to cut down these peasants. He cut down one after another until fifteen had perished. The peasants retreated in fear giving Petros the opportunity to confront Sprasian.

With one swing of his sword he broke Sprasian's blade in half.

Sprasian shocked and confused yelled, "Petros?"

Petros replied, "Hello, old friend. Your days as a brigand have now ended."

Petros pointed his sword at Sprasian's face while two soldiers came up and bound the pirate king.

Petros said to the soldiers binding Sprasian, "Take him back to his royal quarters and place him under heavy guard until I return. We have to finish purging this island of pirates."

One of the soldiers said, "As you command, Petros." and hauled Sprasian away.

Petros turned to the soldiers who had secured the room and said, "We need to secure the city first. After that we will prepare to attack Port Caprica. Elias, see to it that the city is ours for the keeping."

Elias nodded and left with a group of soldiers. Petros then called one of the citizens over who appeared to be leading the peasants. "Why were we not opposed by a greater force?"

The citizen walked up and explained, "Sprasian sent out eight of his twelve ships to raid the surrounding waters and small ports. 3200 pirates have filled those ships. 1000 remain in Port Caprica, which left over 3000 brigands here in Port Verdes. They were completely caught off guard by this assault. I would be remiss if I did not say thank you on behalf of all Remarians for what you have done today. We have been freed from Sprasian's heavy yoke."

A soft eyed Petros said, "You are very welcome. Unfortunately, I believe that we will have to turn you back over to King Melmot since this was his land."

The peasants in the throne room overheard the conversation and one screamed, "NO! We will never go back to Parrus!" The crowd of people came to an uproar over this news.

Petros yelled, "Silence!" and the room became calm.

The peasant that Petros was speaking with explained in a bolder tone, "King Melmot abandoned us and left us under the tyranny of Sprasian. When he abandoned us he forfeited these lands. What kingdom would allow a foreign force to enter it and take part of its lands? They put up no fight and did not protect their citizens. Instead King Melmot chose cowardice and sold us into slavery! He is not our king! We desire to be citizens of Methos. We want a just king to rule over us that will defend his people."

After these things were said by this peasant every citizen cried out,

“Long live Methos and long live King Justinian!

Petros cracked a smile and then spoke for all to hear in the throne room. “If this is the wish of the citizens of the Island of Remar, then we will most certainly accept you into the Methosian ranks.”

A great roar was heard in the throne room from all the cheering citizens. Petros addressed the leader, “Now, send word out to all the people of the island that Sprasian has been removed from power. Tell them that they are now free. Let word spread throughout the island as we prepare to defend against the return of the eight brigand ships and commence an assault on Port Caprica to liberate the island of this tyranny completely. Appoint amongst yourselves leaders that are men of wisdom, devotion, integrity, and courage. We will work with these leaders to restore order and rebuild the infrastructure. Let us meet with these leaders tomorrow in the throne room to discuss how we will proceed forward.”

The citizens left and word began to spread throughout the very large island like a fire consuming dried straw.

Petros and Spiros went back into the royal quarters where Sprasian was being held. As they entered, Sprasian was being attended to by Katherine his nurse.

Petros and Spiros entered the room with force and ordered Katherine to leave. In a firm voice she said, “I must finish attending to his wounds first. I would treat my persecutor no different than I would treat my liberator.”

The men were left without argument and said, "Yes. By all means, please finish giving the care your patient needs."

Sprasian was unconcerned about the coming interrogation but hoped that Katherine would take more time in tending to him. She had kept returning to his aid despite his harsh words to her weeks earlier, but she was soon finished, took leave of the men, and Petros then took the stage.

"Alright, old friend, when are these eight ships coming back to dock?"

Sprasian yelled, "Why would I tell you, a mere slave, eternally bound to a king?"

"Sprasian, I have liberty because I serve in the capacity that I was created. I don't serve outside of it. I know that you hate me for administering those lashes on you in the public square. You were suffering the consequences for your actions. I had no joy in giving out that bit of discipline. Please know that they were not administered in malice, but rather in love. We desired to keep you from an unrighteous path by showing you that transgressions bring pain and suffering."

Sprasian smiled and countered, "Truly? Then why did I become a pirate that was the scourge of Athanasia?"

Spiros then spoke up. "You chose that path of rebellion. By the looks of you I see a man who is already suffering the consequences of his actions with two arrow wounds in his body. If you live by the sword, you die by the sword, Sprasian."

Sprasian countered, "Am I dead?"

Spiros responded, "The people here want to take you out to the square and hang you by the arms on the gallows and let people beat you with sticks for your transgressions and likely leave you there as a sign to others. The very violence you have lived by has only brought violence back in return."

Images of the men of the city flowing into his room not more than an hour before returned to Sprasian's mind. For the first time he began to fear what was going to happen to him, and what the citizens of Remar would do to him if Petros and Spiros turned him over.

"Spiros, find the dungeon and place him down there under heavy guard. He needs some time alone to think and we don't want him harmed as he is King Justinian's nephew and adopted son. He may be the scourge of Athanasia, but his uncle loves him despite his transgressions. I will check on him later after the city is secured and we prepare our forces to defend against this Bremus who will at some point return."

While Sprasian was escorted down to the dungeon, Elias sent out detachments of troops to finish off any stragglers still loyal to the pirates in the city. He and his other forces had a few skirmishes throughout the city, but overpowered them quickly, as the people were still willing to help fight.

The city was secured within hours. In all of the fighting 117 Methosian soldiers had perished and 24 were wounded. The losses for the brigands were many times greater as 2300 were killed and 234 were wounded, while the rest surrendered or escaped. It was a massacre of which the small pirate nation had never seen.

There were 20 brigands that were able to escape. These 20 escaped unnoticed on a small boat with a sail when the attack had commenced on Remar. They were hoping to sail out and find Bremus and warn him of what had happened.

16 - The Waters of Northwest Parrus

Arsinian, who was trailing the Methosian force by several hours stumbled upon Bremus as three ships were spotted coming to the lone Portusian vessel. Bremus' ships were taking flanking positions and moving very quickly. Arsinian ordered his troops to stand down and had them raise a white flag on the mast. Within 10 minutes The *Sea Serpent* pulled along the side of Arsinian's ship. A bridge was extended across to Arsinian's surrendering vessel, allowing Bremus and a host of men to walk across and the board the ship.

"I like it when people make a raid easy for me," said Bremus with a smug grin. "What are you transporting for us to take?"

Arsinian walked up to him, looked him in the eyes and said, "I come to strike a bargain with you."

Bremus began to laugh as he replied, "You can't believe that you are in any position to make a deal."

Arsinian countered, "King Argos has fallen and all of his family was murdered by King Justinian. King Mardok is now the ruler of Portus and has declared war against Methos with 11 other kingdoms. We seek to disrupt his waters and desire for you to pirate them. We will set you and all of your men up in our kingdom with everything that you need. We will allow you to pillage Methos with our protection. In order to make the deal more attractive we will pay you the sum of 500,000 gold pieces to move your army across the map to Portus. Do you think that I am in a position to make a deal now, Sprasian?"

Bremus tilted his head and quickly corrected him, "I am, Bremus, the leader of the Remarian Brigands. Sprasian was killed in a raid a few weeks ago, so now I am the new leader."

Arsinian's brow furrowed at the news of Sprasian's untimely death, but was not deterred. "Sprasian would have done this for a mere 500,000 gold pieces, but I like to think big," said Bremus with an enormous grin on his face. "If what you say is true, then I want 750,000 gold pieces and we keep all the plunder."

Arsinian thought, "This is easier than I surmised. They are slaves to gold." Arsinian then countered Bremus' offer, "You may keep all that you plunder, but I think 700,000 would be more than sufficient."

Bremus quickly countered, "750,000 or there is no deal and we will kill everyone on the ship."

Arsinian burst into laughter, "You are a shrewd negotiator, Bremus. 750,000 gold pieces it is."

Bremus smiled and then exclaimed boldly, "Where is my money?

"Arsinian nodded and six soldiers brought up three chests of gold containing the amount that was agreed upon. "There is your gold, Bremus. I am glad that we could make a deal. Count it if you like? Every coin will be there. However, I will warn you now that if you betray us and break our deal, then we will send an invasion force so great that no ship will be able to escape. We will destroy every one of your ships and kill every single man allied with you. We will hunt every brigand down in your army across all of Athanasia and show them no mercy. You will be shown even less mercy when we capture you, Bremus. Do I make myself clear?"

Bremus had never been spoken to like that in his life. "Is that a threat?" replied Bremus.

Arsinian looked at Bremus in the eyes and patted him on the shoulder, "No, that is simply the way things are now."

Bremus realized that this was one bargain that he had to keep. He believed Arsinian and knew that they could never fend off an attack from the Portusian military. He hated being under someone else's control that was more powerful, but he could not pass up the temptation of such a great deal. There would be protection, lodgings, provisions, as well as, pillaging the richest kingdom In all of Athanasia, and acquire 750,000 gold pieces to do it.

With these things in mind, Bremus said, "Agreed! Grab the money boys and lets go back home."

Arsinian smiled at him and said, "I knew you were a man of great wisdom."

Bremus gave a half-hearted bow and asked, "What is your name that I may thank you for your altruism?"

Arsinian said, "I am one of the Adelphos. My name is Arsinian!"

Upon hearing this, Bremus took a step back as the countenance on his face fell.

"Many thanks, my lord, Arsinian. We will gather our things from Remar and will sail for Portus at once!"

Bremus took his money and had all eight of his ships head back to Port Verdes. He told the men with him, "It is time to supplant Sprasian and move my army to Portus. He is weak and frail, making him no longer fit to do his job."

The men nodded in agreement and pledged their allegiance to Bremus.

As Bremus hurried back to Remar he began plotting his overthrow of Sprasian knowing that a successful assassination attempt on Sprasian would not warrant much if any retribution amongst their ranks.

As he plotted his rebellion Bremus saw a small ship heading towards them. It looked like one of their own, but he could not be certain. "First mate, steer the ship towards the small vessel. It looks like it is one of our vessels," said Bremus.

The ship pulled alongside the vessel, lowered a rope, and had some of the men on the ship pulled up. Bremus yelled at the brigand in charge, "What are you doing out here in this ship?"

The pirate said, "Port Verdes has fallen! Methosian troops have stormed the city and taken it from our hands. They stormed the palace and have most certainly captured or killed Sprasian."

Bremus said, "This is bittersweet news, but I don't have to kill Sprasian now. The Methosian's and Remarian's will see to that."

"First mate!" yelled Bremus.

A stocky man with brown hair came to Bremus and said, "Aye, captain!"

Bremus continued, "We will be changing our heading and will make way to our new home in Portus. Sprasian is dead, making me the new leader of the pirate nation. All ships are to follow me." Then looking out to the attentive men on the *Sea Serpent* he continued. "Our home is gone so we will take refuge in Portus. We will rebuild our ranks like never before!" Then looking to the men that escaped the Methosian raid, he replied, "Get your men onto our ship and leave this vessel here. We make way to Portus."

17 - Port Verdes, Remar

Back in Port Verdes, Sprasian was sitting on the ground in a dark cell. His mind kept jumping from one memory to the next with the pain of his wounds reminding him of his most recent actions and how they had led him to his current state. Within a matter of hours he went from a king to a prisoner. Now the day of reckoning for all of his transgressions had arrived.

As he sat in his cell he suddenly had a memory come to mind. He was standing at his father's funeral weeping as the royal guard carried Fabian's casket to his tomb. A great chorus of women's voices were heard singing:

"A great warrior has fallen

A great warrior has fallen

Rest your soul for your work is done

Rest your soul for you are free

The city weeps at the loss of its son

The city weeps for the great works you have done

Honor the son of the line of kings

Honor the son who loved his home

A great warrior has fallen so strengthen his kin

A great warrior has fallen please lead him to heaven."

At his father's funeral, King Justinian had been standing close by, saw the grief on the boy's face and walked over to comfort him with Queen Alexis. He knelt down and embraced young Sprasian, who responded back and put his arms around Justinian's neck and buried his head in the king's shoulder.

For that moment the loneliness that Sprasian felt melted away. He felt warmth and love for the first time in his life.

In times of great suffering, love and compassion shown by others stands out like a glistening diamond. This was one of those times for Sprasian and he embraced it with every fiber of his being.

Justinian looked the boy in the eyes. "Do not languish my dear nephew for this too shall pass. Your father may not have known how to show you love, but do know that he did love you. We will not allow you to be orphaned. You are kin. The queen and I are going to adopt you as a son. Know that we will love you and that you never have to fear being alone."

Young Sprasian cried profusely and nuzzled his head into Justinian's chest when he said those words. Queen Alexis then knelt down and hugged the young man as he continued to cry.

While dwelling on this memory Sprasian started to cry in his cell. His head fell into his hands as he muttered, "I am all alone again."

That moment at his father's funeral could not be forgotten even though the contempt in his heart covered up its meaningfulness for so many years. In the wake of his suffering that precious moment was resurrected. As Sprasian began to control his weeping he looked up and saw Katherine standing at the bars of the cell with tears in her eyes. She was coming to tend to Sprasian's wounds and witnessed his flurry of emotion.

"If you would like, I could come back at another hour," said Katherine.

Sprasian cracked a small smile and said, "Please, I could use the company now."

Katherine began to clean the wounds which were looking much better as the scar tissue was forming. In her compassionate manner she asked, "Why are you crying, Sprasian?"

Sprasian answered thoughtfully, "I have had an epiphany. I have carried hatred in my heart for my entire life. Only now am I starting to see how the fruits of my hatred manifested. Everything I have gained through my actions is now counted loss. I should have listened to my Uncle Justinian. He told me that if I sowed seeds of evil, then I will reap their destructive reward. He was right. I sit here now a broken man. I was almost killed in a raid and now my army has been destroyed and the seas and the land that I once controlled are now lost. I have been relegated from a throne to a dark dungeon where I will more than likely spend the rest of my life if I am not hung on the gallows for my crimes."

Katherine put one hand over her heart and the other over her mouth as she was shocked by his honest profession to her. Sprasian looked like a man where the virtue of humility was finally manifesting out of his humiliation. Katherine sensing this said, “Humility is not self-deprecation, nor is it allowing people to walk over you. Humility is not thinking lesser of yourself, rather it is thinking of yourself less. Sprasian, for the first time in your life you are seeing how your actions have impacted so many people in such a bad way.”

Katherine continued, “Never would I have imagined that a man with such a hard heart would soften and utter such liberating words. Now is the time for you to make a choice.” said Katherine. “You are ripe to make a decision that could change your life for the better. You have seen that the life you have lived has been without meaning. You have taken the pain and suffering of your life and have transferred it on others. You have done many cruel and abominable things. Your conscience has awakened and is convicting you of wrongdoing. Now is the time to leave this life of burden that has brought you so low and embrace a new life of freedom. If you do not choose a righteous path now, then your heart will harden and you will become worse than before.”

Sprasian looked up at Katherine and had wide eyes as he hung on every word that Katherine said while she was bandaging him up. “You have given me much to consider Katherine,” answered Sprasian with his head hung low staring at the floor of his cell. “I don’t know that I can admit that the things that I have done are wrong. For it would mean that I have wasted my entire life. That everything I have ever done or gained would be for naught. I am not sure that I can accept that. I feel as if my soul has been placed on a rack and is being stretched to the point of it severing."

Katherine nodded her head. "It wouldn't be easy for anyone to reflect on one's life and admit that it was a chasing after the wind. The truth is never easy to accept."

Sprasian struggled, but a tiny smile cracked on his somber face. He said, "Thank you," and looked away.

Katherine walked out of the cell and thought, "I hope that I planted some seeds that would change his heart, but was I too harsh?" She sighed and hung her head as she exited the dungeon.

Sprasian fell asleep shortly after Katherine re-bandaged his wounds, but an hour later he was abruptly awakened. He saw a man with a light gray cloak walking into the dungeon and passed all the sleeping guards without waking them. He walked up to Sprasian's locked cell and the door opened before him.

Sprasian pressed against the wall, trying to distance himself from whatever was entering the cell. However, he froze when his shackles fell off his hands and feet as if they were never locked.

In a tender voice the visitor said, "Do not fear, Sprasian. Come, follow me."

Sprasian hesitantly stood up and followed the man's command and they walked by a host of sleeping guards and out of the prison.

Sprasian thought that he must be dreaming, but the man knew his thoughts and said, "You are not dreaming, Sprasian."

Despite Sprasian's fear he squeezed out a question. "Who are you?"

The cloaked man took his hood off and said, "Your creator."

A confused Sprasian asked, "Which god are you, for there are so many?"

Sophos calmly replied, "I am the only God. There are no others."

Sprasian trembled at his response, but mustered courage to ask another question. "If you are Sophos, then why are there other gods that people worship?"

Sophos looked at Sprasian with soft eyes and rebuked him in a manner as a father would a son that he loves. "Why would I as the creator produce other gods to receive credit for my creation, glory and majesty? If you were the creator of the universe would you create other gods to be worshipped for the work of your hands?"

Sprasian stood speechless as Sophos' words permeated every fiber of his being, causing him to tremble.

"Sprasian, I created a hole in every man and woman's heart that only I can fill. Everyone has chosen to turn away and tried to fill that hole with something I have created. These statues and images are no more than idols that reflect the desires of their heart. Should I as creator be joyful about other people erecting false images from stone, wood and metals which I created? Should I be joyful about my creation giving credit to these false images? These idols are not representative of me nor do they have anything to do with me.

“People worship them in vain. They are fools, for the very wood they use from a tree to carve an idol they also use this same wood to make a fire to cook their food or stay warm. Then they bow to this idol, pray to it and ask it to deliver them from harm. These people are as blind and foolish as you, Sprasian!”

Sprasian looked as if he were about to say something and then put his hand over his mouth. He bowed to one knee and stared at the ground saying, “Forgive me for questioning your sovereignty, great Sophos. Why have you revealed yourself to me?”

Sophos put his hand on Sprasian’s shoulder. Sprasian felt a tingling sensation, the pain from his wounds disappeared and he felt warmth flowing through his body as if he were an empty vessel that was being filled up.

“Sprasian, you have been one of the most evil and wretched men to have ever lived in Athanasia. You have orphaned children and widowed wives. You have beaten and robbed the strong and the weak. You have treated people with contempt and great malice. You have murdered more people in your short life than many wars combined. You have been a power hungry tyrant who lacks mercy, justice, wisdom, courage, humility, and faith.”

After Sophos said this, Sprasian started remembering all the transgressions that he had committed in his life as a child up until this point as he stood with Sophos. He began to feel a hopelessness and a want to undo everything he had done to others. It was so great that he began to cry and prostrated himself before Sophos.

Sophos continued, "Despite these things I have sought you out to save you from the destructiveness of your life. I want to give you a new life, one that will give you freedom from your transgressions."

Sophos knelt down and put both of his hands on Sprasian's head and the burden that Sprasian couldn't bear lifted immediately. The weight of his transgressions left him and he knew joy, peace, and contentment.

Sprasian rose from the ground quickly and marveled at what just happened, "Any word that I say will not come close to conveying to you what just happened. Please forgive me for my offenses against your kingdom, Lord Sophos. For you, and you alone I have offended and done what is evil in your sight, making you blameless when you judge. The unbearable weight of the shame and guilt of my deeds has dissipated like snow under a hot sun. What do you desire from me, Lord?"

A radiant Sophos said, "Breathe the free air my servant, for you are a new creature. Today begins your new life. I have much work for you to do, but I also have much work to do in you. I am going to put you through a series of tests so as to build your character and temper out the impurities of your life. Temptation will be right there to pull you back into your old life. That is why you must go through this.

“Take a ship with Spiros and 150 valiant men and sail east. These men must not be faint of heart. Be prepared, for the adversity that awaits you will be unlike any ever experienced.”

Sophos turned and walked away from Sprasian out into the courtyard. Sprasian felt very uneasy about this command to sail east, so he followed Sophos. He hesitantly asked, “Lord Sophos, thank you for revealing yourself to me and freeing me from bondage. May I ask why you would send us east? There is nothing but ocean to the east, west, north, and south. Ships have been sent by various kingdoms for years in all directions and only one ever returned. A Parrusian explorer came back after over two years with 275 members of their 300 man crew dead from starvation.”

Sophos looked at him in the eyes and smiled. “Obedience is what I seek. Heed my command. I understand your reservations, but I see a greater picture which you cannot see. Trust that I will not lead you astray.”

Sprasian said, “Yes, my Lord. Please forgive me for questioning you. I will do as you have commanded.”

Sophos said, “Now go and find Petros and tell him everything that I have commanded. He will not believe you until you give him this.”

Sprasian looked down and saw the most beautiful gem that he has ever seen in all of his pillaging. He had heard stories about precious stones from Sophos’ court that were not present on Athanasia. The stone that Sophos had given him was as big as a thumbnail, clear like a diamond, but it radiated a magnificent white light in his hand. It emitted this same light in the hand of Sophos.

"This stone is from my court as you rightly discerned in your thoughts. This stone shows the character of a man's heart by the light it shines in the hand of its possessor. When it shines the white light it shows that the person is of upright character, however if it radiates a red light then it reveals the corrupt nature of that individual's heart. When you show this stone to Petros he will know that you speak the truth and will obey all that I have commanded."

Sprasian looked over to Sophos who started to walk away. "My Lord! How am I going to explain what has happened. They will most assuredly execute me as they will believe that I have escaped."

Sophos turned around and said calmly, "Your test begins now."

Sprasian stuck his arms out, holding his hands up as sweat began to form on his face, "My Lord?"

Sophos smiled, "Trials are meant to purify souls. No one said they would be easy. If you let them, they can either purify your heart or destroy it. Trust that I will never abandon you, Sprasian."

Sprasian dropped his arms, wiped the sweat off his forehead, and said, "Does that mean that I will see you again?"

Suddenly Sophos was encapsulated by a beautiful white light. His humble garb turned into robes of fine white linen outlined in gold. This transfigured Sophos spoke one last time to Sprasian.

“If I choose to see you in this life again, then you will see me. All my servants will most certainly see me in the next.” Sophos then rose into the sky as a bright beacon of light, and disappeared into the stars. Sprasian’s heart was pounding in his chest but he had peace knowing that if he died, he would see his King again. It gave him great hope. The former brigand now decided that he had better figure out a way to contact Petros for the guards and citizens will surely kill him if they believe he has escaped. Thus began Sprasian’s trial.

18 - Port Verdes, Remar

The sun was bright yellow as it crept into the sky over Port Verdes and began to give light over the ancient city. The scum of the brigands had now been washed away, and for the first time in 50 years the people felt free and continued to rejoice all over the island. Even the Port Caprica got word of Port Verdes liberation, and the people rose up against the occupying brigands and overpowered them. The Island of Remar was free. Word had stretched throughout the kingdom of Parrus of Remar's liberation.

People were flocking to Remar like refugees as many felt oppressed by King Melmot. His people were in bondage to him as they were overtaxed, overworked and treated as if their lives lacked any meaning. Shiploads of people were fleeing the kingdom and heading to Remar. Even the Parrusian military was fleeing.

Elias stood at the docks with 300 soldiers taking in the refugees. So far five Parrusian battleships with 300 soldiers each surrendered and pledged allegiance to Methos. Fifty seven other civilian boats had come ashore since the liberation bringing with them 12,000 people. The people were angry at King Melmot and wanted to join the Methosian army to defend Remar. They wanted freedom and were willing to fight for it. After talking to the people and observing their disgust for King Melmot, Elias decided to leave and inform Petros of what was happening.

In the palace, Sprasian made his way back to the prison and snuck back into his cell while the guards were asleep in the middle of the night. He put his chains back on and closed the door to his cell.

When the sun rose Katherine made her way into the dungeon to Sprasian's cell.

As she entered she saw an amazing glow on Sprasian's face. "You look different today, Sprasian."

A smiling Sprasian said, "Indeed, much has happened since you last saw me."

A curious Katherine asked, "What do you mean?"

As she pulled away his bandages on his shoulder and leg she saw that the wounds were completely healed. The only thing that remained were faint scars from the arrows. Katherine's eyes opened wide and she put her hand over her opened mouth. "What happened to you?"

A smiling Sprasian exclaimed, "I was visited by Sophos last night and I am no longer the same man you once knew."

Katherine's eyes grew wide, "You were visited by Sophos? Why did he visit you?"

Sprasian took a deep breath and said, "He has chosen me for a task that he has not yet revealed. He has healed me in some strange way that is hard to describe. The burdens of my past are gone and my physical wounds have healed and the pain is completely gone. All that remains are the scars as a reminder of my suffering, but also a reminder of my healing."

An ecstatic Katherine embraced him, "I had hoped and prayed for this day to come and it is now here."

Sprasian said, "It is indeed here. Thank you. Now I must charge you with a task if you are willing. Sophos has tasked me with a dangerous mission. He freed me from my chains and released me from prison last night. I knew that I would surely be killed if I remained outside the dungeon. I came back into the cell and locked myself up again. However, Lord Sophos had told me that I must talk to Petros. He said Petros would not believe my story unless I give him this."

Sprasian pulled out the beautiful jewel he had received from Sophos. It still emitted a bright white light in his hand.

Katherine's eyes never left the stone as Sprasian put the jewel in her hand. It immediately began emitting a white light as it sat in her palm.

"Katherine, will you go to Petros and present to him what has happened, and if he scoffs at what you say, then show him this jewel?"

With her eyes still locked on the jewel she replied, "Certainly, I would be honored to carry out such a task. Praise Sophos!"

Before Sprasian sent her away to carry out his request he told her, "Thank you for looking after me when I was at death's door. I have never been treated so tenderly before in my life. Your compassion melted my heart and showed me something which I have missed in my 217 years of life. It showed me something that I really longed to have. Thank you for showing mercy to a man that deserved death.

Sprasian looked to the ground and hesitated before saying, “Forgive me for the threats that I uttered to you in my quarters. I was wrong to say those things.”

The statement hung silently in the room for a moment before Katherine responded, “I forgive you, Sprasian.”

She turned to leave the cell, but before leaving remarked, “This has brought great joy to my heart. Never could I have imagined that the most feared brigand in Athanasia would change his ways. It is a miracle.”

She left the cell with her head raised and a glowing smile.

Katherine hurried up to the palace to speak with Petros and share this great news with him. When she walked into the throne room she saw Petros and Elias speaking about something serious.

“If what you say is true, Elias, then we will need to start training men to become soldiers as well as build ships and make weapons. We will have to make King Justinian aware of what has happened.”

Elias nodded his head in agreement. “We can use the 2,000,000 pieces of gold from Sprasian’s treasury to finance our effort. What he gained from evil we will now use for good. I will put some of our best officers in charge of recruitment and training and have them announce it immediately. We can use both our soldiers and the Parrusian army defectors. I would like to go and talk to Captain Broshius about leading our naval effort.

Petros nodded in agreement. "That is very wise, Elias. I believe that we also need someone to focus on feeding this budding army and all the citizens. This island is large and its lands are very fertile. We will need to investigate the other two islands and see what natural resources they provide as well. As the refugees grow day by day we need to put an emphasis on farming, fishing, and cultivation of the animals in the forests for food. Can you also lead an effort into metallurgy as we create armor, swords, and arrows? We will also need to build catapults and other weapons to defend these lands."

Elias replied, "I agree. I will begin to oversee the building of weapons and the cultivation of food. I will let you know what I discover when I have gathered all the information."

Once Elias was gone Katherine approached Petros. "My Lord, Petros, I bring great news from the dungeon. Sprasian has had a change of heart!"

Petros broke out with such a boisterous laugh that Spiros made his way into the room, wondering what had Petros in such a joyous mood.

"It is good to see the lighter side of Petros!" Spiros said.

When Petros regained his composure he replied to Katherine, "Are you sure he is not trying to lure you into helping him escape? He has gotten more wicked with every year of his life. This must be a prevarication."

She looked at Petros and smiled, "He said that you would say this, but please listen to what I am about to say. There was a mysterious glow about him this morning when I went to change his bandages and clean his healing wounds. He was full of joy and peace. As I unwrapped his bandages I found that his wounds had healed entirely with very light scars as a reminder of where he was wounded. I asked him what happened to him and he exclaimed that Sophos had visited him last night. He said that Sophos had pardoned him of the wicked life he had led and transformed his soul. He said that Sophos has commanded him to go on some sort of mission of which he desires to share with you."

The smile on Petros' face began to fade as he listened to Katherine's words.

"Sophos visited Sprasian? Did Sprasian burst into flames when Sophos entered his cell?" Everyone in the room could hear the conversation and began bursting out into laughter when they heard Petros' comment.

"He said that you wouldn't believe him, so he told me to give you this." Katherine quickly pulled up the precious jewel that emanated a bright white light in her hand and showed it to Petros whose eyes locked on the gem. She handed Petros the stone and in Petros' hand a white light began to glisten.

Petros turned to the jewel in his hand and said, "Katherine, please forgive me for mocking you and not believing the truth in which you so adamantly conveyed to me. This stone can only be found in the royal court of Sophos. Only Sophos can transport something from his heavenly court to the realm of Athanasia."

The whole crowd stood in amazement and inched closer to see the jewel. Petros called Spiros and a few of the city leaders who witnessed this to follow him to the dungeon.

"Katherine, I would like you to come along as well," added Petros.

Petros made his way down to the dungeon and as he came up to the guards he ordered them to open the door to Sprasian's cell and to take off his shackles. Petros looked at Sprasian while he was being unshackled and thought something did indeed look different about him.

"Sprasian, show me your wounds." Sprasian pulled down his shirt from his shoulder and Petros saw a faint scar. Then Sprasian lifted his pant leg and showed another faint scar from where the other arrow had hit him.

"Is there any pain? Do you have full mobility?" asked Petros.

Sprasian grinned and raised his arm up and down while replying, "I have no more pain and I have full mobility. This is the strongest that I have ever felt in my life."

Petros' jaw began to drop as he surveyed Sprasian's wounds. "Never in all the ages of men, would I have ever thought that Sprasian would ever leave his wicked ways. A man that has shown no mercy in his life has now been pardoned by his creator. What a glorious day this is, old friend!" Sprasian smiled and the two embraced.

"Tell me all that happened, Sprasian."

"Sophos revealed himself to me and made me into a new man. He has tasked me to take Spiros and 150 brave men and sail east. He told me that I would face great adversity that he would use to temper my character."

Petros shook his head and said, "But there is no land to the north, south, east or west? No one has ever found any land. There must be something out there that he desires you to confront or this may be your death sentence."

Sprasian nodded slightly, "I am apprehensive about what I will encounter if I encounter anything at all. However, I am ready to move forward and see what trials I must face."

Petros patted him on the shoulder, "So be it."

Petros turned to the party that followed him. "Spiros, look for 150 valiant men that wish to take this voyage of great peril. We do not want men faint of heart. We want men that know the danger that they are entering so that only the most courageous will step forward. We will give you a Parrusian battle cruiser for your voyage."

He turned back to face Sprasian and took him by the shoulders. Petros began to tell Sprasian the whole account of what Mardok had done and the impending war that was upon them.

"If you by some miracle return to Remar and we are not here, then you will know that Mardok was victorious."

Sprasian nodded.

Petros exclaimed, "Alright! Come, let us make way to the docks in preparation for your departure."

As Sprasian exited the cell he grabbed the hand of Katherine. "We are going to need someone skilled in medicine to accompany us on this voyage. If there is indeed great peril as I was told, then we will need someone to tend to our wounds. I would like for you to accompany us, lady Katherine. You have great knowledge about medicine and great compassion for those that ail."

Katherine had never left Remar in her life and the thought of doing so to set sail for a truly unknown destination caused a tightness in her chest and a want to say, "no."

However, in this instance she replied to Sprasian, "My feelings are saying, 'no', however, my feelings do not rule me, nor are they anchored to the truth. It will be good for me to go on this adventure as I have never left Remar. My mother and father died from disease many years ago and my siblings have married and moved to other kingdoms as they disliked King Melmot. I very much desire to accompany you on your voyage, Sprasian."

Sprasian smiled as he replied, "I knew you would accept. You have great courage in you. You try to hide it, but it is there ready to be unleashed."

She smiled and allowed Sprasian to guide her to the docks.

At this, their party walked from the palace down the beautiful white cobblestone roads towards the dock when they noticed a new attitude amongst the people. The citizens of Port Verdes were in the streets setting up markets. You could see enthusiastic men in training with wooden swords with some of the Methosian officers and soldiers. Blacksmith's were forging sharp ornate swords and armor. The smell of fresh cut wood emanated in the air as men hauled trees down to the marina to start building new warships. Their freedom fostered a new hope which made them want to contribute to the protection of this new Remar and the two surrounding islands.

When they reached the docks they found many valiant men training to be soldiers and others building warships. Petros found a scaffold that was being used to build a ship and climbed to the top of its platform. With his loud voice he caught the attention of those who were near.

"Soldiers of Methos! Men of Parrus! Today I beseech you to listen to my words. Lord Sophos himself has commanded that Sprasian, accompanied by Spiros, is to lead 150 of the most valiant men on a mission of great peril. There is a very strong possibility that whomever makes this voyage will lose their life. I say this not to scare people from volunteering, but rather to accept only those who are not faint of heart. A man of resolve will not cower in the face of great turmoil, but rather will embrace it using discretion. Are there any men here today that desire to serve their creator?"

No one said a word. It was so quiet that you could hear the blacksmith's clanging of steel far away in the background.

Petros broke the silence, "Sprasian is a new man. He has been pardoned of his transgressions and given a special task."

A voice in the crowd said, "Where are they sailing?

Petros made a one word reply, "East!"

Then the silence turned into clamor as people knew that there was no land in any direction outside of Athanasia.

"That is suicide!" yelled one spectator.

Another yelled, "There is no land east of Athanasia!"

Still another yelled, "Why should we go on a voyage that is led by the very man that has oppressed us!"

People began yelling and screaming at this point as they couldn't believe that anyone would send them to sail east with a tyrant. Petros in a voice that drowned out the multitude yelled, "Silence!"

A hush came over the crowd. Petros remarked, "You are being asked to take a step of faith. Who is willing?"

The crowd became so silent that you could hear the blacksmith's clinking on steel yet again, but only for a moment before a Methosian man walked forward.

He was small, with downcast eyes, and spoke softly, "I will go." He paused, then with more boldness said, "I have lost everything in my life including my family because I only cared for myself. I believe Petros when he says that this kinsman of Justinian has reformed. I too have been reformed by Sophos and I will gladly yield my life in service of our creator."

Murmurs and light laughter ran through the crowd.

"I have no skill with a sword or great strength. I am but a lowly cook who only learned this trade from my time in the king's prison. I would gladly lay down my life to serve such a worthy cause. If you will take me, I would like to go."

The crowd grew silent again before Petros said to the man, "We will have you! Your face is very familiar to me. Where do I know you and what is your name?"

I was pardoned by King Justinian for my evasion of the king's taxes. I was the prisoner who was visited by Sophos and changed forever. My name is Dulas."

Petros' eyes opened as if he had had a great epiphany. "I remember you! How blessed we are to have you!"

Petros exclaimed, "People of Methos, this is what faith looks like. It is free of fear. This man does not have the look of a warrior, but he has the heart of one. I would sooner go into battle with 1,000 men like him than 1,000 warriors."

The people began to murmur again, but this time a Methosian

soldier spoke up. “If this man is willing to give up his life, then how can I not? I have much to learn from Dulas.”

The soldier stepped forward next to Dulas. Dulas’ courage and grateful heart encouraged others to start stepping forward. When all was said and done 80 Methosian soldiers, 60 Parrusian soldiers, 8 citizens of Remar, 1 Methosian cook and 1 nurse (Katherine) stepped forward.

19 - Salem, Portus

In Portus, King Mardok's new creed had taken effect. The moral code and all moral laws were removed. Statues of Mardok were erected and the temples of Sophos were defaced and turned into temples worshipping Mardok.

In the city markets merchants were stealing from their customers and their customers were stealing from the merchants. Merchants would lie and sell faulty goods and services while citizens would grab goods and other merchandise off tables and run. All of this went unpunished by law.

Jordan and Marcus, the father and son who had helped find Spiros a ship to escape, were walking through the marketplace in great fear as they witnessed immense depravity. They watched a man get beaten unconscious in front of his young son because two men wanted his money pouch. The man believed that they had a right to his money and that there was nothing wrong with stealing or the assault.

Jordan asked, “Father, what is happening?”

Marcus replied, “King Mardok's new decrees are in effect.”

Jordan shook his head and asked, “I thought laws were meant to protect people, not harm them.”

Marcus shook his head in disbelief as he replied, "They are meant to protect people, my son, but they also reveal the character in one's heart." He paused and looked over at the man who had been beaten. He continued while looking at the man, "This lawlessness is a reflection of King Mardok's heart. He is unjust." He paused for a moment while watching the man's son weep, but continued. "There is a greater law that governs us all, and we must abide in it. Come, let us do good to this man."

Marcus walked over with his son in tow and helped up the man who had been robbed. Jordan went and put his arm around the man's crying son who could not have been over four years old. Marcus thought to himself, "Why did no one come to even assist the man after he was robbed?" Marcus pulled the bloodied man up to his feet and put his left arm around the now semi-conscious man's neck. The four walked slowly to an inn around the corner.

When they reached the inn, Marcus found a bench for all four to sit outside. He tore a piece of his shirt and dipped it in a water trough outside the inn. He wiped the blood off the man's face who was now fully conscious. The man asked, "Where is my son?"

The son broke away from Jordan's care and screamed, "Papa," as he ran and embraced his father. His son began to feel safe in his father's embrace as he nestled his head into his shoulder.

"Thank you for your kindness, sir." said the man.

Marcus asked him, "Where are you from?"

The man replied, I am from the port city of Circe."

Marcus said, "That is in northeastern Portus. You are far from home."

The man nodded with the torn cloth over his right eye. "I came to see King Mardok and carry news back to Circe of his new laws and the upcoming war against Methos. I was trying to find a carriage to take my son and I back to Circe when two men overheard my conversation with others and said that they could assist me. They brought me here and then demanded that I give them all of my money citing Mardok's new decree. When I refused they beat me and took it for themselves. Now my son and I have no ability to travel home."

Marcus asked, "What is your name?"

He replied, "My name is Stephen and this is my son, Jonus."

Marcus wanted to help Stephen and his son, so he said, "Please excuse me for a moment."

Marcus took Jordan aside and said, "Jordan, this man has no provisions or even a way back to his home. What do you think we should do?"

Jordan replied, "We don't have much money, father. There is no way we can help them."

Marcus responded, "If we don't help them, then who will? Will you consider giving them your horse?"

Jordan immediately crossed his arms and held his head in the air and said, "No."

Marcus then replied, "Jordan, I will respect your decision, but I want you to think about it one more time. Take your feelings out of this situation and put yourself in their predicament. They are far from home and have no way of returning. His son is scared and no one else has come to their aid. With this being said, can we help them?"

Jordan dropped his arms and lowered his head and looked over at Stephen who had wrapped his arms around his son while rocking back and forth. Jordan replied, "I want to help them, father. They need help like Spiros did. We were the only people that helped him."

Marcus smiled at his son. "Indeed."

They walked back over to Stephen and Jonus and sat next to them. "Stephen, my son would like to give you his horse to travel back to Circe. I have four gold coins and I want you to take them to help pay for your travels."

"You would do this for complete strangers?" replied Stephen.

Marcus and Jordan nodded and said, "Yes."

Stephen's head dropped as he stared at the ground and then looked back up at Marcus. "Why would you do this for complete strangers?"

Marcus replied, "How can we stand and do nothing?"

The man stood up with his son in his arms and hugged Marcus and then Jordan. “Bless you.” he said.

Marcus gave Stephen his gold coins and retrieved their horse from the stable at the inn. The man mounted the horse and Marcus handed him his son whom he put in front of him. Stephen turned to Marcus and Jordan before he left and said, “I will never forget the sacrifice you made today on behalf of a stranger.”

Stephen turned the horse and road off down the busy street. Marcus and Jordan began walking away from the Inn. Marcus said to his son, “I am proud of you, Jordan.” Jordan’s face lit up with a large grin as they continued to walk.

After a few minutes Jordan asked his father, “What are we going to do to survive? We have no money or a way of bringing our fish back to market.

Marcus said, “The market has become a dangerous place, and as such it may be best that we avoid doing business here.”

#

Mardok stood on his royal balcony smiling and drinking ale while watching the decline of Portus. The Portusian’s had become lovers of self, and as such they raged when they didn’t get what their crooked hearts desired. Mardok watched as people would kill or beat each other for material possessions. Hatred was great in Portus since King Argos died and his family murdered. Murder in the kingdom had risen since Mardok took over and declared war on Methos and any other kingdom that did not join him.

Mardok muttered as he sipped his ale while gazing, “Good. Good. Hatred is running deep in the people’s hearts. It is ready to be harnessed.”

Mardok turned his head to the side and yelled, “General Romus! It is time to corral this hatred and turn it on Justinian and all the people of Methos.”

Romus hurried to the side of his king. “What is your command, Sire?”

Mardok turned to Romus. “General, are my troops ready?”

Romus replied, “Yes they are, my Lord. We have 17 million Portusian soldiers at your disposal. They are angry and ready to march! ”

Mardok smiled, “And what of my fellow kingdoms who have pledged their armies to fight under my authority?”

Romus grinned, “They are all ready to march and only await your command. The generals are in the war chambers planning the offensive. Would you like to see how we plan to carry out our campaign against Athanasia?”

Mardok snickered, “But of course. Take me there immediately as I wish to partake as a warrior king. I want everyone to see my courage.”

The two then made their way to the war room to discuss the plan of attack with the 11 other generals under Mardok’s command.

#

In Methos, King Justinian was listening to his generals.

“We do not have the strength of arms to defend our kingdom from the attack of 12 nations. We estimate that they will have around 40 million soldiers. Up to this date with vigorous recruiting our army stands at eight million soldiers. Our ally Solcis has two million soldiers. We are outnumbered four to one and have too large a border to defend against. It will stretch our forces out which will make us weak and defenseless,” said General Tobias.

General Tobias was the head Methosian General. He was known as the best military commander and strategist that ever lived in Athanasia. He received this distinction because he had never lost a battle as a commander, nor has he lost any of the 18 wars he has overseen. He was trusted by the king not only for these distinctions, but because he was the mastermind behind the rescue of Queen Alexis and the liberation of Solcis from its tyrant king.

King Justinian asked, “What would you propose in light of this grim news?”

General Tobias’ voice resonated through the room as he replied, “We need to protect our supply lines, and food and water resources. I have mapped those areas here.”

He pointed to a large map with white crystals marking out these key defense points. “We also are blessed with natural terrain that gives us a great defensive advantage. The mountains and rivers give invading armies only certain points with which they can invade. I count ten in all aside from the ocean. We need to defend these key points. However, we are going to have to withdraw from certain points of our land which would be foolish to defend against such a large host. Unfortunately, that means that we cannot defend the cities in those areas. We must evacuate these cities and withdraw our forces so that we can concentrate our strength in these points and on the ocean."

King Justinian lowered his head and replied, "You are wise, Tobias. Make it so. Start the evacuation and move our defenses to these strategic points. These areas are where we will make our stand while still being able to help our ally Solcis. Also, send out five ships to Parrus to check on Petros, Elias, and Spiros. I desire a report as soon as they are found. Something was going to come of their voyage that may be significant to this war. My hope is that they are still alive."

General Tobias bowed his head. "As you wish, my Lord."

Tobias quickly left to begin implementation of their strategy. He sent the fastest riders in his army to every corner of Methos to inform them of the evacuation and he sent separate messages to his generals informing them of the battle plan. Time was of the essence and it wouldn't be long until the unified armies of Athanasia would march on Methos.

At the same time these things were taking place in Methos and Portus, on the Island of Remar the voyage to the ends of the planet was about to begin. Spiros and Sprasian were fast becoming friends as everything was ready for their departure.

“You do realize that everyone on this voyage is taking a step of faith and is willing to lose their life to make that step,” said Spiros.

Sprasian nodded back “I do understand. I cannot believe that Sophos would send us on a voyage east only to die at sea. I have to believe that there is something out there, that there is something that he desires us to find. I do not know what it is, but I trust that he would not lead us on an idle voyage.”

Spiros smiled, “You speak like a wise man. I am amazed at how much you have changed. Never would I have imagined that this day would ever come.”

All the voyagers were on the Parrusian battleship named the *“Morning Star”.* They could only pack eight months of food and water which was too small of a provision for this long voyage, but it was hoped that they would be able to catch some fish or by some chance stumble across land.

Petros came up to Sprasian and said, “Good luck, old friend. Nothing has pleased my heart more than to see this metamorphosis in your life. You have spent most of your life on the seas, so you should lead this voyage. Everyone aboard is depending on your leadership to protect them from harm. Their lives are in your hands.”

Sprasian was taken aback by his statement for he didn’t feel that he could or even should lead. “I don’t think that I am ready, nor deserving of such an honor. My whole life up to this point has been a chasing after the wind. It was meaningless. I have not earned the right to lead these people or this vessel. I have made so many bad decisions in my life that I fear that I will make some fatal decision that will cost everyone their lives."

Petros smiled at the young man and put his right hand on Sprasian's shoulder. He looked him in the eyes and said, "You are right. You do not deserve to lead this voyage. You have not accomplished any good work that even entitles you to be a captain of a ship that transports fodder."

"Thanks for your honesty, Petros! I had forgotten that you hold nothing back," said a grinning Sprasian.

Petros smiled and replied, "You may not have earned or deserved this, but you have been found worthy to lead. Your very declination of this position shows that you are fit to lead. It is because you understood that your authority as a leader would be to serve the people. You understand that leading is not for your glory. Like my fallen brother Mardok who is now the King of Portus believes, or like many of the kings and leaders of Athanasia."

Sprasian replied, "How are you so certain of this?"

"It is very easy, Sprasian. You can recognize their beliefs by their actions," responded Petros. "They believe that the people of their kingdoms exist to provide them with position. Your uncle believes that your position as a leader exists to serve the people. My old friend, Sophos would never have entrusted you to go on this voyage unless he knew that you would look out for the lives of others before your very own. You have finally learned that you cannot believe in yourself because all Athanasians are prone to failure. We all make mistakes, so we cannot trust in our own abilities, wisdom, or strength.

Sprasian replied, "So if I cannot trust myself, then what do I do?"

"Lean on Sophos and that will be all you need to make tough decisions or endure any peril. If the creator of the universe says you can do this, then there is no reason for you to doubt his decision to lead or the abilities that he has given you. Your strength will come from outside yourself, not within, Sprasian. I cannot wait to see how you blossom in time."

Sprasian nodded his head and put his hand on Petros' shoulder to embrace him. "Thank you for your uplifting words, old friend."

Sprasian broke his grip and asked one final question. "Because of my past, do you think that anyone would follow me on this voyage?"

Petros responded, "In truth, I am sure that no one will desire to follow you. There will need to be brave men that are willing to take a step of faith. Even then, they will carry reservations about you until you prove them wrong. This is out of your control, Sprasian. If Sophos truly called you to sail east, then he will provide you with the men necessary to carry out his will despite their apprehensions."

Sprasian took a deep breath and nodded his head, "You are a wise counselor, Petros. I can see why my Uncle Justinian trusts you so much."

Spiros watched Sprasian with soft eyes from a distance. He was moved to see a man of great pride and wickedness become a new creation.

20 - Port Verdes, Remar

As the *Morning Star* set sail east, Remar and its two neighboring islands were becoming populated with Parrusian refugees fleeing the insanity of King Melmot. Petros was now looking at 10,000 Parrusian soldiers that had defected with 15 warships, including the admiral of the Parrusian fleet. As it stood, over 115,000 people had flooded Remar and its neighboring islands, and more came each day.

Petros was training new recruits with some of the Methosian and Parrusian troops when Elias approached him. “Petros, I spoke to the natives about the three islands. We have plenty of freshwater from the three rivers and lake that grace Remar.”

Petros brushed the sweat from his eyebrows and asked, “What of the fishing, farming, and livestock?”

Elias nodded, “I have been able to gather many fishermen to fish the seas, lakes, and rivers. There were many farmers on the island and many more that have defected. I will place them accordingly. We have gathered others to hunt and cultivate the animal life. Our biggest challenge now will be to find homes for all of these people.”

Petros sat down on the ground with Elias joining him. “What do you suggest, Elias?”

Elias replied, “We are amassing quite a large army. I believe it would be prudent to set up military strongholds and barracks around Remar and on the neighboring islands. It is time to start building cities so that we can house the multitude of people coming in every day. We should give everyone incentive to build the infrastructure. If one helps to build the strongholds or cities, then they may choose a plot of land to own in which they can build their home. Instead of having to pay gold for workers we will give them land in exchange."

Petros looked at him and said, "Find the officials of the island and make it so in the name of King Justinian. Now, I must get back to work and help train these men for battle. Our ranks grow more every day. Some 75,000 men have volunteered to join the Methosian army including the Parrusian military defectors."

Elias smiled, "It looks like Mardok is going to be in for a fight!" He stood up and made his way to speak to the city officials to attend to the development of the infrastructure.

Petros walked over to a group of 1000 men carrying wooden swords. Behind him one could hear the clanging of iron against steal as the blacksmiths worked tirelessly to arm the new Methosian military in Remar. Petros walked up to this next group assisted by some Methosian soldiers who were ready to learn swordsmanship.

"Soldiers of Methos! Today you will be taught skill with a blade. Skill in and of itself is not enough to survive a battle. Bring to mind what you hold dearest in this world. You, what do you hold dearest?" Petros pointed toward one of the men standing directly in front of him.

“My wife and children. I will not allow the hand of tyranny to jeopardize their lives!”

Petros yelled, “Well said! Now you,” he pointed to another man, “What do you hold dearest?”

The man stuttered initially, but his voice strengthened with each word he spoke. “I am a single man with no family. I hold freedom from tyranny closest to my heart! I willingly give my life to whatever end for freedom!”

Petros sung this man’s praises. “That’s the spirit! You have the heart of a courageous warrior!”

Petros then looked to another man standing in the front. “What say you? What do you hold dearest?” His powerful voice carried for all to hear.

“Honoring my creator, Sophos! He is a beacon of goodness and purity of which I will gladly fight for against the evils of this world!”

Petros shouted, “Well done! There is no more noble deed then to fight for one’s sovereign. All you men have expressed why you are willing to give up your lives. These are only three of the truths that emanate from your heart. I know that each man here owns a different reason as to why he stands before me today.

“Remember these words! In battle you will remember these things as you fight shoulder to shoulder. If you have no reason to fight then you will not survive long in battle no matter how great your skill. That is your first lesson men. War is an ugly thing. It can bring out the best or the worst in all of us. Adversity is the test of who possesses courage and who possesses fear. Now it is our job to temper the fear out of your life and bring courage to the forefront. Soldiers of Methos, are you ready?"

A great eruption of the 1000 trainees and the soldiers standing around could be heard. "For Methos! For Methos! For Methos!" They all chanted. Petros and the Methosian soldiers with him took small groups aside and started to teach them how to wield a sword. They taught them offensive and defensive motions that they would need in the heat of battle. Petros was filled with excitement, not because of the coming war, but because he hated evil and the tyranny it bred. He would instill this value into every soldier he trained.

21 - Salem, Portus

In Portus, the alliance of the 12 kingdoms had marched on the seven neutral kingdoms. They met little resistance as these kingdoms had scaled back their military over the years. Mardok looked on these seven nations as cowards that were not willing to fight for anything.

As the invasion into these seven kingdoms began something ominous followed. General Romus had just conquered Praxis. His force stood in the throne room having killed the palace guard. Only the Adelphos remained as they slew any soldier that came near their king.

Romus began to walk towards the throne where the king stood with his sword unsheathed. The Adelphos saw his approach and made way hastily to confront Romus.

Romus screamed out to his fast approaching foes, "King Mardok has asked that you fulfill your oaths that you have made to him! He has commanded that you destroy the king and his family so that there are no more heirs to the throne of Praxis!"

The four Adelphos reached his position and the leader grabbed Romus by the throat. "How do we know that King Mardok has made this decree?"

Romus began to cough from the pressure and pulled a piece of paper from a small brown satchel. With all of the strength he could muster he said, “Here is King Mardok’s decree stamped with his royal signet!”

The head guardian released Romus from his grip and pushed him to the side as he coughed. The leader broke the seal, looked down at the decree and read its contents.

“By order of King Mardok, all Adelphos that have pledged their loyalty to their new king must execute their king whom they have sworn to protect and all of his heirs. This is a test of your loyalty to me. All Adelphos that carry out my command will be richly rewarded. Those that fail to do so will be destroyed.”

Underneath the command was the signet ring stamp of Mardok authorizing this measure. The four Adelphos turned around and charged their king.

The king of Praxis’ mouth and eyes were wide open as he had heard the words and watched his most trusted protectors make way to destroy he and his family.

The king yelled, “No! No!” as he was struck down by one of the Adelphos.

His protectors knew where to find their former king’s family. They marched down a secret passageway behind a fire place that took them to a clearing where his family was preparing to escape under the protection of some of the castle guard.

A host of Portusian soldiers followed the Adelphos to help destroy any resistance. There were only 40 palace guards to defend the king's family against four Adelphos and 100 soldiers.

The Adelphos charged the king's family and cut down seven guards that stood in the way of them carrying out King Mardok's decree. The other guards were vanquished by the Portusian military as they fought to the last man despite the impossibility of victory.

The Portusian military rounded up every member of the king's family, while the Adelphos walked amongst the family to make sure that every member was accounted for. The lead Adelphos said, "All of the king's line is here. Commence the executions!"

Terror seized the family and screams could be heard all the way back to the castle. Romus could hear them from the balcony where he stood with a captain in his army.

"Sir," asked the captain who seemed uneasy upon hearing the screams in the distance. "Why are we executing all of the king's family? These men, women and children have done nothing to deserve execution."

Romus responded with a smile, "Don't worry about this, captain. This was a command from our king. He has decreed that this be done. To disobey a direct order from the king would be considered an act of treason, thereby punishable by death."

That answer did not satisfy the young captain. He was visibly shaken as he heard the screams in the distance. His palms were sweating and his eyes drooped with sadness. He could not think of anything else to say because it could cost him his life.

Romus then patted the captain on the shoulder and said, “Captain Kalides, we must destroy their royal line so that no one can come back and start an insurrection to claim back their throne. These lands now belong to Portus and we desire to keep them peaceful under King Mardok for eternity. King Mardok doesn’t want anyone to come back and try to reclaim these lands. These were evil people whose lack of response to injustice showed that their allegiance lie with Justinian. They must be removed like Justinian. All of these neutral king’s and their families must be destroyed.”

Romus smiled and then walked away.

The horrified captain just stood and looked off in the distance while tears began to form in his eyes with every scream that he heard from the king’s family.

“The king of Praxis’ family did nothing wrong. What manner of malevolent evil is this?” whispered the despondent captain to himself.

Mardok was able to sweep through these kingdoms thanks to the help that he had on the inside. Specifically, the help that he had received from the Adelphos that chose to betray their kings. Mardok’s armies would march into the opposing kingdoms and the Adelphos that guarded those kings would kill them and their families leaving no heirs. In return he would make them lords over provinces once Athanasia was united under his banner. It was a pact they had made, sealed with the blood of the kings they killed. After the blitz on these kingdoms the first piece of his plan had been unsealed and come to fruition.

The alliance pillaged these lands and absorbed them under Mardok's leadership. In the kingdoms under siege the people who were not killed were left to become slaves. The next phase would lead Mardok to attack Methos and Solcis. It was going to take some weeks to secure the newly annexed lands and reorganize the army to march on these two kingdoms.

#

In Parrus, King Melmot was in his banquet hall with his dogs dressed in fine silk clothing eating some of the choicest meat in all the land. As he sat and conversed with his animals over dinner, his chief vizier entered the hall. All four of King Melmot's Adelphos were in by his side listening to all that was being said.

"My Lord, I have news about Remar," said the vizier.

The king's gaze seemed to almost go through his vizier as he looked up and asked, "What of Remar?"

The vizier contemplated how to present this information delicately.

"My Lord, a force of soldiers from Methos attacked Remar and destroyed Sprasian and his army. The island is under the control of these Methosian troops."

King Melmot smiled. "Sprasian is vanquished? What wonderful news. The bane of my existence has been destroyed. King Justinian finally listened to my endless pleas to deal with his scourge of a nephew. Now we can have our islands back."

The vizier's palms began to sweat and he had to clear his throat as he looked at the king and then the Adelphos. The Adelphos normally wore a stoic expression with their eyes facing forward, but they now looked directly at the vizier as if he were speaking to them.

"My Lord, the people did not want them to leave after the Methosian soldiers liberated the islands. They," his vizier paused for a moment, "have asked to live under the Methosian banner."

The king shook his head. "Why would they want to be part of the Methosian kingdom?"

Sweat began trickling down the vizier's face as he answered, "Well, my Lord, many of our soldiers and citizens here on the main island have defected and sought refuge on Remar. Some tens of thousands flee every day."

The king's face turned blood red. "WHAT? Tell me why they are leaving, vizier!"

The vizier took a step back as the Adelphos looked at each other.

"My Lord, please understand that this is not what I think or say." The vizier breathed in deeply and said, "The people have said that they hate you, that you are a coward and lack the courage necessary to defeat Sprasian. They believe that you care nothing for their own interests as they starve while your canines eat better than they."

The king's fury boiled over when he replied, "Prepare my army, we shall see who the coward is when I invade Remar and destroy everyone for their insolence."

The vizier then spoke quickly in spite of his fear.

"My Lord, we don't have the provisions to mount an assault and take the islands back. We lack the necessary food to feed our soldiers for such an assault. We have no intelligence of how great a host they have on Remar."

The Adelphos turned and the one named Corsica spoke, "Our land has been invaded, we must take it back, my King!"

The enraged Melmot shouted, "Make it so!"

The vizier bowed and said, "Yes, my Lord."

He then walked out and began making preparations with the Parrusian generals to send 300,000 soldiers to take back their land.

Corsica smiled and said, "There is much wisdom in your decision, my King."

The king didn't say anything at first but he eventually smiled and said, "Of course I am a king of great wisdom who cares about the needs of his people."

He then took some food from his plate and gave it to one of the dogs sitting in a chair next to him. His royal dinner party continued without any more interruptions.

#

On the Methosian border in the north a battle erupted. The Portusian soldiers that marched into Methos numbered at around 50,000. They stormed across and pillaged a border town of 10,000 Methosians called Korvis. When they were finished they burned part of the city to the ground and kept marching on without concern of those they were leaving behind injured and homeless. It was just as King Mardok had ordered.

The commander of these invaders had no intentions of falling back across the border, and the further they went, the more they made known that they claimed this land for Portus.

As they continued their progress they sent word back to Portus for more soldiers so that they could move further into Methos. However, word of this attack reached the Methosian commander in the area and he began gathering his force of 60,000 soldiers and marched to push this force out of Methos. They were a day's march from Korvis, but his men were so filled with anger and adrenalin that they made the march in less than a day. They set up camp outside the city and began to draw up battle plans.

The commander was in his tent viewing a map of the area and commanded, "I know that there are enemy scouts watching our position. I need them eliminated. Send some of our elite soldiers to handle this task."

The captain responded, "Yes, commander."

The commander then gave one last command, "Have a soldier

dress in the clothes of one of these vanquished scouts to infiltrate the Portusian ranks. Have him take back a false report to their commander, while observing their positions and plan of attack. When he feels that he has something of value, have him leave their camp and bring this intelligence to me."

The captain replied, "I will instruct them properly, sir," and then turned and walked out of the tent.

Within an hour a small unit charged with this task clothed themselves to look like the forest. Most had sackcloth that had leaves or even bushes sewn into them. The soldiers would put this covering over their back and blend in with other bushes or leaf filled areas. Others went without the sackcloth cover, but wore brown sackcloth with green leaves or small branches down into their garment. They planned on burying themselves under dirt, plants, and fallen branches, or hiding on high limbs of trees or in trees with hollow trunks. This force moved very close to the town, spread themselves out, and hid.

After a few hours, a gentle crackling of leaves and sticks could be heard by one of the Methosian soldiers on a large tree limb that shielded him with its foliage. Another close by could hear the careful steps too. He lay on the ground underneath his sackcloth covered with leaves, moss, and small bushes. The sackcloth covered his entire body while he lay in wait on the side of a trail. Within minutes a man emerged on a horse and dismounted. He found a tall tree and began to scale it to one of the highest points and looked in the direction of the Methosian camp.

The Methosian soldiers knew that this was their chance to infiltrate the Portusian positions. They had to be careful as the scout wore a horn that he would blow in case he was spotted and chased. After an hour the scout climbed down from the tree slowly. As he walked to his horse he was hit on top of the head by a rock and fell to the ground unconscious.

The soldier that struck the scout quickly climbed down the tree as his partner revealed himself from the side of the road, and both converged on the unconscious man.

The soldier that had knocked the man unconscious whispered, "Let's get him off the road."

The other soldier commented as they carried the unconscious scout off the road, "That was a perfect throw, Ian."

They grabbed the Portusian soldier and moved him behind a great tree, secured him with rope, and gagged him with cloth.

The soldier from the tree (Ian) then whispered again, "I will wear all that he has and will communicate to the Portusian commander a false report that 50,000 Methosian troops are coming from the west. They will send multiple scouts to verify my report. Find our hiding brethren and alert them to this. See to it that every one of these scouts does not return to the Portusian commander, then return to camp and inform our commander."

The camouflaged man nodded and made ready to carry out his task as Ian dressed in the clothes of the Portusian scout, mounted the horse, and road for the captured town. The other Methosian soldier took his captive and found others from his group and informed them of what was to take place. Two men carried the unconscious man back to their camp to extract information. Twenty eight other men began to reposition themselves and move westward so as to take out every scout that approached.

Within an hour the two Methosian soldiers made it to the camp with their prisoner and summoned the commander.

"Commander Mylaius! We have news from the front. One of our troops has taken the identity of one of the enemy and here is the Portusian scout whose place he has taken. He is going to report that 50,000 troops are coming from the west. He said that the Portusian's would send out several scouts to verify, and told us to take these men out. When they don't return it will be believed that our false report is true and he will adjust his host accordingly for battle."

"Excellent work!" said Mylaius. "There are 50,000 soldiers that are marching towards the border and are west of Korvis. Make haste and alert Commander Gilliam who oversees this force that we are going to come from the east and north to catch them off guard. In doing so, we will be cutting off their supply line and reinforcements. We will push them west into Methos towards Commander Gilliam. They will be flanked from both sides and should be easy to defeat."

Mylaius looked over towards one of the soldiers and said, "Make haste to Commander Gilliam and inform him of our battle plan." The soldier bowed and quickly made his way to his horse.

Mylaius then rallied his captains and informed them of the battle plan. They then began mobilizing the soldiers and marched east out of the scout's range. They sent 30,000 troops north to make their way around the city, so that they could surround the invading army after they had sealed the border. The other 30,000 remained east and were ready to move when the order was given.

22 - Korvis, Methos

In the enemy camp Ian was dressed in the Portusian scout's clothes. He made his way towards the Portusian commander's tent. It was a large tent made of leather that flew a white flag with an embroidered eagle. When he approached the tent he saw the commander drawing up plans with his captains.

"My lord, I bring grave news," said Ian.

"What news have you, scout?"

Ian walked up to the map and began showing them where the enemy was to be while studying their battle plans.

"My lord, the Methosian forces gathered to the south have quickly broken camp and made haste to the west. It is my belief that they are planning an attack from the west."

The commander tilted his head and squinted his eyes as he asked, "How many soldiers do you estimate were in this force?"

Ian replied firmly, "I estimate between thirty five to forty thousand soldiers."

The commander looked at one of his captain's and said, "Send five scouts to the west to investigate this claim and begin preparing our forces to defend the west. Send two more scouts south to authenticate that the Methosian army has broken camp."

The commander then looked at Ian. "Scout, point to me where you saw the troops gathering."

Ian pointed to detachments that he claimed to see in the west and southwest. He was actually pointing them towards the positions where he believed the soldiers from his group would be hiding.

The spy was dismissed and seven other scouts were dispatched. Ian with his new found information made his way to the eastern side of the city, and quickly went out of sight into the woods without the soldiers on duty seeing him disappear.

#

In the west, Commander Gilliam had mobilized his soldiers as they broke camp. The men were full of energy as they wanted to repay Portus for what they did to the citizens of Korvis. They marched steadily east, not wanting to spoil the ambush by getting into position too quickly. Commander Mylaius wanted Commander Gilliam to reach Korvis after the fighting had already started so that the Portusian Commander would think that no forces were actually coming from the west. Mylaius hoped that the Portusian commander would move the bulk of his forces to the west and potentially some to the south with the bad intelligence. This would leave no significant forces to defend the north or east sides of Korvis.

Commander Mylaius ordered his northern force to march south against the enemy force after they had sealed the border. His force in the east began marching west at a slower pace so as not to expose their position.

In the west, the Portusian scouts staggered themselves over a radius of several miles and were camouflaged as they went. Two of the scouts climbed up tall trees, miles apart on a ridge in order to give them a better vision of the Methosian army. One scout could not see the Methosian army after spending an hour in the tree so he made his way down and was immediately shot in the chest with the arrow from a crossbow. Two Methosian soldiers came out from under a bush and inspected the scout to ensure that he was deceased. They left the body on the ground and hid back under their camouflaged bush.

The other Portusian scout that perched himself in a tree sat over 100 feet off the ground. As the scout looked west he was immediately struck by an arrow in his side and fell from the tree to his death. Three men came out of the woods, one with a bow and the other two with crossbows. They began tracking the other scouts. They were not sure how many were left, but they had to find them all for the deception to work.

North of Korvis the host of 30,000 soldiers were marching to the main road which they would secure before marching south on the Portusian invasion force. As the force came to the main road they were met by one of their scouts. A young inexperienced captain named Alexander was whom the scout shared the information.

“Captain Alexander,” replied the scout. “There are 50,000 Portusian soldiers marching down the road from Portus to Korvis.”

Alexander muttered to himself, "50,000 soldiers? How can we outmaneuver such a large host?"

Alexander looked down to the ground and held his fist up to his lips, tapping them gently. The scout asked, "Captain, what would you have us do?"

Alexander did not answer the scout, but continued to think. Suddenly, his eyes opened wide and his head popped up screaming, "I need a lieutenant!"

A man came running over quickly. "Yes, captain." said the lieutenant.

"I am changing the plans. I have just been informed that a force of 50,000 soldiers are closing in on our border, headed to Korvis. We cannot hold them at the border for it is open plains and they outnumber us almost two to one. We are going to have to abandon our plans for the offensive in Korvis and make plans to stop this force."

All of Alexander's lieutenants overheard Alexander and gathered around him. Seeing this, Alexander addressed them all, "The enemy has come upon us. Our force is too small and the geography is not conducive to stopping their advance. We will cross through the forest and make our stand at the bridge that crosses the Peirus River. A direct charge onto flat terrain against a host of soldiers that large would be a death sentence. The Veros Bridge is what will give us an advantage in stopping their advance."

Alexander paused for a moment and had yet another idea.

"Have 100 cavalry soldiers cut through the forest and find the section of the road that goes through the bog. Have them cut down as many trees as they can to slow this force down. This will give us extra time to move into position and prepare our defense. Lastly, send 2,000 archers that are willing to jeopardize their lives."

The officers began to laugh as they thought Alexander was jesting. Alexander snapped, "Did I say something humorous? We are at war. There is nothing humorous about war."

The officers fell silent and dropped their heads. Alexander continued. "As I was saying, before I was so rudely interrupted. Send 2,000 archers and split them up equally on the east and west sides of the road. Have them positioned after the roadblock, but in the forest right where the bog ends."

One of the lieutenants spoke up. "Sir, shouldn't we position them at the roadblock so that the enemy will be easy targets?"

Alexander responded, "You make a very good argument lieutenant, however, I want to do something unpredictable. When they see the roadblock they will automatically assume that there will be an ambush and prepare a defense. They will send their troops into the forest and bog as a countermeasure and will sweep the area. If we do it after the roadblock it will catch them off guard thereby irritating their commander and soldiers more. My goal is not to stop them, but rather to make them mentally unprepared for battle. I want them looking over their shoulders or becoming enraged. A fearful or angry man does not make a good warrior in battle."

A smile crept on to the lieutenant's face as he now understood Alexander's rationale.

"Now make haste as we don't have much time!" exclaimed Alexander.

The Methosian force marched quickly through the forest towards the bridge. Alexander dispatched 100 cavalry soldiers to make their way towards the section of the road that contained the bog some distance away from the enemy. Their orders were to put obstructions in the way to slow the Portusian advance. These soldiers quickly made their way to an area of the road which was less than a mile inside the bog. To try to go around the road would prove dangerous and almost impossible for the Portusians. It would slow the advance down exponentially.

The cavaliers cautiously moved through the bog with ropes tied to their waists which were tied to their steeds or nearby trees. They did not want to sink to their doom if they came across quicksand or a deep part of the water. They began cutting down large trees near the road with a sense of great urgency. One by one they chopped down these ancient trees and blocked the road. When they were finished they mounted their horses and galloped as fast as they could towards the bridge. They finished the blockade shortly before the Portusian army made its way to their position. They all galloped swiftly away towards the Veros Bridge, full of adrenalin, ready for a fight. They wore large grins knowing that the first part of Alexander's plan was a success.

The blockade worked as the Portusian army could not move forward. The Portusian commander ordered, "Defensive positions! Be ready, as this may be an ambush."

He waited for a 15 minutes as his eyes panned across the bog. He ordered, "Scouts, survey the perimeter."

The scouts went down the road and into the bog, but could find no evidence of an enemy force. After an hour the scouts gave the commander their report. The commander ordered, "We are all clear." He continued. "I need 100 men with axes and rope and one dozen horses to clear the road."

After an hour the road was cleared and the Portusian commander ordered his army to continue their march. However, they kept their eyes open for any sign of ambush.

Meanwhile, 2.5 miles down the road 2000 Methosian archers burrowed into position immediately outside of the bog. They wanted to use this ground advantage to keep the enemy somewhat contained within the bog, so as to make them easy targets. The terrain outside the bog was full of tall hills with many trees. The archers took the high ground and were able to conceal themselves around the trees.

Many thousands of Alexander's men had crossed the Veros Bridge, but there were many thousands more in waiting. It was now up to the archers to halt the Portusian march.

As the front of the Portusian military crossed out of the bog, arrows began raining down upon them. The first strike of 2,000 arrows killed almost all of the soldiers that crossed out of the bog and inflicted serious injuries on those who escaped death.

The arrows then began raining down from both sides of the road at those that had not crossed out of the bog yet. The men were able to put their shields up as they witnessed the first volley in front of them. There were much fewer casualties on the second volley of arrows as there was a scream of "Ambush! Ambush!" being called out through the ranks. Every Portusian soldier took immediate defensive positions.

To counter the Portusian's huddling up, the archers began firing arrows with flaming tar onto their position. As the arrows hit, their flaming splatter would catch men and wagons on fire. Very quickly the Portusian's that caught fire began breaking rank and opening up holes in their defense that would allow more arrows to break through. Men began jumping into the bog to put the fire on their bodies out. Horses began panicking from the fire and knocked many of the soldiers on the road into the bog, including their masters.

The Methosian archers continued their barrage of flaming arrows onto the enemy position. The lieutenant in charge looked to his corporal and said, "It has been five minutes. Fire the flaming green arrow into the sky to alert our forces on the western side of the road to dispatch their first 100 soldiers to Alexander."

The corporal replied, "What if they don't see it, sir?"

The lieutenant replied, "The commanding officer on the other side of the road has a spotter that will alert him when the flaming arrow is seen."

The corporal nodded, lit his arrow and fired it high into the sky. He then turned and released the first group of 100 archers.

On the western side of the road the spotter sat high up in a tall tree on a sturdy branch looking up at the sky. When he saw the flaming green arrow he immediately dropped one of the large brown cones that grew on the tree. A soldier watched it hit the ground and roll over to his feet. The soldier commanded, "Men, the first arrow has been fired. You know your assigned groups. The first group must depart immediately. Second group, be on the ready." Immediately a group of 100 archers made haste down the hill through the woods away from the battle.

The Portusian commander immediately sent word for the archers to be brought forward from the back of the line. He couldn't send ground forces into the woods because of the bog, so he hoped that his archers would be able to counter this attack thereby allowing his ground forces to move out of the bog and into the woods to vanquish this enemy.

Within 15 minutes of this attack 600 Methosian archers had departed and made their way to the Veros Bridge. They had easily vanquished over 1,000 Portusian soldiers. The arrows were not raining as heavy as before as they needed to conserve them. Whenever a group of archers left for the bridge they would give those remaining some extra arrows. They were being fired intermittently which continued to keep the force at bay.

As time passed, there were only 100 archers left on each side. They began firing at a more consistent pace since they were now so few. When it appeared that five minutes had passed they began igniting all of their remaining flaming arrows and firing on the Portusian positions. They hoped that these would cause enough of a distraction that they could make their way through the woods away from their pursuers.

The arrows set ablaze men, animals, wagons and anything else they hit. One wagon in the front became completely engulfed in flames and the only way around it was through the bog.

The Methosian archers then fled away from the Portusian army just before the enemy archers arrived. The enemy arrows fell short of the escaping Methosian's who were well on their way to a safer location. After several volleys of arrows the Portusian archers stopped firing. The infantry then went forward out of the bog and made their way into the forest to try to find their attackers. When no Methosian's could be found they made their way back to their commander and told him of the news.

The commander's face turned red as he shouted, "When I find this army and its leader I will leave none alive, not even their wounded!"

Many of the men in the front became fearful, while others that were out of range of the arrows became incensed with anger.

"Men! We will repay this act of cowardice with the shedding of their blood! Get back into formation, dump the bodies into the bog, and take the wounded to the rear."

A lieutenant came up to the commander and said, "Sir, we lost over 1700 men and have over 300 wounded."

The commander gnashed his teeth upon hearing this and shouted to his captain, “Prepare the men to march double time to Korvis! We will repay Methos for their cowardice!”

“Yes, Commander Soros!” replied the captain.

The Portusian army regrouped and marched rapidly towards Korvis.

23 - The Peirus River in Northern Methos

At the bridge over the Peirus River the entire Methosian force had crossed while the archers began staggering to their position in groups of 200. Only the last group of archers to depart the bog did not return to their ranks.

"Captain Alexander," replied a lieutenant. "The men have all crossed except for the last group of archers to leave the bog. How should we proceed?"

Alexander put his hand on his chin and began looking down at the ground.

After a few minutes the lieutenant asked again, "Sir, are you even listening to me?"

Alexander frowned as he looked up at his officer, "Can't you see that I am trying to figure out what to do next? Do you so lack discernment that you cannot tell that I am deep in thought?"

"But, sir." replied the lieutenant. "We do not have time to sit and think. The Portusian army is almost upon us?"

Alexander put his head in his hand and shook it. "Lieutenant, can you not see how important my next command is? If I am pressured to make a rash decision it could cost us the day?"

“Very well, Captain Alexander. I will wait for your command,” said the lieutenant.

Alexander replied, “Thank you! That is all I ask,” as he resumed his previous position of thought.

The lieutenant began to pace and his face began to turn red. Alexander looked up at the lieutenant and said, “If you are going to pace, could you do it on the bridge so that you do not distract my thoughts.”

The red faced lieutenant nodded, walked over to the bridge, kneeled and started to hit his head against the cobblestone bridge. He was wearing his helmet, so a small clank could be heard with every tap. Alexander’s face turned red as he popped his head up and yelled, “For the love of all that his good and pure, would you please stop clanking your head against the bridge?” he paused before continuing. “Lieutenant, if you have something to say, please come over here and tell me.”

The lieutenant jumped up to his feet and hurried to Alexander. “Captain Alexander, I mean no disrespect, but time is of the essence. You may have never been in combat, but you have been trained in strategy. We can either burn the bridge or defend it. Which should we do?”

Alexander looked at the lieutenant, “Thank you for your direct response, lieutenant. What is your name?”

“Colarian, sir,” replied the lieutenant.

After a brief pause Colarian continued, "Sir, your unorthodox plan has worked and got us here. Now let us capitalize on it."

Alexander shook his head. "Very well, lieutenant. I am leaving you here with 10,000 soldiers to defend the bridge. If we burn it then we still have to deal with 50,000 Portusian troops roaming in Methos. We have two forces to expel now. One here, and one in Korvis."

Colarian replied, "Sir?"

Alexander continued, "You will have 3,000 archers and 7000 soldiers at your disposal, which is more than enough to hold the bridge. A phalanx strategy should work well with keeping their army halted. I will take the other 20,000 soldiers to Korvis as we must execute the plan of Mylaius. His forces will be in jeopardy if we do not go."

Colarian asked, "So we are to just hold the bridge?"

Alexander answered, "Yes. Once we have Korvis I will send reinforcements to your aid."

Colarian responded, "Then we will hold it, sir." He turned to walk away, but then turned back around and asked, "Captain, why did you spend so much time thinking about what to do here?"

Alexander answered, "I knew what to do, Colarian. I just did not know whom I should choose to do it." Alexander paused as Colarian's eyes opened wide. "You were the only one to challenge me. When you started banging your head against the bridge, I knew that you were the man for the job."

Colarian replied, “So this was a test.”

Alexander nodded.

Colarian smiled, “Are you insane?”

Alexander replied, “Actually, I call it genius.”

The two snickered for a moment before Alexander abruptly changed the subject. “Colarian, I will leave you with most of the archers, long spearman, heavy shields and swordsman necessary to hold the bridge. I must take the horseman, some archers and light infantry south. May Sophos guide you.”

The two quickly parted ways as Colarian began to set up his force for defense of the bridge.

#

In the woods west of Korvis remained three Portusian scouts. All three scouts were tracked by the elite Methosian soldiers and eliminated. However, there were two scouts that went south and saw that the Methosian army had left.

The two scouts went and inspected the camp. The first scout said, “It looks like their tracks head to the east.”

The other scout responded, “Then it is a trap. We have to get back to camp and warn the commander.”

The first scout said, “Then we must split up and go separate ways, so that at least one of us can make it back.”

The other scout responded, "Why do you say that?"

The first scout answered, "We are being watched. We must leave quickly."

As they ran into the forest an arrow came down from the sky and hit one of the men in the shoulder. He fell down and two men arose from the ground 30 feet away, picked him up and carried him off.

The other scout was harder to follow and harder to hit when found. He would dodge or duck when he heard arrows fired from their bows in the trees.

While he was able to avoid capture the scout was not sure of successfully getting back to his commander. Yet, he then realized that he may be close enough for his horn to be heard, so he stopped and put the horn to his lips.

No sooner had this happened then did an arrow hit the horn as it touched his lips, shattering it.

One of the elite soldiers tracking the scout said, "What an amazing shot!"

The soldier that fired the shot then commented, "I was aiming for his head!"

The scout's fear of death seemed to give him the energy to continue at his sprint like pace. The Methosian soldiers kept after him, but could only get within 100 feet. At this speed he would make it back to the camp within an hour. As he ran, the two elite soldiers continued their pursuit. The one carrying the bow fired an arrow while running after the scout. The arrow was on target to hit the scout in the head and end the pursuit. However, the enemy scout tripped over a stump and as he fell face first to the ground the arrow grazed his head cutting some brown hair off the top. The sheer force of the fall knocked the wind out of him as he hit the ground. His body rolled from the momentum off the path and down a steep hill towards a stream. As the scout rolled uncontrollably down the hill he hit his head on a rock, knocking him unconscious. His body rolled until it finally came to rest on a log in the stream below. He draped over the log while the force from his landing jarred the log loose from where it rested, and the water current started to take the log downstream.

The soldiers saw him fall hard and roll down the hill, and upon reaching the bank, they saw the man floating away on the log.

The soldiers just looked and shook their heads in amazement. “That must be the most fortunate man to ever grace Athanasia! It is almost as if some force is protecting his life.”

His fellow soldier standing next to him shook his head and said, “How?”

His partner then replied back, “Do you realize that we were eluded by an unconscious man? How does a man that was knocked unconscious escape his pursuers?”

The other soldier grinned and said, “We will be the subject of every joke when we tell our brethren and commander what happened.”

The other soldier's face turned red as his eyes opened wide knowing that they would never live down this moment. "We must go after him to whatever end. I cannot bear the shame of letting this scout get away."

The other soldier nodded and they started their ungraceful descent down this steep hill. They rolled and tumbled hitting trees and rocks all the way down until they reached the stream.

24 - The Peirus River (Veros Bridge) Northern Methos

In Methos, the land surrounding the bridge that crosses the Peirus had steep hills with many trees and rocks. On the top of the hills, on each side of the road ran 100 Methosian archers who were just moments ahead of the Portusian army. Both groups of archers only had a few arrows left in their quivers. The remaining archers on each hilltop realized that the Portusian military would reach the bridge before they could slide down the hill and cross to rejoin their forces. Rather than being killed or captured, the ranking officer in each of these groups decided to stay on the high ground where they would be safer, and have a chance to cause a minor distraction.

One of the archers on the east side saw something glimmer in the trees and thought it could be their comrades. The archer unsheathed his sword and reflected it against the sun towards the west. In the distance he saw an archer reveal himself for a moment and then duck back into hiding.

"Lieutenant, the other group is in hiding on the top of the hill on the other side of the road," said the enthusiastic archer.

The lieutenant replied, "Then we will definitely make our stand here. We will take cover here so as not to be seen and then fire on their archers when the battle begins. My hope is that our comrades on the other side will follow our lead and cause confusion."

He continued, "Men, we are going to draw their fire from our force on the other side of the bridge. We will use their arrows against them since we have so few left. Be careful not to get hit when you gather them."

Moments later the Portusian army came into sight. The lieutenant gestured to all of his men to take cover.

Colarian saw the approaching force and began to call out orders. The battle over the Peirus River was about to begin. The bridge was a little over a quarter mile in length and about 150 feet wide. Colarian had one large phalanx lined up that covered the width of the bridge.

As Colarian looked across the bridge he saw the Portusian archers in the front. The archers began moving off to the left and right side of the road as they were taking positions in the back. When the archers were in position, the Portusian infantry followed and moved towards the bridge in battle formation. Behind the infantry followed the cavalry which consisted of 5,000 horsemen. In the very back were battering rams and a siege tower.

Colarian shouted when he saw the Portusian's preparing for battle, "Archers, ready!

He then shouted to the infantry, "You are just inside their archer's range of fire! Stay low and keep your shields over your heads! The archers will keep their infantry from advancing."

The Methosian soldiers took their positions on and around the bridge while the archers had their bows ready to fire.

Commander Soros who was in the center of his army yelled, “Archers, commence firing! Infantry, forward march!”

The 5,000 Portusian archers began firing barrage after barrage as their infantry marched forward to engage the Methosian phalanx on the bridge. The sound of arrows hitting the metal shields almost resembled in sound a hard rain falling on a tin roof to the Methosian infantry.

When the Portusian infantry came into range Colarian shouted, “Fire!”

The Methosian archers began pounding the enemy infantry and caused immediate and immense casualties. They marched forward quickly with little protection from their shields. The casualties were so many that they had to stop their advance on the bridge and take cover behind their shields. The Methosians had few casualties as every area of their formation was covered by a shield. So much so, that it looked like one continuous piece of steel.

As the Portusian infantry was held in check by the Methosian archers, Commander Soros ordered 2,500 archers to move into position to attack their Methosian counterparts while the other 2,500 archers were to continue to pound the Methosian phalanx.

Colarian had walked up the hill directly behind his position to see what their commander was planning on the other side of the bridge. He saw part of the Portusian archery force moving forward, so he yelled to his archers, “Archers, prepare to fire on the Portusian archers on my command!”

The enemy archers were not in range yet, but the Portusian infantry was no longer under fire and now moved hastily to engage the Methosian phalanx.

Across the bridge on the east hill the Methosian archery lieutenant saw the enemy archers advance. He commanded, “Fire on the Portusian archers!” After firing an arrow he said aloud, “I hope that those on the western hill will follow suit.”

One hundred arrows descended upon the advancing Portusian archers who were completely unaware of their presence. The arrows pierced many men whether wounding or killing them. Another barrage of arrows came down on their position and struck down many more archers, causing confusion in their ranks.

The lieutenant of the Portusian archers ordered an immediate stop and then ordered several hundred of his archers to commence firing at the top of the hill. The Methosian’s were dug in very well as they hid under and behind large rocks and trees. The only problem with their strategy is that they would have to reveal themselves in the open to take the enemy arrows for their own use.

After a few barrages they began gathering arrows from around their positions. They pulled them from trees or picked them up off the ground. When they were spotted the Portusian archers commenced firing again, but all were able to retreat back into their positions safely.

Commander Soros saw that something was going on and sent word to find out what had happened. No sooner had this occurred did the Methosian archers hidden on the western hill commence firing on the enemy archers that were attacking the Methosian phalanx. They struck down many archers in their first barrage and then caused many more to fall on their second. The lieutenant in command ordered 500 archers to begin firing at the top of the western hill. He had not seen them, but based on the trajectory it would have appeared to come from that position.

As confusion swirled around the Portusian army as to what was happening. Colarian witnessed the force causing the confusion and acted immediately.

He yelled to his archers, "Archers, begin firing at the Portusian infantry advancing on the bridge!"

They fired barrage after barrage and began to decimate the enemy force on the bridge. The casualties had gotten so heavy that the advance stopped and the captain leading the attack called for an immediate retreat. As they retreated out of range, the archers let out a great roar of excitement as they had stopped the advance of the first attack. Colarian smiled as he shook his fist in the air with great elation. The Methosian infantry started to celebrate as well.

When Commander Soros realized what was happening he ordered his men to regroup. "Have 500 soldiers storm the western hill and order 500 archers to give them covering fire. Do the same on the eastern hill. This should root out those maggots!"

Soros paused for a moment, “Have the archers by the east hill finish their advance and fire on the Methosian archers across the river. Have the archers by the west hill commence firing at the enemy on the bridge.”

The Portusian soldiers tried climbing the steep hills on either side to reach their enemies, but the terrain was very loose and steep. The Methosian archers now with a large supply of arrows compliments of the Portusian army began picking off these unfortunate soldiers. The covering fire of the Portusian archers didn’t seem to help because the Methosians had the high ground advantage and were tucked away safely in their surroundings.

The Portusian soldiers advanced onto the bridge and were met with a barrage of arrows from the Methosian archers. They tried putting their shields up, but were struck down regardless.

As the Portusian infantry took a beating on the bridge the Methosian phalanx remained well protected under their shields in a tight formation. They looked almost like a turtle in the safety of his shell as the arrows didn’t seem to be penetrating their formation.

A few moments later the Methosian archers stopped firing on the Portusian infantry and directed their attention to the enemy archers approaching the river bank. Colarian yelled out, “Fire!”

A barrage of arrows left the Methosian side of the river and began pounding the Portusian archers who were now in range. A myriad of enemy archers fell to the ground while Colarian called out, “Fire at will!”

to his men.

Commander Soros called out to his archers after the first barrage, "Return fire!"

After they struck down many of the Methosian archers he ordered, "Fire at will!"

With the archers on both sides consumed with each other the battle on the bridge was about to commence. The Methosian phalanx was only a quarter of the way on the bridge standing their ground and remaining concealed under their shields from the enemy archers. The Portusian infantry rushed the Methosian wall of shields and a great crash of metal could be heard from the impact. Intense fighting began as Methosian swords came from behind the shields and started piercing the enemy soldiers down one by one.

The Portusians in the front were caught by the wall and had no room to fight as they had so many soldiers behind them limiting their movement. It was so easy to kill the Portusians that many of the soldiers were not even looking as they thrust their sword from behind the shield wall. Every strike hit an enemy soldier to the point where the bodies were just piling up in front of them.

A Methosian sergeant by the name of Turk was fighting in the very front of the phalanx. His arm was sore and trembling as he continued to hold his shield to protect the soldiers behind him as they engaged the enemy. Screams and shrieks of pain rung without ceasing from the mouths of the Portusian soldiers as they fell. Sweat was beading down his face as he gritted his teeth and pushed forward to hold his place. The officer in charge of the front line was yelling orders from behind him and thrusting his sword into the Portusians on the other side of Turk's shield. "Hold the line, men! Keep your shields up!"

The soldier to the right of Turk lost his balance and fell down and he was immediately impaled by the Portusian soldier that stood in front of him. The Portusian soldier took advantage of the opening and looked to create a larger one by striking Turk down. Turk unsheathed his sword with his right hand as he continued to lean against his shield and blocked the strike. The officer behind him thrust his sword into the enemy soldier and then picked up a shield to plug the hole in the line. He shouted, "Keep your swords moving! Lay waste to these vermin!"

Turk witnessed the bodies of the enemy soldiers pile up waist high. This made it hard for the Portusians to push forward, so they began leaping from the top of the bodies onto the top of the phalanx. The enemy soldiers hit the overhead shields and fell into the phalanx and were immediately cut down. One soldier fell in behind Turk, and as he came down he ran his sword through the officer holding the shield on the front line, but was quickly killed by a Methosian soldier. A Portusian soldier then used the opening to kill another shield bearing Methosian. A hole started to open up on the front line. The Portusians began to flood towards the hole to exploit the breach. Turk moved off the line and engaged the enemy soldiers to try to close the hole. He cut down a Portusian engaged with another soldier. He then blocked a strike with his shield from another enemy soldier and struck him down with his sword. Turk turned his head and yelled, "Pick up the shields and reform the line!"

When he turned around he was tackled by an enemy soldier. He dropped his shield and sword while the enemy soldier climbed on top of him striking him in the face. Turk managed to pull out his dagger and bury it in the enemy soldier's chest. The enemy soldier fell over dead on top of him, pinning his body to the ground. The Portusian soldiers did not notice Turk as they stepped on the body of their fallen comrade to infiltrate the front line.

Turk tried to turn his head to see what was happening behind him. He witnessed two more Methosian soldiers fall, opening a larger hole in the phalanx. He then heard someone shout, "Spears!" He witnessed Methosian spearman impaling all the Portusians fighting around the broken line. As the enemy soldiers fell they began to fall back and pile up on Turk. He had trouble breathing as the bodies fell over top of him and the weight slowly grew heavier. He managed to turn his body slightly under the pile which gave him the ability to breathe somewhat better. No matter how hard he tried he could not free himself or move any further. His breathing began to slow down as he heard muffled screams of soldiers dying in the background. Turk began to hyperventilate trying to free himself until he finally lost consciousness. Little did he know that the spearman were able to push back the enemy allowing new shield bearers to reform the line.

The Portusian archers could only fire on the middle to the back of the phalanx so as not to hit any of their soldiers. They were not hitting many of Methosians because there were not gaps in the wall of shields around them.

After over an hour of fighting, Colarian saw hanging heads and exhaustion on the faces of the Portusians as they could not break the phalanx. He called out to the archers, "I need 300 archers to begin firing at the Portusian infantry on the bridge."

The archers began firing and the enemy soldiers began to fall. The enemy soldiers panicked and began pushing and shoving their own soldiers out of the way to flee off the bridge. As a result, many were inadvertently pushed off the bridge into the river, sinking to their deaths because of the weight of their armor. Others began trampling over other soldiers to try to escape the confined area of the bridge for the river bank.

The Portusian infantry began a full retreat from the bridge as panic had stricken their ranks. Commander Soros was livid as he screamed, "Soldiers of Portus, where is your courage?"

Commander Soros balled his fists and growled. After his growl he yelled, "Archers, fall back!" All the fighting between the two sides had eventually stopped, except for the skirmishes on the east and west hills that continued.

Soros barked, "Officers! Get your worthless bodies over to me to plan a new strategy."

Seeing Soros withdraw and re-group, Colarian ordered, "I want 300 to gather both the Methosian and Portusian wounded from the bridge. Do not kill these men unless they refuse to come peacefully."

As the search for the wounded began, bodies were being moved around. When Turk's body was eventually uncovered they noticed that he was still breathing, so they awakened him with an ancient stink weed. Two soldiers hoisted him up and helped him off the bridge. The soldiers were able to recover 42 wounded Methosians and 128 Portusians. They began tending to the wounds of their comrades, but also the wounds of their enemies.

One of the wounded was an enemy lieutenant named Kregan. He asked his captors, "Why are you tending to our wounds?"

One of the soldiers bandaging up Kregan's gashed left leg said, "It is written in the ancient writings that we should love our enemies and not hate them. We are instructed to show love to those who hate us."

Kregan's thought to himself, "I surely would not have done the same for them. I would have left them for dead or finished them off."

Kregan asked again, "Why would you make me well, knowing that I would certainly show you no mercy if we meet in battle again? If I found you wounded I would certainly not help you."

The soldier that was wrapping the wound stopped, took a deep breath and sat back before he spoke. Looking Kregan in the eyes he said, "That thought has certainly crossed my mind."

He paused for a moment to gather his thoughts and then said, "Hatred is a cruel master. If you allow it, it will consume your whole life. If I hate my enemy, than I am no different than any other person in this world. If I love my enemy then I am free from the tyranny of hatred's rule in my life. If I serve him by doing good and not evil, he is receiving grace, because it is something unmerited that one can never earn or deserve."

"Don't you feel any bitterness?" replied Kregan.

The soldier replied, "At first, I did not desire to do this but have found that eventually my emotions will follow my actions allowing kindness to root instead of bitterness."

The soldier then introduced himself, "My name is Telis. What is your name?"

The lieutenant replied, "I am Kregan."

Telis put his arm on Kregan's shoulder and smiled, "You are going to live Kregan. It was nice to make your acquaintance my friend."

The casualties from the battle thus far were heavy both for Colarian and Soros. Colarian was told by one of his officer's that they had lost 1054 men and had 152 wounded. Almost 1,000 of these were archers and the rest were infantry.

On the Portusian side Soros received a report of a staggering number of dead to add to the men they had already lost in the bog. The toll for the Portusians at the Peirus River was 5,284 dead and 460 wounded. Over 1,800 of the dead were archers. The rest were infantry that died either on the bridge or were struck down by the Methosian archers on the top of the adjacent hills. Soros gnashed his teeth and said, "I want their commander's head on a plate."

25 - Korvis, Methos

In Korvis, the Portusian commander looked to an officer standing by his side and asked, "Why haven't we seen any Methosian soldiers marching from the south or west? Why have no scouts reported back?"

The officer standing by his side, exclaimed, "I am not sure, my lord."

The commander looked to his officer and said, "I am beginning to think that we were given bad intelligence. Take the troops in the south and move them to the eastern side of the city. My instincts tell me that we are about to be ambushed."

The officer replied, "As you wish, sir!"

As the officer carried the message to the ranks of the Portusian army a lone rider hastily made his way to Commander Grim.

"Commander! The Methosians are coming from the east and are only one mile away!" said the soldier.

Commander Grim's eyes opened wide. "How do you know this, soldier?"

The soldier pulled out a sword with the Methosian insignia on it and threw it on the ground.

"We found one of their scouts a half mile away. We killed the scout and headed east where we found the Methosian army moving under cover. We rode back as fast as we could to warn you!"

Commander Grim ordered, "Move half the archers to the east and set up half of the infantry and cavalry in front of them. Have the rest of our force stay in position in the west as I believe they are trying to create a two-front battle. Take these orders out to my captains in the field now. Tell each of them not to leave their positions when they are situated, but to make the Methosians come to them. It is a trap and we must not take the bait."

"Yes, sir!" yelled out the soldier as he turned his horse and rode off to carry out the order.

The Methosian army advancing in the west was only five miles away from Korvis approaching at a rapid pace. Commander Mylaius led his force to the eastern side of the city and was one mile away from the enemy camp.

Commander Grim's occupation force in Korvis was moving swiftly into position. Their force wouldn't have time to dig in, but would be in position by the time the Methosians arrived.

As Commander Mylaius' force approached Korvis he saw the Portusians moving into position in the east. Mylaius commented to the captain with him, "I am not surprised that they discovered our approach, but I hope that they are unaware of Alexander coming from the north. I was hoping that he would be here by now." He paused and looked to the north for a few moments.

“Captain, take the cavalry to the right of our force and attempt to flank their position from the north when I give the order. Have the archers and catapults set up behind our front line and have them soften up the enemy positions. We will not advance any soldiers until either Alexander’s force or Commander Gilliam’s force engage.”

Within a half an hour the Methosians were in position. As they came into position the Portusian archers began firing on the Methosian infantry which stood in the front. The soldiers formed a tight formation as they hid behind and under their shields. Not many arrows made it through the shields as the Methosian infantry became an armored wall.

Commander Mylaius called out, “Catapults, prepare to fire on the Portusian infantry and cavalry!”

The catapults were loaded with tar balls, which were set ablaze. Mylaius yelled, “Fire!”

The seven Methosian catapults fired on the Portusian positions. As the tar started to descend onto their position some of the Portusians began to break ranks to avoid the impact.

The tar had a couple of direct hits that struck their infantry, while the others that missed exploded when they made contact with the ground, sending flaming tar within a 40 foot radius of where it impacted. Many infantry and cavalry were struck and set ablaze. Even some of the archers were hit and set on fire.

The Portusian captain looked down to the archers, made eye contact with their lieutenant and nodded. The lieutenant commanded,

"Archers! Load your arrows with tar and pitch." When they loaded their arrows the lieutenant barked, "Forward quickly!" The archers ran forward until their arrows would be in range of the catapults. The lieutenant ordered, "Ignite arrows!" After a few seconds he yelled, "Fire!"

Thousands of arrows sailed through the air to the Methosian catapult positions. The Portusian lieutenant yelled to his archers, "Fall back now!"

All the Portusian archers began to retreat out of range, but Commander Mylaius was prepared for this. He commanded, "Archers, commence firing on the Portusian bowmen!"

The Portusian arrows hit first and set ablaze all of the Methosian catapults, killing almost all of the soldiers who manned them. The Methosian arrows descended on the Portusian archers and struck half of them down before they could get out of range. Men on both sides succumbed to the arrows as they fell from the sky into their targets. The catapults were useless for Methos as they fought to put out the blazes on each one.

Commander Mylaius quickly surveyed the situation. Speaking to his lieutenants he said, "We need a new plan of attack. We could mount a charge that will overtake their position. We may have lost our catapults, but we now outnumber their archers."

As quickly as Mylaius had conveyed his thoughts did he hear fighting coming from the city. He looked over to the commotion and realized it was Alexander. His force of 20,000 was engaging the sparse Portusian forces from the north. The Portusians quickly took part of their force in the east to block the advance of the enemy descending from the north, but it was too late.

Arrows began raining down on the unestablished Portusian position from Alexander's archers. The lack of time to prepare for an unexpected assault combined with arrows pounding enemy positions gave Alexander's cavalry enough room to break through. They quickly trampled through the enemy lines and made way to the eastern side of the city to engage Portusian archers that were keeping Mylaius at bay.

The archers saw the approaching horsemen and were only able to fire one volley of arrows that struck many cavaliers down. However, they didn't have time for a second as those that made it past the first volley began trampling over and cutting down the archers.

As Mylaius witnessed this he drew his sword and screamed out, "All forces charge!"

The Portusians held off the first advance of Mylaius's force. They had the terrain advantage as the Methosians had to charge up an incline with many obstacles blocking a direct path. The Portusians held firm as the Methosians were winded from the charge.

A seasoned Portusian captain named Lydas commanded this front against Mylaius. Lydas was well prepared for the Methosian charge. As the Methosians started to run up the incline Lydas blew his horn twice, signaling archers to come out from behind the ramparts to fire on the

Methosians. The confined space allowed the archers easy targets as one Methosian fell after another. Despite this, the Methosians continued to advance prompting Lydas to call these archers back behind the line.

As the Methosians made their way through the ramparts they noticed many Portusian soldiers that looked to have fallen by the hands of the Methosian archers. Arrows were embedded in their lifeless bodies. The infantry pressed on and clashed with the Portusians at the top of the incline. Lydas stood on the front line with his troops and engaged the enemy. He struck down the first Methosian that he engaged. Both armies were now embroiled in a face to face battle that stretched down the entire front line.

Lydas struck another enemy soldier down, but the Portusian soldiers on each side of him were cut down. With no defense, Lydas raised his shield and blocked the attack of one and used his sword to deflect the strike of another. Lydas put his shield up to block another attack, but this time he fell down on his back when his shield was struck. The other Methosian soldier knocked the sword out of his hand leaving him scrambling to get his body behind the shield for protection. Suddenly, a Portusian soldier thrust at the enemy to Lydas's left. The enemy soldier spun away from the strike and chopped the Portusian down. The other enemy soldier swung his sword and knocked the shield out of Lydas' hand, while slicing his arm in the process. Lydas screamed as he tried to push his body backwards using his legs and one good arm. As the Methosian soldier raised his sword to finish Lydas, two Portusian spearman thrust their spears into their enemy and his companion. Lydas lay down with his back to the ground, closed his eyes and took a deep breath.

Lydas then used his one good arm to grab a horn on his belt. He lifted it to his lips and blew three short bursts. After the horn blew, the Portusian soldiers that had appeared to be slain at the front of the ramparts by Methosian archers all rose from the ground and attacked their enemy from behind. The Methosian infantry was surrounded.

Mylaius blew his horn signaling the Methosian forces to fall back. The Portusians cut down Methosian after Methosian. Mylaius screamed, "Men, Follow my lead!"

Mylaius pulled out his dagger, fell to his knees and stabbed a Portusian in the leg that was engaged with one of his soldiers. The man screamed and fell to the ground, while Mylaius repeated this action two more times. It opened up a small hole in the enemy line which he and his men exploited by filling it and cutting a path through the Portusians. Within a few minutes several of these holes in the Portusian line formed and the Methosians were able to slash, cut and muscle their way out of the kill box.

Once the men had escaped and regroup outside the ramparts, Mylaius led the next charge, which energized his men. Mylaius stormed up the hill into waiting enemy infantry and blocked an enemy's strike with his sword. He then punched the Portusian in the face and impaled him with his sword.

Mylaius approached another enemy soldier and dodged his sword thrust which left the Portusian open for a strike at the hand of Mylaius.

Mylaius spun around and cut his enemy down from behind. He then impaled another enemy soldier and blocked an incoming strike from another, before cutting him down as well.

Mylaius and his infantry broke through the first line of the enemy defense as they made their way back into the ramparts. Ferocious screams, grunts and the sounds of steel meeting steel emanated into the ears of all the warriors. Mylaius continued to strike down enemy after enemy. More and more enemy soldiers descended on his position by the command of Lydas in hopes of killing this valiant commander and discouraging his forces.

Some of Mylaius' soldiers fell on his left and right flank leaving him open for attack. Thirty Portusian soldiers made haste to his position. He killed the first two, but the sheer numbers of swords coming at him simultaneously was too much and he was killed on the battlefield.

When their leader went down the Methosian resolve intensified. An old lieutenant by the name of Griggs took command and led the charge with the infantry. He led a group of valiant men to retrieve Mylaius' body. In a matter of minutes this group of men had pushed back the Portusians and recovered Mylaius's body and quickly took it off the battlefield.

Griggs had some light infantry that carried bows into the battle. He ordered them to climb onto the ramparts and fire on the Portusian soldiers while the infantry charged. These bowmen unleashed a flurry of arrows that killed so many Portusians that a panic fell amongst their ranks.

When Lydas saw what was happening he ordered the archers by his side to begin firing on the Methosian bowmen. However, the Portusian line had broken, giving the Methosians the advantage. Griggs led his soldiers to the top of the incline and engaged what was left of Lydas' soldiers. Lydas yelled, "Retreat into the city!" As his forces retreated, a group of Methosian soldiers that penetrated through the line in the northern part of the city engaged them. They were led by Alexander.

Lydas yelled, "Make haste to our forces in the west!"

The forces did not make it very far before they were cut down by the Methosian soldiers. Lydas stopped his retreat and made eye contact with Alexander. "Come finish the job, Methosian scum!"

Alexander charged Lydas and swung his sword at Lydas' head with all the strength he could muster. Lydas blocked the strike, but the sheer force knocked him backward a few steps where he fell over the body of a dead soldier. As he hit the ground Alexander knocked the sword from Lydas' hand and then finished him with a thrust into his body. Alexander looked up and commanded, "Soldiers of Methos, pursue the enemy and make safe the eastern side of Korvis."

Within a few hours the north and east sides of the city had been secured by the Methosian forces as they now marched on the west. Alexander was now the new commander. Their attack split the Portusian forces and choked off the remaining eastern troops' flight to the western side of the city.

Alexander regrouped the soldiers and began the assault through the city on the remaining Portusian soldiers in the western side. Commander Gilliam sent word to Alexander that he had already begun to engage the enemy in the west. He ordered a full assault with all his remaining forces.

Alexander led his men into the city streets to finish this battle. The battle was fierce as the streets were full of soldiers and room was limited because of buildings. Fighting was taking place in the city square, on the roof tops and even inside homes and businesses. The Portusians were holding their own initially in the city because it was not an open field. They could not feel the effects of being outnumbered because the confined areas made it congested and worked to their advantage.

Alexander recognized this and took a force house by house and then street by street clearing and securing the western half of the city section by section. The Portusians were unwilling to surrender, so the fighting became so furious that at one point Alexander was seen striking down soldiers who were pinned in on the corner of a roof and refused to surrender. They would not jump and commit suicide, but would fight to the death.

Alexander was having success clearing the streets, but it was costing him many soldiers' lives to do so. As the battle raged on the citizens began to rise up against their captors and this proved to be the turning point. They picked up swords and bows from fallen soldiers, hammers, cast iron pots, and pans and any other object they could find to injure someone. The citizens were scattered within the Portusian ranks, so this caused a great deal of chaos amongst the enemy soldiers. Panic broke out as their lines faltered and they began turning on one another in the heat of the moment thinking their own brethren were the enemy.

Commander Grim was surrounded and had no hope of escape. After watching this dramatic turn of events and seeing many of his men fall helplessly to arrows or the sword, he began to grieve as there was no hope for victory, so he decided to surrender. He raised a white flag and went to Alexander while his captain raised a white flag and rode to Commander Gilliam. The remaining 6,000 Portusian soldiers gave up and followed their commander and laid down all of their weapons.

Alexander searched out commander Gilliam after the surrender. When he found him he asked, "Commander Gilliam, we have a force holding off 50,000 Portusians at the Veros Bridge on the Peirus River, can you lend your forces to turn back our enemy and save our soldiers? Without their bravery in holding the Portusians on the bridge we would not have been able to take the city back."

Commander Gilliam without any hesitation said, "Yes! Captain Coda, gather all our forces and make haste to the bridge at the Peirus River. We have some brothers of ours whose valor was responsible for this victory today. They need our help most desperately."

26 - The Peirus River (Veros Bridge) Northern Methos

On the cobblestone bridge the Portusian army made another advance and this time they tried by sending heavy cavalry. Colarian had the phalanx on the bridge but hidden beneath this wall of shields were 16 foot spears carried by long spearman.

As the enemy approached, the bridge began to shake from all the weight and power of the Portusian cavalry charge. The soldiers in the front locked their shields to form a powerful wall of soldiers that was now united and awaited the impact.

The cavalry charged with ferocity towards the shield laden Methosian front line. Just before the point of impact a shout could be heard and the long spearman extended their spears from behind the wall of shields. An enormous crash resulted from the impact of the cavalry hitting the spears and the wall of shields. Horses could be heard screaming as well as soldiers.

The spears and shields were able to stop some of the cavalry, however as the horseman continued, the momentum started to break through the Methosian line. The initial wall of shields was broken and the enemy began to pour further into the broken ranks, dissolving the advantage the Methosian army had held. The Methosians were in such a tight formation that the momentum from the enemy cavalry started to push the soldiers on the edge of the bridge over to be carried away by the current as they sunk.

A group of Methosian spearman led by Sergeant Turk near the rear of the phalanx made their way to the front to push back the enemy. They were carrying 10 foot spears to subdue the new Portusian threat. Turk witnessed several horsemen in front of him cutting down one Methosian after another. Turk yelled to his men, “Take them down!”

The spearmen quickly began to encircle the horsemen. Turk led first by driving his spear into the chest of the horse in front of him. The horse rose on its hind legs shrieking as two more spearman thrust into its under belly. The rider fell off the horse and was slain by surrounding Methosian infantry. One of the spearman in another group jabbed an enemy horse in the side trying to bring it to the ground. Its rider broke the spear with his sword and then turned his horse, cutting down the spearman in one stroke. The horse was writhing in pain, but the rider managed to keep him on its feet. Two more men in Turks detachment brought the horse down with spear strikes to its front legs. Turk then took his spear and impaled the Portusian cavalier.

The next horsemen they engaged was bucking and trampling any soldier that came near him. As Turk approached, the rider turned his horse and bucked him in the chest with his hind legs. Turks armor absorbed the blow, but indented in his chest. The rider looked to finish Turk off by raising the horse’s front legs and bringing the full weight down on his body. With only a moment to spare Turk took a deep breath and lifted his spear up while the hilt of it was leveraged against the bridge. The horse came down on the spear and shrieked in agony before it stumbled and fell on top of two Methosian soldiers. The rider fell to the ground and was immediately slain by a Methosian soldier.

Meanwhile, Turk gasped for air while he tried to unstrap his armor. He could not remove it from his chest as he took in less air with each breath. Turk turned his head and looked at the scene on the bridge which would disappear into darkness and then reappear again. He finally looked up to the sky and held his arm up grasping at the air with his hand. As his arm fell to the ground a soldier appeared over him, unsheathed his dagger and cut the straps off his armor, pulling it off his body. Turk's torso rose from the ground as he inhaled air like that of a man who had been trapped under water, but was able to escape and reach the surface.

The soldier helped Turk to his feet and wrapped his arm around his shoulder. He looked under Turks tunic and saw a huge bruise. When he touched it Turk screamed in pain as it was obvious that his ribs were broken. Turk looked up at the battle and witnessed the spearman neutralizing the enemy cavalry. The Portusian cavalry had lost its momentum and were now confined to small pockets of fighting along the bridge. The infantry pushed forward and helped to expel the enemy cavaliers.

A full retreat was ordered as the cavalry was being cut down and unable to hold their position on the bridge. As the cavalry retreated off the bridge the Portusian infantry stormed it. The Methosians were in disarray as the phalanx was now broken and there was no time to reform the line.

Commander Soros yelled, “Archers, commence firing on the bridge.” Soros turned to one of his captains and said, “Let us see them deflect our arrows now.”

Many Methosian soldiers began to fall at the hand of the archers. However, Colarian ordered half of the Methosian archers to fire at the enemy on the bridge and the other half to engage the Portusians firing on their infantry. An unexpected benefit were the archers on the top of the east and west hills that overlooked the battle, as they had plenty of arrows from their exchanges with the Portusian archers. They changed their strategy and began concentrating their fire on the Portusian archers again to take some of the stress off their forces. Arrows could be seen flying and darting over the entire river area.

The Portusian infantry still could not scale either hill because it was so steep and slippery from the broken rock debris. The Portusian archers could still not hit the Methosians that were dug in on the top of each hill. Very quickly the Portusian archers became easy targets and started falling in small groups, which eventually mounted up to heavy casualties.

Initially both the Methosian and Portusian infantry suffered some heavy losses from the archers on the opposing sides. However, as the Portusian archers by the west hill were being bombarded with arrows from two directions, their numbers began to dwindle. As a result, the Methosian casualties began to dwindle. These Portusian archers began to now direct their fire from the Methosian infantry to the archers firing at them.

The remaining enemy archers by the east hill began firing at the Methosians firing on the Portusian infantry. The Methosian archers immediately broke away from their assault and started to fire upon the Portusian archers.

As Colarian surveyed the battlefield he could see many slain archers on both sides of the bridge. Colarian turned to one of his lieutenants as he surveyed the field. "It appears that the archer's role in this battle has come to an end. The weight will now be placed on the infantry to hold." Colarian unsheathed his sword, "Lieutenant, rally our full strength to the bridge."

Colarian ran down to the bridge while his lieutenant blew one long blast on a horn. All the remaining soldiers rallied to the bridge in one last effort to hold their position until reinforcements arrived.

Colarian made his way to the front and led the charge. He yelled, "Soldiers of Methos, follow me! We must hold the line!"

Within moments both sides had engaged in battle. Colarian struck down two soldiers with his sword before it was knocked out of his hand by an enemy solider. Colarian went to his knee with his shield up so that it would protect his full body in the crouched position. His shield absorbed the Portusian's strike, but thinking quickly he grabbed an arrow out of a fallen soldier and with an upward thrust stabbed his adversary in the chest. He then took his foe's sword and struck down an enemy soldier that approached from his left.

Colarian dropped back off the line and began to survey the field. The center and left flanks were holding up, but the right began to fall, so Colarian made his way to the right flank of his force on the bridge.

As Colarian reached the right flank he back-handed with his shield the first enemy soldier that he came across. The momentum from the strike knocked the soldier off the right side of the bridge where he began to drown. Colarian then blocked an enemy strike with his shield and impaled the man with his sword. He blocked a sword strike of the next soldier he encountered. Colarian struck the enemy in the head with his shield which disoriented him, and then struck him down with a blow to his side.

As Colarian struck one soldier down after another, he saw a Portusian with great skill striking down any Methosian that engaged him. This was why the right flank was crumbling and causing his men to lose heart. Colarian knew that he had to engage this foe if they were to hold the bridge.

Colarian made his way over to this soldier by striking down two enemy soldiers in his way. This skilled Portusian just finished cutting another Methosian down, and when he looked up, they both made eye contact. The Portusian grinned and began his approach to Colarian.

The Portusian champion grabbed a second sword as he reached Colarian. “What is the name of my next victim?”

Colarian replied, “Tell me your name first and I will give you mine.”

The man opened his eyes wide like that of a crazed lunatic and said, "Death!"

Colarian smirked and then replied, "Very well, 'Death', I am Colarian and I come to ensure that you embody your name today!"

The soldier called "Death" then charged at Colarian swinging the sword in his right hand at Colarian's head. Colarian blocked the blow with his sword. However, "Death" then thrust the sword in his left hand at Colarian, which he dodged with a spin. Colarian used the momentum from his spin to strike "Death" in the face with his shield, breaking his nose. "Death's" eyes produced tears and closed up from the blow that broke his nose. He could not see very well, so Colarian took the opportunity to finish off his opponent. He thrust his sword at his opponent, but the enemy was able to knock the death blow away with the sword in his right hand.

Colarian tried to strike him down again, but the man in his temporarily blind position blocked it again. Since "Death" was on the defensive and holding up nicely, Colarian decided to take a different approach. He struck at "Death" with his sword again, which was subsequently blocked, but then slammed the shield on the man's foot. "Death" let out a scream of agony that could be heard over the entire battle.

"Death's" nostrils flared as he swung his sword at Colarian with all of his might and knocked the sword out of the lieutenant's hand. Colarian then put up his shield as his enemy swung again. The sheer force of the swing sent Colarian staggering backwards when it struck his shield. He eventually fell down on his back and scrambled for another sword as “Death” hobbled after him.

“Death” caught up to him and swung his swords at Colarian who blocked the strikes with his shield. The sheer force of the blow knocked Colarian several feet back where he tripped and fell over a body.

As Colarian lie on the ground he saw a 10 foot spear by his side. He quickly got up and threw his sword at the hobbling “Death”. “Death” blocked the blow, but this bought Colarian enough time to pick up the spear. Colarian then flung the shield at “Death” while at the same time using this distraction to ram the spear into the stomach of his foe. “Death” fell to his knees gasping for air and then to the ground where he perished.

An exhausted Colarian picked up a sword from a fallen soldier and surveyed the battle on the bridge. The right flank was holding and the men of Methos had gained courage as the Portusian champion was now slain.

Colarian took a deep breath and then rushed back into battle. The fight raged on for hours, and eventually the Methosians were able to start pushing the Portusians back. The Portusians began to panic and within moments began a full retreat.

Colarian yelled, “Do not give chase! Save your strength!” He looked to his officers who gathered around him and commanded, “Have your men reform the line. Use whatever few moments we have to take a respite before their next offensive.”

The Methosians reformed the line in the phalanx formation and began to take a breather. Several minutes later the enemy forces began gathering again. The Portusian commander had one final trick up his sleeve. Soros barked, “Bring forth the siege tower.”

The siege tower behind their ranks had been brought up. The tower had not been meant for battle in the field, but they moved it knowing that the Methosians would not be able to stop this massive structure. The tower provided a perfect cover for the men pushing it along as it took up the entire width of the bridge.

Colarian’s jaw dropped as he stared at the tower. One of his lieutenants asked, “What are your orders, sir?”

Colarian squatted down and looked up at the tower as it crossed the threshold of the bridge. He dropped his head and looked down at the ground where many bodies lay. The lieutenant asked again. “Sir, what are your orders? We cannot stand here and push against the tower without being crushed.”

As Colarian stared at the ground and tried to think of a counter measure, he saw several arrows lying in bodies around him. Colarian’s eyes opened wide and his head rose looking at the tower. He stood up and ordered, “Have the remaining archers tear up pieces of cloth to wrap around their arrows. Have them add tar and pitch to the cloth, light them and then fire at the tower.”

The command went out to the archers and they fired the flaming arrows at the tower. Some arrows sailed off course due to the weight of the cloth, but many found their mark. Small spots of fire could be seen on the tower, and they began to grow larger and larger until the entire structure was engulfed in flames. The burning heap of the tower now became a blockade as it crashed down onto the bridge.

Colarian rallied his men around him, "Soldiers of Methos! Today you have looked into the face of overwhelming odds and have shown no fear. I wish I could convey the admiration I have for all of you. Your valor and zeal are an inspiration to me."

The men gave Colarian their full attention and nodded with every word that proceeded from his mouth. "I know that you are tired. I know that the fighting has intensified with every attack, yet you still manage to hold your ground and turn the enemy away. Soldiers of Methos, will you continue to hold this bridge for your king and people!"

The soldiers roared, "YES!"

Colarian continued as his voice echoed across the river into the enemy camp, "Will you fight to the death!"

The soldiers screamed, "YES!"

Across the river the Portusian troops were faint of heart as their heads hung low reminiscent of the sun that was starting to set. The voice of Colarian and the screams of the Methosian soldiers as they rallied around him were defeat in the ears of the Portusians.

Commander Soros articulated to his officers, "The countenance on the men's faces is low. We still have over 2 hours of light left that we can use to claim this bridge." He pointed to the trees. "I had some soldiers cut down some trees during our last engagement. These trees have already been stripped of their limbs and cut into sections. I had the men take some wagons and convert them into battering rams using these stumps. Move these rams up into position. We are going to take this bridge."

The siege tower had burned down and was just a smoldering pile but the Methosians had formed ranks once more to prepare for another attack. Commander Soros ordered the rams forward followed by the foot soldiers and cavalry intermingled. The battering rams shielded the men that were pushing them. Portusian soldiers on the left and right flank of the rams used their shields to protect the ram operators from being hit and incapacitated by the arrows.

This next attack started gaining steam and they were running at such a speed that they crunched through the charred wood of what had been the tower. As they continued forward they were met by a group of Methosian soldiers that covered the width of the bridge with their shields locked as one. Arrows were flying from behind them at the battering rams and advancing enemy force.

The battering rams broke through this initial line of soldiers, but were slowed down as they became obstacles and soldiers began attacking the men around the rams. As the Portusians pushed forward the Methosian forces slowed them down, but could not stop them. Different pieces of the shield wall were taking hits from the rams and the speed was more than the Methosians could handle. Before, they could halt a very slow moving tower, but these weighted carts, with sharp points and wooden spikes on their fronts were plowing through the line. This allowed the Portusian soldiers to better engage the Methosians and take advantage of their greater numbers.

Colarian blew three bursts into his horn signaling his soldiers to fall back. Slowly, the Methosians made their way to their side of the bridge and the archers focused on the coming troops, while the soldiers formed a semicircle around the bridge's entrance.

As the Portusian cavalry made it across the bridge from behind the ram they started to push the Methosian soldiers back allowing for more of their troops to storm the banks. Now the Portusian soldiers had the upper hand because they were able to get a large portion of their army on the other side of the banks.

The sheer numbers of the Portusians pushed the Methosian soldiers back and began to route them. Colarian knew that the battle had been lost and signaled the retreat by blowing a long burst into his horn. The Methosian soldiers began to retreat, but the Portusians pursued their enemy.

Commander Soros commanded, "Kill them all, including the wounded."

Soros' men began executing those they had captured or wounded as they continued pursuing the remnants of the Methosian force.

The Portusian soldiers began cheering that their enemy was on the run. The Methosians were easy targets as the enemy soldiers celebrated every kill.

Commander Soros screamed, "Victory is ours! Bring me their commander's head on a pike!"

Soros found a Methosian soldier who was mortally wounded, but still alive moving his arms around. Soros planted his sword in his chest with a smirk on his face.

As Portusian soldiers were giving chase to their enemy up a large hill by the river, they heard a different horn blow from the top of this hill. Within moments 5,000 Methosian cavalry began rushing down the hill, running over the Portusian enemy making their way to the bridge to stop the flow of any more troops. After the horsemen followed waves of foot soldiers descending down the hill. The Methosians had sent a host of 50,000 soldiers to aid Colarian's force.

Panic struck the hearts of the Portusian soldiers who had grasped victory only to have it taken away from them, as they had no counter attack for this mighty host. These 50,000 reinforcements proved to be too much as they cut down every Portusian soldier that crossed the bridge. They then chased the remaining forces until they had scattered, so much so that they were less of an army and more of a group of men running back to Portus.

27 - Port Verdes, Remar

On the Island of Remar, Petros was overseeing a group of soldiers in training, watching on one in particular who happened to be an excellent swordsman. This young man was always able to best the others in sparing but he had never seen a battle. Petros wanted to test the young soldier. He grabbed a bow and arrow and told the man to spar with a slightly larger opponent, but while the sparring took place Petros fired a shot that was so close that it buzzed the young man's ear. The soldier froze in fear when this happened and his opponent landed what would have been a fatal blow had they actually been in battle.

Petros yelled, "You cannot go into war fearing anything. If you do, then you will lose your life. War will expose your fears, so you must overcome them before they overcome you!"

He looked over at this swordsman and yelled, "Again!"

They started to spar once more. Petros grabbed an arrow as they sparred and fired another shot that almost grazed his ear. The swordsman panicked, lost sight of his opponent, and again was struck with another death blow had this been in a battle.

"Again!" barked Petros.

The soldier held his head low as he raised his sword to fight. His hand squeezed the hilt so hard that it began to turn white. The rattled soldier began to spar again more timid than before as he tried to watch his opponent and Petros at the same time. Petros took another arrow and fired it by his head for a third time. The soldier panicked and dropped his sword and received yet another death blow, but this one sent him to the ground.

Petros drew a clear picture of what can be expected in war. "Soldiers of Methos, what you have witnessed here is what will happen if fear overcomes you. War is an ugly thing. It can make cowards of the greatest of men. You have to learn to not give into fear as the chaos abounds around you. You must always be cognizant of your surroundings, but never allow what is happening to distract you. If you lose focus and become distracted then you will not live to see tomorrow!"

Petros paused for a short moment. His eyes began to soften as he looked at the men who were attentive to his every word. "You may think me a cruel and malicious man for firing those arrows at his head, however, what you must understand is that I have seen war and its many ugly faces. What I did is nothing compared to what you will see on the battlefield. I did this because I care for you soldiers. Someone that cares for you does not hide the truth from you nor does he fail to prepare you for adversity. You will hear screams of your brethren falling to the ground and see arrows darting through the air. If you become distracted by these things, then you will lose your life like this young swordsman would have if this was a real battle."

Looking around, Petros continued, "Discipline and resolve are what is needed to counter fear. Discipline helps you to keep focus and not be distracted from your task at hand. Discipline is what instructs a warrior to operate by principle, not desire or feelings. That is why we train. Constant practice and simulation will make what you learn second nature and thus better prepare you for the horror you will experience. Please understand that I am trying to preserve your lives by being so hard."

Petros then took a seat on a nearby stump of wood and gave one last pearl of wisdom. "Resolve is rooted in the truth. A man of resolve will never crack under pressure of fear no matter how great the temptation because he leans on truth. You have heard it said that, 'the truth shall set you free'. It sets you free because you are not subject to the bondage of lies. The truth is this, we are fighting a grievous evil that looks to destroy and enslave our families. If we firmly believe this, then there is nothing that we will not do to protect our families from this evil. Truth is a firm foundation that you can trust because it will not bend to the left or to the right. It is not relative, but absolute. Better to die fighting for truth then to live and follow a lie. There is freedom in the truth. Men of Methos, what are the absolute truths that will give you resolve in the fight?"

The men were quiet for a moment and then the swordsman who just failed Petros' test spoke.

"I was a slave. I was treated like a filthy rag. Slavery is not right and no country should be built on the backs of slaves. It is a great evil of which I will not go back to. I was taken from my family and robbed of a mother and father and siblings that loved me. This happened more than 80 years ago when I was seven. I will fight to whatever end to ensure that King Melmot or this King Mardok never enslave another person again."

Petros smiled and affirmed this young soldier. "Well said, my friend."

Petros continued. "Is there anyone else that would like to share an absolute truth that will give them resolve in battle?"

Another soldier came forward. "I believe that I can speak for many of the Parrusians here that have lived in this depraved kingdom that is devoid of any morality. Slavery was accepted, stealing is not punished, lying is commonplace, murder is rampant, material possessions have become our idols. I want to fight for this Sophos that you have spoken of, because he is the opposite of these things. These evils are what many of the kingdoms of Athanasia embody. He is truth, so he will never bend nor waiver for anyone nor anything. If he will never bend nor waiver, then neither shall I bend nor waiver. I will gladly surrender my life to fight for this truth because it is there to protect me, not destroy me. It gives me hope."

All the soldiers gave a verbal approval to what this soldier said.

Petros responded, "My brothers, you have brought great joy to my heart. You have encouraged me with your openness and willingness to share. It sounds as if you have come to understand what it is that you are truly fighting for. If you keep the truth in focus then you will never fall into the clutches of fear. When you take your eye off the truth then fear will storm into your life like a thief and will cause your downfall. Well done, my brothers!" Petros left them to continue their training and went to see over more soldiers that were preparing for the coming conflict.

#

On the main Isle of Parrus the army was hesitantly preparing for battle. A great rift was in place as the result of friends and family choosing opposite sides and the conflict within the soldiers of rebelling against a ruler they had known for so long. Yet, it was the character of that ruler that made rebellion much easier.

As this large armada prepared to depart from Parrus, some of the commanders and ships captains talked of defecting as well. One was overheard saying, "King Melmot uses the people of Parrus to provide him with position. The people in his eyes are only a means to an end." While another said, "Melmot values his dogs more than the lives of people. How can a man elevate an animal above a person?" Those that heard these comments nodded their heads in agreement.

A commander approached the chief vizier of Parrus and exclaimed, "Our soldiers have no desire to fight for their king or against their brethren. Our force of 300,000 soldiers is beginning to crumble before the battle has even started. We will not win this war. The men will not fight."

The vizier nodded and said, "I know, but it is by the king's command. Whether we like it or not, we are bound to it."

Unexpectedly, all the ships began to leave the dock with their full accompaniment of soldiers. There had been given no order for the ships to depart as they were making their final preparations for the siege of the island. Those displays of rebellion ignited like a fire around the entire fleet until almost every ship had left without orders for Remar. When they approached the island all the Parrusian ships raised a white flag and surrendered. Even the king's own vizier who was tasked to invade the island surrendered. The entire populations of all three of the now Methosian acquired islands were stunned as ships sailed into the harbors surrendering to Petros.

On the island the chief vizier was making his way to Petros who was close by as he desired to make his acquaintance. The chief vizier of King Melmot approached Petros and Elias and said, "We have no more pride left in us. We were once an army that boasted of great glory, but now we have been relegated to errand boys. Our nation is a disgrace and we would sooner run than lay down our lives for it. We have 300,000 men, 1,000 boats, and many provisions that we surrender to King Justinian of Methos. Please tell your servants how we may be of assistance during these dark days. For our puppet king follows this King Mardok who is a lover of self and hater of men."

Petros furrowed his brow and stared at the man for a few moments. Then he asked a probing question, "What tipped the scales for King Melmot's chief vizier to leave his service?"

The vizier replied, "I was tallying the rations that had not yet been loaded on my ship when I saw a little girl and her mother staring at the crates of food intently. Their bodies looked deathly thin as they wasted away from starvation. The night before I watched King Melmot do what he has done every night for many years; he gives elaborate feasts to his dogs and treats them as if they are human beings. I have been haunted by the image of the mother and daughter and knew in my heart that I could no longer serve King Melmot. I gave them some fruit and a little grain and told them to hurry off and eat."

Petros' eyes perked up as he enthusiastically replied, "You are most welcome here! We welcome you with open arms to our humble land. If you are willing, we can use your soldiers and boats for defense and most certainly use your provisions to feed our growing army."

The two men smiled and grabbed the right shoulder of the other. The vizier said, "I am most willing!"

Petros replied, "Come, you are all friends of Methos."

The next day the five ships of reinforcements from Methos appeared. This continued to help strengthen the forces in Remar. Petros sent a ship back to Methos to inform King Justinian of the glorious turn of events in Parrus, including the redemption of Sprasian.

28 - The Eastern Athanasian Ocean

The *Morning Star* had been on the water for several weeks and had not seen a speck of land. No birds were seen either, which indicated that the likelihood of land being nearby was low. It was quite boring as they had not hit any storms, nor was their much to do on the ship. From time to time some of the soldiers would have sparring matches with wooden swords so as to stay sharp in their skills. They also had archery contests in which they tried to hit the smallest of objects while the ship rocked and the wind blew. In the evenings they would tell stories or read books from the small library in the captain's quarters.

Sprasian had just come out of his quarters and looked like a much different man. His hair had been cut very short, while his face was cleanly shaven. Spiros and Katherine noticed Sprasian as he walked up and took the wheel of the ship.

"What happened to you, Sprasian?" said Spiros.

Sprasian smiled and replied, "What do you mean?"

Katherine then approached Sprasian and said, "What has happened to your beard and long hair?"

Sprasian looked ahead as he steered the ship and replied, "I cut them off."

Katherine replied, “Why?”

Sprasian continued to look ahead and responded, “Because I am not the same man that I once was. I am no longer a son of perdition. The heart of the swine has been changed.”

Spiros replied, “Ah, you cite the ancient writings. Indeed, you are no longer the same man.”

A few hours later Spiros and Katherine were talking around the mast of the ship. Sprasian was speaking about his wounded and destructive past and had everyone’s full attention. “I have stopped blaming my father and have taken full responsibility for all my actions.”

Katherine asked, “Do you still hate your father?”

Sprasian replied, “No, I have forgiven him. I love him very much and wish that I had one more opportunity to speak with him.”

Spiros asked, “What would you say?”

Sprasian smiled, “That I love him.”

Spiros replied, “That is all that you would say? You wouldn’t tell him that you had forgiven him or bring up the wounds that he inflicted upon you?”

Sprasian responded, “No. I have already forgiven him and wouldn’t want to waste that last opportunity together reminding him of how he hurt me. Rather, I would desire to sit down and bond with him by asking about my mother and his love for her. I would like to know about his life growing up with Justinian and if he has any fatherly wisdom for me."

Spiros responded, "That is not the response that I thought you would give. I see great wisdom in you, Sprasian."

Sprasian thanked Spiros and headed back to his quarters thinking of all the different questions that he would ask his father if he had one more chance to speak to him.

One day, Katherine was watching some of the soldiers sparing on the deck with wooden swords. Sprasian walked up to Katherine and asked, "Would you like to learn how to wield a sword?"

Katherine looked at Sprasian and opened her mouth as if she was about to say something, then she turned her head back to the soldiers and said, "No."

Sprasian replied, "It would be wise to learn."

Katherine responded, "Why do I need to learn how to use a sword?"

Sprasian smiled, "There are many evil people out there that cannot be reasoned with. They are only satisfied in doing evil. They cannot go to sleep at night unless they do something evil. You never know what type of peril lurks around the corner."

Katherine put her hands behind her back, but agreed with Sprasian's point. "I am frightened by the thought that I may have to kill someone."

Sprasian replied, “Do not be frightened Katherine, as your attacker will not be frightened from taking your life.”

He handed her a practice sword, but Katherine kept her hands behind her back. Sprasian smiled and said, “It is understandable if you do not want to do this.” Katherine slowly brought her hands from behind her back and grabbed the wooden sword.

Sprasian responded, “I am going to teach you how to hold the sword first and then we will practice defensive movements. In order to go on the offensive, one must learn how to defend themselves first. After you learn the defensive movements I will show you how to turn those into offensive movements.”

Katherine started out poorly as she just held the wooden sword in front of her. Sprasian swung his wooden sword and knocked Katherine’s out of her hand. She immediately pulled her hands back in a panic and said, “Ouch, the vibration hurt my hand.”

Sprasian smiled and said, “I see that we have a lot of work to do.”

Katherine scrunched her nose at Sprasian and picked up her wooden sword and started swinging it at him. Sprasian dodged to the left and the right as she tried to strike him.

“Katherine, stop swinging at me so that I can teach you!” said Sprasian as he dodged yet another blow.

Katherine frowned at him as she swung her sword one word at a time at Sprasian, “Don’t. You. Ever. Do. That. Again!”

Katherine's last swing hit Sprasian on the leg. He winced as he dropped down to a knee, prompting Katherine to pull back, drop her sword and put her hands over her mouth. She asked, "Are you okay?"

Sprasian picked up the sword and gave it back to her. "Yes, I am fine." He looked at Katherine in the eyes. "First lesson; if you allow your emotions to control you, they will lead you to your destruction."

Sprasian paused for a moment. "Katherine, I know that you are uncomfortable doing this and I shouldn't take that for granted. My whole reasoning was to see how you would respond to an offense." He then quipped, "And we have much work to do."

The tension on Katherine's face broke as she started to smile and then giggle. "All is forgiven, brigand."

Sprasian smiled and nodded his head, "Very well. Are you ready?"

Katherine nodded her head and Sprasian began to instruct her. "We are going to do some repetition. I am going to show you how to block an overhead strike, a thrust and then a slash. Then I will teach you how to go on the offensive."

Sprasian paused for a moment in thought and then said, "I'll start with how to block an overhead strike.

"When I come over the shoulder with my sword towards your head or upper torso you must take your sword with both hands and raise it up to where it is parallel to the ground above eye level. The higher it is, the less likely you are to be struck."

Sprasian asked her, “Do you understand?”

Katherine replied, “Yes.”

Sprasian smiled, “Very well, here were go.”

Sprasian came over the head with a strike and Katherine blocked it. He did it again and again and she blocked it. He encouraged and instructed her as she was blocking his strikes, “Well done! Good block! Keep your sword parallel to the ground! Keep your sword above eye level! Well done!”

As time went on Katherine’s heart eased and she fully embraced the training.

It was soon that she was having fun learning how to defend herself with the wooden sword and her skill began to match her enjoyment.

During one of their training sessions, Sprasian took the wooden sword in his right hand and swung it at her head. Katherine countered by taking her sword and lifting it high in front of her face, stopping the blow. Sprasian then countered by thrusting at her abdomen, to which she countered by sliding to her right and swinging her sword down overtop of Sprasian’s hilt connecting with his hand. Sprasian dropped his sword and screamed.

As he cried out in pain the men of the ship that witnessed this began to laugh. “Forgive me, Sprasian! Please forgive me! I did not mean to hurt you.”

She ran over to Sprasian and grabbed his hand. As Sprasian

grimaced and pulled it away he said, "Don't apologize, Katherine! What you did was perfect. You learn very quickly and that is to be commended." He smiled, "I will get over the pain and humiliation of this defeat."

Katherine grabbed his injured hand and inspected the wound. Her soft touch made the pain Sprasian was feeling dissipate. Katherine said, "Try bending your wrist up and down."

Sprasian did as he was instructed. Katherine replied, "You have full mobility which means nothing was broken. You should soak your wrist in cold sea water or with a compress, which will help the swelling to go down."

Sprasian slowly nodded his head at Katherine. She let go of his wrist and replied, "Are you alright, Sprasian?"

Sprasian quickly came to his senses now that the soft touch of her hands was gone. "Yes, thank you for your help. I will go to my quarters and apply a compress."

Katherine replied, "Very well."

Sprasian walked away thinking about the softness of Katherine's touch. It was so soothing that he wanted to go back to his quarters and lay down in his bed. However, the memory of Katherine's touch abruptly disappeared as Sprasian entered his quarters and saw Spiros sitting in a comfortable chair by the fire. He was sipping on ale and Sprasian decided to join him.

“Sprasian, do you really believe there is land east? Sailors have searched for years for land and have found none. What makes you think that things will turn out different this time around?”

Sprasian smiled, “It sounds like you have a lack of faith, Spiros.” He grinned, “You of all people should know about faith.”

Sprasian continued, “Since my change of heart I have started to remember the wisdom my uncle Justinian shared with me. It amazes me that things he taught me so many years ago as a youth have revived in me. On one occasion he taught me about faith as he said, ‘If you put faith in yourself and in your abilities you will always fall short.’

“When he told me about this he explained that we don’t have faith in and of ourselves to triumph over the uncertainties of this world. Our strength comes from Sophos to triumph over the adversities of this world that constantly bombard us. He said that true faith gives way to hope, and that hope is rooted in certainty, not uncertainty. I must believe by faith that Sophos has a task for us to complete. That we aren’t going out to sea aimlessly to die of dehydration and starvation. I must by faith believe that there is some land out there that he desires us to find. I cannot discern the reasoning. I must believe that we are not sailing east in vain.”

Spiros nodded, “You are right. You have shown greater faith than I have shown. I am grappling with why this evil has happened to me.”

Sprasian responded, “I am grappling with why this good has been shown to me.”

The two raised their mugs and took a drink as they continued to converse. After an hour of talking about various things from Sprasian's childhood to what they think the war would do to Athanasia, Spiros left the room. It wasn't long after he had gone that Sprasian slipped into a vision.

However, what he saw wasn't the room but he was on the deck, steering the ship with tall, black storm clouds directly ahead of them. It was unlike any storm he'd seen. It was rushing toward them rather than floating in the sky. Yet, while he tried to steer the ship in another direction to avoid this storm, wherever he went so too did the storm.

Purple lightning and long booms of thunder began to wash over the sea as the clouds swallowed the sky. The storm had finally overtaken the ship, bringing with it winds and rains, and waves that sought to overturn the vessel and devour the men in the sea. Sprasian, Spiros, and his men fought the storm with great valor as they tried to hold their course, working to keep the ship afloat.

Sprasian was yelling words of encouragement to his men. "Stay the course men! We will overcome this adversity and come out better as a result! Do not fear what lies ahead! Victory awaits us!" Sprasian then awoke sweating, startled, shocked, and breathing deeply.

Sprasian continued breathing heavily as the reality of the vision was still around him, but he remembered that Sophos had said that he would be tested and tried.

A few moments later Spiros entered back into the quarters and saw a pale Sprasian sitting up.

“Sprasian, you look like a man who has seen an apparition,” commented Spiros.

Sprasian looked up to Spiros and said, “I had a strange vision in which I was on the deck of this ship and we were heading into a storm that we could not steer around. We had to go into it.”

Spiros said nothing for a moment studying Sprasian, but broke his silence by saying, “That is similar to a vision that I had weeks ago.”

Sprasian replied, “Well, you are an Adelphos, you are gifted with the ability to discern things that we Athanasian’s cannot. Do you know its meaning?”

Spiros shook his head and said, “I cannot understand the full meaning of the vision. It could be literal, it could be metaphorical or both. It appears that there will be some sort of adversity coming our way, but whatever the meaning, only time will tell.”

29 - The Forest East of Korvis

The two elite Methosian soldiers continued their pursuit of the escaped Portusian soldier. The Methosian with the bow and arrow had a clean shot at the Portusian soldier's body on the log floating down the stream. However, the scout regained consciousness and saw them as the Methosian soldier discharged his arrow at the scout's head. Just before the arrow would impact his head an osprey swooped down to grab a fish and was struck and killed just two feet in front of him.

The soldier without the bow screamed, "Drat! There cannot be a man in all of creation with as much good fortune as this man."

The soldier dropped his bow and his jaw while gazing at the scout who would not die. The Portusian scout waved and screamed back at them, "You men have to be the most unfortunate marksmen in the whole Methosian army!" He laughed as he continued to float away at a faster speed.

Yet, as the scout floated and the men pursued, they heard a low thundering sound that began to get louder.

The man on the log spun around to see the river that would have been his escape, disappear, transforming into the beginning of a waterfall. The scout began to kick his feet and flail his arms as he screamed, "Help! Someone throw me a rope. You cannot leave me to die."

The Methosian soldiers followed the banks of this stream towards the falls taunting the man. “How fortunate do you feel now, fool?” said one of the soldiers.

“You can’t just leave me to die. I thought that Methosian soldiers were men of honor?” said the scout.

The soldier with the bow yelled, “We are men of honor. We are also men of justice. Hopefully, you can understand our position.” His companion nodded his head in agreeance with every word.

The scout shouted, “What?”

As the enemy scout approached the drop off of the falls, the sound became so loud that his screams were drowned out. The soldiers quickly sought a path to the bottom of the falls as the scout dropped down out of their sight. The men ran and climbed through trees and over rocks until they came to the bottom of the waterfall. It was there that they found the scout washed up on the bank. He had fallen 70 feet, was battered, but was still alive. He was coughing and moving very slowly as the Methosian soldiers unsheathed their swords and put them in his face.

“It looks like your good fortune has just run out.” said the soldier without the bow.

The scout sighed and just lay on the ground. The soldier with the bow said, “Because of your good fortune I think that we will make you our prisoner, not our victim. What is our trophy’s name?”

The scout looked at them and said, "I'll give you mine if you tell me yours."

The soldiers nodded in agreement.

"My name is Gio," replied the scout. "What are the names of my captors?"

The soldier with the bow said, "I am Tiberius and this is Gregorian."

"Well, you have captured me, so why are you not going to kill me?" said Gio

Tiberius answered, "I think you have some important information that we may be able to extract from you. We were ordered to eliminate the scouts, but we are miles away from the battlefield. Come, there is a small town just over this ridge. We will go there for provisions and make our way back to our camp."

As the three men walked to the town they began to converse more. They found that Gio believed that Justinian murdered King Argos' family as was told by Mardok. They argued back to him that Justinian had no desire for the Portusian throne and that he was a righteous king who would never murder anyone because he followed the ways of Sophos. They told him how Mardok set Justinian up as the scapegoat to usurp the throne from King Argos. However, they were not able to convince Gio that what he was told by Mardok was a lie.

"How can you say that your king is a follower of Sophos and the ancient writings in light of the evidence against him?" said Gio.

Gregorian answered, “Sophos revealed himself to Justinian and warned him of a great evil in Athanasia. Sophos would not have come to a murderous usurper to warn him of a great evil that has arisen.”

Gio replied, “Sophos revealed himself to Justinian?”

Gregorian continued, “If you were a follower of Sophos then you might be incensed by the blasphemy uttered by Mardok on top of the temple in Telemicha. Mardok cursed Sophos and claimed that he would take his throne. Is that something that would be spoken by an individual that has no desire to not usurp a throne?”

Gio was silent when he heard this. He looked down at the ground and spoke, “How do I know that you speak the truth?”

Tiberius responded, “Because I was present when he spoke those words on the temple. By chance I was selected as one of the elite guards assigned to the temple that day to protect King Justinian. Mardok is no follower of Sophos. If he was, he would have known his place.”

Gregorian commented, “The creation said it was greater than its creator, there is no greater blasphemy. If Justinian uttered those words, we would no longer be allied to him because our allegiance is to Sophos first.”

Gio frowned and hung his head when he replied, “If what you say is true, then I too would choose Sophos over my king. He is my sovereign.”

Gio continued, “It is good to meet fellow servants of our creator.”

Tiberius replied, “Truly?” he paused and looked at both Gio and Gregorian before he continued, “If what you say is true, we almost killed one of our own brothers. What a dark day that would have been if we killed you.”

Gio retorted, “It was your poor marksmanship that saved the day.”

Tiberius clenched his fists, but when Gregorian started to laugh he lightened up and snickered.

As they were going up over the hill that overlooked the town of Adair they heard some commotion. Gregorian asked, “Did you hear that?” Gio and Tiberious nodded.

Tiberius whispered, “It sounds like weeping and yelling. Come, let us investigate.”

They quickly made their way to a group of trees on the top of the hill and from there they saw Portusian soldiers taking seven bound men, three women, and two children to an open field near them.

They could hear the Portusian officer in charge yelling, “Lord Mardok has decreed that any captives found unwilling to serve the kingdom of Portus will forfeit their lives and the lives of their families!”

Many of the citizens of the town were around the scene yelling, crying, and begging the men to stop.

A family of three was huddled together in fear as they stood to be executed. The man had a wife and one son who was a child. The Portusian officer asked the father in a loud voice for all to hear, “Today, you are being charged with treason for swearing allegiance to the usurper King Justinian. What say you to these charges?"

The father's eyes were red as one who had been grieving for some time. He replied, "We will never serve your malevolent King Mardok. Our allegiance is to Methos alone."

The officer smirked and asked aloud, "Is this how you all feel?"

All those that stood to be executed began to nod. The officer quipped, "I tried to show you all mercy today, let the record show that they have declined this act."

There was a momentary silence after the officer's comments. Suddenly, the young boy standing to be executed remarked, "We will never bow down to the likes of the tyrant King Mardok!"

The officer furrowed his brow and his jaw dropped from his face as he turned and looked at the boy. He replied, "You are a brave little swine, aren't you?"

The boy held his head up as he began to fight back against the fear that was trying to grip him. The officer continued, "I think that I am going to kill your mother and father first, so that it will be the last memory you have before you die."

At that moment, the father raised his head high and looked the officer directly in the eyes and said, "What you are doing today is murder, and you will not escape judgment! Make no mistake, you are not taking our lives, rather we are giving them up willingly!"

The officer began grinding his teeth and squeezing the hilt of his sword upon hearing these words. He looked over at his soldiers and said, "Commence with the executions!"

The Portusian soldiers approached the family and broke their embrace so that they all stood apart. All twelve people were now separated and had one soldier that stood in front of each of them. The soldiers unsheathed their swords and the officer in command gave the execution order.

The father then screamed, "Long live Sophos and long live King Justinian!"

Gio, Tiberius, and Gregorian watched as the Portusian executioners stepped forward and ended the lives of these 12 people. The three men turned pale faced by what they had just witnessed.

Gregorian whispered with a scowl on his face, "The Portusians are beasts, let us end this one's life in retribution for their wickedness," as he motioned to Gio.

Tiberius replied, "No. Gio was not the one who murdered those people. Those men chose to murder and Gio should not suffer the consequences for the transgressions of others. Those soldiers will pay for what they have done."

Gio spoke to Gregorian, "I did not enlist in the Portusian military to savagely murder innocent people. I signed up for retribution against the murder of King Argos and his family. I do not condone this behavior nor would I ever follow an order like this from King Mardok."

Tiberius replied, “Then understand that your King Mardok is the murderer. He made the decree to kill those that refuse to willingly serve him. Justinian would never make such an order or commit such an act. Mardok is the one that murdered King Argos’ family. Since you said that you read the ancient writings you will understand the truth where it states, ‘That a bad tree cannot bear good fruit nor can a good tree bear bad fruit.’ Mardok is a bad tree.”

Then from behind they heard a voice. “If you say one more word you will be killed. Drop your weapons and place your hands on the ground in front of you!”

Tiberius and Gregorian did as they were told. Several Portusian soldiers came forth and struck both men, bound them, and they began walking down the hill to where the executions had taken place.

The Portusian soldier in command asked Gio, “Who are you? You dress like a Portusian scout.”

Gio responded, “I was a Portusian scout for the army that had marched into Methos and destroyed the city of Korvis. I was sent out to see where the assault on our position would come from when I was chased by those two Methosian soldiers. I was the only scout to escape, but they captured me so that I could not take word back to my commander to warn them of the ambush. They kept me alive so as to interrogate me on the military positions and plans of Portus.”

The officer replied, “Did you tell them anything?”

Gio exclaimed, “No.”

The officer said, "Good, I think it would be fitting if you were given the honor to slay your captors. There is no better feeling than to deal retribution to those that sought to harm you."

After a brief pause Gio nodded his head. The officer cut his bonds and gave him a sword.

"Come, we have one more group of executions to carry out today. We will add these two men into the group."

Seven Portusian soldiers escorted Gio, Tiberius, and Gregorian down the hill to the execution field where 13 other soldiers stood. Many townspeople remained as there was one more execution slated for the day. Three women waited with their hands bound in the field. As the soldiers reached these three women they stood Tiberius and Gregorian next to them, while delivering a parting strike to both of their rib cages.

"People of Adair! Before you we have three women that have committed treason by refusing to serve the Kingdom of Portus. Next to them are two Methosian soldiers found on the hill above us holding a Portusian soldier captive. These are all offenses punishable by death. Gio, you may have your vengeance," ordered the lieutenant.

Gio moved up to Tiberius and Gregorian with his sword as the lieutenant stood next to him. The three women started crying as they could sense that their end was near.

Gio looked at Tiberius and Gregorian, then away, wiping sweat off his brow. He then looked to the lieutenant and then the three women. Tiberius saw the color drain from Gio's face, as he kept looking back and forth between the lieutenant and the five captives.

"Gio, commence with the executions now! That is an order!" barked the lieutenant.

Gio raised his sword to strike Tiberius but his arms went limp and the sword hung loosely in his hand at his side.

The lieutenant yelled, "If you do not carry out these executions then you will forfeit your life!"

Finally, Gio brought his sword back up to strike down Tiberius to the lieutenant's delight. As he raised the sword over his shoulder he screamed and brought the sword down over the ropes that bound Tiberius's hands freeing him. Tiberius quickly grabbed daggers hidden on his hips and threw them at the two soldiers standing behind him, killing them both. After freeing Tiberius, Gio swung his sword at the lieutenant, slashing him across his upper torso, killing him. Tiberius then freed Gregorian and they picked up the dead soldiers' swords, and charged into battle with Gio as Portusian soldiers swarmed on their position.

Gio took on one soldier while Tiberius and Gregorian took on the rest of their adversaries. Tiberius ran at one soldier closing on his position. The enemy soldier swung his sword at Tiberius' upper torso, which Tiberius countered by ducking into a roll under the swing. Tiberius stood up and struck the soldier down from behind.

Tiberius grabbed the shield of the soldier he had slain and flung it at the head of the nearest Portusian soldier knocking him to the ground.

He struck the soldier on the ground with his sword and then moved to the next. He took along the fallen soldier's sword and charged his attackers.

He blocked his next attacker's strike, and with the sword in his other hand struck him down.

Gregorian dodged to the left of a sword thrust from the first soldier he encountered. The miss by the soldier left him exposed and Gregorian slashed him deeply across his side. Gregorian then picked up the sword of his slain foe and followed Tiberius' lead with the attack. As his attackers closed on him he blocked and then struck with ease at the executioners who seemed poorly trained. He blocked one soldier's strike with the sword in his left hand and then impaled him with the sword in his right. As one soldier approached him from behind, he spun around and blocked the strike and then impaled his enemy with his other sword. He then pulled his sword out of his slain enemy and continued to engage the remaining Portusian soldiers. When the two were finished with their exhibition in swordsmanship, all of their foes were vanquished with the exception of one.

Gio was still fighting the one soldier he had engaged. They were going back and forth while Tiberius and Gregorian approached crossing their arms and tapping their feet. The men seemed evenly matched as one couldn't seem to best the other. Gregorian was tired of waiting, so he took the hilt of his sword and hit the enemy soldier on the back of his head, knocking him unconscious.

Gio said, "I had everything under control!"

Gregorian replied, “Of course you did. If we would have waited any longer for you to vanquish your opponent we would have died of extremely old age.”

Tiberius and Gregorian began taking the clothing and armor off two of the soldiers.

Looking at the women Tiberius explained, “If you remain here they will kill you. Come, take that hill west, and when you come to the falls follow the stream to the Methosian encampment which will be around the city of Korvis. Tell them that Tiberius sends you in his stead. Tell them what has happened to your city and the atrocities that have been committed. They will send help to liberate your city from these heathens.” The women nodded and made their way quickly up the hill and out of site.

The townspeople that happened to be there for the executions rejoiced at what he said. Tiberius picked up his bow and arrows that had been confiscated from him and began walking to the forest where Gio and Gregorian waited.

As Tiberius departed he said, “If the Portusians asked what happened, tell them a force of militia overpowered their soldiers. Tell them that the militia retreated south after the ambush. You must also get rid of the soldier that is unconscious or he will make a report when he regains consciousness that will uncover your story.”

Tiberius caught up with Gio and Gregorian and told them, “We must head to the northern road that leads to Portus.”

Gio responded, “They will send messengers for reinforcements.”

“Precisely. We will intercept these messengers so that word of this request never reaches their ears. We will then put on the Portusian clothing and armor so as to enter the ranks of their army. Our story must be that we scattered from the Methosian route at Korvis.”

Gio replied, “How do you know that the Portusian forces were routed there? We knew exactly where the Methosian forces were coming.”

Gregorian replied, “That bump on your head must have knocked something loose. We made it appear as if there were forces coming from the west with false intelligence. They were most assuredly routed as they were outnumbered by 50,000 soldiers and were probably attacked from the west, north, and east. They would have been caught completely by surprise.”

Tiberius looked at Gio and changed the subject, “Why didn’t you kill us when you had the chance?”

Gio looked him in the eye when he said, “I was forced to make a decision not based on my allegiance, but rather based on integrity. To have heard why these people were being executed and to witness the slaughter made me ashamed to be fighting for our new king. They are murderers.”

Tiberius asked, “So these Portusian soldiers committed murder?”

Gio answered, “Yes, those soldiers committed those acts in hatred which is a reflection of our king. King Mardok decreed these executions. They would have had me execute those three women, and you, my brothers. I would rather die before compromising my integrity. That is why I set you free. I knew that you would help me protect the lives of those three women even if it cost us our own."

Gregorian responded, "Gio, it appears that we share the same integrity as you. For if our forces would have committed the same acts against three Portusian women, then we would have freed you and fought to the death for their lives."

Tiberius then added, "You see, we share the same values even though we do not share the same kings. We share these values because we serve a kingdom not of this world."

30 - Biscus, Methos

On the western front of Athanasia, Bremus had gotten settled as the pirate king. He was given three bases from which he could work inside Portus. He was meeting with his first in command going over plans to sack Biscus.

“Where do our numbers stand, Tacitus?” asked Bremus.

“Your army stands at 70,000, Bremus,”replied Tacitus.

Bremus smiled and smashed his fist on the table. That number is 10 times greater than what Sprasian boasted. I am greater than even the late Sprasian.” He paused before continuing, “Though, I am unsure of how we could amass such an army so quickly? It is almost as if someone were aiding our efforts. Tacitus, you found me the same day I entered Portus. How?”

“I was convinced by a man over 100 years ago that things in Athanasia needed to change. The kings were feeble men who did not know how to govern. They inherited their position. It was not earned or deserved. I swore my allegiance to this man as did countless others. No longer would my voice be snuffed out as an individual, but now as a part of something greater I could make resonate loudly throughout the land,” answered Tacitus.

Bremus asked, “Who was this man?”

He is the man who hired you and gave you lands and protection in Portus. He is an immortal named, Mardok. He is the new king of Portus," grinned Tacitus.

"You sound as if you are an acolyte of this new king." quipped Bremus.

"I am," said Tacitus. "If you sat down with him for only a few moments he would speak to every desire of your heart. He would show you the importance of getting what you want in this life. He is not a man. He is a god."

Bremus tilted his head as he looked at Tacitus and thought, "This man is loyal to me only because he is loyal to Mardok."

Bremus asked Tacitus, "What if King Mardok wanted to kill me? Would you protect me?"

Tacitus replied, "No. I would do as he commanded." Tacitus tried to lighten the heaviness of his answer by saying, "Be glad that you are held in high regard by King Mardok."

Bremus thought to himself, "What have I done? There is no amount of gold or power great enough to make me subject to anyone. If my men are not loyal to me then I have no power."

Tacitus saw the countenance on Bremus' face fall, so he changed the subject. "Bremus, I have a note from Arsinian that I would like to read that will give you some direction. It reads, 'To the Pirate King, Bremus. You are meant to wreak havoc on Methos. Do whatever your heart desires. Show no mercy and take all you care to carry. Whatever you pillage is yours to keep, but remember where your allegiance lies.'

Tacitus then explained, "Our goal is to help King Mardok overthrow Methos. On the table is our plan of attack on the island of Biscus. It is undefended, but in view of the isle of Telemicha where Sophos' filthy temple stands. We are to take control of those islands and use it as a staging point for an invasion of Telemicha and Patras."

Bremus looked at Tacitus, "Who is giving the orders around here. You, or me?"

Tacitus replied, "Neither. Only King Mardok.

Bremus smirked and said, "What if I defy these orders?"

Tacitus waived his finger at Bremus as he replied, "Oh, I would not recommend that. If you disobey, my orders are clear. You are to be executed, and your dead corpse will be hung in the city square as a reminder of what happens to any that disobey King Mardok."

The pirates in the room drew their swords and started to walk towards Bremus. Bremus put his hand on the hilt of his sword and squeezed tightly. He thought, "If I draw it, then I am a dead man and lose all that I have gained."

Bremus took his hand off the hilt and said, "Very well, Tacitus. I will do as King Mardok has instructed."

The pirates sheathed their swords as Tacitus said, "I see much wisdom in your decision, Bremus. Mardok is a mighty god and worthy of reverence."

Bremus looked at the map and said, "Take 50 ships, which should give us 15,000 men. There are only 30,000 people on the island and there is no military garrison. We should be able to capture this entire island within a matter of hours with very little resistance. We will invade from the northern and southern ports where most of the population lies."

Tacitus clapped his hands. "Bravo. That is an excellent strategy, Bremus. I will go get the men ready for our invasion."

Tacitus bowed his head to Bremus and left the room.

The next day the water around the shores of Biscus was clogged with ships as men began to spill onto the beach and race into the towns and communities. They were met with small pockets of resistance that quickly fell to the large host of pirates. They pillaged towns taking all of the money, jewelry, and clothing they could find. They confiscated all of the livestock, food supply, and small crops for their own use. They executed people that resisted them and burned their homes to the ground to deter any more resistance or rebellion. The pirates pillaged the entire island and left it in ruins in only one day.

Bremus took the island and established it as a base of operation for the 15,000 pirates. He enslaved the people that they did not kill and made them build boats, fish, and raise their livestock and crops for his pirate army.

Bremus sent word of his conquest to Arsinian so that preparations could begin jointly with the Portusian navy to assault Telemicha and then the capital city of Patras.

Justinian was alerted to the siege of Biscus by soldiers stationed on Telemicha who witnessed it from a distance. In his chambers he told one of his commanders, "I know that our forces are spread thin. I knew that I should have put soldiers on the island to defend the people. I have failed them as their king. Now the enemy is going to use it as a staging point to invade Patras."

The commander replied, "We need to keep our borders strong, my Lord."

Justinian replied, "If we take the island back then we can thwart a direct naval assault on Patras. Make haste and gather 15,000 soldiers to launch an assault on Biscus."

The commander replied, "But, my Lord."

Justinian exclaimed, "Do as I have ordered commander."

The commander bowed and left Justinian's chambers.

As Justinian prepared to leave, Queen Alexis gave him words of encouragement. "It is a noble thing that you are doing. You are demonstrating leadership in its truest form by serving your people rather than the people serving you. The people need you to be strong in this dark hour. There will be good that will come from this."

King Justinian embraced his wife and kissed her. "Thank you, Alexis. I love you."

“When will you liberate Biscus?” asked Alexis.

“We are going to lay siege in the evening. My scouts tell me that most of the pirates get drunk off ale and pass out in the early hours of the morning. We are going to attack the island the same way that Bremus did, by splitting our forces and going ashore in the northern and southern ports.”

Justinian departed late that evening and sailed to their northern and southern positions and waited until midnight to commence the attack.

Justinian spoke to his ship’s captain with Brackus and Lucian in the captain’s quarters prior to midnight. “Is everything ready for our assault?”

“Yes, my Lord. Everything is ready.” replied the captain.

The captain paused and then looked outside the window in his quarters to gauge the position of the moon.

“I believe it is now time to commence the assault, my Lord. Should we proceed?”

Justinian commanded, “Yes, launch the attack.”

At midnight, the ships hurried in from both sides of the island and dropped off the invasion force. As they reached the cities people could hear the march of soldiers and could see the gleam of silver helmets and shields in the moonlight.

The pirates had only left a small band of men on watch and were quickly made aware of the presence of the enemy as they began calling out, "To arms!"

The pirates were engaged in drinking when the alarm was being raised, but was drowned out by the revelry as Justinian's force began to file onto the island.

As Justinian's soldiers marched into the southern port he yelled, "Take back our island!"

As he led his force into the city with his soldiers behind him, they were engaged by a small band of pirates. He quickly took down the first pirate that met him by blocking his blow with his sword and then pummeling the pirate with a blow to his head with his shield. He then engaged another pirate and blocked the enemy strike with his shield and struck him down with his sword.

As Justinian and his forces proceeded deeper into the city, the fighting grew more intense as the pirates became aware that they were under siege. In the midst of the fighting Justinian was separated from his soldiers. His protectors Lucian and Brackus had gotten pushed away in the ruckus.

Lucian yelled to a few soldiers around him, "You men, follow me. The king is in danger."

Lucian, Brackus, and the soldiers that accompanied them were moving forward cutting down the pirates, but it was not fast enough to make it to Justinian as many foes stood in their way.

Meanwhile, Justinian blocked an enemy strike with his shield and then kicked his foe in the stomach and kneed him in the face, knocking him unconscious. He then clashed with two more pirates, slashing one across the chest and thrusting his sword into the other.

Lucian and Brackus were fighting what seemed like an endless group of enemies as they progressed forward, but not at the pace they desired. They kept their eyes on Justinian as they fought. Justinian was holding his own, but it was only a matter of time before he would be overtaken.

Lucian and Brackus took their frustration out on the pirates as they fought. Lucian blocked a strike from a pirate with his shield and struck him dead. He took his fallen foe's body and then threw it into the crowd of pirates in front of him, knocking many to the ground. Brackus then blocked an enemy strike and punched his foe so hard that he knocked him unconscious. Brackus picked the man up and followed Lucian's lead by throwing him into the crowd of pirates knocking several to the ground. Many of the pirates had never seen the strength of the Adelphos before and some became hesitant when it came to rushing into battle. This gave the Methosian soldiers an opportunity to gain ground to Justinian's position.

As Lucian and Brackus continued fighting they saw Justinian striking down pirate after pirate, but finally it looked like they were about to surround him. Seeing they were about 40 feet from his position, Lucian yelled to Brackus, "Quickly, get on my shoulders!"

Lucian bent down and picked up a mace from a fallen pirate while

Brackus mounted his shoulders. Lucian handed the mace to Brackus and said, "Throw it!"

Brackus looked and saw a pirate approaching Justinian from behind, so he reared his arm back and threw the mace with all of his strength. It flew end over end before striking the pirate in the back saving the life of Justinian.

Brackus then turned his head and yelled to several archers firing from an elevated position, "Archers, protect your king!"

Brackus then motioned to Justinian's position and yelled, "Fire!"

The archers began firing at will, striking down pirates that were attempting to outflank the king. They did not fire upon those that Justinian was directly engaged with for fear of striking their king.

Brackus dropped off Lucian's shoulders and picked up a long shield from a fallen Methosian soldier. He turned it sideways and began to push forward into the line of pirates using his brute strength. The line moved back slowly until Lucian began chopping his way through the pirates. As each pirate fell, the resistance against Brackus became less and less as the line began to crumble. The Methosian soldiers followed the lead of the two Adelphos and a powerful surge began to manifest. Within moments a hole started to open in the front line as Brackus continued pushing forward while Lucian and the soldiers continued to push and thrust their swords into the enemy.

Finally, the line was breached with one final push that sent Brackus falling forward with Lucian and some soldiers. The two Adelphos and the soldiers then fought their way to come to the aid of their king, while the rest of the soldiers exploited the hole and began to flank the enemy.

Justinian was getting pummeled by the enemy. His foes were so many that he could no longer go on the offensive, but rather only defend himself with his shield and sword. Justinian was getting pushed backwards when he fell over the body of a fallen foe and landed on his back. One pirate swung his sword knocking Justinian's out of his hand, while another swung a mace that went under the shield knocking it away.

A grinning pirate then said, "I will get a hefty reward for bringing Bremus back the head of a king."

He swung his sword down at Justinian's head, but it stopped just inches from Justinian's face. It was Lucian. He stopped the strike with his sword while a Methosian soldier came from the side and struck the pirate down. The pirate with the mace swung it at Lucian's head while another pirate tried to impale Justinian. Brackus then appeared and blocked the mace strike while Lucian blocked the sword thrust of the other pirate by deflecting it away from Justinian's body. The Methosian soldier with them then struck the pirate with the sword down and Lucian struck down the pirate with the mace.

The three men then put themselves in front of Justinian like a wall and were fighting off the pirate attack. Justinian then stood, grabbed his sword, and re-engaged in the battle. Shortly after this the Methosian forces rejoined their king and continued to move forward with the expulsion of these brigands from the Island of Biscus.

After the front line was broken by the Methosian soldiers the pirates began to retreat. There were still some pockets of fighting in the city from pirates who could not escape or those that chose not to escape and fought to the death. Nonetheless, the city was liberated in the early hours of the morning.

Justinian ordered a march north once the city was completely secure to meet their other force and hopefully vanquish all that remained of the pirates.

The second invasion force which struck the northern city on the Island of Biscus was successful in routing the enemy as the pirates were in full retreat. There were about 1000 pirates that fled to the south while Justinian gave chase to about 500 moving north. Eventually the pirates were surrounded by both Methosian invasion forces with only a few hundred having survived as they surrendered to Methos.

With the battle over, Justinian went back into the southern city. He was greeted with hugs and kisses from men, women, and children. One little girl brought tears to his eyes as she approached the king and hugged his legs saying, "Thank you for saving our family." Justinian lifted her up and she gave him a kiss on his cheek and hugged his neck.

As Justinian continued to assess the damage inflicted to the island and its inhabitants by the pirates, the praises continued. One man shouted. "I knew you would come. The product of my faith can now be seen!"

Another woman yelled, "Thank you, great King! You never forsook your servants even though we were tempted to despair. We knew you would come."

Justinian wanted to stay with the people so he could share in their joy but he knew one small victory was not the end of a great war so he left 5,000 soldiers on the island to defend it from anymore attacks.

Justinian sailed to Telemicha and fell to his knees on the top of the tower of Sophos. As the sun was setting he said, "Thank you, Sophos, for this victory today." I should have lost my life, but you spared me."

He then prostrated himself on the marble floor of the temple and sat in that position for hours giving thanks silently.

Queen Alexis made her way to the tower when she heard of the victory at Biscus. Justinian was startled when he heard, "I am so proud of you, Justinian. You set an example today of what a selfless ruler must do as king. It will not soon be forgotten."

Justinian stood up, embraced his wife, and said, "I am grateful to have you by my side, Alexis. Your encouragement is a cure to the anxieties that vex my soul."

31 - Northern Methos

On the other side of Methos were Tiberius, Gregorian, and Gio hiding in the woods near the border of Portus. They could hear the rush of the river off in the distance as they hid in the brush off the main road, waiting for the messengers from Adair. They had been patient and it was only a short time before they heard the galloping of two horses coming up the road from Adair.

“Tiberius, here they come,” whispered Gregorian.

Tiberius looked at Gio and Gregorian. “Get ready.”

The ground began to shake and a light rumble gradually became louder and louder as the horsemen approached. Tiberius pulled out his bow and arrow and fired it at the first messenger hitting him in the chest. He fell off his horse and dropped to the ground like a heavy sack of potatoes. Tiberius then aimed and fired at the next messenger hitting him in the gut, sending him from his horse to the ground. This soldier began screaming as his body writhed in pain, but eventually calmed as he succumbed to his wound.

Gio and Gregorian were able to go out and grab the horses and pull them off the road. They then pulled the two deceased soldiers off the road and hid them in the brush. They waited, listening for the sound of more hoof beats, but there was only silence.

"Quickly, let us make our way into Portus," said Gio.

Gregorian and Tiberius changed into the Portusian military uniforms as they were ready to enter Portus. The trio made their way into Portus untouched, and were eventually greeted by some Portusian soldiers who asked them what had happened.

"We were routed at Korvis and are part of the remnant that was able to escape," said Gio.

"Very well, please follow us as our commander will need to hear what you know." replied the lead soldier.

As the trio walked, they stayed at a distance behind those that were leading them. As they walked into a nearby camp many of the Portusian soldiers wore scowls on their faces as they passed by. They could not help but notice the constant clanging of countless blacksmiths forging swords and shields. They continued to observe their surroundings as they walked and they noticed three siege towers and several battering rams getting their finishing touches. It became obvious that this was an invasion force whose purpose was to raze the cities of Methos to the ground.

Tiberius whispered, "We have descended into a dark land. What has happened to our brethren in Portus?"

As the three observed the camp they were eventually escorted into to the commander's tent.

As they walked in they were greeted by a tall man with black hair, dark eyes, and a scar on the left side of his face that stretched from his nose across his cheek up to the top of his ear. He was missing an ear lobe on his right ear and sported a crooked nose.

"What of our army at Korvis?" said the commander.

Gio replied, "They have been routed and we are some of those that were able to escape with our lives."

The commander stared the men down with a scowl. "I don't believe you."

The commander squinted his eyes at each of them as if he were looking for some signal that would reveal any deceit. He quickly broke his gaze and said, "What direction did they come from?"

Tiberius spoke up. "They came from the east and west and probably the north."

The commander interrupted, "Probably the north? How can you not tell from which direction your enemy is descending upon you?"

"My lord," said Tiberius, "we found our friend Gio in the woods to the south scouting the next troop movement of Methos. The Methosians had broken camp, so he thought that a fight would happen in Korvis--"

The commander looked at Tiberius and said, "Spare me the commentary, soldier. The only reason you are not receiving lashes for speaking out of turn is because you said something that peaked my interest. You will speak only when spoken too! Am I clear, soldier?"

Tiberius nodded in agreement.

The commander looked at Gio again and asked, "Tell me what you encountered? Is this true, Gio?"

Gio answered, "Yes, it is! I was sent to corroborate the report from a scout that came from the west. This scout reported a force making way to the west of Korvis. I was told to go south with a companion as that was the last known position of the enemy. When we made it there, the camp was empty."

The commander responded, "Please tell me what you did next?"

Gio continued, "All the soldiers were gone, so we made haste back to Korvis to warn our commander. It was at this point that we were hunted by several Methosian soldiers lying in wait to kill any scouts that came to the camp. My counterpart was killed, and I was eventually unable to avoid capture as I was cornered by two Methosian soldiers. Just as they were about to kill me, Tiberius and Gregorian darted out of the forest and destroyed my would-be executioners."

The commander then looked at Tiberius and Gregorian and said, "How did you manage to find Gio and destroy those trying to take his life?"

Tiberius replied, "We had been routed far before Gio was pursued. The Methosian armies came from what felt like every direction. We were taken by surprise, not to mention that they outnumbered us two to one. After we were routed, we were able to escape to the south since they had no forces coming from that direction. That is how we stumbled across Gio."

"What is your name, soldier?" asked the commander.

Tiberius replied, "I am Tiberius and this is Gregorian."

"I had an Uncle named Tiberius. We called him Uncle Tibe. He was a jolly fellow that had an affinity for eating pork. Do you have an affinity for eating pork?"

Tiberius squinted and looked at Gregorian and then back at the commander and said, "Yes?"

The commander smiled and began to soften his tone from his previous sequence of rigid questions. "Were there any others that escaped to the south or that joined you?"

Tiberius responded, "They did give chase and caught many of those that ran to the south, but there were others that were able escape. We made our way to the southeast as we wanted to try to turn back north to Portus. The others fled to the south further into the lion's den."

The commander's eyes widened as he sat forward in his chair, "Is this true, Gregorian?"

"Every single word," replied Gregorian.

The commander motioned to an officer that stood by the tent's exit, "Lieutenant, send scouts to Korvis to survey the area so that we can corroborate this story."

The lieutenant replied, "Yes, Commander Lisban," and then

departed the tent.

Commander Lisban turned to Tiberius, Gregorian, and Gio and said, “Your story seems believable, but I want to verify what you have said.”

Gio responded, “That is more than fair, Commander Lisban.”

Lisban smiled and then continued, “Since you have given me some very important intelligence I see no harm in bringing you up to speed with our efforts since you will be part of our ranks now. We control the border town in Methos called Adair. Justinian had pulled his people and forces back to protect areas that are strategic for military defense, including food and water supply. Many people refused to leave despite the warning, so we have entered into Methos with little resistance. We have taken some of these border towns into our control and will use them as staging points as we conduct our assault on Methos.”

Lisban paused as he walked over to a table and then continued, “I would be inclined to send soldiers into Methos to find any more of our separated forces, but it may not be wise. If they have indeed taken Korvis back then they will have forces scouting the nearby areas. I cannot risk our manpower to round up any other stragglers. I think that we may need to send reinforcements to Adair in light of this. The Methosians could send forces to Adair and we cannot afford that.”

Lisban stamped a parchment on the table and hand it to Gio, “We will welcome you men into our army. Understand that we will send you three with a force of 10,000 soldiers into Adair since you are familiar with the geography around it.”

The three bowed their heads and said, "As you wish, Commander Lisban."

Lisban continued, "You will report to Lieutenant Boldar. I must warn you that he is rather unorthodox. I would highly suggest that you do what he tells you if you want to keep your lives. That is all."

He turned to a man beside him, "Corporal, introduce these men to Lieutenant Boldar."

The trio exited the tent and stayed out of ear shot of the corporal. Gregorian asked, "Was it odd that he told you about a gleeful relative who liked to eat pork and was more than likely morbidly obese?"

Tiberius replied, "It was. I felt very uncomfortable. I could not read what he hoped to achieve by telling me about his uncle."

Gio replied, "Well, imagine if he didn't like his uncle who bore your name, we would probably all be dead right now."

The trio started to chuckle as Tiberius quipped, "He probably would have taken pleasure in stuffing pork down my throat until I got the meat sweats."

Gregorian laughed as he remarked, "Then he would have probably skewered and roasted you."

The trio snickered as they were eventually delivered to a lieutenant who was in the midst of flogging two soldiers.

"You pieces of rubbish better sharpen your swords better next time," yelled Boldar.

The corporal spoke up saying, "My lord, here are three new recruits being put under your command."

After the short introduction, the corporal turned and walked away as the men waited for Boldar to hear their first command.

"Just do as you're told and you won't be subjected to this punishment. Anyone who takes issue with my authority I give the opportunity to challenge me for my position, since he thinks he knows better. If he comes up short in his challenge, then he is killed. Have I made myself clear?"

The three responded back, "Yes, sir!"

He turned and said, "Good!"

"Lieutenant Boldar, I believe you to be a coward. You couldn't lead ants to an outdoor feast!"

The lieutenant spun, looking Tiberius in the eyes, his face growing red. "You dare challenge me for my position only seconds after you met me!"

"You are a city without walls, Boldar!" responded Tiberius.

Boldar grabbed his sword and charged towards Tiberius. Tiberius unsheathed his sword as a swarm of soldiers circled them. Gregorian and Gio backed off as the two locked swords. Tiberius blocked Boldar's strike, countered, and punched him in the face. Boldar stumbled back disoriented but this only made him angrier.

No soldier had even laid a hand on Boldar before, so the soldiers watching were pleasantly surprised by this start. Tiberius kept his breathing slow, his eyes on his opponent, and his footing solid.

Boldar charged Tiberius and took a swing at his head but he didn't have the footing for a quick strike. Tiberius ducked the sword and kicked his opponent's legs causing him to fall to the ground. The soldiers began to cheer for Tiberius. Gio started a cheer of "Ti-be! Ti-be! Ti-be!" that started to spread around the circle of soldiers watching the match.

Yet, Boldar took to his feet again and charged Tiberius screaming as he ran. Tiberius blocked his strike this time, and the two began to take strikes at the other which were subsequently defended by the opposing party. Tiberius' strikes were much stronger and allowed him to get the upper hand forcing Boldar to backtrack to this superior swordsman.

Boldar pulled his sword back and swiped at Tiberius' legs. Tiberius jumped in the air while planting his sword in the ground and holding on to the hilt. Boldar's sword met Tiberius's sword and Tiberius's feet came down on top of the flat of Boldar's sword, dragging the sword and its bearer to the ground. Tiberius then gave Boldar a kick to the face and that caused him to release the grip on his weapon. Tiberius left his sword in the ground as the two then locked up in hand to hand combat.

Many of Tiberius' punches went unanswered until Boldar grabbed him, hugging him close so he could no longer strike him with any force.

The Portusian soldiers were cheering with every blow that was laid on their lieutenant. Finally, Boldar pulled a small dagger from his boot. Someone in the crowd yelled, "Dagger!" alerting Tiberius, who grabbed Boldar's wrist and twisted, causing him to drop the dagger. Tiberius landed a final punch just behind Boldar's ear, who then slumped over and fell to the ground flat on his back.

The Portusian soldiers gave a great cheer and swarmed Tiberius as he said, "It looks like I have been promoted to lieutenant!"

All the soldiers began clapping and cheering "Ti-be! Ti-be! Ti-be!"

Tiberius walked over to his sword and pulled it from the ground. Looking at all of the men around him he pronounced his first command. "My first order as your new commander is to demote your former Lieutenant Boldar to the lowest position in our ranks. Every man will rank above him. If he refuses any of your orders, then he will suffer in the same way that he has treated you. You will be allowed to publicly flog him for his insubordination."

Boldar had regained consciousness but was still sitting on the ground wincing in pain.

Tiberius said to him, "Boldar, this moment you are assigned to clean the cavalry's horse stables. You will need to clean their stables using only your hands. If you are caught using a shovel to remove the waste, then you will be publicly flogged for disobeying an order."

Tiberius looked over to the soldiers who had been flogged. "Will you oversee this task? You may do anything to him you like except take his life." The two men began to smirk upon hearing this as they looked over at Boldar.

One said "It would be our pleasure to oversee his rehabilitation!" With that, they grabbed Boldar from the ground and drug him by his arms to the stables.

Tiberius walked over to Gio and Gregorian and together they began to head back to camp. Gio remarked, "You should go tell Commander Lisban of your victory. He would most surely have a feast of pork in your honor."

The three began to laugh, but never spoke of what the rank that Tiberius now held meant or how it would benefit Methos.

The next day they began the march that was ordered by Commander Lisban to Adair. As they moved out Tiberius thought, "How can I stop this force from reaching Adair? The small force that liberates Adair will be crushed if they are there when we arrive."

As they were heading back down the road from which they had come, it struck him that the two soldiers they had killed the day before would be in the woods. He looked to the soldier attending him and said, "Ride to the front and bring me two scouts. Make sure that Gio is one of those scouts."

"Yes, lieutenant." said the aide.

Several minutes later the aide galloped back on his horse with Gio and another scout in tow. "You called, Lieutenant Tiberius?" answered Gio.

Tiberius looking at Gio ordered, “Yes. Gio, I want the two of you to scout the forest area before the road opens to the city. My gut tells me that something is amiss.”

Gio’s eyes opened wide momentarily upon hearing this. He answered back, “I know the forest well. I know exactly what areas to scout to see if there is a Methosian snare waiting for us.”

Gio gave Tiberius a nod and left with the scout. As they made their way down the road near the city, Gio abruptly stopped. He held a hand up, looked at his companion and put a finger up to his lips. He started to look to the forest to the left of the road and then the forest to the right of the road.

“Do you smell that?” said Gio looking at his fellow scout.

“Smell what?” replied the scout.

Gio answered, “I smell something rotting and I don’t believe it is an animal. Quickly, scour the forest to the left of the road, and I will investigate the forest on the right.”

As Gio searched the woods where he found the body of one of Portusian riders decomposing. Moments later he heard his fellow scout yell, “Sir, come quickly.”

Gio hurried across the road into the forest and found the man and whispered, “Keep your voice down. There may be Methosians watching us.”

Gio looked down and saw the body of the other slain rider. He looked up to his partner and said, “I found a dead man on the other side.”

The scout whispered, “He is Portusian. He wears a ring with the insignia of Portus on it.”

Gio replied, “So did the other man. We need to report back to Lieutenant Tiberius immediately. I think we are being watched.”

The scouts eyes opened wide and his face turned pale. Gio whispered, “We must make haste back to Tiberius.”

The two made their way out of the woods and ran a long distance back to their force marching on Adair. When both men reached Tiberius they were out of breath and fell to their knees. Gio said, “Dead. Portusian. Soldiers.” between breathes as he pointed down the road.

Tiberius looked to a man on this right and said, “Sergeant. Prepare the men for battle.”

The Sergeant rode down the ranks on his course calling out. “To arms! To arms! Prepare for battle.”

Once the men were battle ready they marched down the road to Adair. After some hours had passed the soldiers had arrived where the bodies were found. Tiberius ordered a full stop.

Tiberius looked down to Gio and said, “Gio, I want you and Gregorian to go to the edge of the forest and spy out what the Methosians are planning.”

The two men entered the woods and headed south towards Adair. Tiberius then called out, “I need 100 soldiers to check out the forest on both sides of the roads.” He looked to the officers gathered around him and said, “Get the men in defensive positions until we know there is no threat.”

Then men nodded and left Tiberius quickly to bark out the order.

When Gio and Gregorian reached the edge of the forest, they looked out and saw Methosian soldiers stacking the bodies of Portusian soldiers into a pile and then lighting them on fire. Gregorian whispered, “It appears that the city has been liberated. The citizens are emptying the Adair.

The duo looked off into the distance at the hill in the west and saw the three women they had rescued from execution standing next to some Methosian soldiers. Both men smiled as Gio whispered, “They did it.”

As they gazed at the women Gregorian commented, “In the midst of the storm of our execution I did not realize that those were the fairest women I have ever beheld.”

Gio said, “It is tragic that it was under such dire circumstances that we met.”

Gregorian commented, “Those beautiful women are also women of noble character. They would rather have died than to serve Mardok. They found the Methosian force at Korvis and lead them to liberate the city.”

Gio nodded his head, "When put in the crucible their character showed them to be women without compromise. They are as rare as precious jewels. Worthy of marriage.

"Are you betrothed, Gio?" asked Gregorian.

"No, but I think that I may have found her in the woman whose head is beautifully draped with red hair," answered Gio.

"Good," remarked Gregorian, "because the woman with the golden mane has captivated me." After a brief pause, he continued, "That leaves Tiberius the dark haired beauty. He is fond of dark haired women."

Gio replied, "How do you know?"

"We have spent a lot of time together on missions which has joined us to become like brothers," answered Gregorian.

Gio abruptly changed the subject, "This has been a pleasant respite from our stresses, but we must get back to Tiberius immediately to inform him of what has happened. Come, we have no time to waste."

The duo quickly made their way back to the Portusian force down the road. Upon their return, Gio feigned fear and yelled out, "Hurry men, Adair has been taken back by Methos. Where is Lieutenant Tiberius? They have a large force of at least 50,000 soldiers and they looked to be preparing to move north to our position!"

Tiberius made his way to Gio and locked eyes as the soldiers around them began to chatter. Tiberius gave Gio the slightest of nods, which was returned.

Tiberius called out to his men, "I order a full withdrawal. Let us make haste back to Portus before we are overcome by this great host. We must let our commander know of what has happened so that we can prepare our next move."

The army hastily marched back to Portus, and while they went Tiberius called Gregorian and Gio over and spoke to them in a hushed voice, "What really happened?"

Gregorian responded, "A small force of less than 1,000 men took Adair back as we reached the city. There were no soldiers that were able to escape. It appeared that they ordered a mandatory evacuation of the town."

Tiberius smiled, "Good. Now we have to figure out what we must do from here. We have been given a great opportunity to throw Mardok's plans into disarray by being in leadership in the Portusian military. We must make the most of it."

32 - Somewhere in the Eastern Athanasian Ocean

The *Morning Star* had been on the sea for six months. It was a rather smooth voyage, but the crew started to grow more fearful the longer they seemed to drift to an unknown destination. They had officially run out of food and water three days earlier and during the course of their voyage the skies were surprisingly dry.

Sprasian had the ship drop anchor and set out a boat to fish, but nothing was caught.

"How could you take us on a voyage to our doom!" said one of the ship's crewmen.

Spiros spoke up to all of the grumbling. "Men of Methos, you must not lose heart. We must have faith that Sophos would not send us to our deaths. We must stay the course."

Another man yelled, "How do you know that we are not being punished for following Sprasian? He has lived a destructive life devoid of any goodness!"

Spiros yelled, "Sprasian is not the same man anymore! You know this to be true! He is not leading us astray. He is following the command of Sophos. I know that you are thirsty and hungry. I know that this suffering is causing some delusion but you must keep your focus."

The crewmen became incensed and started making their way towards Sprasian. "If we kill him now maybe Sophos will spare our lives for following him."

Spiros took Katherine away for he did not want any harm to befall her. Sprasian then stepped forward and spoke to the men candidly.

"Men of the *Morning Star*, I too am hungry and thirsty! I too am feeling faint! We must not waiver. We have come too far to waiver. Killing me will not end your suffering. We must trust that Sophos always keeps his word."

One of the crewmen answered, "We are finished following you. We are going to take control of the ship and do what we think is right. That means that you must go!"

Dulas, the man who was pardoned by Justinian, spoke up.

"Stop! Men of the *Morning Star* have you forgotten that you willingly volunteered to put your life in peril? No one forced you to follow Sprasian. Each one of us made that decision of our own accord. Stop placing the blame for this adversity on Sprasian. We chose to follow Sprasian to whatever end. Therefore we are to blame for this decision."

The men quieted down as Dulas' words seemed to permeate all of their ailing hearts. However, some of the crew still voiced their want to throw Sprasian overboard.

"What are we to do then? I still believe that Sprasian is the reason we are suffering. If we kill him, then maybe our fortune will change?" asked one crewmember.

Dulas spoke one last time. "Men of the *Morning Star*, I would like to make a proposal to you. If we have not found food, water, and land by tomorrow, then we can throw him from the ship. Let us give him one more day. What say you?"

The crew began to grumble as Dulas' words continued to strike a chord in them, but it could not change their hearts. "Very well then, we will give Sprasian one more day to lead us to food, water, and land. If we do not find it by tomorrow, then we will cast him into the sea." said another crewman.

Sprasian nodded his head and walked to the wheel with a heavy heart as he began to steer the ship. As he hung his head he began to question in his mind, "What purpose does Sophos have leading us to our deaths? What good is going to come out of this suffering and my death?"

As Sprasian steered the ship he looked up to the heavens and muttered, "I have less than one day to live. If you are going to do something, then it has to be now. I am resigned to my fate either way. If I die, then I die. I will not fight my persecutors, but will surrender myself willingly. If I am to die, give me the strength to die well." Sprasian stayed up the entire night guiding the ship so that if it was his last day, he would be doing that which he loved.

At sunrise the next morning Sprasian was still at the wheel with only half of a day left to live. Katherine awoke early in the morning and stayed by his side encouraging him. The deck was devoid of anyone and the only sound that could be heard was the blowing of the wind on the ocean.

The reality of his death started to sink into every fiber of his being as his eyes were drooped and his stare was blank. A tear began to form in his eye and then trickled down the side of his face. He thought to himself, "I only just begun to really live."

While wrestling with his thoughts Sprasian closed his eyes, took a deep breath and exhaled easily. When he opened his eyes he saw what looked to be a tiny bump on the ocean that was southeast of their position.

He screamed out, "Get someone up to the crow's nest immediately!"

Every member of the crew awoke and opened their eyes in great excitement as they ran up to the deck. They had not heard this word "land" in over six months and the word was hope. However, if this was not land then it would hasten Sprasian's death.

Very quickly one of the stronger crewmen scaled to the top of the crow's nest. Sprasian yelled, "Look to the southeast."

The crewman looked to the southeast and leaned forward as far as he could without falling. He yelled, "I see land! Sprasian is right! I see land!"

A loud cheer erupted from the crew as Sprasian changed their heading toward this speck of land.

The excitement of the crew could be seen as they ran around the deck, getting ready to go ashore. It wasn't long after seeing land that they reached the island, dropped their anchor, and rowed boats hastily to the shore.

The island was small, only about 10 miles in diameter. When they reached the shore, men began falling on the ground and kissing it. They were rolling in the sand and mud grateful for what they had found overlooking the fact they were the first people to ever discover land in the east.

Spiros took in the moment with a grin. While he didn't need food and water, he was happy that the needs of the people would be met and they found relief from uncertainty.

Everyone was quick to pick up the fallen coconuts beneath the numerous coconut trees and open them for their water and fruit.

"Spiros can you cut the top off of this coconut?" said one of the crew members holding a large coconut in front of him.

Spiros shrugged, "I don't think the swords of Helios were created for opening coconuts, but since they can cut anything I suppose it wouldn't hurt."

Spiros swung his sword as the soldier held it in front of him, lopping off the top. The soldier then put the opening up to his mouth and began to gulp down its contents. Other soldiers began to line up in front of Spiros asking for the same service.

After the men had their fill they set up camp. Spiros, Sprasian, Katherine and a few other men decided to scout the island to look for any life or resources. Sprasian pointed down the shore, “Look over there! That part of the beach is teaming with crabs.”

The crew quickly brought wooden pales over and began to fill them with as many crabs as they could hold. One of the men called out, “Dulas! Get a fire started and help us clean and cook these crabs.”

Another commented, “I cannot wait to sink my teeth into some delicious meat.”

Sprasian and his small group walked inland and began to make their way through the brush. Sprasian lifted his hand and everyone stopped. Katherine asked, “What is it, Sprasian?”

He answered, “I think that I hear wild boar.”

He moved a few feet ahead to a small clearing and saw wild boars feeding on some brush. Sprasian turned around and said, “It looks like pork will be on the menu tomorrow.”

Those in the party cheered at their good fortune. Sprasian then ordered, “Let us continue inland to find water. There has to be some source of fresh water other than coconuts. These boar could not live without a water source.”

As they continued they stumbled upon an open area with a large pool of water in the center. Sprasian walked up to the pool fell to his knees, cupped his hand, and scooped up some water to his mouth. He took some into his mouth swished it around and then swallowed.

“It is fresh!” said Sprasian. The whole party with the exception of Spiros ran up and started to drink from this pool to quench their thirsts. Katherine began splashing water into her face while all the men dipped their heads in the water and pulled it out.

Spiros commented, “This is a refreshing moment for you mortals, but maybe we should let the others know so that they can bring barrels ashore and store it for our voyage.”

Sprasian said, “Very well. Once we have our fill we will head back to camp and alert the others.”

Later in the day on the beach everyone was enjoying their cooked crab and coconuts as there was plenty to go around. Everyone bore a smile and many were laughing, while some were singing songs. One of the crew members stood up and said, “May I have everyone’s attention.”

When everyone quieted he said, “Sprasian, forgive us for doubting you and desiring to take your life. We should have trusted you. Thank you for finding this land.”

Sprasian responded, “Don’t thank me thank Sophos. He came through for us in the eleventh hour. He told us to voyage east in faith. I am learning that when we are in the storms of life, that we are given little oases along the way that will help to strengthen us so that we continue the journey and not lose heart."

All of the men nodded and replied, "Here, here!"

Everyone enjoyed a peaceful night's sleep with full stomachs. In the morning some men went out into the shallow blue waters to fish while others fished in boats around the island. Wherever the men fished their nets seemed to be bursting with fish. This continued to encourage the men as all of these resources would aid them in their voyage east. So they gathered all that they could take with them.

They later discovered by the fresh water pool on the island that there were a multitude of pineapple trees and two banana trees. They began pulling all of the fruit off of the trees and taking it with them. What wasn't eaten was stored on the ship with the other food reserves.

Other men on the island went hunting for the wild boars and seagulls and noticed that the seagulls were nesting on the island, leading them to believe that finding more land might be unlikely. The men began gathering the eggs from empty nests and when the hunting party returned, they brought back 75 wild boars and 100 seagulls. They were also able to procure some 216 seagull eggs. Each one of these boars weighed around 500lbs, so they had a large quantity of meat to store and take with them for the voyage. They were able to extract salt from the ocean to use cure and preserve the meat.

That night they feasted in preparation for the journey that would soon come. Sprasian stood up and made an announcement, "Men, we have three more days on this island, so feast while you can and store while we have resources. We have much work to do in preparation for the next test we face."

All the men nodded as Sprasian excused himself with Katherine, Spiros and a few others to visit the fresh water pool.

When they reached the pool the moon was full and was casting a pale silver reflection on the water. Everyone sat in the sand and put their feet in the pool relaxing from the day's work before their last chore.

"Katherine, where in all of Athanasia did this island come from?" said Sprasian breaking the silence.

Katherine smiled at him, "I do not know, but it appeared at the perfect time."

Several minutes of silence ensued before Katherine opened up to Sprasian.

"Sprasian, I am afraid of sailing into the unknown. I am alive today, but could perish tomorrow. This adversity is one that I have never experienced."

Sprasian smiled, "It is natural to fear the unknown. I struggle with this too but these troubles and trials have caused me to really appreciate and enjoy the blessing of this oasis and my life."

Katherine replied, "You are quite the encourager, aren't you?"

Sprasian smiled and turned away looking at the pool in front of him. He saw something glimmer from the corner of his eye. As he took a closer look he saw the moonlight reflecting on something metallic.

“Katherine, I think I see something shiny in the pool.” He reached into the water and fumbled around. When he had pulled his hand out he had what appeared to be a gold coin. After turning it in his fingers for a moment Sprasian looked to see if he could find any others, but nothing appeared.

Spiros then came over and looked at the coin. “I have been alive for tens of thousands of years and I do not know the origin of this coin.”

The coin was two inches in diameter, and had a bust of a man on one side and of a woman on the other. The man had short hair and a scowl on his face, but in the background was a dragon whose head came around the man and rested on his right shoulder.

On the other side of the coin the woman had long hair and also wore a scowl. She held a book in one hand, and above her other hand was a levitating ball. On either side of her head were two dragons with their mouths wide open as if they were roaring.

“What is the Kingdom of Locknar? Who is King Lorgos and Queen Azriel? These are not Athanasians. This has to be from a land east of here,” said Spiros as he analyzed the coin.

He continued, “This is an unparalleled discovery. There must be another kingdom to the east.”

Sprasian said, “Come, let’s take it to the camp and see if any of the men may have seen anything like this."

Sprasian and his small group returned to camp and showed the coin to the rest of the men who remained clueless to its origin. As everyone wrestled with the meaning of the coins inscription, Spiros stopped the discussion. "Men, let us retire for the night for we have much work to do to prepare for our departure in three days. We can check the pool tomorrow to see if we can find anything else. You are starting to vex your minds about things we have yet to discover." said Spiros.

As everyone retired to sleep on the ship a soft rain began to fall. This was the first rain they had seen since the voyage started. They quickly grabbed barrels and brought them onto the deck of the ship to catch the water. As the rain continued the soft pitter patter of the drops could be heard throughout the ship which gave the men a comforting and peaceful sleep. This simple pleasure of life, just listening to rain drops fall, brought great comfort and pleasure to everyone on the *Morning Star*.

In the morning the sky was clear and the sun was blazing as a team of men went hunting again for wild boars. Since they had the light of day Sprasian, Spiros, and Katherine went to the pool again to see if they could find anything else that might give them a clue of what was further beyond the island.

The pool was breaming over with water from the rain that fell during the night. They waded into the water, dove under, and felt around but could not find anything else.

"Well, let us just be grateful for what we have discovered. This one coin has given us some insight. There is a kingdom out there somewhere," said Spiros.

As they made their way back to the ship the quartermaster approached and informed them that they have enough food and water for an eight month voyage. They piled the extra supplies wherever they could find space on the ship. After their rest on the island and the coin suggesting that there was something beyond the seemingly endless sea, they were ready for another long voyage.

Sprasian said, "Let us just enjoy the final two days on the island. We should not hunt anymore boars as we will have to come back this way again if we intend to return to Athanasia. I am not sure how they were introduced to this island, so we need to let them continue to inhabit it."

Two days later the ship was ready to leave for the voyage east. Everyone was rested and ready to make way to find this land called Locknar, but there was an unspoken anxiety among the crew as to what they might find.

As they set sail the men had thankful hearts for this land that they had discovered. They planted a Methosian flag as they claimed it for their kingdom, and they hoped to see it again.

33 - Port Verdes, Remar

On the Island of Remar, Petros was planning an attack on Parrus. The Parrusian vizier, Elias and Petros were standing at a table outside with a map of the area around the Parrusian capital.

Petros asked the vizier, “If what you say is true, then there are no soldiers left in Parrus outside of the palace guard. How many men remain in the palace guard?”

The vizier answered, “I would estimate around 500 men. There were once 2,000, but that number has dwindled since the liberation of Remar.”

Petros asked, “What of the Adelphos that protect Melmot? Did you notice anything about their demeanor or counsel that might point to them being in league with Mardok?”

The vizier answered, “Yes. I didn’t see the point of my job as they seemed to convince him to do the opposite of any of my counsel.”

Elias replied, “This will be a more dangerous mission than I thought. It is a tall task for the two of us to engage four of our brothers in battle.”

Petros replied, “I do not fear these treasonous monsters. They have betrayed their creator!"

Elias responded, "Then let us engage them together."

Petros pointed to the castle and asked the vizier, "We must plan our strategy for the assault now. Do you know of any weaknesses that we can exploit that would give us the element of surprise?"

The vizier pointed to an area close to the castle and answered, "There is a secret passage that is used to take the king to safety if they were ever overthrown. I know the passage very well. It is a remote location by an inlet where our king could escape by boat. The passage leads from his very bedroom to this isolated location. I can take you there."

Petros said, "Very well. We will need three boats to execute the plan. We will disembark on a small boat while the other ships go to the main port and march on the palace. I want the vizier, Elias and seven soldiers to accompany us on this secret assault"

The men nodded while Petros turned to address the many soldiers around them who were in training. "Men of Methos! It is our understanding that there are no soldiers left to fight for Parrus except the palace guard. Therefore, now is the time to strike and remove this puppet king so that we can liberate all Parrusians. However, we will have to engage the immortals that protect him. These Adelphos are dangerous and give no regard to human life, and I want to be upfront with the risks; many men will probably die in this assault, so I wanted to make it clear before anyone volunteers. We need men who are stout in heart."

There was a silence over the soldiers that stood around them. "If we can supplant King Melmot we will be able to win the kingdom back to the people," explained Elias.

The soldiers began shaking their heads, one by one both Methosian soldiers and Parrusian soldiers volunteered until 1000 soldiers were counted.

As they set sail the next day there was a quietness in the air. All that could be heard was the blowing of the wind on the sea for the entire voyage. As the ships entered the main island of Parrus, the lead ship dropped a boat with ten men close to the shore. The vizier pointed and said, "Row to that inlet."

The men rowed to the inlet and took the boat ashore. As the men disembarked the boat Petros asked, "Where is this passage you spoke of?"

The vizier pointed to a section of forest right off the water with enormous trees. As this expeditionary unit approached the trees Petros commented, "Are those Megalos trees?"

The vizier smiled and said, "Indeed." The men gazed at these majestic trees for a few moments before the vizier interrupted, "Follow me."

The vizier led them to one of the Megalos trees and began to navigate over its giant roots. Upon reaching one particular root he pulled on what looked like a small shoot, which was actually a switch. A small door cracked open a few inches at the base of the tree. The vizier pushed against the door and it slowly slid open revealing a stairwell. The vizier, Petros, Elias and the rest entered and began ascending through a dark passageway. The vizier grabbed an unlit torch on the wall that was covered in cobwebs. The vizier gave the torch to Elias and then grabbed a piece of quartz sitting on the wall. Next to it was small piece of metal that looked like a file. He took the file and started striking it against the quartz in front of the torch. After his third try it began to spark, and those sparks eventually lit the torch. The other men grabbed the other torches on the walls and lit them.

Petros looked at the vizier and extended his arm to the stairwell saying, "After you."

After an hour of scaling the stairs they reached the palace and the king's chambers which was behind the throne room. As they entered the king's chambers they heard some conversation coming from the throne room, so they held their position before they advanced out.

Elias and Petros exchanged glances as the tone in the men's voices suggested something to be wrong. Petros walked out to King Melmot's balcony to see if he might get a better idea of what was happening. When he peaked outside towards the road he saw parts of their invasion force on their knees with their hands behind their heads. He immediately looked out towards the ocean and saw two of their ships burning. The other was docked and under heavy guard.

He returned and whispered, "There is nothing out of the ordinary happening."

But then Petros' actions contradicted his words as he closed the panel that led into the room and wedged some of the furniture in the room against it.

The vizier said, "Why are you blocking our escape?"

Petros ordered, "Blockade the doors."

"What are you doing? They will hear us," said the vizier.

Petros looked at him, "They already know that we are here. You betrayed us."

The vizier's eyes opened wide as he screamed, "Help! They are in here! Help!" He unsheathed his sword and started swinging at Petros, but Petros blocked his attacks and with one blow he slew the traitor.

Immediately, loud thuds rang through the room as soldiers began to try and break through the doors leading into the king's chambers. The door to the secret passage with which they entered also began to rumble.

"All right men, let's take these sheets from the bed, tie them together, and rappel from the balcony to the ground," ordered Petros.

The soldiers began to work quickly as the crashes against the door began to grow louder. The rattling of hinges and splintering of wood told them their enemy would soon be in the room. When they had joined some of the sheets and blankets together they tied them to one of the pillars on the balcony and threw the line to the ground. The balcony overlooked a side road that lead to the courtyard. Petros ordered, "Men, rappel down the sheets and set up a perimeter."

The men quickly climbed down one by one and Elias grabbed one of the torches in the room and began to set all he could aflame. Putting fire to the bed, curtains, and furniture soon left a radiant orange glow as Elias ran out and slid down the line behind Petros. As they descended the soldiers that were guarding their captured brethren began to break ranks and head to their position.

Petros, Elias, and their men then began defending themselves from the attack of the soldiers that had left their ranks.

Petros blocked a strike from an attacker, kicked him in the stomach and struck the man in the back of his head with the hilt of his sword.

Elias dodged a sword thrust of one attacker by spinning to his left, and coming out of the spin he slashed his opponent down. He then immediately blocked a strike to his head from one attacker and then blocked another strike to his torso from another. One of Methosian soldiers came to Elias' aid and cut down one of his attackers. Having been freed up, Elias struck down his second attacker. The next attacker swung his sword at Elias' head. Elias blocked the strike and the Methosian soldier fighting next to him struck the man down.

Those that had been taken captive now only had a few guards watching over them. One of the captive soldiers took his bound hands and extended his arm over the head of one of the guards using the leverage from the binds to pull the man down and begin choking him. Upon seeing this, the rest of the captives were inspired and revolted against the few remaining guards. One or two captives were slain in this attempt, but their numbers were too many and they were able to subdue the guards.

The men quickly began cutting their bonds with the swords they had procured from the guards and charged out of the courtyard into the skirmish. They picked up any object they could find as a weapon, from stones in the king's pond to helmets on the deceased captors heads, and used them to combat their enemy.

Petros, Elias, and their men were able to hold their position against the Parrusians just long enough to allow their recently liberated cohorts to take the enemy from behind. Some guards turned to fight and were greeted by a strike in the face from a helmet or rock. Within moments there were no remaining Parrusian guards standing.

Petros ordered, "Men, let us retreat out of the city."

The men began running down the side road away from the courtyard and out of the city.

Petros and Elias were the last to leave. As they looked up they saw all four of the Adelphos standing on the balcony as torrential flames and smoke could be seen behind them.

Petros yelled out, "We will see you again traitors! The next time we meet will be your end!"

The two Adelphos then turned and ran behind their soldiers as they exited the city into the forest.

In the forest the men took a quick breather by a stream to do a head count. Elias counted 130 men which meant they had lost almost

90% of their force.

"What happened?" questioned Elias to any man that would answer.

One soldier spoke up and said, "We were met by the enemy fleet before we even made it to shore. The first two ships were boarded and overrun by the enemy. We had no choice but to surrender as we were surrounded by two dozen ships. They burned the two ships and killed everyone aboard. They struck down many of us when we lay down our weapons and surrendered. However, those of us they let live were then escorted under heavy guard to the palace. That was when we saw you rappelling down from the king's terrace."

Elias looked to Petros, "What do we do now?"

Petros looked off to the distance at the palace blurted out his first thought. "We cannot get off this island without a boat, so either we try to track one down or we are stranded here. If we are indeed stranded, then we must somehow blend in. We may be able to lead an insurrection within the kingdom of Parrus, as you all know that they are dissatisfied with King Melmot's leadership. It only takes a tiny spark to ignite an unstoppable fire and we cannot only be the spark, but fan the flames."

One of the soldiers replied, "Then let us stand our ground here and fight in the shadows."

All the men gave their approval.

Petros responded, “Very well then, we will be the spark. Let us now move before our enemy tracks us down.” The men began running again through the forest as they headed west away from the capital city.

In the castle the Adelphos stood in anger as they hit stone walls, putting their fist through them. “How did they escape? yelled one.

“We must try to track them down before they become a great thorn in our flesh.” yelled another.

One of the other Adelphos commented, “We only have about 10,000 soldiers at our disposal. The rest have defected. This was our best chance at destroying Elias and Petros.”

Then the immortal named Corsica ordered, “Each one of you take 1,000 loyal soldiers and track these men down. We cannot have them loose in Parrus.”

34 - Northern Methosian Border

In Methos, Bremus' army was sailing down the rivers that crossed into Methos. He was pillaging the river towns and stopping their supplies from being sent downstream to the Methosians. He would burn the towns when he was finished taking all that he could and would head back out to the ocean to plunder supply ships and fight against the Methosian navy.

King Justinian was preparing for the defense of Methos as Mardok's forces were primed to charge their enemy. Justinian made his way to the front lines because neither he nor his kingdom could afford to leave anything on the table in the defense of their city.

On the other side of the border stood Mardok with his massive invasion force.

"Men of Portus, today begins the payback of the treacherous act that was committed against our kingdom by the ruthless tyrant King Justinian. He and his people are murderers and will pay for trying to usurp the throne of King Argos. We will show no mercy to his soldiers or to the people of Methos!"

All the soldiers yelled and threw their fists into the air. When the cheers died down Mardok addressed one more issue. He turned to Arsinian, "Bring the prisoner here for everyone to see."

Arsinian departed momentarily, but returned with Commander Soros who lost the battle over the bridge at the Peirus River.

Mardok unsheathed his sword and then spoke. "Men of Portus! Failure will not be an option. Only victory will be accepted. This commander that stands before you lost an important battle that cost us many soldiers. Men of Portus, here is the punishment for anyone that surrenders or retreats like this cowardly commander."

King Mardok then took his sword and impaled Commander Soros. The crowd began to cheer and raise their swords in the air as the commander fell to the ground.

"Men of Portus, prepare for battle!" ordered Mardok.

Arsinian came up to Mardok, "All of our generals on both the land and sea are preparing to march or sail into combat in Methos and Solcis. Our enemies are outnumbered over four to one."

Mardok smiled and then said, "Excellent, Arsinian! This war should be over in a matter of weeks and I will be the sole ruler of Athanasia. Every knee in Athanasia will bow and worship me as their king and their God."

The two began to walk to their positions as the Portusian military was beginning to start its attack.

Mardok asked him, "How many ground invasions will be under way when we start our march?"

Arsinian ran his hand through his long dark black hair and said, "By lighting that pyre of wood over there you will send a signal to other pyre watchman to light their wood who are spread out all across Athanasia. This reaction will serve as a command to all our generals to commence the attack. It will be as close to a simultaneous attack as can be planned. Seven invasion forces will converge on Methos to attack and gain control of what we planned. There will be two invasion forces marching into Solcis. This is an unstoppable host, my Lord. We have countless soldiers waiting in reserve if by some miracle we are unable to take either of these kingdoms. Once our navy takes control of their waters, the supply ships for our ground forces will move from their holding positions and meet up with these ground forces to give them what they need to destroy Methos and Solcis."

Mardok exclaimed, "Perfect! Arsinian, I will reward you greatly with a province of your own to rule for your faithfulness to me. However, if this fails, then I will hold you accountable. I have not forgotten how you failed me in my quarters when King Argos' messenger overheard our plot." Mardok clenched his fists and his face turned dark red. "You knew Argos' messenger was on his way, and your lack of attention forced me to move my plan up by three weeks!"

Arsinian hung his head down as he replied, "Yes, my King. Please forgive me. He was supposed to be dispatched later in the day after our meeting with Romus. I will not fail you again, my Lord."

Upon hearing this Mardok's face regained his olive complexion as he replied, "Good. There is no more room for error. You were my first convert and I hold you in high regard."

As the two men parted Mardok mumbled to himself, “I want Justinian torn in two for his insolence. No one challenges me and lives.”

#

On the Peirus River, the spies Tiberius, Gregorian, and Gio had been ordered to build a dam. The Portusians wanted to cut off the water supply to Methos so that they would have no drinking water and more importantly so that they could not water their crops. Any river that ran into Methos from Portus had men working feverishly to dam them up. Of the 32 rivers in Methos, there were only 10 that originated in the kingdom, while 21 flowed from Portus to Methos and one flowed from Solcis into Methos.

As Tiberius’ men built the dam he asked one of the engineers, “Is there anything that could break this dam?”

The engineer answered. “The only way that this dam will not work is if it is not built to specifications. If there are any quality problems in its construction, then it could possibly collapse, but I am overseeing every detail, and once it’s complete, it will stand for 1000 years.”

Tiberius thanked the engineer and went to find Gio and Gregorian to speak about how they could do this without exposing their loyalties.

As Tiberius walked he reasoned, “Methos and Solcis are not strong enough to defeat Mardok. Sabotaging a dam will not create a lasting effect that would save the kingdom.”

Within a few moments he reached Gio and Gregorian. Tiberius

paused and looked around the area for a moment to make sure that no one was listening.

"My friends, I have figured out a way to sabotage the dam, but the only way to win the war for Athanasia is to assassinate Mardok," explained Tiberius.

He continued, "I have a plan to procure a sword of Helios that could cost us our lives. If we survive, then we will most certainly die when we carry out the assassination attempt. Are you willing to die to save Athanasia and all that is good in this world?"

Gio and Gregorian shook their heads and were silent for a few moments as they both stared down at the ground.

Gregorian broke the silence first, "Life will not be worth living when Mardok takes over Athanasia. It will become a cesspool of all that is evil. I would rather die than allow that to happen."

Gio responded, "What greater love is there than to give up one's life so as to spare the lives of countless others. I will lay down my life to stop evil from being victorious."

Tiberius smiled, "Very well, my friends, the matter is settled. Let us go and deliberate so that Athanasia might be saved."

35 - Somewhere in the Eastern Athanasian Ocean

On the *Morning Star*, the months of sailing were about to turn into the first year. Their food supply had dwindled over the six months of the current leg of this voyage, but they still had enough food in storage to last over two months. They were also running into storms and showers which replenished the water they had in storage, so fear for the basic necessities of life was less of an issue. Every person on this voyage still longed to see land and wondered if their eyes would ever gaze upon it again.

As Sprasian was steering the ship he saw what looked like a storm moving west. It seemed as if it covered the entire eastern sky. He yelled, “I need all the crew on deck now.”

As the crew filled the deck Spiros and Katherine appeared behind him. Katherine asked, “Why are you calling us together, Sprasian?”

Spiros looked out at the horizon and pointed to black skies in east. “It looks like there is a tempest coming our way.”

When the crew finally assembled Sprasian began to speak. “Men of Methos, There is a squall that is headed in our direction. I have endured many storms, but none with the looks of this. I want to be forthright so that your minds are prepared for what we are about face. We need everything in the ship secured by either rope or nails. I will need several sets up shackles nailed into the deck around the wheel for the men who will help me to steer the ship."

Sprasian paused and looked from left to right across the ship at each man's face. Prepare you minds for what we are about to embrace so that you will not despair and fall into fear. You are the most gallant men I have ever had the pleasure to captain." He paused for a brief moment and the continued, "And this includes you even trying to throw me overboard to be food for the sharks."

Then men broke out into to laughter as Sprasian's jest lightened the mood. Smiles crept onto the faces of the crew and heads began to be held high.

Sprasian finished his speech by saying, "Be strong and courageous men. This storm will pass and we will be all the mightier for it."

The men cheered and quickly emptied the deck and began to fasten anything not stationary to the ship.

"Katherine, I want you to stay in my quarters tonight. It will be the safest part of the ship. Brace yourself for this is a wicked storm that approaches. I will be guiding the ship through the storm until we are safe."

Katherine's eyes fell as she replied, "Will this storm sink the ship?"

Sprasian smiled, "I certainly hope not. I have already escaped death on three occasions."

Katherine laughed and then responded, "You have such confidence in the face of peril. That is a noble quality."

Sprasian returned the compliment saying, "You have the same quality, Katherine. When you rebuked me in my quarters for my brigand ways you did not fear for your life. You are a woman of noble character."

Those words caught Katherine by surprise and so moved her that she gave Sprasian a warm embrace. Sprasian's eyes opened wide and he held his arms out as someone not knowing how to respond. After his initial hesitation he returned the hug. The embrace helped him forget about his anxiety over the approaching storm.

Katherine pulled away and said, "I hope that my embrace didn't make you feel uncomfortable."

Sprasian stammered in his reply. "No." Sprasian paused for a moment and then continued, "It has been a very long time since I have felt a warm embrace. I had forgotten how they felt. I believe that the last embrace I remember was from Queen Alexis when I was but a child. You made me feel very comfortable as it brought back pleasant memories from my childhood."

Sprasian turned to walk away when Katherine blurted, "Be careful."

Sprasian looked back at her with a smile and said, "I will not."

Katherine's mouth opened wide as her eyes fell. Sprasian continued, "Because I am going into a tempest."

Katherine laughed and pushed him saying, “Off with you and your foolishness.”

As the storm approached, Spiros stood close by Sprasian as the two friends had grown close over the last year of sailing the ocean.

As the two looked into the horizon of the approaching tempest they held their heads high with a slight grin on their faces. Sprasian commented to Spiros, “I don’t believe that I have ever felt this way when going into any storm of life.”

Spiros replied, “Indeed, it is only natural to fall into fear when facing any peril. However, I believe that this storm will only last for a time, and that we will surely see the sun shine on the other end.”

Sprasian replied, “I feel the same way, my friend.”

The waves and wind started to strengthen as they were getting closer.

Spiros said, “Does this remind you of the dream we had, Sprasian?”

Sprasian had the question on his mind. “It does have some sort of semblance to our dreams doesn’t it? However, there were some subtle differences. Whatever manifested itself that night seemed different than an actual storm. It felt malevolent and had great power of which we had never seen. Wherever we attempted to steer the ship was not enough to navigate around this foul squall.”

Spiros paused for a moment. “Enduring the storm is what we must do now. We cannot stop it, so we must patiently endure it. Every man on the ship had his character refined when they endured no food or water for four days or landfall for over six months. It strengthened them for this adversity. If we survive this tempest, then it will prepare us for the next one to come."

Sprasian decided to give Spiros the wheel for a moment as he wanted to check on Katherine one last time. As he entered the quarters he saw that Katherine's face looked pale. Her eyes and head were hanging low as her body was shaking intermittently.

He took Katherine's hand and opened the door and led her out to the deck to look at the storm.

Katherine's voice shook as she said, "It looks so dark and cold. All the light of the sun is in full retreat."

Sprasian replied, "It may rule our course, but it certainly does not rule our destiny. This darkness will only last for but a moment and then we will see the light."

Sprasian continued, "I want you to face this storm like I am. This is no different than facing the storms of life that lack wind and rain; the storms that take away our health, our livelihood, loved ones, or that turn us over to those who seek to persecute us. We must be courageous and endure their fury. Do not fear Katherine, for the storms of life are temporary."

Katherine replied, "You words are of great comfort to me."

A smile cracked on Sprasian's face as he said, "Thank you. Come now, it is time for you to brace for the storm. He walked her up to his quarters and then returned to the wheel as the wind and waves became more furious. Heavy rain drops started falling and pelting the ship as the fury of the wind caused them to fly at a high velocity.

"Hold tight men as the storm is upon us!" said Sprasian as his voice boomed over the storm.

Immediately, great waves started crashing against the ship. Sprasian and Spiros held the wheel steady so that they would not be knocked off course or abruptly turned into a vulnerable position that would allow the waves to sink them.

The first eight hour shift went by and Sprasian and Spiros seemed to get more strength and courage even as the storm grew worse and worse. It seemed as if they were enjoying themselves. They would scream encouraging things to the men on deck. Sprasian was heard saying, "Be strong and courageous my brothers for we are mightier than this squall!"

Spiros would yell, "Keep up the good work men! You are truly mighty warriors!" Their words of encouragement strengthened the crew that was assisting them.

As the storm raged, some of the waves hit the ship so hard that it threw men to the deck. They would have slid to their doom if it were not for the shackles bolted into the floor. Each time a man took a fall one of the other men who had firm footing would help the man back up to the wheel.

After 10 hours Sprasian noticed that the men looked tired, so he asked, “Men, do you need a respite?”

The men shook their heads as one of them said, “We will not leave your side.”

The *Morning Star* had been in the storm for 18 hours when Sprasian decided to do a shift change. Everyone was breathing heavy and losing their footing, falling to the deck, with the exception of Spiros. “Sprasian yelled out to his men, “We need some rest! Come, let us go inside and get some food and drink!”

The men all nodded their heads in agreement. One of the crew members walked to a door to the left by the steering column. He opened it and called for seven men. He took off his shackles at the door and put it on the foot of his replacement. He went inside while the replacement went to the steering column amidst the rocking of the boat. When he made it to the steering column another crewman left and went to the door and traded places with a reserve. They continued this process until Sprasian finally made it in. Outside were Spiros and seven new fresh crewmen.

The men went to a room in the back of the ship that was used for relief. It had hammocks, windows, a fireplace, and chairs fastened to the walls of the ship. The men were rocking back and forth just trying to make it to a place to rest. Sprasian was able to make it to a cupboard. He unlocked it and took out some cured boar and pineapple (Sprasian had the crew uproot some of the pineapple trees and place them in barrels filled with soil so that they could cultivate some food at sea). He started handing it out to the men as they sat in a chair or lay in a hammock and they devoured the food in gulps. Shortly after eating everyone in the room fell fast asleep from exhaustion.

Sprasian was awakened three hours later from what felt like the ship taking a large descent. Rubbing his eyes, he said, "Men, let us arise and head back out into the fray!"

All the men awakened and slowly got up from their positions of rest. Sprasian made his way to door that led to the deck. He opened it and saw water flying everywhere and men being tossed to the deck of the ship.

"Spiros! We are coming back out!" yelled Sprasian.

One by one the current team of men fighting this storm as their relief came to the door and traded places.

At the 32 hour mark the men began to struggle. A large tempest on the ocean doesn't last longer than 12-18 hours so the mental and physical toll on Sprasian and the men caused them to grow weary.

"When is this storm going to end?" yelled one.

Spiros yelled, "Do not lose heart men! We have suffered the worst that this storm can offer for 32 hours! I believe that we are near the end of this beast! Stay strong as we have not come all this way for nothing! To give up now would be to throw away all that we have gained!"

At the 38 hour mark there still was no break in the waves or wind. The ship was taking a beating, but was holding strong. Sprasian thought to himself, “How much longer must we endure this ferocious storm. My men’s courage hangs by a thread and the ship may not last another day.”

At the 48 hour mark the men were holding on with every ounce of energy. Their knuckles were turning white as they held the wheel in place. One of the men noticed something. “Captain Sprasian, does it feel like the ship is steadying and that the rain is beginning to withdraw?”

Sprasian looked out at the waves to the right and left of the ship. He exclaimed, “The waves appear to be smaller and the drops feel smaller.”

An hour later the waves were down further, the rain had stopped, and the wind was almost back to normal. Sprasian began to embrace all the men that had helped him on the deck. Enduring the storm built a strong camaraderie amongst Sprasian and his men. Katherine came out of Sprasian’s quarters and gave him a long embrace. “I knew you would do it, Sprasian.” As she let go of him the sun started to break through the clouds and shine on the ship.

The ship had taken on water, so the men worked at getting the water out of the lower decks. Sprasian went to the wheel and checked their course. He saw that they had been taken off course, and they were now headed on a more northeastern track. Sprasian told the crew, “Stay the course. We did not know if there was any land east. We are shooting arrows in the dark. Who knows if this storm directed us to where we will find land?”

“I trust your judgment, Sprasian,” said Spiros. All the men nodded and said, “We all trust your judgment, Sprasian.”

Sprasian then excused himself from the crew and Katherine to get some much needed sleep. He lay down on his bed in his quarters and slipped into a deep sleep.

He awoke one day later and grabbed some of the cured ham in his quarters and devoured it, then cracked open a coconut and gulped down its contents. When he had finished his food he strutted out to the deck to check their course.

Spiros was on the wheel at the time when Sprasian approached. Spiros commented, “You realize that you have been asleep an entire day?”

Sprasian rubbed his eyes as he was still in a groggy state and asked, “Have you seen any sign of land?”

Spiros quipped, “If I had found anything you would have been the first to know.”

Sprasian laughed and patted his hand on Spiros’ shoulder. He then turned away to seek out Katherine.

When he found her, she asked him, “Were you ever tempted to give up during the storm?”

He dropped his head and answered, “I was fighting discouragement. As a boy I was told by my father that I was worthless and would never amount to anything. If I was the runner-up in a contest, he told me that I should have gotten first prize. If I won the contest he would point out my flaws and tell me that I could have done better. He never said, 'Well done, my son.' That is all I ever wanted to hear. While we were fighting the tempest the words that he had spoken to me would manifest in my thoughts. Who would have thought that words spoken to me as a child would still haunt me today?"

Katherine affixed her eyes on Sprasian and grabbed his hands as she responded, "People do not understand that ill-timed and malicious words can last a lifetime. I would rather be wounded physically than have someone I love wound me with their words.

Sprasian nodded his head softly in agreement and said, "I believe I see that now for the first time in my life."

Katherine continued, "The only reason the men with you never gave in to fatigue or gave in to fear was because you encouraged them. I was holding on for dear life in your quarters during the storm. I could not see you, but I heard your voice faintly calling out to the men, 'Be strong and courageous! You are doing a marvelous job! Well done, men!' These faint words that I heard encouraged me to believe that everything would be all right. I could even hear Spiros yelling out words of affirmation. These men will remember your words for a lifetime."

Sprasian replied, "You could hear that?

Katherine answered, "Yes!"

Sprasian replied, "Your words are like medicine to my wounds." He rubbed his eyes with both of his hands and then ran them from the front of his head to the back. He simply replied, "Please excuse me, Katherine," and went back to his quarters to ponder her words.

The next morning Sprasian was up early at the helm. There was a great fog that had covered the ocean. Sprasian had the crew drop the sail, but hold its course as they now crept forward.

Two hours later the sun could be seen cutting its way through the fog.

Sprasian continued slowly forward as Katherine and Spiros joined him. As they all looked out the fog revealed an anomaly only for a moment. Sprasian saw something that looked black and gray in front of him for a split second and then it was covered up by the fog.

"Did you see that?" shouted Sprasian.

"What did you see?" replied Spiros.

"I saw something that looked like stone very far away." answered Sprasian.

An excited Sprasian had Spiros take the wheel and began to scale the heights of the ship to the crow's nest. Sprasian searched for an opening in the fog again to see if what he saw was real. As he gazed forward a break in the fog occurred.

He yelled down to Spiros, "Drop the sails and anchor now!"

With that command the anchor began its descent.

"What do you see Sprasian?" yelled Spiros in return.

Sprasian did not answer, but climbed down from the crow's nest hastily.

When Sprasian finished his descent he went to the wheel and said, "Everyone, look forward."

The entire crew gazed out into the white mist. Many of the crew began to gather around Sprasian and look out over the sea. The fog was being broken up by the rising sun and started to dissipate fast. After a minute of searching a large patch opened up and revealed an enormous wall as far as the eye could see.

ABOUT THE AUTHOR

Thomas Coutouzis was born on May 8, 1974 in East Lansing, Michigan. Thomas's parents moved to Fayetteville, North Carolina in 1977 where he grew up until he graduated high school. Thomas attended East Carolina University in Greenville, NC from 1992-1996 and graduated with his bachelor's degree in Business Administration with a concentration in Marketing. After graduation Thomas moved to Raleigh, NC where he worked in various roles in Marketing and Advertising. It was during this time that he became involved in the Big Brothers Big Sisters organization as a mentor. He mentored little brothers JJ from 2000-2006 and Damion from 2006 to 2013. He was later given the President's Award for Service by Cokie Robert's on behalf of George W. Bush. Shortly after, Thomas was married to his lovely bride Kathy on February 28th, 2009. They have two children, Chloe and Micah. Thomas and his family currently reside in Fuquay Varina, NC and attend Fellowship Baptist Church in Willow Springs, NC. As a Christian, Thomas has a passion to teach the Bible expositionally. This style of teaching helps to interpret correct context and meaning by going verse by verse through the bible. Thomas is of Greek heritage so he enjoyed studying the ancient Greek and was able to glean an even greater understanding than the English translation presents. Thomas's desire to teach scripture prompted a desire to write books. He loved God's word so much that he wanted to convey it to people in writing, but how? After praying, God reminded him of when he was a child in school writing fantasy tales when given a writing assignment. Thomas believed this was the avenue that the Lord wanted him to take. He would write a partial allegory, but not a full allegory like Pilgrim's Progress. He wrote "Athanasia: The Great Insurrection" in three months and went through seven rounds of revisions over a five year period. On April 4, 2016 he published his book independently after some 50+ rejections from agents and publishers. This book is the first book in a six book series.

Made in the USA
Monee, IL
06 March 2020

22796516R00245